Dzanc Books

Best of the Web 2009

**DZANC
BOOKS**

1334 Woodbourne Street
Westland, MI 48186
www.dzancbooks.org
info@dzancbooks.org

Published 2009 by Dzanc Books
Book design by Steven Seighman

06 07 08 09 10 11 5 4 3 2 1
First Edition July 2009

ISBN – 13: 978-0-9815899-7-8

Printed in the United States of America

Dzanc Books

Best of the Web 2009

Guest Editor
Lee K. Abbott

Series Editor
Nathan Leslie

**DZANC
BOOKS**

1334 Woodbourne St.
Westland, MI 48186
www.dzancbooks.org

Contents

Series Introduction
by Nathan Leslie

You had a bad 2008. Who didn't? Everyone did. Well, not everyone—you know that's not true. Obama had a great 2008. Biden had a great 2008. You didn't. You lost money. A lot of money. You realize now that our national greed accomplished what Al Qaeda couldn't—a deep, bruising, lasting blow to our economic system. Your 2009 doesn't look promising. You recently got "laid-off" or you know people who did. Something about that phrase rubs you the wrong way—like referring to death as "passing." (When you took a course back as an undergraduate you hoped to "pass." How can "pass" also="dead"?) You figure, let's see what the folks at Dzanc Books came up with this year. Why not read a few stories and poems and essays from online mags, here in book form? Why not indulge? You spent much of the latter half of 2008 worrying. Now that active fretting is a constant national state you can ignore the white noise, if only for a bit. You can relax and enjoy. There is something to be said for just allowing yourself pleasure.

You read last year's *Best of the Web*. Or maybe you missed it; maybe it flew under your radar. Maybe the election and the economic collapse garnered more of your attention. Maybe you're just curious now for the first time. You consider yourself an eclectic reader, adventurous. You like to dabble. You scan through the table of contents. Some names are familiar. Many are new. Colorful. Unique. Full-throttled. Energetic. *Avatar Review. Fawlt. Wigleaf. Centrilfugal Eye.*

There is comfort in a book, in a physical object you can lift and carry and flip through casually. You consider yourself tech savvy, at least savvy enough. If you had any money you'd consider a Kindle; you just pause at the yet-another-screen facet. You find yourself all too often staring at a computer monitor, even when you don't want to. Sometimes you feel queasy. But a book—a book is something you can sink into, escape into. You consider yourself traditional in this way. And at any rate you'd like a little escape from all the bad news. This is a good place, you think; gems seem to await you. You're just ready for the immersion, the loss of self.

You no longer doubt the validity of on-line magazines. At one point you did. You wondered if online magazines were just some kind of vanity publishing scheme. But now you know better. As a wise man once said, "Everything is Everything." In fact, the print versus online distinction seems nitpicky to you now, small-minded, narrow. So pre-recession, so when-we-had-the-luxury-to-worry-about-such-things. So 20th century.

You begin reading. You notice the sudden prevalence of "you." The second person is everywhere, or at least more widespread than it once was. Is the second person the new first person? What is this all about? You scratch your head. Are folks suddenly attempting to pay homage to *Bright Lights, Big City*? It's not as if this is exclusive to fiction, you notice. The nonfiction. The poetry. You, you, you.

You gather your thoughts, speculate. Is it a focused distillation of the author-reader relationship? Is it the equivalent of hand-held camera in the films of the '70s? Are writers so concerned now with holding the waning attention span of readers that they seek immediate involvement? Is it just one of those fleeting trends (using footnotes as homage to David Foster Wallace; maniacal, over-the-top George Saundersesque sentences; the crimped Anne Beattie style)? Who knows? Whatever the case may be, "you" is the star of the show several times over. This makes you feel...unsure initially, then ecstatic, then simply *involved*. It's something new.

You were happy to read a few months back that the N.E.A. reported that the percentage of American adults who read novels, short stories, poems or plays actually rose from 46.7 percent in 2002 to 50.2 percent in 2008. You are suspicious. You'd like to take a gander at their numbers. They don't match up with what you observe day-to-day. Your beloved *Washington Post Book World* just ceased publishing. If more people are reading, why would a major national newspaper stop running reviews? And what percentage of this body of creative work was Scott Turow or Danielle Steele, or Harry Potter? Nevertheless, the N.E.A. does give you some hope. Perhaps there is a shift to a slower, more thoughtful public—you'd like that. Even if this public no longer has print newspapers much less print book reviews in these newspapers at their disposal.

Still, you wonder what percentage of those who read literary magazines are writers themselves? It's good that writers read, you think. However, if writers are to scuttle out of the literary cave in which they life, you think they could also use readers who aren't writers. Readers who just like to read—for fun, for their own enjoyment, for their own edification— you think, are what we should really be striving for. They are the audience we aspire to.

You read for a while. This anthology features such a wide array of work, you think. The flash fiction bounds from the page—the fractious "Forearm and Elbow," surreal "I Would Tell You." You realize most other anthologies ignore flash fiction entirely. The fiction is of the highest quality, you think. You notice the familiar names: Stephen Dixon, Peter Markus, Karen Heuler, Michael Czyzniejewski and many more. *Brevity* dominates the nonfiction category—a testament to their commitment to short, lyrical works of personal narrative, you realize. You notice this year's anthology also features several works on literary giants—Melville and Borges. The poetry, of course, is various and sundry and likewise speaks to the wide array of poems online. This said, you notice *Agni, Arsenic Lobster, Convergence,* and *Cortland Review* make the strongest showing this year.

This is scintillating work, you think. It glows. It activates. The words are alive on the page—no beautifully scribed but equally withered specimens here.

Still, you know we have so much ground to gain. You read a poll in which the average child 8-17 plays 3.2 video games per hour, whereas only 27 percent read a book as much as 2 or 3 times a week. So reading is up among adults, but the next generation shrugs and sinks in front of the screen. You realize you are fretting again. How will online magazines help turn the tide? Kids use computers more than adults; where are the online magazines for younger readers? You wonder, are anthologies such as this merely denying the future of quasi-literacy? You wonder, is that future already upon us? It's depressing. Yet, there is hope. This anthology is a step in the right direction.

You need a break from reading. You return to your computer. You check your e-mail. You check your work e-mail. You check your other e-mail. You check your Facebook. You think of all your Facebook friends—how different they are. Some are writers. Some are paper-pushers. Some are aunts and cousins and sisters. Some are college classmates or ex-lovers. You realize that despite the fact that you sit at your computer so often you do communicate with people more than ever—even if you never see them. It's so easy. It's so easy to take for granted.

One quick stroke of the keypad and click send—there, it's done. Status update: you are loving *Best of the Web 2009*. The word is out there. There is, at least, that. You walk away from the computer screen and brew yourself some tea. You take a sip. You sink back into your favorite reading chair. Open the book. The words leap into your cornea. Almost imperceptibly you lean forward. You breathe and read, read and breathe.

Nathan Leslie
March, 2009

Introduction: The Best of the Web 2009
by Lee K. Abbott

First some teaching, then some preaching.

At some point in every workshop I teach, we discover a snob. That is, we uncover among us someone who thinks that one kind of writing is superior to all others—yes, a hierarchy, at the top of which stands (drum roll, Ringo!) Literature. I have a colleague, an otherwise smart and sensitive soul, who believes this nonsense. No science fiction, she says to her charges. No romance writing. No mystery stories. No gothic tales. No horror. No westerns. And, please, no action adventures. In other words, no fun, just more quiet and polite narratives about stumbling upon The Meaning of Life, however crosswise and subtle, at the kitchen sink.

With humility (sure, pal), I tell my students that my colleague is as wrong as Republicans. Imagine, I say, our tribe without Jane Austen (romance writer extraordinaire), or Elmore Leonard, or Edgar Allen Poe, or Cormac McCarthy, or Richard Price. The moral is this (nowadays, everything that pleases comes with a moral): good writing is good writing, no matter where we find it. Want to rule out futuristic fiction? Then you're going to have to get rid of, say, *Fiskadoro* by Dennis Johnson, and I am not keen to do so. The detective story is beneath you? Then *adios* James M. Cain. Fantasy is jejune, a redoubt for the pimply geek you've always been? Then *sayonara* Gabriel Garcia Marquez. Well, you get the point.

A similar divide, methinks, characterizes the relative merits of writing that appears on the Web and that which appears in hard copy—page versus pixel, if you will. Among my academic confederates, the Web is a suspiciously cheap and recklessly democratic phenomenon. It is, they fear, without gatekeepers (yup, putatively dispassionate and judicious editors, the folks born to say "no"). In private, the mossbacks among us will tell you that anyone with a computer, basic cyber-savvy, and the money to purchase a domain name can put up an e-zine or the like. Given such givens, quality can't be guaranteed, and thus Li-tra-chure is already in the handcart headed for hell. For these folks, the medium is indeed the message.

For others, me happily among them, the message is the message. That is, it ain't where; it's what.

What, of course, makes many demands, some onerous, on *Who*. You have to cerebrate, analyze, reflect, and perhaps re-evaluate your own standards for excellence. Here's another notion I have to provoke: imagine that there are as many kinds of fiction—sorry, poets, the "liar's art" is what I know best—as there are vegetables. Now, think of the vegetable you like least (the brussels sprout anyone?). I hold that my job is to tell the good sprout from the bad, personal taste be damned. So what if I don't like stories with ice fishing. So what if I've already read too many stories set in Vienna. So what if I have no use for fiction about mermaids. My responsibility, in an effort to know best from better and better from bad, is to put aside my prejudices, my crotchets, and preferences. Confronted with a story about a talking milk bottle, I am obliged to say more than "Oh, please, enough already."

Which again brings me, courtesy of the twisted logic I am the fortunate victim of, to the Web—and what I like about it.

1. Space (no, not outer). The Web has room for, in my case, the especially long story—that 100-page monstrosity, say, that almost no commercial, bricks-and-mortar periodical can accommodate. Can't sell enough advertising to afford such efforts.

2. Freedom. The Web is a fine home for the offensive, the transgressive, the experimental, the indelicate, and the dangerous. You can bet your bippy (vocabulary from an earlier and equally anarchic age in entertainment) that *the Georgia Review* is not going to publish a story its trustees think they will be embarrassed by. (The late Donald Barthelme used to say it was "difficult to find a point of view kinky enough to call your own." The Web, I assert, is just the place for the unique or nearly so, for the minority opinion, for the unfashionable, for the hopelessly retrograde, for the derelict and delinquent, for the visionary, for the fanciful, and for the heedless and headstrong.)

3. Frequency. Want to publish daily, then do so. No investment in paper, glue, ink, and postage. No deep pockets needed (just, I am tempted to snark, pocket protectors).

4.   Immortality. The hard-copy magazines and books I've been published in will one day rot (sigh). My Xs and Os, however, will last forever in the ether, provided the servers survive nuclear winter.

Finally—I have, if you can't tell, ascended to the pulpit here, one arm now sawing the air for emphasis—I think that our republic is better off for having a new medium that can show us, as John Updike used to say, how we live in the here and now. As a species, we're better off for having more perspectives to consult. As consumers, we're better off for having such inexpensive access to the "willed words" that are yarns and lyrics and arguments, (have you bought a hard cover book lately?). As writers, we're better off for having still more places to say our say. And, yes, we're better off, brothers and sisters, for having yet more language, albeit English this time, to believe in.

The Boy and the Colgante
by Jeff Parker
from *Waccamaw*

For an external outdoor flagpole, one need not necessarily go with the Illuminator Hurricane Series to wit a flagged wind speed of 220 miles per hour plus if one is not in, say, Florida. And I am nowhere near Florida. I am in what Floridians think of as the anti-Florida if they ever think of a place like this, if they even know about what might exist not a few hours north of the Vermont border of the United States of America. I *wish* for Florida.

I am in Roberval, Quebec, Canada, the long-distance swimming capital of the world, a place to wit there are creatures heretofore unbeknown to me which is called a French Redneck. The French Redneck is very much like the American Redneck we know and love but for the obvious fact it speaks French. I will not even tell you how I landed here other than to inuit (which is a kind of indian here) to the fact that it is on a count of the boy, that lacking-in-character son of mine, who loves America not even enough to put his butt on the line for it, who because I love him enough to put my butt on the line for him have put it so. I am now here and am technically considered an accomplice by the laws of the good country which I love should I ever return which I can't see because how would it look to the people who share my views and whose sons are not lacking in character? To wit there are days I have no idea what I am doing here. It is an uninteresting and unfortunate little tale, I'll spare you.

One does not necessarily need go with the Illuminator Hurricane Series, flagged wind speed of 220 miles per hour plus, but I am going with it. I am installing a fifty foot exposed height, ten-inch diameter butt, four-inch diameter top, and while this pole easily supports the fifteen-by-ten-foot flag I am settling for the twelve-by-eight so as not to make the neighbors feel *too* bad, which still will be tough because it's spun polyester, the most durable flag material on the market, with sewn stripes and embroidered stars. The beauty of the Illuminator, where usually a regular flag pole top caps out, the Illuminator orbs a fixture to wit powers a 120-volt halogen or 12-volt Zenon to alight the

7

whole shebang through the night, when it will flap over this suburban Roberval neighborhood in a Zenon—I am going with the Zenon—glow.

I am going with all this, because the flags decorating—and that's just it, flags are symbols and idols and not decoration—the French Redneck porches of every house around us have begun to irritate me. They are of two sorts, mostly the crimson zit of a maple leaf, *printed* mind you on a nylon scrap, popping in the wind. The Quebec flag I can stomach, four little reproductions of that thing, reminds me of a Webelos badge, and at minimum cloth with stitching. Got some symmetry. With that I can pert deal. I'm all right in general with Canada. Sure, the maple leafs. And then when they speak English it's all turned around. There's the *sawrys* and the way that the first *a* in two-*a* words gets backward. The *dra*ma of driving a *Maz*da. But I intend to make a statement this morning when the semi, an actual semi comes down the street with the pole chained to the trailer and the flag folded down and boxed the size of a nice dining room table.

I have already dug and wired the hole and the boy is stirring six bags of Quickcrete in a wheel barrel. Though he is not, as we say, altogether with the program, he understands that he owes me something here. The semi guys help us stand it in and run some support lines to the house and before long we are ceremoniously raising the flag of the US of A, flicking a switch and illuminating it just before dusk when the French Rednecks on all sides, step off the porches, summoned like moths, except French-speaking and Canadian moths instead of the kind you would expect, so in about a round way they're like exactly what you would expect except different in some small and altogether disconcertive way.

After a few moments all of them are in my yard, standing next to me and the boy at the base of Illuminator Hurricane, and they are all speaking in French. The boy talks to an Asian redneck, who lives right next door. Imagine it, an Asian with maple leafs and Webelos all over his house, speaking perfect French. That is something.

"Ne *boo* play," I say. "What? What is it, boy?"

"They seem impressed," the boy says. "They say it's a fire hazard."

"That's Zenon," I say, "Less heat than Halogen. Emits."

The boy says something to them and the Asian French Redneck mouths the word "Zenon."

8

I mouth the words "Illuminator Hurricane, motherfucker."

The non-Asian French Redneck from the other side what knocks on my door at three am, saying something in frog.

"*Sawry*, eh?" I say. "*Sawry.*"

He continues. The boy appears. Him and the non-Asian French Redneck talk. I can't tell you what they're saying, but I can say for fact that you can hear the country in the way a French Redneck talks. It's like yak butter or meat jelly. You don't know exactly what it is but you know it's there.

"He says the light from the flagpole is shining into his bedroom, Dad," the boy says.

I study the French Redneck. You can see in his eye the belief that everyone who ever did anything important in the world—invent electricity or the name for a dish of fries in gravy and cheese or the solid-body guitar or went to space, wiped out polio, sacrificed their line for braided-hair virgins—I imagine his belief that everyone who ever did any of those important things was French like him, just like blacks with blacks and Jews with Jews, Peruvians with Peruvians. The French Redneck looks like REO Speedwagon. He wears jeans that are too long on him and a Ducks Unlimited t-shirt. He's got hairy toes. He drives a pick-up.

He says another thing, and the boy doesn't translate.

"*Sawry*, eh," I say. I flick the porch switch, which the Illuminator is wired into.

The boy goes back to bed. I stand at the door until I hear the non-Asian French Redneck's front door closed. Then I count off sixty seconds, just how long I reckon it takes him to get those jeans off and back cozy into bed. I flick the porch switch again and go to shower where we have this shower head that opens up to a monsoon and the water hits the tub with such force you can only barely make out the pounding on the door. But I have only my upper body soaped down when I notice something I can't believe I missed before. In the pocket corner of the shower head we picked up from the dollar store just a few days un, there's a stamp in the metal: "Made in Tehran."

And suddenly I'm up in the sky, aught from space, seeing my own house with X-Ray vision, the Illuminator casting a shadow of that gorgeous flapping flag down on my roof, and I see through all the Canadian-made shingles, to the bathroom where a turkey named me is standing in the shower, the water kept in by a curtain hung from a rod made in the place where my country is getting its war on next. I snatch it down and reach for my towel.

The boy and I are building a rock garden around the base of the Illuminator Hurricane the morning when the water meter reader comes down the drive. He speaks in French. The boy tries to step in, translate. I put my hand over his mouth.

"It's around back," I say. "But they just read the thing to wit a week ago."

"You don't speak French, sir?" he says.

"Dramamine," I say.

"Excuse me."

"I'm fluent beginner Canadia."

"I am here from city works. We received some complaints. And I'm sorry to say, but this, it's against see city code. It must come down." He looks up at the flag.

"That's the Illuminator Hurricane."

"Yes. I am afraid Robervale law is nothing in the residential region over eight meters."

"It's under eight."

"This is at least fifteen meters, sir."

"You didn't measure it."

"I can measure it, if you like."

"I think you'll find it's under eight meters if you do."

The French city works guy stands there a moment before fishing a tape measure from his back pocket, stepping into my new rock garden and running it up the pole. I rake the red and brown and yellow maple leafs into a pile by the rock garden then sit on the rocks and one by one tear them along the veins, listening to the plinking of his metal tape measure on the Illuminator Hurricane.

"You see, sir, it is almost fifteen and a half."

"Oh, shit," I say. "I thought you meant feet. It said on the box it was under eight football fields, American football of course. I'm not Argonaut of Blue Bombering here. It's all confusing, but I don't think anyone minds."

"We are receiving many solicitations on this matter." A gust of wind whips the flag. "I am afraid it is the law and the rules. If you do not take it down, we will start to fine one hundred and fifty dollars per day. It is an expensive rent for a flagpole."

"A hundred and fifty per? Let me think about that. Is that cash?"

I knew what this guy was thinking. But it wasn't that even. I'm just into the spectacular, and if anything in the world is not spectacular, it is a Canadian flag. Run one of them up this pole and it'll look all wrong flapping in the Zenon of the Illuminator. It just doesn't carry the weight. And that comes across I guess, which is why they're all after me about it.

"Let me ask you this: If I hang one of those maple leaf pus bubbles from this pole, can I keep it?"

"We are having laws here, sir. It is not a negotiable. But I may ask you, this is about genitalia? You have big American penis and this is how you show it to us all?" He smiles.

"I'm not going to accept that," I say. "I will take the Illuminator Hurricane down to avoid you fining me, but until my dick is fifty feet long with a queen-size flag draped off it, a Zenon bulb for a tip, you better take that back."

Me and the boy stand in the yard staring up the Illuminator Flagpole after the city guy leaves. The boy won't admit, but I can see that it stirs something in him too.

"Going down to a twenty-five-footer isn't going to hurt us, dad," the boy says.

"What is going to hurt us, boy?" I say. "Come on."

We drive to the dollar store.

To wit the boy makes a stupid point. You can't go down in size by half and expect it not to hurt you in dramatic effect. And I don't even know rightly if they make the Illuminator in twenty-five-foot. And what then? Put floodlights on it from the roof overhang? Might as well cross the border and go to jail free. Maybe it's where we both belong.

I count the Canadian flags on porches and mailboxes and hanging off siding. They might be postage stamps as much as they're flags. Got zero meaning. A leaf is not a symbol. It's a picture, a drawing. At best you get nature off it. But you take an American flag and you know an American flag is in the room with you, or on the street with you, or in the neighborhood. You can *feel* an American flag, especially when presented all fifty-foot Illuminator Hurricane and all.

At the dollar store, the boy wanders the aisles. I tell the woman straight off, "Ma'am, I am not speaking French with you. But I am returning this Iranian flag pole on the count of it's Iranian."

She seems puzzled, then twirls it behind the counter like a baton.

"No exchange."

"I don't want to exchange. I'm giving it back. Just take it. And accept my friendly customer-service suggestion to discontinue the stocking of this and all Tehran product."

"Made in Iran?" she says. Her co-worker comes over and they speak in French. Theirs is not redneck French. Something different. You can hear it in the expression.

The boy appears at my side. "What are you doing, Dad?"

"I'm returning this Iranian curtain rod."

"Why's it Iranian?"

"That's the most natural question you've asked in a time."

The woman points to the metal stamp on the rod and shows it to the boy.

"It says, 'Made in Taiwan,' dad."

"What'd you say to me?" I have a look, hold it up to my face and pull it back. "Still don't want it." I drop it on the counter and walk out, wait for the boy in the car.

The boy drives. Little piles of snow form peaks on the sides of the road. He slips a CD out of his breast pocket. The CD has a metal ring through it, looped around a silver thread. The CD has an American flag print and the letters "USA". The bilingual packaging says "Hanging CD / CD Colgante."

"I got you something, dad," he says. "It's not a fifty-foot flagpole, I know."

"Some kind of decoration?" I say.

"It's only a decoration if you put it facing out. If it faces you, then it's just for you. All anyone else sees is the reflective back of a CD. Here."

He takes it out and hangs it over the mirror. We drive and it swings from the rear-view, slicing the air between us.

"What's *colgante* mean in frog?"

"It's Spanish. It means hanging, or pendant."

"Why's it Spanish?"

"I don't know."

It was another stupid notion the boy had. It was clearly a decoration. But something about it endeared me to wit I respected its Spanish, the second language of the USA.

"Music on there?" I ask.

The boy shrugs. I pry the metal ring off the colgante with my side teeth. I feed it into the CD player and there's a long silence while the player tries to read it. The boy turns the volume knob all the way up and then it starts. The "Star Spangled Banner" played on little Mexican guitars, a maraca keeping the beat.

He turns it down, and I slap the back of his hand.

"Jam that colgante, boy!" I say.

We ride the streets like that, windows down so the cool air bites, the "Star Spangled Banner" playing on repeat. I picture myself busting up the cement base of the Illuminator Hurricane with the sledgehammer when we get home. I picture the boy, while I am busting, propping his feet on the sofa and eating what's called here a Wagon Wheel but is a Moon Pie. Though it seems to be my lot, bringing up things that in the end I will tear down, I start to feel a little good again, riding around like that, picturing only the immediate future, with the "Star Spangled Banner" cranking, with my boy and the colgante.

The World As You Left It
by Helen Wickes

from *AGNI Online*

The strands of hair in the brush and
the indentation in the pillow, your dog
snoring on the bed, the unkind note
on the dresser top, the red silk rose
the body guys left for us, the curtains
full of dust, swinging, as a bird lands
on the stone wall, the summer heat
bears down, and eight geese take off
from the pond, and as his backhoe idles,
the guy smokes, while in the distance
there's the endless hum of cars,
and a small plane sets loose a glider
in the afternoon, into the quiet
of all that space opening out.

All that space opening out
in the afternoon quiet, as overhead,
a small plane sets loose a glider,
and in the distance the endless hum
of cars, and nearer, the guy lighting
his smoke, his backhoe idle, as geese
rise from the pond, the summer heat
bearing down, a bird on the wall,
the curtains full of sunlight and dust,
in the room where the body guys left
a silk rose, there's the unkind note
on the dresser top, your dog snoring
on the bed, the indentation in the pillow,
and four strands of hair in the brush.

Landlord
by Blake Butler
from *Memorious*

She had the pink house in the gristle around her heart. I lived on the fourth
floor where the ceiling trembled. The rent was high. The floors were warped.
I slept in one room and ate in another. Most days I never moved—though in
warmer weather I'd crawl behind her eyes and watch the men with mouths and
fingers. I'd watch her watch the TV. Cartoons and QVC. She once ordered a
cheese grater. She did not use it to grate cheese. Most nights when she got home
she filled the bathtub. Underwater her heartbeat grew distended. Sometimes
she soaked in money. More often I tried not to think at all. There were others
living on my floor, though in the hall we avoided each other's eyes. At night
another tenant played a trumpet. Not a song but wounded skronk. You could
hear it through her skin. I wonder what her mother thought. I was concerned
about her future. I shaved my face on her smaller bones. Her blood bubbled at
the windows. Insects skittered. Some knew language. Some knew my name. In
the short term she had seasons. Rain of liquor, sweat or suds. Snow of dead
cells. Pop of muscle. Hairdryer sun. Certain weekends I grew blisters. I combed
the crud out of my hair. I continued to have faith in our future despite many
nights awry. The doorbell buzzed for no reason. The carpet molded. The sockets
sparked and squealed and leaked. I begged my requests into the air vents: (a)
fix the deadbolt; (b) *find the mailman;* (c) *install a finer light.* The answers
arrived in short marks on my forearms: (a) *keep your teeth clean;* (b) *wake up
sooner;* (c) *there is nothing here to see.*

When My Girlfriend Lost the Weight
by Matt Getty
from *FRiGG*

When my girlfriend weighed 143 pounds, she stopped eating.

We'd just moved in together after dating for a year. I'd just realized I didn't know shit about her. We had stopped leaving the room to fart months ago, had already owned up to our love for reality TV, already kissed with bad breath. But we'd never shopped for furniture together. I'd never seen how she reacted to dropping Chinese food on a rug.

In Ikea a fight over a long boxy dining room table almost got physical.

"Why the hell would we need a dining room table when we don't even have a dining room?" I asked.

"The table creates the room," she answered, "just like a family creates a home. If you don't know that, I don't know what the fuck I'm doing with you. I don't know what the fuck I'm doing with my life." She called me a jackass, called me a motherfucker, called me the whole list of dirty names, started making up some of her own.

I stood there baffled. People walking by could have thrown futons into my mouth. I barely recognized her. Her face had gone from red to purple. She was trembling, holding her arms stiffly at her sides, her hands flared. Little judo chops she struggled to hold back from my neck. This suddenly was my girlfriend.

Our third night in the new apartment, she toppled a Tupperware container of kung pao chicken onto a Persian rug I had yet to notice. She'd been eating on the couch.

She cried. I laughed nervously, unsure what to do.

"Shit!" she shouted, standing up and stamping her foot into the rug, chicken, and peanuts. "My whole life is shit! Shit! Shit!"

She crouched over the mess and sobbed. I knelt down beside her, touched her shoulders, said nothing.

The first half of that kung pao chicken was the last thing she ever ate.

✦

When my girlfriend weighed 142 pounds, we had a little talk about the kung pao chicken incident.

"I'm not a happy person," she said.

"You've done a hell of a job faking it up to now," I said. "Hats off on that."

"This is bigger than you and me," she said. "It's more than that, but I guess it's all ours now. Can you handle that?"

"Sure. I could have the dining room table delivered here by four o'clock this Saturday. I looked on the Web. You can order it online."

"It's not about the table. But it is about the table. I don't know. I've got baggage, but I don't know what it is."

"Leather perhaps. Maybe nylon? You can order luggage online too. Are we taking a trip?" I smiled weakly.

She didn't. "You don't understand what I'm saying, do you?"

"Not a word of it."

She frowned. Tiny dimples had a field day on her chin. "Just promise we won't get bored," she said. "Promise we won't become furniture to each other. Promise you'll take me dancing."

"OK, OK, and do I have to?"

✦

When my girlfriend weighed 139 pounds, she started talking about her body parts as if they didn't belong to her. "Look at this ass," she said. "Look at these thighs."

Then she started addressing them directly. "What do I got to do to get rid of you?" she said, staring down at a roll of stomach skin she'd pinched between her fingers.

Then she demanded answers, started shouting. "Answer me, lard sticks!" she screamed at her legs. "Get the fuck out of my life, you saggy pudge lumps," she hissed at her breasts.

I disguised my voice and answered for them. They needed someone to take their side. "We don't want any trouble," I said in a high-pitched Southern accent I thought appropriate for her breasts. "Evolution and gravity are powerful foes. When did softness cease to be a quality women valued?"

Her legs I gave a thick Scottish brogue, her arms a Midwestern drawl, her stomach a child's voice, innocent and sincere, emanating, I imagined, from her navel. "I'm where you began," it pleaded. "You can't hate me."

She only got more worked up, spitting curse words at herself, dissecting her body into an anatomy of anger.

I walked into the other room, left her alone, her body silent. Hers to do with as she wished.

※

When my girlfriend weighed 132 pounds, she asked me how she looked.

"Thin," I told her. "You look thin."

"Do I look unhealthily thin?" she asked.

"No."

"Damn it!" She punched my arm. "How can you say that to me?"

※

When my girlfriend weighed 124 pounds, she was the happiest I'd ever seen her. We went to her sister's lesbian wedding. I was supposed to meet her whole family, but her parents didn't come. "Daddy doesn't approve of the whole lesbian thing," she told me. It was the first hint I got about her father. "Sometimes I think my sister's doing all this just to piss him off."

I'd never been to a lesbian wedding before, but I was open-minded. Both brides looked lovely. My girlfriend's sister, a wide-hipped sturdy butch in a navy-blue pants suit, her betrothed, a short, curvy Eastern European with a fake orange tan, penciled in eyebrows, and a giant poofy wedding gown.

Everyone asked my girlfriend if she'd lost weight. Old friends whispered the question to her during the ceremony. In the receiving line her sister slapped her ass and demanded to know her secret. As we danced to an unbelievably loud Neil Diamond medley at the reception, a silver-haired aunt shouted the question into her face.

"What?" my girlfriend asked, as if she couldn't hear.

The aunt screamed louder. "Have! You! Lost! Weight!"

"What?" my girlfriend asked over and over, smiling as her aunt repeated it two more times, then laughing herself to tears just to hear it shouted again and again and again.

❈

When my girlfriend weighed 118 pounds, she started asking me to look at other women's asses. To study them, really. To contemplate them for much longer than I'd ever thought possible.

"Look at her ass," she'd tell me as we stood in a subway car, waited on line at a movie theatre, or strolled down a crowded sidewalk. "Is my ass bigger than hers?"

She wouldn't take a quick "no."

"You've got to really look at it," she would tell me. "That woman right there, stare at her ass for seven minutes and then get back to me."

I stared at big asses, small asses. Round, flat, short, and long asses. Asses that looked as firm and solid as an unripe apple, and soft, saggy asses that had given up the fight years ago and, in that, seemed to possess a kind of stoic wisdom.

The more I looked, the more I loved them all. There was vulnerability and strength in every single one. Some remnant of the child making faces behind the adult's back. Thumbing its nose at every staring fool. Each ass was proud, each ass defiant.

So I never had to lie. "No," I told my girlfriend again and again. "Yours is definitely smaller than that one too."

❈

When my girlfriend weighed 112 pounds, she told me it was time to meet her parents.

She warned me about her father. "Everyone calls him 'Colonel,' but he's never been in the military," she said, nodding slowly.

She told me he was a difficult man. He had a way of getting what he wanted. Usually it involved making physical threats to innocent bystanders.

She told me he used to be an airline pilot, but he was forced into retirement after he kicked a passenger because a stewardess wouldn't laugh at one of his jokes. But I shouldn't mention that. Or her sister's marriage. Shouldn't mention cats or dogs because he hated small animals, thought pets were a sign of weakness, preferred to pretend they didn't exist. And I shouldn't look him in the eye when he eats, shouldn't let my fork touch my teeth.

After a while she wrote me a list. I looked at it and laughed.

"This isn't a joke," she said. "I grew up with this man."

❊

When my girlfriend weighed 107 pounds, we took her mother and father to a pricy steakhouse. Her father insisted on ordering for everyone. Even a few people at another table. He seemed not to notice his daughter's weight loss, her hollow cheeks, the caved-in eyes, the shoulders that looked like they could cut glass.

When I couldn't finish my rib eye, he called me a communist.

I laughed.

He didn't.

The remnants of grizzle and fat remained on my plate uneaten. He banged on the table and ranted about the failure of socialism across history. "You think you know what's going on in Cuba?" he shouted. "You know what Castro wants you to know and that's it. Now eat your goddamned steak."

I laughed again, softer this time. If laughter could be asked as a question, that's the sound I was making.

Then he threatened to assault a busboy if I didn't finish. I looked at my girlfriend, her plate untouched, completely ignored by her father. I looked at her mother, her plate clean as a surgeon's sink. They looked down at the table and shook their heads.

I choked down my last scraps of meat.

❊

When my girlfriend weighed 96 pounds, I took her swing dancing. We didn't know what we were doing, but I just spun her around, threw her in the air like a baton, and everyone went nuts.

Truth told, they probably didn't know what they were doing either. The swing dance fad had ended years ago, so mostly these were just people who still had the clothes.

They couldn't get enough of us, though. The more savage and violent our movements got, the more they cheered. I threw my girlfriend behind my back with one hand, turned and caught her with the other. I held her by her shoulders and swung her through the air, bent her waist around my neck and spun her all the way down to my ankles.

They screamed and applauded.

They were in a frenzy by the time we left. Men begging to dance with her, women pawing at her clothes. I had the feeling that if I would have snapped her over my knee, they would have carried me off on their shoulders.

☀

When my girlfriend weighed 83 pounds, people began to stare.

A little girl coming up the other way on the escalator at the mall looked at her and cried. Her mother turned the little girl's head away, glanced briefly at my girlfriend, and then stared daggers at me.

☀

When my girlfriend weighed 76 pounds, I tried to force-feed her in her sleep. I waited until she was unconscious. Then I got out a pint of chocolate ice cream. I whispered the names of flavors into her ears until her lips parted and her tongue peeked out past her teeth.

"Rocky Road," I whispered. "French Vanilla, Caramel Swirl."

I spooned the ice cream in slowly, and for a few seconds I thought it was actually going to work. Then she woke up gagging and pissed as hell.

She said it was a betrayal. Accused me of "gastronomic rape" as she wiped melted ice cream off her face.

"Whether I eat or not is my choice," she said. "Not yours. Got it?"

I didn't say anything. Drops of melting ice cream fell from the spoon to the bed spread.

"This is me," she said. "I'm not some damsel in distress, and this is not some dragon for you to slay. OK? I don't need you to rescue me. I just need your support."

21

Part of me felt like she had a point, and part of me felt like, "Fuck her." It didn't matter. They both added up to the same thing. "OK," I said. "Don't eat. It's your choice."

❀

When my girlfriend weighed between 70 and 60 pounds, I lost her in the apartment for three days. I didn't find her until her sister came to visit with her lesbian wife. I folded out the sofa-bed and there she was, curled up with a pile of coins and a spare set of keys in the space between the cushions and the floor.

She said she'd been calling out for days, but her voice had grown weak from the drastic weight loss. Even as she cussed me out for leaving her in the couch all week, it sounded like she was whispering.

The visit was strained and tense. My girlfriend's sister got drunk early each afternoon and spent most of the evenings snoring on the couch. Her lesbian wife couldn't stop staring at my girlfriend. "What do you do to stay so thin?" she asked.

"I don't eat," my girlfriend said.

"What, your boyfriend doesn't let you?" she asked. "He beat you up if you get too fat?"

My girlfriend didn't answer. Just laughed uneasily. Her sister's lesbian wife looked down at her own waist, slid her hands over her hips, and then looked at me, smiling.

❀

When my girlfriend weighed 58 pounds, I cheated on her with her sister's lesbian wife. My girlfriend was lost in the couch again. Her sister was passed out. I could hear my girlfriend calling me faintly between her sister's snores, but I ignored her. Maybe I was still mad over the whole "gastronomic rape" thing. Maybe I was sick of having a girlfriend who didn't eat.

Her sister's lesbian wife found me in the bedroom looking at fake celebrity porn on the computer. I tried to close the browser and hide what I was doing, but she asked me questions about their bodies, asked me to go to other Web sites where they had pictures of large half-naked women being punched and choked by men half their size.

She asked me if I pressured my girlfriend to lose the weight, if I pushed her to be so thin. She let her hand linger on mine as we both reached for the mouse at the same time.

"Tell me I'm fat," she demanded as she turned and straddled me in the chair. "Call me a pig."

She tore at the buttons on her blouse, and I felt myself growing hard against her thigh.

"Tell me to lose some weight," she begged. "I'm a cow. A big fat horse. Say it."

She was neither overweight nor attractive. But it had been so long since I'd held anything other than bone against my body.

I gave up. I told her she was a big gross whale, and we fell back onto the bed and had strange and angry sex.

Afterwards I slept soundly for the first time in weeks. I dreamt of trees, fruit, living things.

✾

When my girlfriend weighed 52 pounds, I started using her as a coat rack. She asked me to do it. Her knobby shoulders offered themselves up as perfect pegs, so we hung coats on them.

She loved it. Loved having jackets and hats piled on her, umbrellas hooked to her fingers. Soon she asked for shirts and pants to be added.

"I'm made for clothes now," she said, begging me in whispered shouts to empty the closets again, cover her in her clothes, then my clothes. "Everything fits. Everything."

She disappeared in clothing. You'd look at her standing in the corner, and all you saw was a pile of clothes.

"I want to be the clothes," called her muffled whisper from beneath the pile. "More clothes, less me."

✾

When my girlfriend weighed 47 pounds, I told her I'd been unfaithful with her sister's lesbian wife. It was hard to tell if she was angry or not. Her voice had

23

gotten so soft that everything she said was just a long hiss. I leaned in close so she could scream into my ear.

"Tell me everything about it," she asked. "Every detail."

I did.

She laughed, and her voice sounded clear and full for a moment.

Then we tried to make love for the last time. It was complicated and sometimes painful. We were all elbows, ankles, and knees. Angular. Our bodies struggling to join in an intricate erotic geometry.

"How was it for you?" she asked me when we finally gave up.

"Pound for pound, it was the best sex I ever had," I said.

She smiled, and I knew we'd be fine.

⁂

When my girlfriend weighed 43 pounds, her family finally held an intervention. Her sister said her father had been keeping any of them from saying anything. He'd said she was just doing it to get attention. If they ignored it, she would start eating again. But when her voice started getting too weak to take his phone calls, he decided to get serious.

Family and friends crowded our apartment, ate our food, drank soda. It was like a party, only angry.

"You wanted our attention? Fine, you got it," my girlfriend's father said, pacing back and forth in front of her as she lay folded up next to me on the sofa, staring off into space.

Her mother mostly just cried, put her head in her hands, and said "why" a few times. Some other family members tried to talk, but her father held the floor.

"If this is part of your non-violent, make friends with the world bullshit, let me just tell you, you're off base," he said. "Eating is the cycle of life, sweetheart. The real deal. Not that horseshit they sing about in Disney cartoons. You need to eat. You need to kill. It's a universal imperative. The moral contract is based on murder. You kill, you live, life runs through you and gets shit out to kill or be killed again. You opt out of that circle, and you're not protecting anything, you're not stopping death. You're putting the breaks on life."

My girlfriend said nothing.

A lot of people shot questions in my direction. "How could you let this happen?" "What kind of man are you?"

"The kind that doesn't force-feed his girlfriend in her sleep?" I offered. They weren't hearing it. Almost everybody seemed to blame me, thought I'd caused it somehow—except for my girlfriend's sister's lesbian wife, who'd gained some weight since I last saw her. "I don't think he had anything to do with it," she said, shooting me a dirty look and then looking at my girlfriend and widening her eyes suggestively.

"Oh, shut up," said my girlfriend. "I know he fucked you, and I don't care. Truth is, I don't care what the lot of you has to say. My body, my business. My weight, my business. You were all so happy for me 60 pounds ago, so keep smiling. It really doesn't matter, because I'm not doing this for any of you. I'm doing it for me."

It was a great speech. Too bad no one heard it. Once she'd dipped below 50 pounds, her voice had grown so weak that you couldn't really hear her unless you pressed your ear to her mouth. Even sitting right next to her, I could just barely make it out.

꧁

When my girlfriend weighed 42 pounds, she started to thin out in places I never thought you could. Her ears actually looked smaller. Then her nose, her eyes, her entire skull. Her shoulders narrowed, her hips collapsed, her ribs curved in towards one another. It was like her bones were losing weight.

꧁

When my girlfriend weighed 41 pounds, she started using my "pound for pound" line as if she'd made it up herself. It irked me at first, but I let her get away with it. She didn't have much. When people expressed concern over her health, she said, "Pound for pound, I'm the healthiest I've ever been."

When people stared, she said, "Pound for pound. I'm the sexiest woman in America."

When large men walked past her on the sidewalk, she said, "Pound for pound, I'm the best boxer on the planet."

Nobody could hear her but me. I'd grown used to her tiny voice by now, could hear it clearly on a crowded street, in my sleep, when she wasn't even talking.

Hearing the phrase so often eventually got me curious. "What does it really mean, though?" I asked her. "To be the best at something 'pound for pound.' I understand what's implied. But the words themselves...what do they really mean?"

"It's simple," she answered. "It means because I have less pounds but an equal amount of me. Each one of my pounds is worth more."

"So then you're not just disappearing," I said. "You're growing more dense. You're intensifying with each pound you lose."

"There's more of me in each pound," she said thoughtfully, considering the implications of the phrase for the first time. "Pound for pound, I'm the most me I've ever been."

※

When my girlfriend weighed 38 pounds, she couldn't wear clothes anymore. She cried for an hour. Soaked herself so bad her fingertips pruned. We eventually got her some clothes from a toy store. Not Barbie clothes. They were actually too anatomically correct. We had to stitch together the stuff they made for those new dolls with the giant heads, huge feet, and tiny waists. At this point the Barbies were actually more lifelike than my girlfriend.

It was a shame. Barbie's wardrobe had a bit more variety. Everything my girlfriend wore now was either covered in glitter or prominently featured words like "brat" or "kitten" in swollen curlicue letters.

※

When my girlfriend weighed 34 pounds, I took her country line-dancing. She fractured her shin on her first stomp-kick turn. We had to go home early.

I carried her to the car effortlessly. I'd carried her before but this was different. She felt so light—the opposite of a burden. I held her in my arms, and I felt like I was floating.

❈

When my girlfriend weighed 31 pounds, I begged her to eat. I even tried to trick her by putting her old clothes on a plate.

"You are what you eat," I offered.

She ate half a cashmere sweater and threw up.

❈

When my girlfriend weighed 26 pounds, she told me how it all started.

"It started with that table," she said. "I knew it was stupid the whole time. That was part of it too. Me knowing it was stupid."

"Does it help if I tell you that I knew it was stupid too?" I asked.

"Shut up. This is important. I'm going to say something important now." She paused, ran her finger over her lip. "That's really how I was feeling then too. Like I wanted this to be important. We were moving in together, and it was like we were doing grown-up stuff, you know? Not wanting to get that table, it was like you weren't on the same page. But it was also like I felt, if this was going to be important, I'd have to make a big deal out of it."

"And you did a great job of that."

She shushed me angrily and slapped my knee, her fingers so thin they tickled. "So when I dropped that kung pao chicken, I thought about how you always hear how it's the little things that really break your back, and I thought, What if this was one of those little things for me? And I just thought for a second, What if, because of this, I never ate again? So at first I just played with the idea. But the longer I went, the more real it got. Then at one point I realized it was the one thing that no one could take away from me. The one thing no one could protect me from. The one thing that demanded nothing from me. Does that make any sense?"

"Sure," I said. "Makes perfect sense. That and the fact that you're just real fucked up."

"Of course." She smiled, leaned in, and kissed me. Her lips had disappeared weeks ago. All I felt were her teeth, hard and true behind a thin veil of dry skin.

❀

When my girlfriend weighed 18 pounds, I took her dancing at an ultra-trendy downtown club. We waited in line for twenty minutes, me in my best suit, her in a plush burgundy dress we'd gotten that day at Toys 'R Us.

Then a bouncer offered us a deal. Apparently, they needed a temporary extra section in the velvet rope. Someone was getting more from the club's basement storage room, but he wanted to know if my girlfriend could fill in in the meantime. "I'll get you inside in like ten minutes," he said flexing his meaty neck from side to side.

There were hundreds of people ahead of us. My girlfriend nodded, and we followed him to the front of the line.

She stretched as far as she could, hooking her feet into the ring atop one short metal pillar as she clung with her fingers to another. Groups of two or three, sometimes more, would walk up against her and stop. The bouncer would look them over without moving his head. Then he would unhook my girlfriend's feet, lift her up, and let them in, or just wave them away if he didn't like what he saw.

Sometimes it almost got ugly. Two college-aged fraternity types waved their arms and leaned against my girlfriend when the bouncer said he'd let in the girl they brought but not them. A group of four short European men dressed in black tried to peel her fingers away and sneak in when the bouncer wasn't looking, but my girlfriend held tight until he turned around and chased them out of the alley. Anytime anyone was refused, they walked away looking not at the bouncer who'd ordered them away, but at my girlfriend, the soft barrier between in and out, the border between their desire and their inadequacy.

When they'd finally found their spare length of rope and offered to let us inside, my girlfriend refused. "I'd like to keep at it and finish up the night," she said to both me and the bouncer. I told him what she'd said, and he just shrugged.

We stayed long into the night. After the crowds had left my girlfriend seemed almost lost.

"That's it," said the bouncer. "We don't need the ropes anymore. I'd tell you guys to head on in, but it's last call."

I told him we'd just be heading home, but my girlfriend didn't move. She looked like she was going to cry. "What's the matter?" I asked her.

"The way they all looked at me . . . I'd never felt such hatred and such longing at the same time," she said. "It was wonderful."

❀

When my girlfriend weighed 14 pounds, her father called me drunk and in tears. He said he was calling for her, but she hadn't been strong enough to hold a telephone in weeks. For a while I could hold it up to her ear, and she'd scream as loud as she could, but as her voice got weaker and weaker, that had become pointless.

Her father knew all this, but when I explained it to him again and tried to rush him off the phone, he just kept talking as if it were me he'd really wanted to talk to all along.

"Do you know what it's like to raise daughters?" he asked me.

"No, sir," I said. "No, Colonel, I mean."

"More than anything in this grand shit-stain of a world, daughters will teach you what an asshole you are. You see the world through their eyes. Only you know the truth. You smash those two things together and you take a look at yourself . . . It ain't pretty. Now, both of them are busy erasing themselves from my life, and that's all I'm left with—me through their eyes, the truth."

❀

When my girlfriend weighed 11 pounds, I didn't knock her over when I sneezed. Not because that would have been physically impossible, but because when I gasped before the sneeze I inhaled her down to her ankles.

Her feet hung from my mouth like the ends of thick, undercooked noodles. I tickled them before coughing her back up, and I felt her laughter rumble deep inside my belly as if it were my own.

❀

When my girlfriend weighed 9 pounds, her father called back to tell me more. He didn't even bother to ask for her this time, just went right into it.

"When they were little, they wanted to be princesses," he said weakly, struggling not to cry. "But I made them play as knights. I wanted them to be strong. I wanted them to know they could do anything men did. So I built a dragon in the basement—out of the legs of their dolls and the head of some pony with rainbow colored hair. For swords I made them use their plastic high-heel dress-up shoes. They wanted to make friends with the dragon, but I told them they had to kill it . . ."

He explained the rest of what he did. The argument over whether a dragon could ever be friends with a knight. How he piled their dolls in front of the dragon's head, said it was going to breathe fire on their dolls if they didn't kill it, actually got a can of hairspray and a lighter.

"It was only supposed to scare them," he said. "But you play with fire . . . What can you expect?"

The flame caught one of the doll's toes. They went up quickly. I could see it. Clothes burning like cheap paper. Plastic faces melting, collapsing in on themselves.

"That shook them into a frenzy," he explained. "I got what I wanted. They beat that dragon to shit with their little shoes. They were still at it after I'd put out the fire. Their eyes were crammed with rage. For just a hair of a second I thought I'd taught them something important. Then, of course, I saw that they weren't looking at the dragon. They were looking at me."

*

When my girlfriend weighed 8 pounds, I held her like a baby. Curled her up in my arms, her body brittle but unbreaking. I looked into her deep-set eyes, her face a death's head wrapped in skin, and I sang to her. It was a lullaby about sleeping, falling, dying.

Aren't they all?

*

When my girlfriend weighed 3 pounds, I took her dancing on my back. Took off my shirt, put on some Al Green records, and said, "Have at it."

I could just barely feel her. Her feet tickled my bare skin like thin fibers from a feather. I laughed so hard I cried.

Getty

❋

When my girlfriend weighed 1 pound, I noticed her for the first time. Like we were just now meeting.

I introduced myself, and when I shook her hand, barbed and delicate like the foot of a baby bird, there was no longer any mystery. I understood her with the clarity we reserve for strangers.
She was finally what she was.

❋

When my girlfriend disappeared, I found out her sister's lesbian wife was pregnant. My girlfriend's father told me. He'd been calling every day for the last week. We'd had some good talks.

"I'm trying to be OK with the whole dyke thing," he said. "Maybe she doesn't have to be erased if I can deal with it. Maybe this baby just shows they really can do anything a man and woman can do. I wonder how they pulled that off, though. I'm not up on all the latest procedures."

I wanted to tell him there weren't any procedures, the baby was mine, the truth would come out, their marriage would end, I would be blamed.

"I got to go," I said. "Just call your daughter. Tell her you love her. Don't call her a dyke."

When I hung up the phone, I asked my girlfriend for advice, walked around the empty apartment talking to nobody, thinking maybe she was still there somewhere, just too thin for me to see, or maybe lost forever in some other piece of furniture.

"I have to do something," I said. "Don't you think? It's my baby, right? They're going to figure that out."

I listened intently for an answer. Still, not moving, not breathing for what seemed like hours, I heard things I'd never heard before. Our neighbors, an old retired couple, singing soft love songs to each other. Children outside teasing one another in cruel whispers. Footsteps of insects crawling in the walls.

Then I heard her voice. Or maybe I imagined it. There was no way to tell anymore.

Over the next week we had some of our best conversations. Our most honest heart to hearts. Sometimes I lost her voice when a car drove by outside, or one of the larger insects scurried through the wall, or she just got tired of talking. But it didn't matter. I'd come to know her well enough to carry both sides of the conversation.

She told me I'd have to take responsibility. I'd have to try to make a family with her sister and her lesbian wife. I'd have to grow up. I'd have to buy a dining room table.

I talked honestly for the first time about my own feelings of inadequacy, my sense of helplessness. How it felt to watch someone I loved waste away. How it felt to be unable, and then even unwilling, to stop it. How it felt to be jealous of her now. To wish I could disappear like her.

❀

When my girlfriend stopped answering me altogether, when I could no longer even imagine her quiet voice, when she'd finally lost all the weight, I flew out to her sister's. I brought a dozen orange roses and a copy of *What to Expect When You're Expecting*. I had big plans.

I slept on the plane most of the way, and as I slept I dreamt of the baby and my girlfriend. They tangled together in that odd half-formed dream logic. One wasting away beside me, the other growing day by day in the dark recesses of a woman who wanted me to make her disappear.

In my dream I was the creator of all of it. Not just the baby, but my girlfriend's weight loss and the strange connection between the two. Then sometimes my girlfriend was the baby, and I was pregnant. Or she was pregnant, and I was the baby making her hungry enough to eat again. In the end, I didn't even know who was pregnant anymore, but the baby was all of us. Me, my girlfriend, my girlfriend's sister, her mother and father, you name it—all of us waiting inside, waiting to be born into a world of stark light and noise.

It all stayed with me long after I woke. Even by the time I rang my girlfriend's sister's doorbell, I wasn't completely sure if it was the baby, my girlfriend, or myself I'd come to claim.

It didn't go as I'd expected. They took the flowers, but they both just stared at the book.

"Is that some kind of sick joke?" my girlfriend's sister asked.

I stammered for a few seconds, trying to explain why I was there. "I want to do the right thing . . . I know it will be hard at first . . . It's for all of us."

"I had a miscarriage about a week ago," said my girlfriend's sister's lesbian wife.

"By miscarriage, she means abortion," said my girlfriend's sister. "But alas the truth is sometimes just too challenging for my wife."

As I sank back onto their love seat, dropping the book on the floor, they started yelling at each other. I'd walked into a fight that had probably been going on since the day they met.

"How could you do that without talking to me?" I interrupted finally.

They both stared at me, mouths open. "Why the hell would she talk to you?" said my girlfriend's sister. Then she laughed. "Oh my God. That's why you're here. That's so cute. I see why my sister liked you."

"I don't get it," I said. "Why didn't you at least tell me?"

"Relax," said my girlfriend's sister, smiling. "My wife fucks a lot of guys. She's one of those Howard Stern lesbians. Half the time, I think she just got into the whole scene because she's too lazy to shave her pits."

I still didn't get it. I kept babbling about my rights as a father until my girlfriend's sister's lesbian wife stepped forward and drew me the picture.

"I'd already known I was knocked up for two weeks when I slept with you," she said. "That's why I did it—to get rid of the baby. I thought you'd make me lose enough weight to have a miscarriage. My wife, God fuck her, says I have an unfounded faith in the power of men to magically transform my life. At least I'm not the one with the daddy issues."

They launched back into the fight that was their love. Chased each other from the living room to the kitchen, to the bathroom. Broke the vase they'd put the orange roses in. Collapsed crying on the stairs, telling each other, "You are my everything."

I told them I was going to get going, apologized for misunderstanding the whole thing, asked if they wanted to keep the book.

They sat down on the sofa opposite me, and I just kept talking, my voice now a creature with its own mind. I told them everything. The fight in Ikea, the kung pao chicken, the asses of other women, the swing dancing, the day we buried my girlfriend in clothes, how I held her like a baby.

Then I told them about my dream on the plane. About me, the baby, my girlfriend, and all of us. Even if it wasn't mine, I told them, they shouldn't have gotten rid of the baby.

"I would have taken it, taken care of it for us," I said. "I would have raised it strong and proud, and complicated, and beautiful for all of us. I would have taught it that dragons are neither our friends nor our foes, but powerful, magical creatures deserving both our fear and our pity. I would have taught it that everything deserves our fear and our pity—even ourselves."

"Would you have taken the swelling and the stretch marks too?" asked my girlfriend's sister's lesbian wife.

"The morning sickness?" asked my girlfriend's sister.

"The varicose veins? The back labor? The torn perineum?"

"The chance of death?"

"I would have done what I could," I said, picking the book up off the floor and laying it on the coffee table between us.

"Exactly," they both said, as if that settled it all.

We sat silently for a few minutes, but it felt like longer. Then they asked me more about my girlfriend. They wanted to know every detail of our last days together.

Then finally they got to the question I could tell they'd been dying to ask the whole time, the question they wanted to ask me as soon as I got in the door. Would have asked me over the phone if I hadn't told them I was coming.

"Before she disappeared," her sister said.

"In the last seconds," said her sister's lesbian wife.

"How did she look?" they both asked in unison, leaning forward on the edge of the sofa, their hands curling together, touching tenderly and casually on the coffee table.

"She was beautiful," I said. "I could barely see her."

An Interview with Matt Getty
Author of *When My Girlfriend Lost the Weight*

1. This is a story that just grabbed me right away; there may even be a certain shock value to this story. Did you find it difficult to write?

At times, yes, but for the most part it came quickly and easily. Originally, I thought it would be flash fiction. I figured I'd just hit five or six weights on my way down to zero and wrap it all up in 1,000 words. But it was just too much fun. I kept finding new ways to play with the basic idea and kept adding new weights.

It only got difficult when I started to wonder what it was all about. Then I sat on it for a long time—2 years actually—before I felt comfortable enough to send it out.

2. What I also find interesting about this story is the first person male point of view. Tell me why you chose this particular method of telling the story.

I think that really just came from the set up. For some reason, I thought it would be interesting to write a story that began every section with the line, "When my girlfriend weighed ..." and that set up kind of dictated the point of view.

But I have been playing with a longer version of this, and I sometimes think of trying two different versions—"When You Lost the Weight" and "When Your Girlfriend Lost the Weight." A few years ago I wrote this little book "You Will Behave," which some people say was the first book written in the second-person future, so sometimes I get all ambitious and think maybe this could be the first gendered book, with alternate versions for men and women. And then I just tell myself to calm down.

3. I read that you were inspired to write this story after reading about Mollie Fancher, who essentially starved herself in the late 19th century. Tell me more about these "fasting girls" and how you were able to take the research you did and write about this very particular woman.

Actually, I'd already written much of this when I came across Mollie Fancher's story. It was really weird because I thought I was writing this ridiculous fantasy, but here there were tons of stories of real women who reportedly went 10 to 20 years without eating. It was actually helpful because when the first draft of "When My Girlfriend Lost the Weight" was done, I was worried about the whole anorexia thing. I kept hearing these imaginary readers in my head scoffing at the story and saying things like, "That's not how anorexia works!" But—and I know this sounds weird—I never wanted this to be about anorexia. Whatever's going on here, I didn't want it to be something that people could point at and say, "Oh, this is this, and this works this way."

So anyway, then I came across these stories of "fasting girls" going all the way back to the Middle Ages, and there was always something mystical attached to it. In the Middle Ages, they had visions, spoke to God, became saints. Then in the 19th century they had ESP or other fringe abilities. Mollie Fancher never left her bedroom, but she was supposedly able to see people miles away and describe what they were doing.

Now, of course, there's a lot of skepticism about whether these women actually ate nothing and actually had these abilities. Whether you believe that or not, however, it's clear that the whole not eating thing has been around a lot longer than these clinical definitions we created to explain them in the 20th century. That kind of gave me the courage to see that the story could be bigger than anorexia, or eating disorders, or psychological explanations. It was liberating.

4. Did you submit this story to other magazines before FRiGG published it? Any particular reactions from previous editors?

I did submit it to *Esquire* and got a really nice rejection. I think they even used the word "mesmerizing," but they said its tone wasn't a good match. Then I sent it straight to FRiGG.

4. What else do you have in the hopper?

I am trying to finish a novel version of this story, though I doubt I'll do the different versions for men and women thing. The plan is to do a chapter for each pound. My most recent short story is about raising a child whose body parts keep falling off. It will be interesting when I find out that that actually happens.

Chamber Music
by Sam Rasnake
from BOXCAR Poetry Review

— after viewing Ingmar Bergman's film trilogy

1. *Through a Glass Darkly*

Is it foolish
to think God
a spider?

a spun moment,
perfect in its
architecture of waiting?
in its raw edge of abandon?

The gull cries
a sudden emptiness
of sea lapping stone.

Wind in heavy grass —
Is that what I carry?

What I carry, I forgive,
what I forgive, I touch
or name or pity

like the fields
soaked with rain,
like voices inside
my mouth, like a love
with no bowl
for keeping.

2. *Winter Light*

Your body, like river-rush
in late November,
craves the early summer.

Our eyes refuse us nothing.

The fence and sky,
tough wings of darkness
expect a storm,
will not be moved.

Sheets thrown back.
The hard gossip we surrender to,
coughed hallelujahs, and guilt
to feed us.

Through a closed window at dusk,
I watch wind jar the hazel tree
by the porch, but hear nothing.

3. *The Silence*

I've no idea where I am.
There's no one to call,
and if there were,
I'd have nothing to tell.

War rumbles through the city
and on the rails.
All the faces are the same.
They speak in tongues, they wear fear
on their shoulders.

There's no one –
But you know this already.

The body I touch is no longer mine.

I spend my time changing words –
translation in a cloud of smoke.
The piano is Bach, Goldberg Variations.

This hotel, with its hint of plush,
massive, severe, is mostly empty.
In the corridor, a passing troupe of dwarfs,
the last one in death mask,
is my pretense for loneliness.

Under my window, a scrawny horse
whose ribs could spell my name
pulls at a wagon, loaded with junk
to sell, over the narrow, dirty street,
from one lost intent to the next.

Theodolite's Survey
by Jordan Zinovich
from *Big Bridge*

In an age when everywoman was expected to slap barefoot and perpetually plump around hearth and homefires (2006 B.D. - BY DUBBYA-EM-DEE!), Theodolite Pope's-Nose was a swollen little pullet who riddled convention by having none of it. She dwelt baldly in the tiny Yankee hamlet of Little Grotty, South Carolina (population 69), having lost her hair-shirt and not bothered to look for it. Her husbandman, Butthole William Bailey (AB for short), was one of fifteen local publicans. They didn't run their taverns, exactly, just drank up the votes.

Theodolite was a trailblazer. One bright morning she clamped her blind left eye to the backend of a moose and searched for a glimmer of hope. She searched HiLo through antecedents and precedents interior the posterior until she scryed a solution, which she dodged in the nick of time. Old New-Gate Prison! Of course! The ancient north-country mineshaft where her granddames tossed burglars, horse thieves, and low-L liberals was the perfect place to career as a floozy. Nearby was an explosives factory slash art center where as a girl she'd seen fascinating bits of art. It all fitted together perfectly. That neighborhood had its hopeful perversities. And so she set off, abandoning Butthole Bill and his spawn to fretting flatulence.

1.

The first crackpot that tripped her on the road was a pimply farmer named Bert Yodél. "Do you yodel?" he asked ingenuously, realizing the fine stream he waded, anti-semitically speaking. Theodolite, of course, was prepared for anything, regardless of what it knew. The boils spangling Berts face signaled his hormonal challenge, but that was okay. They were nicely textured and the goose-eggs on his head made plain that another kind soul had tried beating sense into him. Together they were an aesthetically pleasing combination. Who knew? He might back Ms. Pope's-Nose into a future together - at least until she found wolves to toss him to.

Bert said his upland farm lay below sea level, which suited Theodolite's smelly sense of irony. Finally, the south end of a north-facing horse, she chortled fitfully. Butter-breast-milk while you can, no telling when you'll need next. Time passed quickly around them, silently between Bert's ungodly and echoless shrieks. But four hours proved sufficient. Theodolite abandoned Yodél without waiting for the wolves, tying him to a tree with a note wishing them good luck. At least AB could whinny, she murmured, her ears still ringing. It that a telephone? Maybe I'd better go back and rip out his tongue. Wolves like to eat in peace.

2.

"Angiosperms!" dribbled the next idiot she met, planting himself shallowly in the roadbed, rustling as gently as dinosaurs in the breeze.

Oh ye gods of thieves and travelers, rattled deer famished Theodolite. Send me Sweeney Todd. I have the razor, but lack testicules to swing it.

She paused to survey her situation. From Little Grotty to Old-New Gate Prison looked to become a very, very long-winded road. The idiot looked up from the rut he was pawing and waggled his antlers. A very long-winded road indeed, gnarled Theodolite, walking softly for a big stick.

Cuck you buddy, she sighed, whacking him with singular emphasis, leaving him prostate on the gravitas.

3.

Arriving at a fork in the road she took it. It was a pitchfork - portent to a potent tale of unusual length and vigor; a black tail with a point to it, she could see that. She wondered to whit and whom it had belonged, then didn't care. It was a Sturm und Drangy day with faintly Nietchzean tangs of Goethe in the damp air. Saturated, Theodolite gripped the gasping exercises she'd stolen from a mad Tibetan mendicant who hadn't been tall but was honest and self abusing. What more couldn't a woman want? She wondered, patting her petunias.

The castellated high school in the distance had a distant look about it, marred only by a tiny Hakminster Bey window that suggested little thinking inside. Geodesically speaking, if it doesn't it soon will, she thank grimly, refilling a purse with her downstairs smile. I know the fulvous lechers inhabiting such places mix nuts like kindly blowsy intellectuals. I'll get a snoot full before you jack-robin son. Great practice for Old-New Gate floozing.

Then she thunk again. Why whittle away a peasant forenoon skinning companies of arrested adolescence playing with their piercings? Theodolite thought not. Nix on that, regardless of institutional propriety and manifold crookedness. Somewhere wars were lost. Sometime diplomats were tossing in deep reverence to a break wind. The raspberry was ripe. Gather ye rosehips while ye may, mixed nuts are too damned tedious to sort. In short: Time fugit. She'd never liked high school. History! It was all politics and histrionics. By dubbya-em-dee, who cared? We'll all be dumb as dork-knob soon enough.

Eight chains transit the moon, she sang. Eight rods urge this lunatic on. And so singing she sought her parting amicably, finding it at sunset near the northern horizon. Damn them dubbya-em-dee. Damn them everyone.

Why
by Kathrine Leone Wright
from *Brevity*

What good are you? What do you do? – *Dr. Seuss*

Because language is all we have. Because today my son is eight years old. Because songs run over, over, over and spiral out on their own axis. Because I cannot sing. Because almost nearly half through last century and however much is left to me of this one is all the time I'm allotted. Because neurons fire up the ovens. Because my daughter knows: four times four is sixteen is the square root of divided by.

Because intergalactic dust and gas. Because moon rising, rain. Because the world is held together with duck tape and string, my friend. Because pale light and all. Because when a tree is struck by lightning the tree's growth is altered. A knot sometimes forms where the lightning hit. Because all the same exchange fuckay fuckay. Because for years, perhaps all of their lives the wind would die as they touched.

Because it doesn't cost a dime or an asphalt burn. Because you shouldn't run with sharpies. Because I can make seventy-five pieces of popcorn small enough to fit inside my small mouth.

Because I am of the only ten percent going south with pens. But I can make north, too. Sometimes north is good.

Because words: Belligerent. Marsupial. Jodhpurs. Silversmith.

Because there's no room for chit-chit-chit-chat. Because there's rhythm in them thar hills. Because I was thirty before I learned that feta + cucumbers + tomatoes + plain yogurt dallops = just the thing. (Note to self: Don't forget the kalamata olives.) No one should wait that long. I need to tell them.

Because you should do what can't be done, and then some. Because it takes more than this much time to glean petroleum from the floor. Because energy volts detonate from behind my eyes.

Because it arrived at my door as an empty corrugated box with paisley paper. Because when the box did gymnastics, I threw oily vibrant pastels into the crevices. Because my mother called me in for dinner and inch-thick paint calcified and the box blew into three hundred fifty seven pieces. All red. Ten different reds. Cinnamon. Cimmarron. Fire engine. Fury. The color of my hair. Because. Just that.

Because just when you think there aren't three hundred words left to sling together, you have. Because the same road signs dot Highway 50 and I-95 but each jaunt to the grocery store is new. Because of the wonderful things he does. We're off to see the wizard.

Because you just can't slip your eye under the door, but bees can swarm your belly. Ask my friend Scarlett.

Because I was born where mushroom clouds scattered cancer seeds. Because that red, violent earth runs through my veins like so much caffeine. Because it's an easy trip right back to there.

Because sometimes you just know.

Because it's leaded fuel, antioxidant, free-range. Because no one thinks exactly like each of us. Because ninety words per minute shoot from my fingers. Pow! Because I'm forever chasing what-gets-away. Because words seeped out in dreams are the worst. A notebook by the bed? Fuck that.

Because when I wasn't much taller than half my current height, there were myths and Greek gods and tired tall tales gasped and spewed. Because you only get one ticket. Because when I wasn't tall enough, poems curled off manual typewriters. Today they're retired. Because tomorrow you, too, will be tired.

Because it can slay like a scalpel, a trademark, an AK-47. Goliath. That's who.

Because clarity, obscurity, contradiction, levitation. Because conjugation. To be. To be. To be. It depends on what the meaning of the word *is* is.

Because there are few perfect titles. Do you have a perfect title? Because you could share it and we could all be thermoluminescent. Warm and lovely.

Because once I buried time in a sandbox, found it months later in a plastic baggie. Because chaos, string, relativity explain us. But not enough.

Because a good firm stride and handshake are equally important. Because my mother kept her sewing gene, gave me her sewing machine. Because missing buttons bring down entire closets. Because when I close the last page, the very last page, my head lifts from my spinal cord.

Because the world has much to say. Because the world.

An Ugly Man
by Marcela Fuentes
from *The Vestal Review*

On her lunch break, she dumps Luis for Daniel Towens, the ugliest man in the county.

She and Luis meet at the downtown café Luis hates. He picks a table next to the window to keep an eye on the parking meter. There's an old beater truck in the space he wanted and he grumbles that the guy is probably not even a customer. Nothing but hipsters eat here, he says, artsy gringos and uppity high-spanics like her, who like to spend money when they can make a fucking sandwich at home. He scowls out the café window.

Daniel Towens steps out of the credit union across the street. He stands on the sidewalk waiting for the traffic to clear. Daniel is lanky and mercilessly freckled. He wears dusty green coveralls with National Park Service stitched on the pocket. He has an unfortunate arrangement of teeth. They jut from his mouth like fossilized woodchips.

Fuck that's an ugly guero, Luis says. He thinks it's funny that Daniel is sweet on her. When she frowns Luis flashes a shark grin, all razor and gleam. Fuckin' ugly, he says again, and bites his roast beef sandwich.

She doesn't tell Luis not to be rude. She purses her mouth around her straw and sucks cold lemon water. She pretends she's not listening, although the couple at a nearby table shift to look at him. Her face stiffens with the effort of indifference, lacquers over, smooth as riverbed sand.

In the desert Daniel, glides over rocky caliche and scrub brush. He leads hikers and artists and anthropologists on expeditions through the chaparral, identifying varieties of lichens and cacti, spelunking for prehistoric rock art. But he crosses the street with his face to the ground, hunching his chicken-thin shoulders, a hank of dull hair splayed on his green collar.

He stops, his back to the café window, and digs in his front pocket. The small truck, white and latticed with dried mud, appears to be his. Luis knocks on the glass and waves. Daniel squints. He offers an uncertain closed-lipped smile.

You're funny, she says, standing up. She walks out of the café. Luis says hey-hey-hey, the word tugged out of him in sharp little jerks.

Daniel, she says. She steps into him, so close his head blocks the hard afternoon light. He smells like bluff sage and wind. His eyes are mild as cloud shadows. She sets her mouth on the wilderness of his mouth, lets it open against the rough structures of his teeth.

Powwow
by Darlin' Neal
from *Wigleaf*

At dawn on a day nearing Easter, Lily wanted to sneak around and see if her parents had bought any more presents, any candy or stuffed animals. Yesterday the family had gone down to Grants and done some shopping while Lily had waited in the car. She already knew her mother had bought a giant dictionary because she'd seen it in a cabinet above the couch. They'd been practicing words. Each morning they started with a new one.

She stuck her head out the small trailer window to try and see if her father was already gone to work.

What she saw instead of her father was a Jemez man running barefoot. It filled her with longing to follow, his swift silent movement, his long hair trailing after, the way he headed up the side of the golden red mountain toward the cliffs. Heights made her freeze with fear. She wished to live here long enough that she would know many trails and could work on losing that fear. She wished to live here always.

She stepped out her door and into the kitchen. There would be no sneaking around. Her mother sat there drinking coffee. In the center of the table sat a basket of Easter lilies. "Speculate," her mother said.

Her mother speculated about whether or not they should plant them outside in honor of Lily, to leave something behind that was her name. Would they grow in the mountains? They would never know if the flowers came up the next year and bloomed or not. They were always moving. Any day now, Lily's father would hitch the trailer to the pickup and off they would go, again.

"Speculate, speculate," Lily muttered. She went and turned the TV on with the volume all the way down. Her baby brothers were sleeping on the couch. On the screen a woman sang high and whispery as a mouse. Then pageant girls were doing cartwheels and twirling batons.

"Did the singing wake you last night?" Lily's mother asked.

"Yes, but it was interesting."

Heyya, yahna, heyya, yahna, started running through Lily's head.

"Were they having a pow-wow?" Lily asked, mainly because she liked the way that sounded.

"Some ceremony or the other," her mother said.

There wasn't room to do a cartwheel so Lily braced against the wall and stood on her head. She watched an upside-down woman wearing a tiara. She didn't know how in the world, but this woke one of the babies up.

"You're hyper," her mother said. "Why don't you take your brother and go to the store. You can buy some gum."

Outside, Lily scanned the cliffs looking for runners. She'd seen a funny thing once while riding in a car and she thought of it now. A convertible coming fast around a curve, the side of the mountain plunging on the other side of her, and the driver flew out still holding the wheel, and then back in. "Did you see that?" everyone kept saying. Her mother said, "His eyes were as big as silver dollars."

"Silver dollars, sand dollars," she said now. She walked along the arroyo, carrying her baby brother on her hip. The thin crust of dry earth crunched beneath her feet and turned to the softest powder. She felt it between her toes, wishing she was feeling home. She let the baby down so he could feel it too.

Hives
by Elizabeth Penrose
from *Abyss & Apex*

My babysitter told me she had hives
And showed me a hole in the palm of her hand
Where bees kept going out and coming in,
Their yellow fuzz bright against pink skin.
Then she lifted her dress hem and showed me her thigh
Where a knot of the insects pushed against her nylons
And worried the shining network of threads.
She let me snuggle in fearfully, past hand and leg
As we lay down on my living room floor.
I rested my head upon her breast
To hear the great murmur within her body:
Whole chambers of workers and knots of nestlings
Buzzing around blood vessels and below each organ,
And the queen herself ticked out eggs
In a honeycomb beneath my babysitter's heart.
She was a sweet girl to show me that,
But I could never forget, in all our gentle hours,
The angry rattle that went through her.

Macedonio Fernández: The Man Who Invented Borges
by Marcelo Ballvé

from *The Quarterly Conversation*

I.

In 1921, a well-to-do Argentine family arrived in Buenos Aires on a grand transatlantic ship, the *Reina Victoria Eugenia*. If they were on deck to watch the city come into view after seven years in Europe and a three-week ocean crossing, they would have first seen the curved *art nouveau* facade of the Argentine Yacht Club at the port's entrance, its spire evocative of a lighthouse; then they may have noted the *belle epoque* customs house, which rose higher than the loading cranes and warehouses of the Dársena Norte port complex; and finally, once they arrived at the passenger pier, they would have seen the crowd eagerly awaiting the ship. On that pier, if we are to trust the memory of Jorge Luis Borges, began the most pivotal friendship in Argentina's 20th century literary history.

The family on the ship was Borges's: along with him traveled his father, mother, sister, and paternal grandmother. Among the friends and relatives waiting to greet them was one Macedonio Fernández, a longtime friend of Borges's father who had graduated with him from the University of Buenos Aires law school. This Fernández may have been a lawyer by education, but he was a writer and philosopher by inclination, and had been recently widowed—all circumstances that would contribute to his affinity for the 22-year-old Borges, whom everyone called "Georgie." Likewise, no one ever referred to Fernández by his last name; he was known by his beguiling and unusual first name: Macedonio.

Many years later, this is how Borges would remember his first meeting with Macedonio, who would become Borges's mentor and a sort of intellectual guru to all the poetry and art-addled young men of 1920s Buenos Aires: "When we arrived, a miniscule figure in a bowler hat was waiting for us at Dársena Norte, and I inherited his sumptuous friendship from my father."[1]

1.) Material regarding Borges's recollection of Macedonio's presence on the pier, and the ship's name

The friendship, though it was definitely most intense in the 1920s and cooled afterward, lasted until Macedonio's death in 1952. The words Borges delivered in a eulogy at Macedonio's burial are the most eloquent confirmation of how important this bond was to Borges's development. "In those years," Borges said, referring to the 1920s,

I imitated him, to the point of transcription, to the point of devoted and impassioned plagiarism. I felt: Macedonio is metaphysics, is literature. Whoever preceded him might shine in history, but they were all rough drafts of Macedonio, imperfect previous versions. To not imitate this canon would have represented incredible negligence.

Gabriel del Mazo, Macedonio's cousin, remembers Borges's speech by the family crypt for a different reason. It may have been the first time in the history of the Recoleta Cemetery, a decidedly somber if beautiful necropolis, that attendees at a burial burst into laughter. Borges accomplished this by recalling one of Macedonio's jokes: that gauchos were invented as entertainments for horses.[2]

Humor was one of the hallmarks of Macedonio's writing—a refined and cerebral humor typically flavored with paradox (in one piece he describes a man who is always rushing around so as to be the first one to arrive late). The affinity for the paradoxical proposition is one of the many ways in which Borges took after his old friend, but hardly the only one. Both men were enamored of speculative philosophy, and arguably it was Macedonio who was responsible for making a metaphysician out of Borges. Both writers were incessant explorers of a handful of themes: the inexistence of the individual personality, the elastic nature of time, the permeability of waking life to dreams and vice-versa; one might say: the instability of reality in general. In both writers' work the

and passengers, is taken from two sources: *Macedonio Fernández—Jorge Luis Borges: Correspondencia 1922-1939: Crónica de una amistad*, Carlos García (ed. and notes). Buenos Aires: Corregidor, 2000 (pg. 33); as well as *Macedonio Fernández: La biografía imposible*, by Álvaro Abós. Buenos Aires: Plaza & Janés, 2002 (pg. 99). García's evenhanded and thoroughly annotated and researched book is the best resource I came across for understanding the ins and outs of the friendship.
2.) Borges's speech at the cemetery has been widely reprinted, but is included as the epigraph to the book *Hablan de Macedonio Fernández*, Germán García (ed.). Buenos Aires. Atuel, 1996. The book also includes Gabriel del Mazo's anecdote about laughter at the Recoleta Cemetery (pgs. 34-35). The translation of the fragment from Borges's speech is mine, as are most of the quotes reproduced above in the text.

supposedly bedrock concepts by which we live are revealed to be unstable isotopes, slippery and layered, none being in essence what they appear to be and all of course eminently moldable, especially within the pages of a story, poem, or essay.

There is an ongoing debate in Argentine literary circles about the extent to which Borges was influenced by Macedonio, an eccentric genius who spent the final three decades of his life drifting through Buenos Aires boardinghouses and country hermitages, absorbed in writing and thinking. Some critics believe that without Macedonio's influence, the Borges we know would have never existed. Noé Jitrik, who might be described as the dean of academic literary critics in Argentina, said last year in an interview with Buenos Aires's leading newspaper, *Clarín*, that "Borges is a product of Macedonio."[3]

For other critics, Borges's friendship with Macedonio is instrumental, but hardly determinant. They point out that Borges published his famous short stories in the 1940s, a decade or more after the period in which he was closest to Macedonio. Also, Borges's own reading appetites were omnivorous and prodigious: Who's to say whether he absorbed this or that idea from Macedonio or from a tome in his own library? Also, they regard the debate as somewhat spurious: even if the fodder for Borges's iconic short stories like "Tlön, Uqbar, Orbis Tertius" or "The Circular Ruins" came via Macedonio's influence or idea bank, it's certainly Borges's consummate art as a stylist and storyteller that enabled him to fashion flawless prose from the material.

Whatever the outcome of this critical debate, if there is one, it's clear Macedonio left a deep imprint on Borges, one of the 20th century's great writers. And yet Macedonio Fernández's name and his work are hardly known outside Argentina. What's needed is a proper estimation of Macedonio's legacy; toward this, it's still useful to examine his friendship with

---

3.) Jitrik's quote can be found in the Sept. 7, 2007 edition of Clarín (http://www.clarin.com/diario/2007/09/07/sociedad/s-04501.htm). The quote was given in the context of the publication of one of the twelve volumes of the *Critical History of Argentine Literature*; the volume was entirely devoted to Macedonio. Only one other author was distinguished by having a single volume devoted to his or her work: Argentine founding father figure and 19th-century intellectual Domingo Faustino Sarmiento. The attention given to Macedonio might be interpreted as part of a larger critical effort to push Macedonio out from under Borges's shadow in the Argentine canon. The best academic work I came across arguing Borges's literary reliance on Macedonio and detailing some of Borges's suspicious disavowals of his onetime mentor is *Desencuadernados: vanguardias ex-céntricas en el Río de la Plata*, by Julio Prieto. Buenos Aires: Beatriz Viterbo Editora, 2002.

the much better-known Borges, as well as the ideas they decanted together amidst the general intellectual ferment of 1920s Buenos Aires.[4]

II.

The flowering of the friendship between Borges and Macedonio was quick and intense. Memoirs of the 1920s recall a cafe in the Once neighborhood of Buenos Aires called La Perla where Macedonio would hold court on Saturday evenings. When not finding him in the cafe, young literary men would visit him at his boardinghouse rooms, where Macedonio would offer visitors gourds of yerba mate as well as cookie-like Argentine confections called *alfajores*, which he kept stashed in an old suitcase under the bed. More than one memoir recalls Macedonio's alfajores had a funny tendency to emerge from storage as an unidentifiable blob of crumbs, *dulce de leche*, and chocolate.

Reminiscences also coincide in the portrait they draw of Macedonio: a small and slight but striking man with a dark mustache and flowing white hair, usually swaddled deep in a poncho, fond of strumming a guitar and sinking into silence to meditate upon some point of philosophy, only to emerge from absorption with a brilliant turn of phrase.

Borges was among his most assiduous visitors. In those days Borges had a habit of taking endless walks around Buenos Aires, calling on Macedonio at insomniac hours. Almost immediately, the two men began to exchange writing and ideas.

Before the end of 1921, Borges had included a poem of Macedonio's in an anthology of contemporary Argentine verse he prepared for the Spanish magazine *Cosmópolis*. This publication is, for several reasons, an important indication of the intellectual infatuation the men shared. To begin with, the poem is titled *"Al hijo de un amigo"* or "To the Son of a Friend," and so it is explicitly dedicated to Georgie. On the one hand the poem reads as a summation of Macedonio's metaphysical interests: "Drunk with meaning / Reality works as an open mystery / And succeeds sometimes / In making not only dreams but life / Seem like a dream." But the poem is also interspersed with tributes to Georgie's youth and enthusiasm for life: "The

4.) The U.S. publishing house Open Letter is slated to publish an English translation of Macedonio's posthumous novel *Museo de la Novela de La Eterna* in fall 2009, hopefully creating an English-language readership for Macedonio.

way I saw him yesterday / Greet a woman soul to soul / I came to understand what greeting was." The poem is shot through with affection, but so is the gushing biographical note appended to the end of it, penned by Borges himself:

> *Macedonio Fernández: perhaps the only genius in this anthology. Metaphysician, denier of the I . . . crucible of paradoxes, just and subtle gentleman, undefeatable and polemic chess player, meditative and smiling Don Quijote. . . . . Macedonio is perhaps the only man—a definitive man and not a derivative or secondary thinker—who lives his life in plenitude, without believing that his moments are less real due to the fact that they do not intervene in others' moments as books, fame or citations. A man who prefers to scatter his soul in conversation rather than define himself on the page. It's licit to suppose that for centuries to come psychologists, metaphysicians and diggers in aesthetics will busy themselves rediscovering the bits of genius he already has found, has filed to sharpness, appraised, and not only that: silenced."[5]*

The text is worth quoting at length because it is the first published piece of writing Borges dedicated to his mentor, and it already offers all the ingredients of the Macedonio myth that would later (in the view of critics specialized in Macedonio's work) become a superficial caricature, to the detriment of Macedonio's reputation as a writer. Borges conjures a romantic image of a wizened hermit, devoted to chess and esoteric speculation, a genius in the raw, who does not even bother to capture his creativity in writing or publish it.

The portrait is so compelling it would cling to Macedonio for the rest of his life—and much of his posthumous existence too. Again, those disposed to view Borges's handling of the Macedonio myth with suspicion believe he too conveniently cast Macedonio as a kind of avant-gardist sideshow, rather than a literary innovator. Only posthumously, with the publication in the late 1960s and 1970s of the major novels *Adriana Buenos Aires* and *Museo de la Novela de la Eterna* (Museum of the Eternal's Novel), did Macedonio

---

5.) All the details regarding Borges's 1921 anthology of Argentine verse is to be found in C. García, (pgs. 47-51).

begin to shake off this reputation as an eccentric footnote to Argentine literary history.

Both novels exemplify Macedonio's implacable pursuit, similar to Borges's, of literary forms that went beyond realism and plot, to investigate the bottomless combinatory delirium at the source of art and reality. His *Adriana Buenos Aires* was an experiment in parodying defunct novelistic forms handed down from gothic fiction and romanticism, while suggesting possibilities for literature light years beyond sentimentalism. *Museo de la Novela de la Eterna*, first published in 1967 and impossible to summarize, is best described as an extended experiment in writing an open novel analogous to a piece of music. The prose evokes a dizzying world of aesthetic associations and possibilities in the reader's mind. At every moment it tests the limits between art and life, reality and fiction, as well as form and content.

Macedonio's novels do not satisfy on a narrative level as Borges's stories do, but instead engross us with their constant tinkering under the hood of fiction. They suggest a workshop full of previously unimagined literary contraptions. Even if most of these do not quite make it out of the garage, they still make mind-opening exhibits for anyone with time to visit Macedonio's museum: a kind of early 20th-century World's Fair for possible literatures.

The two men definitely had divergent artistic temperaments. Essentially, Macedonio was erratic and impassioned; Borges was methodical and restrained. Borges's essays and short stories are painstakingly crafted and famously flawless, each carefully prepared for publication. Macedonio spent decades prolifically recording his thoughts and composing wildly experimental novels, but published only three books in his lifetime: a brief meta-novel, a collection of humorous writing, and a compendium of speculative philosophy.[6]

6.) The meta-novel is *Una Novela Que Comienza* (A Novel that Begins), which was published in Chile in 1941. The collection of metaphysical writings is *No Toda es Vigilia la de los Ojos Abiertos* (It's Not All Vigil With Eyes Open), first published in 1928 in Buenos Aires. The collection of humorous writings is *Papeles de Recienvenido* (Papers of Just Arrived), issued in 1929 in Buenos Aires but republished in a revised version by a larger publishing house in 1944. Macedonio did however publish frequently in literary magazines and journals, and much of his production was collected into books during his lifetime and afterward. Beginning in the 1970s, Macedonio's multi-volume complete works have been published by Buenos Aires publisher Corregidor, in editions painstakingly prepared through an exegesis of many years by Macedonio's son Adolfo de Obieta, who died in 2002 at the age of 90.

III.

What united the two men more than anything else was their proclivity for metaphysics, their unflagging interest in examining the nature of reality, the mystery of being, the fabric of time and space.

For the young Borges, still searching for his voice and subjects, Macedonio's boardinghouse room clearly was a sanctuary, a place where he could unburden his heart and simultaneously soak in the consoling and vertiginous rush of philosophical discussion. In 1924, during another trip to Europe, Borges wrote a letter to Macedonio in which he said he would like to talk with him regarding a woman he loves, but then added he'd rather wait until he was back in Buenos Aires, "and say it to you in your berth on Rivadavia Street, amidst yerba, guitar and metaphysics."

Extrapolating from this line, we can imagine many long nights of yerba mate drinking in which the two men engage in metaphysical flights of fancy while not forgetting to periodically descend to earth and talk about their troubles and frustrations. In short, they did what male friends do—banter endlessly, about everything under the sun.

This level of intimacy seems to have lasted until 1928. By this time, Borges had begun to distance himself from his early avant-gardist tendencies, meaning he already would feel less rapport with the perennially iconoclastic Macedonio. For his part, Macedonio had just published his first book, the collection of metaphysical texts *No Toda es Vigilia la de los Ojos Abiertos* (Not All Is Vigil with Open Eyes), and would have been particularly sensitive to any literary cross-currents.

But as is the case with most intellectual friendships that taper off, there was a catalyzing spat. In this case, it involved a less-than-reverential published reference to Macedonio written by Borges's brother-in-law, the critic Guillermo de Torre. In an article published in Spain, he referred to Macedonio as a "man already advanced in years, a kind of frustrated semi-genius writer, whose attitudes have exercised a diffuse influence over the writers of the new generation."

This lukewarm appraisal enraged Macedonio's disciples, who by that time did not include Borges among their inner circle, and they began to lump Borges together with his brother-in-law on the enemy side. One Macedonio devotee, Leopoldo Marechal, fired off a plucky response to the article. In the course of arguing that Macedonio's influence over the new generation was hardly diffuse but ubiquitous and thorough, he also makes a pointed reference to Borges as Macedonio's "spiritual son," who perhaps could do a better job honoring his progenitor.[7]

The spat carried over into other literary magazines, with Macedonio partisans here and there accusing Borges of a less-than-scrupulous appropriation of the older writer's ideas. As one writer put it Borges was playing the role of an "unconfessed Plato" to Macedonio's Socrates.[8]

The two men would patch things up the next year, in 1929. Although they never regained the intimacy they once shared, the exchange in metaphysical ideas still went on. Into the 1930s Macedonio wrote Borges long letters full of scratched out and illegible words, letters detailing extravagant positions on metaphysical problems. In the last extant letter of their correspondence, dating to 1939, Macedonio wrote to console Borges after the death of his father the year before, and stated, among other esoteric asides: "I deny the world as unity, identity, continuity." Toward the end of the letter he added: "I think death has a little twist to it."[9]

IV.

For anyone who has a passing familiarity with Borges's career-making 1940s story collections *Ficciones* and *The Aleph*, the two statements above will strike a chord. Simply taking Macedonio's propositions, and slightly reformulating them, one might come up with a one-sentence summation of many of Borges's famous stories: they portray reality as endlessly mercurial and death as something slightly other than what we might make it out to be.

7.) Leopoldo Marechal's important 1948 novel *Adán Buenosayres* includes Macedonio as a character. So does Ricardo Piglia's novel *Ciudad Ausente*, from 1992. Both are available in English.

8.) My material is from an essay organized around an account of this spat that can be found online "Borges y Macedonio: un incidente de 1928," by Carlos García. Interestingly, the accusation of Borges being an unconfessed Plato to Macedonio's Socrates, which according to García's essay was first made in print by Pedro Juan Vignale in 1933, is continually echoed in the bibliography treating the two men's work and lives in conjunction.

9.) The letter is reproduced in C. García's book, which I cited in the first footnote (pgs. 18-21).

These two themes—the illusive nature of reality, the idea of death as a metaphysical rabbit-hole—are fused in "The Circular Ruins," among the most anthologized of Borges's stories. It is at once an allegory anatomizing religious belief and a devastating diagnosis of life, death, and individuality, which the story says may be nothing more than dreams—self-deceiving phantasmagoria. This is the story's last line: "With relief, with humiliation, with terror, he understood that he also was an illusion, that someone else was dreaming him."

The idea of one's reality as a dream (or someone else's dream), which of course has ancient roots, is a favorite one with Macedonio. He fleshed it out as early as 1924 in *Proa*, a short-lived magazine founded and edited by Borges and a few other writers in his circle. According to an editor's note preceding Macedonio's essay (a note almost certainly written by Borges), it is a "hurried sketch" of Macedonio's metaphysical position. Like much of Macedonio's writing, the essay, titled "Metaphysics, Critique of Knowledge; Mysticism, Critique of Being," is intricate, dense and brilliant:

> ... *time, space, causality, matter, and I, are nothing, neither forms of judgment or intuitions. The world, being, reality, everything, is a dream without a dreamer; a single dream and the dream of one alone; therefore, the dream of no one, and that much more real to the degree it is entirely a dream.*[10]

Here, Macedonio is rendering a microcosm of all his metaphysical ideas, much as Borges's Aleph is a concentration of all points in space at one ultimately indescribable spot.

If reality is a dream of "one alone," as Macedonio's essay claims, then it is also the dream of "no one," though this may at first appear paradoxical. In Macedonio's world the individual personality does not exist; in his conception, reality as we know it is best described by what he elsewhere calls an *"almismo ayoico,"* or "I-less soulism," a rush of sensation we only imagine to be connected to ourselves.

10.) My edition of Macedonio's essay, which also was included in *No Toda es Vigilia la de los Ojos Abiertos*, comes from a 1968 anthology of Macedonio's writings selected by Carlos Mastronardi, Borges's and Macedonio's friend, fellow metaphysics buff, and poet (and who also, like Macedonio, is currently being re-evaluated by Argentine critics). *Macedonio Fernández: Selección de escritos, Carlos Mastronardi* (ed.). Buenos Aires: Centro Editor de América Latina: 1964. The translation is mine.

Although Macedonio admits there is a practical level to existence in which we must communicate through conventions such as personality, causality, and time, it is the mystical level that is of the essence. On this fundamental level, everything that is sensed must be treated as real but understood to be part and parcel of an endless dream, without knotting oneself up with silly questions such as, "Who am I?" or "What is the purpose of life?" or even, "Is this real?" For Macedonio, the primordial fact is that something is occurring as sensation in the present moment, whether it is dream or waking life. Everything else is sophistry. There is no reality outside of what each of us sense, outside the sensation itself. As he says, "We *are* everything, we don't perceive it."

Among the corollaries of this philosophy is a refutation of death, which Macedonio also explores in this essay. Based on the mystical position he has staked out, the only experience we can know is being in the now. Existence is a succession of present moments and so does not have a past or a future, which are illusions. Since death can only occur in the future, in the moments after we die, or in the past, in the instants or ages before we were born, it follows death does not exist. The Grim Reaper is a phantom we invent to romanticize our lives.

This philosophy, derived from a life reading William James, Immanuel Kant, and Arthur Schopenhauer, was unusual in the context of Macedonio's milieu. It is evidence of Macedonio's powerful and intuitive intelligence that an amateur philosopher studying on his own would have arrived at these idiosyncratic conclusions, albeit expressing them in lyrical language and without any pretense at academic rigor. The dominant philosophical school at the time in Argentina was positivism, diametrically opposed to Macedonio's sketch of a radical, I-denying subjectivity. It's not surprising then that beyond a small circle of writers and artists Macedonio's ideas were assimilated mainly as eccentric expositions rather than serious philosophical reflections.

But clearly, Borges took these ideas seriously, at least as conceptual artifacts that might be induced to produce innovative literature. Whether it was Macedonio's influence or not, he became in his own right a serious reader of philosophers like Schopenhauer (arguably Borges's favorite, and Macedonio's second-favorite after James). Few of Borges's iconic stories lack a metaphysical inflection similar to that contained in Macedonio's metaphysical writings of the 1920s. Again, whether these ideas were taken directly from Macedonio or emerged more spontaneously from Borges's general immersion in the intellectual cutting-edge of his time is a matter for scholars to squabble over.

Neither writer believed in originality in art, so in the deepest and most important sense the question is moot. If Macedonio invented Borges the metaphysician, then it is probably just as valid to say Borges invented Macedonio, the literary man. By his own account, until he met Borges and other young writers and artists participating in the Buenos Aires avant-garde, Macedonio was still writing self-conscious poetry mired in *fin de siecle* conventions. However coy both writers may have occasionally been about influences, they were conscious of the debts owed one another. For Borges's legions of readers it's important simply to know Macedonio played a pivotal role in opening the younger writer's eyes to a wider world, beyond appearances, through veils of illusion.

V.

Reading Borges in the light of Macedonio's ideas enriches Borges, fleshes out the context from which he emerged, and has the overall effect of making Borges more approachable. With Macedonio as a precursor, Borges seems less monstrous, less a preternatural intelligence emerging freakishly in splendid isolation.

There is no contemporaneous writer I have read who enjoys as many correspondences with Borges's writing as Macedonio. With almost every other author, including those in the Argentine canon, Borges seems to offer far fewer points of contact, or if they are to be found they seem far more subterranean and circuitous. Borges looms large as an influencer, but appears to have no clear genealogy and so remains fixed as a distant, cold juggernaut in the literary firmament.

Of course Borges claims certain influences—Edgar Allan Poe, R.L. Stevenson, H.G. Wells, etc.—but these only get us so far. We read these authors' work and Borges's stories side by side and can't quite fathom what might have triggered the quantum leap represented in stories like "The Aleph," or "Funes the Memorious."

Borges's writing, so obnoxiously perfect, can seem an impenetrable construction, much like the city featured in his story "The Immortal," built on a foundation that does "not reveal the least irregularity, the invariable walls not indulging a single door." After a dose of Macedonio, though, the reader suddenly feels empowered to tunnel in with multiple points of entry.

Consider the 17 epic pages of "The Immortal." The cross-references start even before the actual story begins. First, there's the title of the story. Immortality, as before said, was one of Macedonio's favorite ideas to toy with, since he believed death to be as illusive as most of the other concepts we fear or feel buoyed by in this life. Macedonio once described death as a "game . . . that happens and never kills."[11]

After the title we find hovering above the short story's text one of Borges's characteristically erudite epigraphs, this one from Francis Bacon, which begins: "Solomon saith: there is no new thing upon the earth." The quote sums up the story's deeper theme, which is how our notions of history and memory are turned to dust once we consider the mind-boggling ramifications of infinitely elasticized lifetimes: infinite destinies, transmigrating personalities, a leveling of ethics.

After reading this epigraph, a reader familiar with Macedonio can't help but think of his "Prologue to Eternity," included in the first pages of the *Museo de la Novela de la Eterna*, which explores a similar idea, only less solemnly:

> *A popular musical phrase was sung to me by a Romanian woman, and later I rediscovered it ten times in different works and composers from the last 400 years. Without a doubt, things don't begin; or they don't begin when they are invented. Or the world was invented ancient.*

If the world emerged as an ancient thing, as Macedonio says, then clearly, as in "The Immortal," memory's depth perception is an illusion, and the distinction between remembering and foreseeing is doubtful. And both Macedonio's novel and Borges's short story take this idea of relativizing history into the aesthetic plane as well, where it instantly undermines any conception of authorial importance or artistic originality.

11.) *Diccionario de la novela de Macedonio Fernández*, Ricardo Piglia (ed.). Buenos Aires: Fondo de Cultura Económica, 2000 (pg. 64).

In Borges's story, we learn that Homer's poetic output would be reproduced by any human, given an immortal span, since an infinite lifetime necessarily contains all possibilities. In Macedonio's novel, amid countless meta-narratives spinning here and there like so many tops, there's one that plays with the idea of originality, "humanity's eyes placed finally on something never seen," a "novel like none that has ever before been written," "the first good novel," only to tragicomically deflate this utopian notion when the author admits in the end: "I leave behind a perfect theory of the novel, and an imperfect example of its execution."

Other resonances: in "The Immortal" the protagonist explores a sinister palace, in which stairways' steps are all of different heights and exhaust him. According to Borges himself, the idea for these irregular stairways emerged tangentially from Macedonio's most well-known 1920s literary stunt, which seen through the lens of today seems nothing less than a conceptual art piece: his quixotic project to win the Argentine presidency.

To support the campaign, which of course never really got off the ground, Macedonio and his co-conspirators (among them Borges) invented a series of subversive pranks. These would supposedly frustrate citizens into voting for candidate Macedonio, who would then ascend to power and deliver them from the disruptions. Among the absurdist tactics conceived: trolley-cars' handrails would be loosened, small-denomination coins would be minted to be absurdly heavy (recalling the metal cones in Borges's "Tlön, Uqbar, Orbis Tertius" that fit into the palm of the hand but are nearly too heavy to lift), mirrors would reflect only half the face, and stairways would be constructed so that none of their steps were of equal height.[12]

Beyond these surprising biographical connections, there are lines in "The Immortal" that simply gleam as polished avatars, concise coinages, of Macedonio's theories. At the pivot point in the story, when a central enigma is revealed via the unveiling of a troglodyte's secret identity, Borges's narrator states: "We easily accept reality, perhaps because we intuit that nothing is real."

A bit later in the story we find a succinct and poetic rendering of Macedonio's metaphysics canceling out death and individuality: "Nobody is somebody, one immortal man is all men ... I am God, I am a hero, I am

---

12.) The interesting links between Borges's short stories and some of the "subversions" invented for Macedonio's presidential campaign in the 1920s are explored in Julio Prieto's book, cited above (pgs. 61-73).

a philosopher, I am a demon, I am the world, which is a fatiguing manner of saying that I am not."

The philosophical vein running through Borges and Macedonio might be described as mystically-inclined skepticism (though perhaps Macedonio drank more and more eagerly of his own Kool Aid than Borges did). Both were habitual doubters of their own existence, and by extension, also of their novelty as artists. Borges liked to say "I don't write well, I plagiarize well." Macedonio once wrote prophetically of Borges, "he will be what others thought I would be." But if we accept the premise of "The Immortal," perhaps it's immaterial who wrote what, or who became what. Given immortality, there's no doubt each would have written the other's work, with an unshakeable, creeping sense of deja vu.

On the Other Hand
by Michael Czyzniejewski
from *Waccamaw*

It was one of those accidents that resulted in the wrong hand being sewn onto the wrong body. Twice. I have, attached to my left wrist, the left hand of the man whose Buick front-ended my Capri, leaving that guy with my left hand attached to his left wrist. The coolers, they say, got switched on the way to the hospital, or maybe before, everything at the scene a collage of fire, twisted steel, and blood. The hands were just too similar, they explained, and our good, still-attached hands were too mangled to use as guides. Time running thin, they just guessed wrong.

Three weeks went by before anyone noticed. The bandages had to stay on to keep out infection, and during changes, I was either too doped up or the hand was still too damaged for me to notice. Then I just realized it, the day the man with my hand started screaming. Our rooms were next to each other, and he started yelling that he wanted his wedding ring, that he needed to have his wedding ring, that if he didn't have his wedding ring, someone was going to get hurt. I figured they'd probably cut it off for surgery, the swelling making sliding impossible. Maybe there were pieces somewhere, in an envelope, his name scribbled on the front. A couple of hours later, the guy resting with a sedative, I noticed a small dish on my nightstand. Inside sat a wedding band, white gold, thick and enormous, big enough for my thumb. I reached over for it, and just to see how ridiculously small my hands were, I tried to slip it on. It fit. My hand was bigger: much bigger. While this could still be attributed to swelling, I couldn't deny the black stubble on my knuckles; I'm blond, and checking my good hand, my knuckles were bare. At that point, I just knew.

I didn't see the man in the Buick again until we met in a lawyer's office two months later. After I'd discovered the mix-up, they told him what had happened and he became violent, throwing his dinner dishes around the room, pulling out his IV, even grabbing the doctor by the neck and pressing his thumbs into his Adam's apple. The only thing that saved the doctor was the hand, my little hand, too weak to hold tight. After that, they had to move the guy to another room, on another floor, where they could put a guard at his door, keep him away from other patients. The mix up was irreversible, and since I imagined the guy ripping his old hand off my arm and taking it back, I didn't want to meet him, for him to know what I looked like. All that was left was the legalities, who was at fault, who could or could not sue. We sat down at one of those big lawyer tables in one of those big lawyer conference rooms, the Buick man and his council on one side, me and my lawyer on the other. The man with my hand was named Rich, I found out. Rich and I were just there to sign papers, everything explained to us beforehand. I'd get a little money, and his insurance company would pay it. Then Rich and I would be done, except for the small pieces of us we'd left with the other.

After the meeting, Rich and I shook hands and he apologized for drifting into my lane, for causing all this trouble. Then Rich asked if we could hold up each other's old left hands in front of our faces. Why not? I thought, and did. I looked at my old hand, he looked at his, and for a brief instant, the hands brushed together, palm to palm, my little tiny hairless hand on his arm engulfed by his gigantic hairy hand on mine. On my old ring finger was the wedding band, held on tightly with some white yarn, white yarn that had already been stained a sickening color, like pus oozing out from under the ring.

"Do you beat off with it?" Rich asked, our hands still touching.

The lawyers looked up; his giggled, mine didn't. I thought he was kidding and smiled.

"I love beating off with your hand," he said. "It feels like I'm cheating on myself."

I pulled my hand away, his former hand, and that was that. We'd each have a good story to tell, including a prop, and since Rich lived over three hours away, it was unlikely we'd ever see each other again.

Distance didn't keep Rich from contacting me, however. A few days after the settlement meeting, I began receiving e-mails that Rich sent around to people he knew—his friends and family, mostly—e-mails about his wife, who had been diagnosed with ovarian cancer, who was pitching a good fight. Another was about his new vehicle, a Ford Ranger, and he attached a picture of him standing next to it, leaning against the door with a thumbs up. I didn't respond to these e-mails, or bother to ask him to take me off his list. There was only one message that first week, and what's one extra e-mail a week? Telling him to take me off the list would only seem rude. Big deal: I'd get an extra e-mail from the guy with my hand. I'd gotten stranger e-mails—from people with none of my parts—so really, what could it hurt?

Pretty soon, though, I started getting more and more e-mails, one every day, and eventually, more than that. My sister in Las Cruces was like that, sending along everything she found on the Internet, every video, every joke, every odd or cutesy picture. I just erased all that stuff, keeping an eye out for family photos, but for some reason, I started opening Rich's and reading them, just to see what inspired his proliferation. Rich's e-mails weren't like my sister's, no cats in cowboy hats and spurs, no warnings about cell phone numbers going public. Rich sent personal messages to his list of loved ones, and they were mostly just soapbox rants, an ongoing diatribe against everything that irked him. Some were about gas prices, others were about his sports teams losing, and one was about a pizzeria putting canned mushrooms instead of fresh on his pizza. Others were more intense. One was about a drunk woman in his apartment complex who called him a fag every time he walked through the hallway. Rich described the woman as a "... redneck maladroit who proves we need another Civil War," then detailed how he climbed her outside wall that night—to the third floor—and shit on her balcony. Another e-mail was about how he fried a sponge up in butter and put it on his complex's lawn, just to kill a neighbor's dog who was crapping there all the time. (I couldn't help but wonder if the redneck woman would fry up a sponge of her own for Rich.) I was more intrigued than weirded out, and before long, I started forwarding the messages to people I knew, just because they were so crazy. My friend Adam from college posted the one about the shitting on his blog, as Adam was fascinated by reports of public defecation and had to report all news to his readers. If anything, I was starting to enjoy Rich's messages. He was a colorful guy, a colorful guy who just happened to have one of my hands.

When I got a message with the Subject line reading, "My fucking hand," however, I felt some unease. Inside, Rich told the story about how our hands were switched, beginning with "Did I ever tell the story of how I ended up with some other cowboy's hand instead of mine?" With all the sick shit he'd written about, it was only natural that he'd tell the tale of our accident, so when I read that first line, I wasn't even bothered. I'd told a million people since then, especially when they saw the scars, the hugeness of the hand, etc.—just not on e-mail. Of course Rich was going to tell that story. Why wouldn't he?

But the tone of the e-mail got more and more accusatory as it went on. In the first paragraph, Rich's account was for the most part accurate. After that, he drifted from reality, explaining to his list that his little hand would keep him from returning to work, that even if he ever got it to respond the right way, my hand was too small to pipefit. He'd have to collect worker's comp for the rest of his life, or maybe, to quote, "Be some faggot accountant like the guy who has my real hand." I was gay—that much he'd nailed—but was by no means an accountant: I wrote grants for non-profits. Still, a line had been crossed.

For whatever reason, I didn't ask Rich to take me off his list until I got the pictures, the pictures of Rich looking like he was going to maul my old hand. There were about a dozen, and all of them were pretty messed up. One had my old hand on a wood chopping block, Rich posing with an enormous hatchet, poised to bring it down. Another photo dangled my hand above a pot of boiling liquid, something green with an ivory film on top. My hand was placed into all kinds of precarious situations, like almost grabbing a white-hot log in a camp fire, lying underneath the tire of a semi, or reaching into a cage at the zoo, a tiger just inches away. Rich explained to his list that sooner or later, he was going to rid himself of my pussy little girl hand, and he was just trying to figure out how. He even asked the list to write back and vote, claiming he would take their recommendation under serious consideration (though it was not a guaranteed democracy).

I responded immediately. Instead of voting, I sent Rich the following message:

Dear Rich,

Greetings. In case you don't recognize my name, I'm the other person from the accident, the guy with whom you've exchanged hands. While I appreciate the passion and creativity you display in your e-mails, I think my address has been added to your list by mistake. My company employs a strict policy concerning profane or disturbing images being displayed on its computers, so I believe it is in my best interest to be removed from your list as soon as possible.

I hope all is well with you.

Sincerely, _____

I was on my way out to lunch when I sent it, but before I could get to the door, I heard my computer beep, telling me I had new message. It was from Rich and it read:

Dear _____,

Greetings yourself! I can't believe what an incredible ass I am! Wow! You must be completely bugged out by me. Me and my friends have been exchanging these weird e-mails since before e-mails, just trying to gross each other out, shit like that, see how much like a crazy person we can sound like. I think I know what happened: My e-mail migrated to another system, and your address—why do I even have that?—must have been thrown into my contacts box somehow, the box I make my list from. I am so very sorry that this happened. You must think I'm some sort of nutcase! I will remove your address immediately. Don't worry: I'm not crazy! You won't get these anymore.

Apologies,

Rich

P.S. Now I REALLY regret that line about masturbating at the lawyer's office!

I can't explain how relieved I was when I read this. It was strange, how Rich was able to type such a long message in less than five seconds, especially with only one good hand. I couldn't type yet. But the important thing was that this was cleared up. Rich wasn't in my closet at home, wasn't the the-call-is-coming-from-inside-the-house guy. He was just a bit odd, a bit beyond eccentric. And besides, looking back, the jerking-off comment was funny. Especially since it turned out to be true.

The next day, I got another e-mail from Rich, sent to his list, this one much, much worse than anything I'd gotten before. Instead of any rants or photos of my hand in fake danger, what I got was a photo diary of Rich doing real, awful things to my hand. To his hand. The first few showed Rich cleaning it, first with soap and water, then with isopropyl alcohol. Then the photos positioned the hand next to some cutting instruments, scalpels of all shapes and sizes. And then the photos got downright disgusting. Rich took one of the scalpels and traced the surgery scars, cutting right into the keloid, bleeding all rather profusely, risking extended damage to the nerves. I was afraid that the photos would get worse, lead to the hand's amputation, but they did not. Rich made some small incisions, but not anything that would cause permanent damage. It's nothing any sane person would do, but Rich wasn't hinged anymore, no matter what he'd said about his friends and their ongoing gross-out contest. I remember going through a period in my life where I'd call friends up, tell them to turn on channel 46 as soon as possible, leading them right to the Surgery Channel, some poor bastard's insides up on the screen. But I was 19, and I'd only done that three or four times. Rich was cutting into his body, taking pictures, and showing them to people he knew, including his mom, sisters, and some members of his church. I was a practical joker. Rich was fucked up. There was a difference.

I called my lawyer right after I received the photo diary. He'd been pretty happy with the settlement I received, from both Rich's insurance and the hospital, and told me if *anything* ever came up concerning the hand, really stressing the "anything," to call him without hesitation. When I explained what was going on, my lawyer seemed confused. I told the story slowly, even forwarded the photos, and all he said was, "But you feel fine, right?" He told me there was nothing I could do except tell Rich to leave me alone, clearly explaining my desires, and if that didn't work, file for a restraining order. My lawyer didn't handle cases like that, he clarified, but offered to refer me to someone who did. I thanked him. He was not going to help me.

I did take my lawyer's advice and send Rich another message, emphasizing how I really needed to be taken off that list, lying and saying that my boss had been monitoring our e-mail, that he asked me to cease all personal contact on company time. I told Rich I could be fired, but erased that line before I hit Send, as Rich seemed like the type of twisted asshole who would find that funny, me being fired; he'd lost his job as a pipefitter, so maybe that's what he was going for in the first place. I just sent a message reminding him to take me off ASAP, and left it at that.

For some reason, I was confident that this would work.

The next day, the police arrived at my office to arrest me. They entered my cubicle as a gang, the lead officer asking me to stand up and hold out my hands so he could cuff me. Once secured, he pushed me through the mob of policemen—five counting him—past my coworkers, to the elevator, out to their cars. They weren't gentle, weren't careful with my head as they pushed me into the back seat. On the ride to the police station, the officers read my rights and told me I was being charged with breaking and entering and arson. In the interrogation room a couple of hours later, I was told that the Dunkin Donuts on Second had been robbed and burned to the ground. Then they asked me to explain how my fingerprints found their way onto the crowbar that broke through the door and the gas can and cigarette lighter that were found just outside. For a second, I couldn't say a thing, couldn't account for how that was possible.

Then it hit me.

It only took three minutes of explaining to convince the police of what had happened. Even without checking a computer or running any tests, they could see the hands were different, that Rich's fingerprints did not match the ones on my good hand. A newspaper story had run after the accident, making light of the mix-up, and one of the detectives remembered it. "That was you?" he said. All the recovered prints were from a left hand and I obviously didn't have that hand anymore. They even started to treat me well, apologizing for being rough, buying me a coffee and a Twix bar, asking me to help them find Rich. They ran some tests on Rich's old hand, taking his prints and a fingernail sample for DNA. They set me up at a computer and I showed them the e-mails, including the surgery photos, which caused even them to wince when the scalpel broke the skin. I told them Rich had a handlebar mustache, shaved his head bald, and had a yin/yang tattoo on the back of his neck. Once they had everything I could offer, they warned me about further repercussions, as it seemed like Rich had a vendetta out on me. They asked if I wanted an escort back to the office, but I only accepted because the officer would apologize to everyone I worked with, explain they'd made a mistake, that I wasn't a robber or arsonist. Right before I left, a different cop stopped me at the door and said that she'd tried writing to Rich's e-mail to see if he'd respond, but no dice. She also said that the other fifty or so addresses on Rich's family and friends list were fakes, that the providers had no record of any of those people, that those other e-mail addresses never existed. Rich had been sending messages to me and me alone the whole time.

I spent the next week wondering if Rich was going to do something crazy, or by this point, something much crazier. It was a week of looking over my shoulder, adding a lock to my apartment door, of sleeping with a carving knife on my nightstand, an aluminum softball bat next to it on the floor. When I came home I wondered if I was alone or if Rich had somehow broken in, and at every noise I heard, I would jump, reach for another knife, cower behind the kitchen counter, hoping Rich wasn't hiding in the cabinets behind me. I crossed my fingers every time I started my car, as if Rich was suddenly a mob assassin. Little by little, when nothing happened, I started to relax, moving back into my routine. Rich had probably left town, the cops looking for him, and he wouldn't want to risk getting caught. Destroying a Dunkin Donuts was a serious offense. If anything, I'd get another e-mail, maybe an anonymous postcard, but nothing that would expose him, make him too vulnerable.

The cop leading the investigation called me once a week, asking if I'd heard from Rich, if I could remember anything else about him that I'd forgotten. I hadn't. The third week, the cop told me that they were able to find Rich's apartment through his auto insurer. When they tried to pick him up, they found that the address didn't exist, that the numbers didn't go that high on the street that he'd listed. His lawyer couldn't help, either, as he had the same address, and the hospital said that the bills they'd been sending to his insurance provider came back, the company never having heard of Rich.

The cop had found out that Rich had never been married, so the ovarian cancer was made up, too. God only knows why he had that ring. Rich was also absent from every pipefitter union in the state, but he had mentioned to someone in the hospital that he worked as a grant-writer for a non-profit, my exact job description. I started to wonder if maybe Rich had planned the whole caper, targeting me with his big, old Buick Skylark, for some reason wanting our lives intertwined. But that was crazy—we both could have been killed as easily as we weren't. Besides, there was nothing distinguishing about me, nothing that would make me a likely victim, including my tiny hands. My mind was playing tricks with me, I decided, and was determined not to think about it too much.

In the meantime, I started getting full use of my new hand, the fingers bending at my command when at the beginning, it didn't feel like I had fingers anymore at all. I started by picking things up with the thumb and pointer, sort of propping stuff between the two, but before long, I was able to get a hold of larger items, grasp them and actually feel them against my skin. The real barometer was picking up a paper clip, and once I'd done that, I tried typing. That took time, but eventually, it was like Rich's old left hand was my hand, doing exactly what I'd wanted it to do, when I wanted it, no limitation that I could see. It was as if the accident had never happened. For vanity's sake, I would wax off the black hair from the knuckles, trying to match the hand with mine, and was sure to keep my fingernails trimmed, Rich's growing at an incredible rate. Someone who knew what had happened could tell I kept the hand out of sight in public, placing it in my pocket, underneath the table, or even behind my back. Anyone who didn't know would never be able to point that out. It was a gesture, not a sign of insecurity.

I was also growing more and more confident in my personal life. I returned to the gym, and soon after, registered for an online dating network. Since the accident, I was moving in this direction, trying to convince myself that being alone was no longer a choice, maybe more of a bad habit. I didn't receive that many responses to my posting, and after rereading my self-description, I could see why. I took out the information about how long it had been since I'd dated, and what should have been obvious from the get-go, I removed the anecdote about the accident, how I had another man's hand instead of my own. Who would respond to a personal ad that said that? Even better, who would *write* that? I added a picture and used my whole first name instead of my initials, to seem more friendly, more like a person. I wasn't an underwear model, but I had good photos of me, taken for my company's website. I looked dignified in a tie, had just gotten a haircut, and since the photo was taken a year before the accident, I looked much younger, the tiny burn marks and other scars not yet in existence. It was a complete me, a place I wanted to get back to.

This new ad generated a more positive response, though any response at all was a step up. Several of the replies included a "wink," which meant the guy was interested, but only one wrote an actual note, going so far as to ask for a date. There wasn't a picture, and he was seven years older, but we'd both majored in English lit in college, neither of us pursuing careers in teaching or writing; he worked in human resources, for a very large company, and made a comfortable living. I set a time and place, a sports bar chain that featured light beer specials and cheap chicken wings, hoping we'd keep things casual. What was less seductive than beer and wings?

The night of the date, I decided to get there early, have a drink to calm my nerves. I sat at the bar for a half an hour, sipping a gin and tonic, and smoked a cigarette, which I only did when I drank. The bartender grabbed my arm at one point when he noticed me ashing onto a pile of cardboard coasters instead of into the tray. I apologized and settled up, moving to a table in the back of the restaurant area, the best seat at a place like that for two gay men meeting for the first time. I perused the menu and watched the games on the flat screen TVs, marking the scheduled start time of the date with another gin and tonic. My boy was late, and I feared I'd been stood up.

As I stared out the window at the passing traffic, a much, much worse fear came over me, the fear that I wasn't meeting a charming ex-English major who worked in H.R.: I could very well be waiting in the restaurant for Rich. Worse, Rich could be waiting in the parking lot for me to stumble out, angry and embarrassed, my guard down. I started to think, how could it not be Rich? I'd put up my picture. I'd put up my occupation. I'd even used my name. Rich was either going to walk through the door, have me trapped in the back of the restaurant for something nefarious, or he was in the backseat of my car, waiting for me to sit down inside so he could pull the wire over my head and into my throat. I was going to die or Rich was simply going to prolong my torture, reveal the new way in which he would torment me and his old hand.

Just as I was thinking this, a man's voice interrupted, announcing, "You must be _____." The man standing before me had his hand on the chair opposite mine, and for a second, I stared at the hand, his left hand, not saying a word: I fully expected to recognize my hand there, my old hand, attached to the rest of Rich's body.

"Aren't you _____?" the man said again.

Standing in front of me, begging to be acknowledged, was a man fitting the description of my planned date. He was handsome, he was dressed sharply, and most of all, he wasn't Rich.

"Can I sit down?" the man asked.

I apologized for my spacey reception, blaming it on the gin and tonic. My date apologized back, saying he didn't blame me since he was nearly fifteen minutes late.

"I got confused on the way," he said. "I went to the one on Tallmedge instead of this one."

A waitress came and took our drink order, and since I was drunk enough, I ordered a water, insisting my date have something alcoholic. He ordered a gin and tonic, and we told the waitress we'd be ready in a few minutes. I perused the menu even though I knew I was going to get a salad. I was still embarrassed about ignoring him when my date first came in, and could only imagine the look on my face as he stood there, me thinking I was about to die, that something horrible was about to happen. I sat with my back straight, my bad hand, Rich's hand, under the table and in my pocket, the double whammy of disguise. Sooner or later, if things went well, this man was going to see my hand and I'd have to explain, but I was hoping we'd hit it off before that happened, that he'd decide to like me or dislike me based on something besides the hand. Telling him about Rich would come later—much later—like when we were in Hawaii, walking up the aisle at our wedding, and we'd already bought property together, much too late for him to change his mind. Then would be a better time.

The waitress came back much longer than a few minutes later. She put the gin and tonic in front of me and the water in front of my date, an easy mistake since I'd already had three. My date then ordered what I'd wanted, a sesame chicken salad with carrots and walnuts, and not wanting to get the same thing, to seem patronizing or pathetic, I for some reason said, "A dozen wings. Hot as they come."

We spent the time waiting for our food talking about our jobs, each of us glancing up at the screens when the rest of the restaurant cheered, a big play interesting to even me, the most casual of sports fan. I was having a good time, my date was having a good time—as far as I could tell—and it seemed like we'd perhaps be able to extend this past dinner, past domestic beer, hot wings, and big screen TVs. It was one of those things you could just tell, no matter how long it had been since you'd been on a date. This was working. We had a connection.

When our food came, the waitress put our meals in front of us, complemented by silverware, extra napkins, and ketchup. She gave me an extra dish on the side for my bones. She told us to enjoy, asked us if we wanted another round of drinks. We did. As she turned to leave, her apron, filled with change, pens, and straws, twirled around with her and knocked over my water and the bottle of ketchup, sending them tumbling off the edge. As the items floated in mid-air, both my date and I flinched, but neither of us moved—they were falling to my left, and even by instinct, I couldn't bring myself to pull my left hand out, for my date to see it. My date couldn't move, either, though, his right hand, much like my left, frozen under the table. It was as if we both had something to hide.

The ketchup and the water shattered to a smatter of glass, ice, and red paste on the parquet floor. It looked like a horrible accident, like someone could have just died, right there in front of us. Like something much worse than what it really was.

Amongst the Cares
by Jonathan Rice
from *AGNI Online*

It was spring in the Vatican, and uneasy
were the men who waited in the dim
and marbled room for the voice of the castrato.

The phonograph looked like an instrument
of confession, a torturer's tool, or a crippled demon,
the stylus a hissing tongue in the turning canister,

recording everything. Later, I played the *Ave*
for an unlaced woman who lay beneath me. That room
and we in it, were real, in a time before anything

was permanent. Afterwards she scoured her thighs
with handfuls of dried grass, discarding them clutch by clutch
at the roadside. To think of her or what became of her

is useless. I took the song. It is permanent,
witnessed to be unwound from the coiled grooves.

Babyfat
by Claudia Smith
from *NOÖ Journal*

A man is trying to MySpace her. He looks like her father, but not exactly. His online name is The Ancient Mariner. He has a red moustache, and music, all ballads about people lost at sea. It could be her father, the picture is blurry, reminding her of the twenty-something women who take pretty pictures of themselves in mirrors, blurred, at odd angles.

He's in there, a little square, for days and then she friends him and he writes her. She checks to see if he is online. He is. He has six hundred and ninety six friends. He says, You are who I think you are, aren't you?

She writes back. She says, who do you think I am?

It's Wednesday night, which means drinks with the librarians. She is a library assistant, and they are her friends, sort of. She might move to New York. They talk about it, about how they are not what people expect. But, she thinks, they really are. They are laughing because Trish is wearing a tight tee-shirt she made herself. It unzips. It says, I'm All About Easy Access. She gets very drunk, and the other librarians drift away. All they've had is beer, and there's class tomorrow. She tells a man in bicycle shorts her name. She says, "I think my father is trying to fuck me."

The man says, "That isn't a very good line."

One of the librarians takes her to the diner across the street. They drink black coffee.

"You look like someone who sleeps with stuffed animals. I mean that as a compliment," she tells the woman, whose name is Lorelei. "You're much funnier when you're sober," Lorelei tells her. "Drink your coffee."

Yesterday, she'd thought the most interesting thing about Lorelei was her name, and her haircut. Now, she thinks Lorelei is very wise. Lorelei offers her a cigarette and she takes it, even though this is a smoke-free city now and she doesn't even smoke. It feels good to maybe have a friend. Lorelei is plump the way her father would have called babyfat sexy, and her hair is the color of sherry, with bangs cut in zig-zags across her forehead. She wears hand-knit hotpants. They split a cab fare back. Turns out her maybe-friend only lives a few blocks away.

"You should watch what you say to people," Lorelei says. "Not everyone wants to protect you, you know."

Before going to bed, she walks around the apartment complex. People are on their balconies, laughing, smoking, drinking their beer. She can hear an ice maker, and a small dog yelping. Fall snaps at her bare arms and legs. The stars are too bright, they hurt her eyes.

She doesn't go to work the next day. The man who may or may not be her father says he would like to meet women with medium to low self esteem. He has sent her another message. It says, that wasn't me. This is. Talk to me. His profile picture has changed now to a picture of Britney Spears looking sad and pretty. She's wearing a little brown hat. There are posts from other women, some slightly younger than herself. One says, Meet me behind the Diamond Shamrock you know what I'm talking about Blackbeard. Another says, Your song is sweet and soulful. It touched me.

She posts a comment. It says, This man has poor hygiene, and he does not bother to wash his hands after going to the bathroom. He is a landlubber.

She changes the background of her profile to a softly lit pink. She drinks a pot of coffee, feels her heart go pit-pat, pit-pat. The last time she saw him, long ago, they got stoned and he called her little Pete. She wasn't sure what he meant. Peat moss? But it could have been something he'd called someone else, and he forgot. Their kiss was slurpy and his laugh was broken, brittle crumblies. When she goes back to check, he is no longer her friend.

Melville and Bartleby: Facing the End of an Audience
by Jon Thompson
from *Identity Theory*

Everything is again set in motion—called into question—by writing.
—Edmond Jabès

What can we face? The face as mystery, sign, image. "Bartleby" stages the terrible unworkability of faces, the equally terrible unknowability of our own. Facing it, face offs, to turn one's face to the wall, to lose face, to gain it. The tragedy of each is the tragedy of all...

The worker consents or faces death. This is Bartleby's recognition. But in consenting, ironically, he also faces death, the death of the self. It doesn't matter that the self is a fiction. In fact, the murder of the fictive self, the self that finds a place within society, that has basked in social approval, is more tortuous and painful than the death of any actual self. This is what it means to "lose face."

Becoming a pariah is one thing; becoming exiled from who you thought you once were is another. Or is Bartleby's slow, deliberate journey of self-exile a journey to freedom? So: Heaven has levels, degrees. In reality, it is only an *idea*.

The slow, sad spectacle of the self, staging its own death for an audience that doesn't exist.

The audience that has not yet found the means to look about and see that the drama is *in* the clapping, not in the performance, the one loud roar of approval that sweeps aside both the past and the future.

Freedom from external restraint, unto death. "Freedom-from" versus "freedom-in": in this most free of nations, there is no freedom-in being. Your freedom is guaranteed by the right to die by yourself, with whatever self you can covet unencumbered by love or relation. No one would dream of curtailing that freedom. Bartleby: the nineteenth-century ancestor to every homeless person wandering aimlessly on America's streets, each one the sovereign of all he surveys.

Bartleby never *argued* with anyone; he never tried to prove a point, win converts, vanquish foes. What does this lack of rhetorical aggression signify? The fruitlessness of conversion via argumentation? The failure of rhetoric? The contamination of rhetoric by a culture in which most "disinterested" expressions cloak naked self-interest? Bartleby's "I prefer not to" exists as an assertion of will—but not will-to-truth.

The most destructive of all faces: benign tolerance. This is the face of Bartleby's employer. It disguises its own intolerance within a mask of benevolence. Worse: because that intolerance cannot be admitted, it does not exist. And because it does not exist, it is free to become pitiless.

Behind the narrator's courteousness, theatrical benevolence, and good manners lurks the threat of violence. Without these rhetorical forms, manners, forms of self-presentation, capitalist society would be undressed, its violence made manifest. With them, it is dressed up as civilized, moral, benevolent. Bartleby forces it to undress; he forces it to endure the shame of exposure, the danger of self-recognition. Therefore society takes its *revenge* upon Bartleby.

About Bartleby, the narrator says, "No materials exist, for a full and satisfactory biography of this man." In being unknown and unknowable, Bartleby exists as a threat to society's will-to-know, to narrative itself. That which is un-narratable *must* be narrated, must be known.

Everyone, everything must be faced, categorized, reported upon. To be unknown and unknowable is to incur the wrath of custom and law that demands a *modest* amount of submission.

Those about "whom nothing is ascertainable" defy the order of things, which rests on the ability to recognize, ascertain, assess. One death meets another.

"What my own astonished eyes saw of Bartleby, *that* is all I know of him." Astonishment polices reality: it turns it into heaven or hell. Hell is what is unrecognizable; heaven is only a name for what can be recognized.

The voice of *doxa* is the voice of comfort and reassurance. It speaks—not in terms of certainties, but givens. It refuses its own name.

To trade in "bonds," "mortgages" and "title deeds" is to trade in articles of possession. Within this world, language—writing—becomes the guarantor of ownership. The language of the law attempts to contain the irreducible play of meaning in language, its fundamentally mercurial dynamic nature, by means of complete discrimination, complete description. Through exactitude and precision it attempts to forestall all contingency, all unforeseen contexts. Bartleby's refusal to yield his soul defies a social order possessed by the desire to possess everything and to translate its own imperial ambition into an idiom of benevolence and generosity.

The soul is what is withheld; the soul is that which is proffered *without being acknowledged as such*. It is then material and invisible. The achievement of Bartleby is that he maintains, in large part, the invisibility of his soul. This, too, is his tragedy; it is also the tragedy of the society that demands it.

What is safety in a world made "safe" by money? The mansion becomes the mausoleum.

"Poetic enthusiasm" will always be an embarrassment in the face of prudence and method. Prudence—thou knows not what thou art!

In a society in which the lack of "poetic enthusiasm" is judged to be good, any evidence of it will be seen as a weakness, a failure of restraint.

Wall Street. Even the name is mythological: destiny materialized within the flux of numbers rising or falling on the stock exchange. The market depends upon fluctuation, but fluctuation within limits. Wall Street creates walls, as well as the need for them. It also creates a demand for a limit to tolerance. In a market society, tolerance *must* be limited else there will be no profit. To be infinitely tolerant, that is, to be meaningfully tolerant, would require unending expenditure. Thus in market societies, tolerance becomes a most precious commodity; its value is dependent upon it being "cashed in" only rarely.

In 1653, Wall Street was named for a "barricade built by Peter Stuyveysant to protect the early Dutch settlers from the local Indians," writes Peter Geisst in *Wall Street: A History*. Wall Street has always been then a place of barricades, an instrument of separation, a means to distance "entrepreneurial" settlers from the locals, a place of appropriation and exploitation. Indeed, it marks a border, a boundary, a space designed to produce both wealth and alienation. It marks a frontier; a defensive establishment already prepared against the backlash of the people beyond it. It thus exists as a predatory commercial site, though so "normalized" it virtually ceases to look or feel like one. Necessarily, it is a place of self-righteousness; wealth must be a sign of God's favor. Yet there is uneasiness here too, rooted in the partially repressed recognition of the illegitimacy that comes from appropriation, which must always be legitimized. The aggressor must always be the victim.

Through his unorthodoxy, Bartleby challenges the liberal definition of benevolence. His employer, however, writes to convince us of his unsullied liberalism. The reader too is called upon to confirm the narrator's own skewed self-image. In doing so, Melville shows the insecurity of the liberal mind—and its monstrosity. The entire world exists to confirm it in its essential benevolence. But since at some level it *knows* that it is not benevolent, the world exists to prop up a tattered fiction. Everything is sacrificed. The liberal mind: pitiless, egotistical, endlessly benign, endlessly serene.

Wall Street is presented to us as dialectic of "industry and life" by day and "emptiness" and "vacancy" by night. Bartleby shows, by contrast, the emptiness and vacancy of industry itself. Even to the narrator, Wall Street is a "Petra" and a ruined "Carthage."

To blot a document for a scrivener is a mortal sin, for it reminds the reader that the law is not a distant, Olympian arbiter of right and wrong, but a frail, imperfect human institution... lawyers, not surprisingly, want to exorcise blots from their records. As if the law could be unblemished.

The impertinence of Bartleby: he does not *negotiate* the terms of his employment; he decides and acts off his own bat. Despite his mildness, his is the grossest kind of insubordination. Subordinates who take their own preferences in hand and follow them up challenge the legitimacy of authority. Thus the latent, nearly extinguished utopianism of "Bartleby": what would be if all the wretched of the earth declared, "I prefer not to"?

Bartleby alone appears to be self-conscious, undeceived. This degree of self-awareness renders him unfit for labor which depends, to varying degrees, upon a dimming of self-knowledge, self-consciousness. Within American capitalism, self-knowledge brings the individual to a state of unfreedom. Its price: exile. To be self-conscious in America is to become an exile, a social outcast. Individualism becomes the compensatory myth for a society intolerant of it.

What is the black wall that Bartleby sees through his windowpanes? It is nothing but sheer blankness, Necessity, the limitation that he endures, the sum of limitations upon individual desire by the rule of law and social custom. It is the pitilessness of all laws, written and unwritten, that demand conformity and obedience. It is the primal scene of socialization in which the implacable order of things confronts human desire with its inhuman face.

To write the law over and over again, to copy it repeatedly, is to perform the individual's subjection to the law: he is embodying it within language, enabling it to take material form; he is giving it his life force. The scrivener is not writing the law; it is writing itself through him. It is impervious to death and decay; the scrivener, by contrast, is mortal, temporal, frail, corruptible. The scrivener embodies the fate of the subject: to be subjected to the law is to be its subject. Which is synonymous with being subject-less. The irony of Melville's parable: fleeing the death of the subject only hastens it.

The labor of the scrivener: writing without thinking, writing that faithfully and mindlessly duplicates the signifier, writing that has as its sole object the *reproduction* of the word of law—is this not a symbol of the co-opted labor of the intellectual working under the aegis of a reifying capitalism?

Bartleby arrives at his employer's premises as an adult, but an adult without a history. It is this emptiness, this lack of a knowable past, the silence of his past, his solitude and lack of connection that distinguishes him, paradoxically, as history's subject. His silence about his past only amplifies that untold drama. That past, that history, becomes too monumental to be written. It is unrepresentable, but in becoming unrepresentable, it acquires a ghostly presence. History haunts Bartleby. It is unseen but everywhere it makes itself felt with its uncanny presence. (Bartleby, too, becomes a wraith.)

Bartleby is *stricken* with life, with the burden of living.

Why does Bartleby begin his employment with an orgy of productivity? To obliterate the past? To identify himself with social expectation in a failed attempt to conform? The reasons are unknowable, perhaps to himself as well as Melville. *That* is respect for fiction.

Alternatively: Bartleby's orgy of productivity at the beginning of his employment is the sign of the unconsciousness responding to the demands of everyday life. Bartleby's frenzy mimics the law of productivity, becoming a grotesque parody of it. To live as a conformist is to live as a parody, to live as a mimic man. Bartleby prefers to live as a grotesque.

For Bartleby's employer as for most representatives of the law, civil dis-obedience—"I prefer not to"—is a species of madness. In Paradise, refusal has always been a form of heresy, of madness. "What right do you have to reject Eden, my Eden"? (Even Ginger Nut thinks Bartleby is "luny.")

For Bartleby, "reason" is unreason. Its tyranny is met by mildness, mildness that exists as reproach, gentle condemnation, a refusal to enter into the ugly economy of compulsion. Bartleby's mildness, then, is utopian—or at least a faint sign of the utopian in a world degraded by imperatives. By contrast, Turkey affirms his employer's rules "with submission."

Bartleby is regarded by his employer as unreasonable, the very embodiment of unreason. What Bartleby forces us to see is that reason is a fiction authored by certain interests (the legal profession, the middle class, etc.) in order to legitimize themselves. Reason, of course, is always what you have but the other person does not. Since the Enlightenment, reason has been deified as Truth, but in so doing it betrays its own idealization. That which cannot be proven wrong becomes, by definition, an article of faith. We should speak of *reasons* rather than Reason. In actual practice, Reason has little to do with itself.

"Come forth and do your duty" declares Bartleby's employer to Bartleby. Duty: every society induces it to ensure its own reproduction. Duty is needed to overcome the inevitable revulsion toward the menial, the abhorrent, as well as the mundane. Doing one's duty always involves an annihilation of the self—as well as a fulfillment of it.

Without irony, the master looks to the slave for confirmation of his essential benevolence; similarly, the employer demands of his employee that he confirm his employer's sense of tolerance and benevolence. The annoyance Bartleby's employer feels toward Bartleby is, if anything, exceeded by the irritation the other scriveners feel toward Bartleby for "shirking" his work. Turkey and Nipper's inflamed response to Bartleby's *non serviam*—"Shall I go and black out his eyes"—expresses the narrator's own rage against Bartleby, a rage he cannot express himself inasmuch as it would give the lie to his own magnanimity. But it also allows him to act the role of the liberal, long-suffering employer (which in truth he is). "Bartleby" thus explores the psychic organization of labor under capitalism in which the wage earner expresses the anger and frustrations of his boss, which also become *his*. Melville reveals a system in which one class not only exploits another, but it also expects the exploited class to voice the angers, the frustrations, and the point of view of the dominant class, that is, the middle class. For Melville, this system is essentially two-faced. The question of voice or *expression* (the representation of what is internal) then becomes immensely fraught, caught up in the unconscious social imperative to speak for interests that are *not* one's own. In part this explains Bartleby's linguistic miserliness: to speak more would be to invite his speech to be infected by the speech and interests of another class. Bartleby's linguistic minimalism resists this enforced class-based ventriloquism.

Failing to reform Bartleby, his employer takes it upon himself to read Bartleby's protest as an opportunity to exercise his own moral improvement. That he fails is not a sign of his moral turpitude but a sign that moral improvement in a Puritan society is impossible.

Bartleby repossesses his employer's premises. He has a fine indifference for property. Is it any wonder he must die?

"Immediately then the thought came sweeping across me, what miserable friendlessness and loneliness are here revealed." To have his life interpreted for us by one with such suspect motives: this is Bartleby's fate and that of all the dispossessed. He cannot narrate his own life, tell his own story in his own words. In Melville's America, identity is not something you have or own; it is instead something conferred upon you by others. Identity is a function of how you are seen. In a society possessed by the drama of individualism, the social rears its ugly head by silently and efficiently forging an identity for every American, an identity that is never wholly available for inspection and understanding by the individual. The American self: one who thinks he knows himself utterly.

Spectre, spectator, specimen: Bartleby cannot escape the imprisonment of categories, more carceral than mortar.

The narrator says he feels a "bond of a common humanity" with Bartleby, yet his actions do not acknowledge the sanctity of any such bond. This then is the fate of the liberal mind: to feel one thing, but to have that feeling, that liberal sentiment, overborne by the "more practical" demands of class and the conformities a market society exacts.

"Pallid," "miserable," "silent," "pale" "cadaverously gentlemanly": Bartleby is not only deathly in appearance; he is death. Death to social convention, death to social custom, to normative expectation, to social behavior. Negating social expectation, Bartleby is negated. That is, he becomes more like who he is. He approaches the horizon of his identity, which is paradoxically nothing as well as being the unspeakable form of his resistance to social law. This is why the narrator pities him, hates him, loves him. As an object of pity, Bartleby's unspoken critique of everything that narrator stands for (professionalism, class, respectability, tolerance, etc.) does not have to be engaged. Indeed, once made an object of pity his unspoken condemnation can be dismissed as eccentricity or lunacy.

The laws of property permit all kinds of plunder, invasion, appropriation. Because the narrator observes that Bartleby's desk "is mine," it, too, can be penetrated by him. He has in law, if not in ethics, a right to rifle Bartleby's desk. The narrator possesses a will-to-truth vis-à-vis Bartleby: his mysteriousness, his reserve, his enigmatic taciturn character *must* be made explicable. That it is not defies the narrator's complacently bourgeois worldview, which demands attribution, causal hermeneutics, simplicity, clarity. Bartleby gives this will-to-truth, which is also a will-to-power, no relief. What knowledge cannot know it must dismiss, pity or deligitimize as contemptible or a mere object of curiosity.

Bartleby: the exemplary American. He tries—and fails—to make a home for himself within the ever-mutating, ever-the-same precincts of capitalism and ends up being imprisoned by it.

"... standing in one of those deadwall reveries of his": the reverie, long the ally of American self-invention, self-fashioning, can also be its undoing, especially when reverie becomes a substitute for doing. Bartleby is Benjamin Franklin's nemesis, the presence of a horrific unproductivity in American culture that Franklin sought to annihilate or at least shame out of existence. The narrator (Benjamin Franklin's alter ego in the story) initially feels pity for Bartleby, a pity that transmogrifies into repulsion. It is not only that Bartleby represents an entirely different principle of living; it is that he cannot be changed to be in alignment with the narrator's complacent establishment values ("What I saw that morning persuaded me that the scrivener was the victim of an innate and incurable disorder.") Hence Bartleby must be cast out.

The initial test of Bartleby's excommunication will be whether he will divulge the particulars of his deliberately veiled history. If he refuses to do so, the narrator is determined to fine him. Significantly, he is *not* first asked to become more efficient. He is asked to reveal his soul, to become transparent before the gaze of his employer, to lose his identity as a separate, equal, and distinctive life, indeed to lose his private history. He is asked, in short, to become a case, an aggregate of facts, an object of narration, a known story, an *employee* instead of an individual. To the question, "Will you tell me anything about yourself?" Bartleby responds "I would prefer not to."

Bartleby's presence, his example, is a contagion that must be contained. Within the highly conventionalized world of employer-employee relations, preference cannot be allowed to have much more than a rhetorical significance. Preference speaks to individual will, which in Melville's America, exists only ideologically, or at the level of enunciation. Individual will haunts America, its brick and mortar, its devil-deal with Wall Street, its boom times and its bust ones; it is dead, but its uneasy spirit is everywhere, a reminder of what has been lost, or perhaps what once was envisioned but never realized.

In the face of society's "thou must," Bartleby heroically maintains his own sense of will. He cannot be bribed to conform; he will not acknowledge the coercion of politeness, the ascendancy of manners. Yet he is not free. Obedience to social law and defiance of it are seen by Melville to be equally constraining. Defying social law defines Bartleby, almost absolutely. Wherever he turns there are walls. Bartleby is an individual who cannot free himself from his narrator, even from his author. Melvillean tragedy: narration itself as a form of subjection, unless the reader rewrites the story...

Self-interest, too, dictates the ultimate removal of Bartleby from the narrator's law offices; the narrator decides he cannot afford generosity beyond the recognized border of conventional liberalism: the silent uncooperative presence of Bartleby has begun to affect his "professional reputation." In a society actuated in the main by the profit motive, self-interest will always be the cardinal value; other pretenders exist, but none command the same degree of allegiance.

"What earthly right do you have to stay here? Do you pay any rent? Do you pay my taxes? Or is this property yours?" In nineteenth-century America, as now, rights are, in practice, guaranteed by money and property, not by "higher" ethical, legal, or constitutional principles. Melville's postmortem on the body politic reveals not so much a divide between ethical and political life but a conquest of ethical principles by capitalist premises such that thinking beyond them requires an immense act of the imagination. By 1854, the "cash-payment nexus" had thoroughly colonized America; the only space outside it was the space of the imagination. The great achievement of capitalism is that it forces its dissidents and critics into exile, it forces us to inhabit the territory of the imagination, which it then delegitimizes as unreal, as mythical, a place of childish fantasy, a land of improbability. From whence will come the beast, slouching toward Bethlehem.

Horror—that Bartleby should dispossess his employer. He worries that "...in the end [he might] perhaps outlive me, and claim possession of my office by right of his perpetual occupancy." Fear of dispossession leads to dispossession. Fear the devil! Possession, the devil! Legitimacy, the devil!

From valued employee to recalcitrant employee to enigma to apparition: by the end of the story Bartleby is made to metaphorse again: in a final incarnation he is seen to be an "intolerable incubus." This is no exaggeration; he is an incubus. He haunts the living by his mere *being*. Merely being in a nonconformist fashion becomes an affront to bourgeois propriety, to professional decorum, to normativity itself. Bartleby becomes burdened with the socially unsaid in America, particularly the gap between our idealistic image of the American body politic and the harsher reality. Bartleby is—the worst sin of all—an embarrassment. He embarrasses the narrator's notion of himself as a generous individual; he embarrasses society's pretense to be a society in which action is grounded in principle. His mere presence *mocks* the American claim to have established a uniquely free polity.

"Bartleby" is about the magical power, the horrific power, of representation to transform lives. The narrator defines Bartleby's life; his definition of Bartleby as an outsider, an "intolerable incubus," becomes material, actual, in the body of Bartleby, wraithlike in prison, by the wall, awaiting death. In representing others as inhuman, supernatural, mythical, fantastic, they are metamorphosed into fiends, spirits, ghosts, devils, diseases, witches. Via this magic they can be annihilated, burned, slaughtered, converted, exorcised, chained, imprisoned, starved and mocked—made to gabble, made to flee, made to fly.

Once Bartleby's employer deserts his law offices, he is finally able to separate himself from any sense of responsibility to Bartleby. But his departure does not signify a new disavowal of Bartleby, only the acting out of a disavowal that has already taken place. The disavowal merely becomes visible, public, as he makes clear to the new occupant of his former premises on Wall Street: "'I am very sorry, sir,' said I, with assured tranquillity, but an inward tremor, '"but really the man you allude to is nothing to me—he is no relation or apprentice of mine, that you should hold me responsible for him.'" What fear there is here: fear of a social contract that would bind one individual to another, make one responsible to another, or merely genuinely responsive to another. Bartleby's employer is desperate that he not be made "responsible for him." He expresses a horror toward social responsibility. "Bartleby" is in this sense a dramatization of the American horror toward the notion of the social as the environment in which individual destiny receives completion. It ironizes—despairingly!—the narrator's desire for the social to be replaced by an environment in which individuals pursue their ambitions limited only by the pressures of economic necessity, class, and a legal system firmly rooted in the prerogatives of wealth and property.

Within this vision, the social makes no demands on individuals vis-à-vis other ones, and should not. It is a space populated only by a single individual and his solipsistic ambitions. Yet the emptiness of this social space demands the most rigorous policing. It must not be filled up, certainly not by a vision of the social as fulfilling. The social is defined by Melville as the space of the prison yard, demarcated by "the surrounding walls, of amazing thickness."

Ironically, in so privatizing the dream of the social as a source of support and enrichment, the social domain actually is reduced to becoming barren, coercive and exploitative. Melville's irony: horror at the horror we have allowed the social to become.

"As I afterwards learned, the poor scrivener, when told that he must be conducted to the Tombs, offered not the slightest obstacle, but, in his pale, unmoving way, silently acquiesced." The shameless of false pity, false piety! Bartleby acquiesces in the face of death. Pity is death too—in this sense, Bartleby's removal to the Tombs is merely the actualization of the living death that he has already endured. Bartleby faces this fate without flinching. He acquiesces not only because he knows his end is inevitable, but because it is the ineluctable fulfillment of the social law, of social life. (To say that the social does not exist in "Bartleby" would be to simplify and to miss a finer irony. The social exists—but it exists in its purest form only negatively, punitively; it exists as a coercive power applied to those who violate the law of unfettered individualism or the law that sanctifies existence as a process of accumulation.)

Bartleby is imprisoned with other social discontents as a way punishing him for resisting the dictates of individualism. The strongest social taboo in Melville's America is a taboo against thinking beyond the narrow confines of individualism. If you cannot live as an individual conforming to a liberal world-view, then you will die as something unrecognized: a true individual. Whether or not you want to conform then becomes a superannuated consideration.

In refusing to become an object of his employer's gaze, Bartleby be-comes an object of the gaze of murderers and thieves. His dissident behavior is lower than that of the lowest of criminals. How ironic that this most private of individuals should suffer the indignity of having his privacy stripped away, made an object of curiosity, a spectacle for the amusement of society's outcasts (who only violated the letter, not the spirit of the law). Glassed in, he lives under the gaze of society's condemned; his unrecorded sentence is to suffer the loss of privacy endlessly. Having defied the imperatives of materialistic individualism, he is made to endure a degraded and grotesque sociality. This is his "freedom." And in giving him the run of the prison, society can be persuaded of its own generosity. "Being under no disgraceful charge, and quite serene and harmless in all his ways, they had permitted him freely to wander about the prison, and especially, in the inclosed grass-platted yards thereof. And so I found him there, standing all alone in the quietest of the yards, his face towards a high wall, while all around, from the narrow slits of the jail windows, I thought I saw peering out upon him the eyes of murderers and thieves."

Bartleby is never charged with any crime; to charge him with one would be to face the unacknowledgeable, the brutality of the unwritten law of individualism. He is, indeed, "under no disgraceful charge."

Bartleby's face is "toward a high wall," the wall of Necessity, the wall of repression, the wall of the law that condemns Bartleby. Bartleby can see it; he knows what it is. Likewise when saluted by his former employer who visits him in the Tombs, Bartleby replies "'I know you,' he said, without looking around—'and I want nothing to say to you.'"

And the meretriciousness of his former employer's response! "'It was not I that brought you here, Bartleby,' said I, keenly pained at his implied suspicion. 'And to you, this should not be so vile a place. Nothing reproachful attaches to you by being here. And see, it is not so sad a place as one might think. Look, there is the sky, and here is the grass.'" The narrative voice smoothly defines reality. There is no presumption in this—for he belongs to that class that *has* defined reality. For those who do not have to live with the falseness of representation, hell can be a form of heaven.

But there is meretriciousness here, meretriciousness based on an invincible form of self-deceit. While the narrator did not technically remove Bartleby from his premises, his own behavior made that all but inevitable. The narrator will not face his complicity in bringing Bartleby to this end. He will not accept responsibility for it, or for his own actions; his is the voice of individualism: not thou but I! His rhetoric transforms himself into a martyr to Bartleby's unwarranted and unjust suspicion; likewise, it makes a heaven of hell.

In the narrator's last attempt to convert Bartleby to accept the world as it is, he encourages Bartleby to accept the "grub-man" in the Tombs as his servant. Bartleby rejects the role of master just as he rejected the role of servant.

His emaciated, wraith-like body symbolizes his lack of visibility, his social invisibility. Bartleby is out of bounds, beyond the narrator's ability to recognize him. Why then eat? What is there to eat? Eating is a form of hopefulness. It expresses a hope about the future, or at least the belief that the future will be responsive to individual human desire. What is there to sustain Bartleby? His frail body records the cost of defying the social law, which enshrines mastery and slavery as society's modus vivendi. He becomes—another—invisible man.

"'Deranged? Deranged is it? Well, now, upon my word, I thought that friend of yourn was a gentleman forger; they are always pale and genteel-like, them forgers. I can't help pity 'em—can't help it, sir.'" This, the grub man to the narrator, about Bartleby at the story's end. Forgers pass off fake documents as manufactured ones, as "authentic" originals. Forgers thus exist as the doppelganger to scriveners. Scriveners produce copies, but copies recognized as copies. Their copies do not destabilize this economy of authenticity; indeed they affirm it. Bartleby's refusal to work is also a refusal to work as a scrivener, as a worker who supports this economy of authenticity. Has not the law forged itself? Has it not declared itself authentic—indeed the source of authentic behavior for the body politic? Doesn't the law's excessively punitive stance toward forgery betray its own anxiety about its own "authenticity," its own insecurity about its status as the embodiment of transcendent truths about justice? Doesn't Bartleby's wasted body declare the inauthenticity of the law, and the inauthenticity of the lawyer-narrator who presumes to narrate Bartleby's life?

"Dead letters! does it not sound like dead men? Conceive a man by nature and misfortune prone to a pallid hopelessness, can any business seem more fitted to heighten it than by continually handling these dead letters, and assorting them for the flames. For by the cart-load they are annually burned. Sometimes from out the folded paper the pale clerk takes a ring—the finger it was meant for, perhaps, moulders in the grave; a bank note sent in swiftest charity—he whom it would relieve, nor eats nor hungers any more; pardon for those who died despairing; hope for those who died unhoping; good tidings for those who died stifled by unrelieved calamities. On errands of life, these letters speed to death. Ah, Bartleby! Ah, humanity!"

The fact that the narrator—the agent of Bartleby's destruction—is also his elegist is a sign of the text's veiled outlook: he signifies either the first shoots of change, or the final cruelty of the dream of a New Jerusalem in the New World.

"Bartleby the Scrivener" is composed of dead letters: the dead letter of the law; the dead letters of a constitutional democracy; the death of individualism; the death of narrative's power to transform social failure; the death of authenticity and benevolence; the death of humanity. Just as dead letters are letters sent too late to those who were despairing, and now are dead, so too "Bartleby" is a dead letter sent to a reading public, which by accepting, indeed internalizing, compromised versions of freedom and community, is also dead.

But the letter itself, like the letters Bartleby consigned to the flames, is also charged with redemptive energy, with the desire to redeem loss and failure. The irony is ineluctable: redemption for those who are beyond it. The imperative is to look at the death-face of the American body politic face on, to see it in all of its ghastly pallor. Seeing—recognition—is the necessary prerequisite for social transformation. Melville's text is haunted by loss, by almost-extinguished hopes. Hauntings terrorize, but they may also be quests for redemption. Just as it awaits a general resurrection of all dead letters, Melville's text awaits, still, its audience.

All references to "Bartleby the Scrivener" are from Herman Melville's *Billy Budd and Other Stories*, edited and introduced by Frederick Busch (New York: Penguin Classics, 1986).

An Interview with Jon Thompson
Author of *Melville and Bartleby: Facing the End of an Audience*

1. Your essay "Melville and Bartleby: Facing the End of an Audience" will probably strike a nerve in readers given the current economic dire straits. Were you thinking of this possible parallel when you wrote it?

Actually not: I wrote the essay a while ago when the economy was booming, but I was mindful of the fact that Melville's short story deals with someone who is a member of what we now refer to as "the underclass" and for them, even a booming economy does not deliver the life—the possibilities—it should. One of the subtleties of "Bartleby" is that it explores and critiques the underlying organization of American society, the structure that makes it what it is. In seeing it as a critique of the limits of liberalism, of tolerance, it goes beyond a criticism of bad times. Or that's my thinking...

2. Is Bartleby a particular kind of American Everyman? Are we all essentially Bartleby?

I see Bartleby as dramatizing some peculiarly American dramas—especially the conflict between individualism and authority in America, which is a very old conflict and very much with us today. Part of the irony that Melville's story addresses with such force and poignancy is that American society sees itself as one which embraces individualism to a unique degree—but as the logic of the story suggests, we Americans are not as tolerant of difference as we like to think. So Bartleby is an Everyman to the limited extent that every American has to deal with the tensions within individualism, but Bartleby is exemplary in that he displays a courage that is highly unusual. If we were all like Bartleby, this country would be very different.

3. "Bartleby the Scrivener" is a widely anthologized story, but I wonder if it still gets actually read. Talk about this if you can.
You're right—it is widely anthologized. Which means that it is widely taught and is required reading in many different kinds of courses. So it is still being read widely on college campuses. Is it still read outside academia? I don't actually know how much it is read by non-students, but I'm sure it is still read.

It does not bother me at all that it is required reading in, say, American literature classes. It is an immensely rich and subtle text; it is useful to have a guide to help read it. To me, that is one of the uses of an education: it requires students to engage texts they probably wouldn't have worked through outside the classroom and that makes all kinds of discovery possible. There are autodidacts still, but it seems there are fewer of them.

4. This particular essay comes from a book-length manuscript you're working on. Can you tell me a bit about this project?

The chapter on "Bartleby" is one of five chapters in a book that looks at American literature and culture from the Puritans—William Bradford—and ends with the brilliant Vietnam War memoir, *Dispatches* by Michael Herr. The book is willfully eccentric and deploys the lyrical structure evident in the "Bartleby" chapter. In this regard, I was inspired by some other eccentric books on American culture—D.H. Lawrence's *Studies in Classic American Literature* and Susan Howe's *My Emily Dickinson*, as well as other writers like Roland Barthes and Maurice Blanchot, who write critically in a very lyrical idiom.

Basically I was interested in exploring some interrelated questions: How have American writers seen their writing as writing? What work do they want it to perform in the real world? What aspirations do they have for it? Relating to all that, how does the writing of some key American writers deal with—evaluate—the violence that is such a key part of American culture? And to what extent can this writing body forth or imagine a different world? The book is called *After Paradise: Essays on the Fate of American Writing*; happily, Shearsman Books will be publishing it early in 2009.

5. What IS the fate of American writing?

This is a question that the book loops back on itself time and again to work out and I've tried to develop a structure in the book that will offer a kind of answer to this question, but an answer that is open-ended and suggestive. So the book itself is the answer to the question, but one way to address it here is to say that the fate of American writing is whatever readers say it is, whatever readers declare it to be in their actions and non-actions. As I see it, the fate of American writing is never an absolutely settled question, but one that books and readers create in their ongoing interactions with one another. A text has the power to re-imagine the world. That can be enormously transformative. or it can be entirely latent—just paper moldering on the shelves. But it is never one thing across time.

Colors
by Cassandra Garbus
from The Cortland Review

1.
Blue

Blue was the color of the room where she lost it. Where the Korean man with the dirty pants nudged into her. His hair smelled of turpentine, and he was a painter too, he claimed, pressing against her in the dark corner of Danceteria. Bodies lurched, the dance floor trembled. "Let's split this joint," he whispered, his small palm on her ass.

A rainy, December night, she shivered on the corner of 8th Avenue. Away from the music, the darkness and flickering lights, he seemed closer to middle age; his skinniness and mangy clothes had fooled her. Clenching his fists against the cold, he waded into the street for a cab.

In the Washington Square Hotel, a black-coated man, a hooker with orange lipstick, and a blond girl with a boy's haircut slept in the lobby armchairs. The Korean man seemed almost embarrassed by her. At seventeen, she was chubby, and her wet hair fell flat against her face. Drunk, after three Long Island Ice Teas, she was on some kind of dare with herself, and she laughed too loudly, her insides braced.

"Where have you taken me?" she kidded foolishly, her hands on her hips.

A musty lamp yellowed the dingy carpeted room. The Korean man flicked on the TV, then bounced on the bed, testing its spring. The cover had burgundy flowers with white stitching. It made a zipping sound when he ran his hand over it.

"Come here." He reeled her in with his index finger.

Whispering words she could not understand, he pressed her down to the bed. A TV news program flashed one emergency after another. An earthquake in Mexico. A shooting in the Bronx. A car which had cruised onto the sidewalk in Brooklyn, killing three people. She felt like a wreck as his body careened into hers.

2.
Red

When she was in love for the first time, she was sure her happiness would never end, and when he finally left her, she was sure the pain was endless. Raking her fingers through his complicated brown curls, she would repeat to herself this is the hair, the head, the shoulders of the one I love. Tracing his wiry stomach, imagining the organs, the liver, the veins, the relentless heart beneath the skin, she would repeat to herself this is the flesh, the meat, the body of my love.

Sex with him felt like the earth, undisguised. Lights on, he pumped slowly in and out of her, testing every sensation. Their slippery hips made funny squishing sounds, and she pressed his wet back down with her palms so that their bones might mesh. But the feeling in her own body came and then went. The harder she concentrated on it, the more it eluded her.

They had athletic sex, trying impossible positions on living room furniture, and he reported on all his sensations. He word-processed at a law firm for money, but he called himself a writer, and so he spent nearly as much time finding the perfect words to describe their sex as they spent actually doing it.

"It's like the heat of August subway stations enveloping the shaft," he would say and then immediately revise his description. At twenty, devoted to painting, to solitary work, she had trouble with words and adored hearing him talk. He would pour over every experience to see it from every angle. He was the only man she'd ever met who liked to dissect his own thoughts so thoroughly. At night, he lay awake, wide-eyed. "Am I really in the heart of it? Am I really living? Is this love?"

Those years with him, she painted canvas after canvas: naked tangled bodies in rich earth tones. Crevasses, orifices, tongues and limbs. Her teacher at Cooper Union chose her work as an example for the class. The first three years, she lost her bids for fellowships, the fourth year she won.

"You're a tough nut. A survivor. An ever-ready bunny." Her lover bloated his cheeks, mocking her for her plumpness, and then he barked out a laugh. He could not bear that her work was going better than his.

"It's okay if I think about other women." He shrugged to her one day from his writing desk, the corners of his lips quivering into a smile. He had suffered another bad writing morning and took pleasure in hurting her.

Naked beneath an old towel, she felt slapped, dazed, even before she fully heard him.

"It's all part of the experience of sex. Fantasies," he informed her.

"I think about other men too," she retorted. In the bathroom, the steam from the shower dizzied her, and she gripped the towel rack for support. It was true, images of other men had flashed through her mind, and it meant nothing. So what if touching her, his mind wandered too? Why should she feel so ashamed?

To acknowledge this, the fragility of love and passing of passion, was simply being mature. Their sex changed into something furious. They pounded against each other, nails digging in, and she concentrated on the corners of the ceiling and thought, this is life, this rage, this disappointment. Afterwards they lay side by side, confessing everything to each other. He remembered everything she'd told him about her childhood and pointed out how she had been both damaged and saved. No one knew her better.

"You're my best friend," she told him, nuzzling against his complicated curls.

3.
White

White was the color of loss, of dawns without him. At five am, she would awaken alone, sheets twisted around her legs, the white morning relentless through the window. Broadway was silent below her. The day had not even begun, but the pain was already there, churning in her heart, rising up into her throat until she howled. Like an animal. Like something ugly.

Hot August in the city, she was immobilized on her couch, hours slipping away. Doctors discovered cancer in one of her father's lungs and they operated immediately. A smoker, a constant worker, he had been raised in the Bronx by immigrant parents who had died together in a fire when he was seven. But he had gone on to comedy, producing three hit television series. His eye for what was funny but harmless had never failed him. He'd made money, outstripped his roots, but now groggy from anesthesia, he mumbled how he had never been happy. Not in his work or either of his marriages.

"But I love you," she argued as if her presence and love could ever be enough to make him happy and prevent him from leaving her.

"Sixty years of life and now this." He waved his arm to the narrow hospital room, the single suit hanging in the closet.

"Some people would say you've had everything," she said. On the windowsill were flowers, dazzling and sexual, which his second ex-wife had delivered.

She reminded him that the doctors had been certain all the cancer had been removed.

"What did I tell you about doctors? Stay out of hospitals," he warned, wagging his finger.

She praised his life of hard work, driving a cab days and nights through college, and then his subsequent successes. Television people called the hospital, and his siblings, whom he had neglected, still visited and cared. One of his shows had recently failed, but there was another one in the works, a comedy about hard knocks at a lonely-heart bar.

"You can be happy," she insisted. Her own happiness seemed to depend on him believing her. But he looked over the shoulder of his hospital gown and refused to speak. It was as if his entire life had boiled down to this, this final bed, the East River trudging away indifferently outside his shut window. She tucked herself away, a tough nut, ever-ready, as her old lover had said only months before, and took care of her father. She read glossy magazines, took walks down the fluorescent halls, staring into the open doors of other rooms, onto other narrow beds. All the nurses knew her by name.

"You're a good daughter," they said to console her, and she soaked in their words, repeated them to herself so she might remember them later.

"My hands are empty," she told the old lover over the phone. She had given in and called him, having resisted for a week. They spoke for an hour, but the ex-lover was too busy writing to see her. Stripped down, raw, she became insatiable. She couldn't get enough of bodies, of sweat, of brief, sad encounters. She faked her pleasure. The men were appropriate to varying degrees. Friends were beginning to marry. She asked gentle-looking cab drivers, her father's age, about the secret to marriage, and tears welled in her eyes when they gave the most simple advice about respect and kindness. Meanwhile her father recovered. He would not die now, not this year.

4.
Silver

Painting, her mind was most engaged. Even if she began in despair, she would soon come alive, stroking the canvas with swirls of colors: purple here, yellow there, an angle to the left obscuring this figure and emphasizing the next. She loved to feel the ropes of her mind pulling, stretching, puzzling; she loved to see, step back and then see again. The whirl of colors, the mess of life.

And afterwards, she had a profound sense of ease and rest.

Her canvases were vibrant with color. Tone and hue were everything. It did not matter whether the figure emerged or receded into the splattered color blocks. Eventually the colors, the impression of a dream or nightmare, despair or hope, were all that mattered.

She had one show at an East Village gallery, Mud Fish. She'd agonized over the selection of her work, sure she would later realize other options were far better. Quick witty titles had always escaped her. All her paintings were numbered and named, "Memory." She could not tell if she was a genius or de- luded. Work was everything, she thought, the most pleasurable part of life.

The gallery was packed with friends and friends of friends and her divorced parents, who stood on opposite sides of the tiny room, watching each other. Still, for a moment, at the show, she felt bubbly and alive, discussing her own work. Everyone gathered around her and stomped their feet as she re- ceived her champagne toast. Face flushed, fingers tingling, she floated around the room. She knew this feeling would end, and so even as she lived it, she was recording it to herself: this is what it was like to shine.

5.
Black

She dressed up for the sculptor in leather and lace.

"Look how sexy you are," he whispered, and in the mirror, her own body and his excitement turned her on. Sometimes he tied her wrists to the bedposts, and she would never admit to anyone how her body trembled before he touched her, first gently and then harshly. In the morning though, rage throbbed in her throat, a crimson behind her eyes, and she could hardly speak. She lay in bed with the lights out, eyes squeezed shut, wishing to be obliterated. Years ago beneath the flashing TV lights at the Washington Square Hotel, she had been sure she would die inside permanently, but now she knew these moments of despair would pass.

As the daylight progressed, the sculptor's tenderness slowly soothed her anger away. Within a day, she might feel ten different ways.

"I'd do anything for you," he said, kissing her awake. Saturday mornings, he went to the deli on Avenue A and served her pancakes and fresh orange juice in bed and fruit from the farmers market, which he perused for hours. "What cherries, what avocado," he would say flushed with his news. She could eat all she wanted with him, all the pancakes, all the syrup. He liked her as she was, soft around the edges.

"Everyone's jealous of me," he would tell her as she dressed for their weekend afternoons together, browsing thrift shops. She wore work boots, fishnets and a bright orange skirt. Joke clothes, but sexy, the sculptor thought.

Though she had pushed her work with dealers and galleries, she had never gotten another solo show. A critic after Mud Fish had called her color-work imitative and glib. Her days seemed consumed by her day job, answering phones at a law firm. Still the sculptor believed in her completely, encouraged her work. For her birthday, he made a series of clay images of her, and for Valentine's Day, he built a stark iron sculpture of a man, bony and bent.

"This is who I'd be without you," he said, though women always wanted him. He had dark hair and lean cheeks. Black angular sweaters draped his wiry shoulders.

"I wake up furious," she told him after sex one morning when the bitterness in her throat was unbearable. "I hate what you do to me."

"You hate it?" He blinked at her, keeping his voice even. "You're so critical. I'm always doing something wrong."

He withdrew from her, touching her only occasionally and tentatively. Even though she apologized, he became even more silent and inexpressive. Evenings he slipped away from her, drinking beer in front of the television and laughing to himself. But this despair was familiar to her, not at all alarming. She had never been attracted to anyone who was mild or facile or clear. The sculptor was still as devoted to her as ever. He worked as a carpenter, and his dream was still to build them a home, a beautiful home of wood and glass in Upstate New York, where he'd been born. Every time she doubted his ambitions, he won something, an award for his art, a grant, an important exhibit.

"I want to please you, to give you everything," he told her.

"You already do," she insisted though, really, she wasn't sure.

6.
Beige

But he did build her that home, a home with space and light and tall windows overlooking the Hudson River. They cooked dinner together in their tranquil kitchen, and in the evening, she read books or watched TV beside him. Though she had sworn never to leave the City, she found moments of expansion walking silently with him through the woods. The crunch of their boots, the branches snapping against their jackets, the honorable trees swaying above them.

She taught English as a Second Language to dishwashers at neighboring resorts. She often gave them time she wasn't paid for and spent her evenings devising lesson plans. She had class parties for their birthdays and bought them small presents that, to them, seemed extravagant. They were grossly mistreated by the resort management, and she wrote letters on their behalf. Her days were busy and purposeful, and her relief at not painting surprised her. When she returned to her art on weekends, her chest tightened with anxiety, and she painted less and less.

Though sex was rare, her life with the sculptor had become one of comfort and kindness and much more peace than she had ever expected. If she ever wondered whether she had lost something, she quickly reminded herself how much easier everything was now, with this home, this steady love. She had made a deal long ago, even before the sculptor: touch was too difficult, and the only way she could live contentedly was to live without it.

At thirty-five years old, she was nearly half way through her life. In the confusion, the whirl of it all, how could there ever be only one good decision? Before her father finally died of cancer, he had warned her that she was too much like him, too lost in doubt. "Go forward," he told her. "Don't get stuck in the mire."

Did this mean she should marry the sculptor? She replayed her father's final moment, the moment when the body stopped. A scream had formed behind her eyes, and then the brassy nurse had pushed in, joking about the heat, unknowing. There was something about the Yankees outside the hall. "You're a good daughter," the nurses had all said.

Her August wedding day was humid and still, the sky a muted gray. The Hudson River threaded the hot valley. Women in light summer dresses fanned themselves. Sweat dripped down her sides, and she had to hold her best friend's arm for support. At the altar, the sculptor looked a little crazy too, his eyes bright and fidgety, his forehead damp. But when she reached the altar, his long fingers grasped hers. "I love you," he mouthed as they turned together to the judge.

"Are you happy?" She held his hand later as they lay on their backs beneath the moonlight.

"Nothing's changed really." He shrugged off the momentousness of ceremony. In the pale light, his white undershirt glowed.

"I mean, we know each other, don't we?" he said. The pillow rustled as he turned towards her, waiting.

Would she open her arms to him, caress his body in the darkness? Would she be kind?

"I'm happy," she said, as if she weren't quite sure, but then she checked herself and squeezed his hand. "I am."

Photographer
by Claudia Emerson
from *The Cortland Review*

It began with the first baby, the house
disappearing threshold by threshold, rooms

milky above the floor only her heel,
the ball of her foot perceived. The one thing real

was the crying; it had a low ceiling
she ducked beneath—but unscalable walls.

Then she found with the second child
a safer room in the camera obscura, handheld,

her eye to them a petaled aperture,
her voice inside the darkcloth muffled

as when they first learned it. Here, too, she steadied,
stilled them in black and white, grayscaled the beestung

eye, the urine-wet bedsheet, vomit, pox,
pout, fever, measles, stitches fresh-black,

bloody nose—the expected shared mishap
and redundant disease. In the evenings

while they slept, she developed the day's film
or printed in the quiet darkroom, their images

under the enlarger, awash in the stopbath,
or hanging from the line to dry. Sometimes

she manipulated their nakedness, blonde hair
and bodies dodged whiter in a mountain stream

she burned dark, thick as crude oil or tar. The children's
expressions fixed in remedial reversals,

she sleeved and catalogued them, her desire,
after all, not so different from any other mother's.

Hidden Child #9
by Lynn Strongin
from *The Centrifugal Eye*

One

In 1951, I became a hidden child, child of a vanished world—akin to hidden boys and girls in Europe, during wartime—self-contained, brooding over the egg of mysticism. I convinced myself that *tomorrow* the light would shine for me. I was hidden, given a number: in a ward of post-polio children, those with spina bifida, and a few with birth defects. I was hidden child #B9: Ward B, bed # 9.

Was there anyone who sought me? How to now translate myself out of this darkness, in which only the eerie, silver cylinder of the iron lung shone, "March of Dimes" stamped on it. *Metal Monster*. We were hidden like shame, stains on sheets or coats, in dark corners, in anonymous wards.

In '51, quiet as an egg, as a pearl in oil, I lay in my hospital cot confiding the atrocities and indignities I endured to my first cousin, Nyrene (now gone), and to the lovely, strange, quiet and compelling Annike, my cubicle-mate.

Summer, that year; a stagnant time: screen porches with grids often ripped, so hardly kept out flies. I saw nothing of grandmother while in the hospital. She lived in her darkened cottage of the soul and mind on Park Avenue. (She *did* take sister Chel in.) Saw nothing of Aunt Flossie.

Stricken, I struck a light: my mysticism did *not* begin after polio, but long before: In my room with iron bedstead, a rat appeared. I fell to my four-year-old knees and prayed. Nobody worried because nobody knew. "The light" was deferred, but enveloped me again seven years later, my enchanted eleventh summer when I ran, flew, swam, a waterbird—dived in a body that would soon leave me, given me by a God, by she who decided to fashion me and then bade me to an unconscious calling.

A few years earlier, Mother Marcelle regularly shampooed Chel and me—rinsing her hair with olive oil, mine with lemon, to bring out the luster in a brunette, the highlights in a blond. Tonight, smelling the olive oil Sweetheart is heating for supper, I recall that scent, float in a time warp to our bathroom half a century ago.

Social activities were suspended during my adolescence. I did, however, learn to light up at age twelve—me, the kid with coke-bottle-green eyes, taught by another girl a year or two older than I. It was while on a stretcher (ours were side-by-side) in a hospital hall, waiting.

Festina lente—"hasten slowly"—I mistype as *Festina Lenten*. Was my life not like Lent? Are not all of ours? The working person was an anomaly to me. There was no male in the home. Someone going out to work was anathema. Going out to a lesson, to perform, to take a lecture—these were other things. Like bathing. Strange, the zinc tub, the smell of char, the memory of war returns, invisible but piercing battle lines.

And if mother, instead of love-making, spent her evenings on a hassock or rickety stepladder reaching for hexagonal boxes, rustling tissue paper with hats, it was not only that hats became her for whom the years had not been kind—a child with polio, a divorcee in the forties—but also because she had worn well. At art and motherhood (to an extent), she had excelled. Is a "good mother" a misnomer?

I rode no cockhorse to Banbury cross. The clay-pit light was blue down south, the bird-wakening signaled by light rather than song. Up north, in our wartime kitchen, the only light I ever remember was also blue—the blue light, harsh like the stumbling buzz of a hacksaw, moved over Chel's back and mine as we were bathed in the kitchen sink. Hidden first by soap, we then emerged. In similar fashion, I emerged after infantile paralysis. I read up on it in a dictionary:

> *"Polio (also called poliomyelitis) is a contagious, historically devastating disease that was virtually eliminated from the Western hemisphere in the second half of the 20th century. Although polio has plagued humans since ancient times, its most extensive outbreak occurred in the first half of the 1900s before the vaccination, created by Jonas Salk, became widely available in 1955."*

In 1951, lying on my back, I read about the first trail-blazing cures for this historical, incurable disease. Historical. Incurable. A word-child, I turned the words over my tongue; looking out above the East River in New York's Cornell Medical Center, high above trees, lofted above tugboats on the river, I sailed—although it was a solemn voyage and the waters alternately wool, silk, taffeta, and liquid iron.

For me, all homecomings mirror this homecoming.

Sweetheart always sees the justifying view of things. All her margins are justified. She has all the answers. I have few. "I am sweating the onions," she says, and I look up and smile at a language I hardly understand.

Neither was I conversant with paralysis, with seeing the world horizontally rather than vertically, and when I sat up, with seeing the world from the eye-level of a five-year-old. Coming home was just for the weekend, initially, but it was like being reborn. The new skin was that of the outer world, but virgin skin softer to the spiritual touch, the physical, than was the straitjacket of pad and gown which I'd worn for half a year at age twelve.

Homecoming was Gertie, our black nanny, in the kitchen boiling a fowl, and her asking "Would you like a backrub, child?"

I explored corners of the West 73rd street brownstone with its round, castle bedroom, as though I had just stepped through the looking-glass. Black and white linoleum imparted a resinous, rain-like smell to things. The furniture I touched like I might an old dog, but it responded with velvet seat-cushions indenting only a bit at the pressure of my finger. The lamplight was soft, golden, diffuse. Unlike the ward's blue-white light which had infiltrated my waking and sleeping.

I copy this next paragraph in the country of my adoption; after my body changed, so did my country— but many years later:

"Polio quietly preyed on thousands of young Canadians. The disease caused paralysis, deformed limbs and in the most severe cases, death by asphyxiation. In Canada, polio was so feared that as recently as the 1950s, it closed schools, emptied streets and banned children under 16 from entering churches and theatres. In 1955 it looked as though a miraculous polio vaccine signaled an end to new cases of the crippling disease. But a recent medical condition known as post-polio syndrome has survivors reliving the sequel to this once-forgotten nightmare."

A Christ-haunted childhood the South bequeathed me—polio-haunted childhood, the North. Signs posting "No visitors, Isolation" hid my child self. Being parent to Chel, parent to Sweetheart—keeping good care of them—further veiled that child behind a mask of pain only now beginning to be ripped open at age seventy.

Two

And at the start of it all, quiet as matches in water, like snow folding over the three of us, stands mother, long-suffering, but able to make magic, to see the white unicorn (the same way her eyes later opened at the moment of death to see the white peacock). Mother stands at a battered sink, pouring the precious half cupful of lemon for my blond hair, olive oil for Chel.

What boxcar might I have ridden in with cattle? What camp been delegated to? Treblinka, Bergen-Belson, like Anne Frank to die in Auschwitz. I did not die. I lived. Or rather, I died and came back to life. Rolling in an old wooden wheelchair into the castle bedroom that winter evening in 1951, I did not ask, *where is my lemon juice, where is Chel's olive oil?* I was transferred to the sagging cot alongside Chel's in the round room — a bed so different from the coarse-linen sheets of the State Hospital — she asked "What was it like?"

A word child— for the first time, words eluded me.

Hidden child, come into the light. I am bed #9. Consider the nine months in the womb; consider circular hideaways from the mechanical devices which replaced miraculously functioning legs. It's amazing how many pulleys, wheels, levers, buttons, hoists, sticks are needed to supplant them.

Mother Marcelle saw to it that I never thought of myself as "crippled." I was arrow-straight, symmetrical, alive. My sugar cube was sunlight; I asked to be wheeled to the hospital roof in Manhattan for a few moments each day by my nurse. My ballast was bravery — I was cocky, brazen, the girl with coke-bottle-green eyes, and put into a woman's ward due to overflow problems despite the massive summer exodus from the cities. I said to the nurse, "I'm a child. I don't belong here. Please get me out, and in with kids."

"When will you come out of hiding?" asked a friend years ago. "You are a jewel looking for a place to shine."

My Australian friend bathes in Dead Sea salts to wash off a love that betrayed her. What would I do if Sweetheart, who people say is like a nun, did that? I would hide my harp under my duffel coat and flee into north winds.

I write a story which I want to be classical, a story of *ones*: one action, one chief character, one emotion, one setting. Few folks alive remember me when I could walk. I hardly remember myself. But we are hard-wired to rise; I wake and am set to run. There is an old grainy black-and-white film of me in 1947 in which I move. Trance-y, I feel, looking at it, the diamond particles of dust dancing in the cone of light. It is a projection from the platform of time past.

Stories of *one* are lovely. But mine are multi-leveled—you can move on Escher-type elevators up and down in them, past florists where snow circles pines, past grain elevators on prairies stored with golden grains.

A child may be hidden, but is a structure nonetheless: like a house, the psyche has many windows, yet is an anomaly, like the white unicorn or albino peacock—feathers exploding within, it's a home with windows but no door.

Three

Sweetheart, at fourteen, a Jillaroo, "showed" in the doorway of her parents' elegant home—a party in progress. She'd returned from the stable, riding boots covered in *merde*. That young, marriageable brunette. She slipped round the back door. Eyes? The windows to the soul. She eyed the guests and felt outcast, strange.

I want to make a hole in the rain today and dart out and visit my daughter's friend who has phase-four lung cancer. I want to be the little window of her soul. The eyes, the eyes!

Sweetheart now comes in and circles me with long pipestem arms. There's a crash down the hall—"Oooh! I must re-balance the load."

Life is theatrical, but our only theater was Monday night movies. And in these "olden days" when I was a child, a milkman came with milk in thin glass bottles at five a.m. So much happened in the olden days; I skimmed the cream off the milk with imagination. Nevermind that Chel and all the world went out—I brought the world in. Don't you see *that's* what's shining under tables and over chairs, a wrap like florist's cellophane over everything? Our father, whose practice was all bedside manner—he did not prescribe—said, "You use everything you have, Indigo."

Mother brought me two inches of ivory to paint upon: these were "A Tale of Two Cities" and "Call of the Wild," but everything was suspended for Alphonse Daudet's *Le Petit Chose*. You could say my mother was a French-woman in a Jewish girl's skin. With the charm of a Southern Belle. Where could she crouch to hide?

My mother had an incomparable beauty. Rosenblum skin. Golden rose—not as English as Sweetheart's, who says, "cut it out" when folk compliment her. (Or did so in her youth, her earlier childhood with me when she arrived and told her parents over the first phone call, "I'm here, mummy and daddy, but I have funny tummy." Everything turned our guts inside-out in the hospital. Porridge looked like something someone could not keep down. Castor oil was heavy as liquid petroleum.)

Lord, let the light shine on us.

"The upholsterer," Sweetheart comes to me with the report, "has been by. She said the small wing chair needed new arm caps and that 'Big Wing' has a soppy seat." The language suits the nursery perfectly.

Sweetheart received a parcel! It was a plastic bag from "Rowing-Leggs," her financial advisor. We hang it, over gales of laughter, on the lamp screw. "They must consider themselves generous, just think," I say.

Sweetheart ducks out into the storm. I envy her the elation, the absolute high of leveling against laser-sharp weather. Ancient Gary Oaks blow, tossed about like Don Quixote's and God's feathers. But God herself, where is she? *O hidden child, your back aches from crouching. Hidden Mama, come out of hiding.*

I turn the Oxford cream-and-vellum pages of a book. "Darling," I say, "did you read that today a deer (in rutting season) burst into a New England schoolroom while they were doing a vocabulary drill? He ended up in the nurse's office. What are bandages, to his unnamed sounds?"

"I'll be," she says, then rises. "Drat-it, another spill on the floor."

Whereas Sweetheart's humor is social, mine seems more a Jewish, familial humor—given somewhat to derision, or laughter through tears. Call them "loving swings." But now, as all my world turns: flatten, lenten, linen and iron, I wish the messiah would come. Smells of pumpkin soup cooking in the kitchen... a child coming home, for whom all homecomings are *that* homecoming.

Cream-colored hatboxes and shoeboxes (old, tea-colored) are silent—contain ancient love letters. I could open a forty-year love letter from my old soldier; I cannot, whatever I do, try on a hat, look in the mirror.

Even if all my life is Lenten, visionary experience began early—long before the first vision, one eye milked over and required cataract surgery—so young, no doubt due to trauma. Long, long ago I began praying "Lord, today make the light for me shine." And it wasn't the light refracted from a mirror, in which a rat scuttled across the room, and a girlchild fell to her knees wishing she'd been a boy and prayed till her knees ached. Nor was it the tiny mirror affixed to the iron lung in which the patient captures the world, tries on a hat.

All my hiding was simply the getting ready to come out and glisten. I was child #9, smooth as pearl and as slowly sinking, though I rose again with each dawn.

·

Coda

Pachebel's *Canon* plays. Sweetheart stands in the doorway.

Grandmother met her once and said, "She's soft-spoken, not at all like modern girls." Mother said, "She has a lovely voice, she'd make a fine telephone operator." She also asked, "Are you living alone? I hope you don't just *meet to eat.*"

Before I revise this, I turn down the light. One burner working up north here, winds howling. Sweetheart's father said she looked like an Inuit child when she was born. "Hair standing all around her face." He used the politically-incorrect term, "Eskimo child."

Sweetheart contemplates her long, tapered fingers. I contemplate her abuse suffered at the hands of a blacksmith, when she was age twelve. Neither of us speak about it. She reminds me of an obedient nun. Hidden child emerges, always slips back inside. My dark swan, I throw salt upon the soup. Dark Salt. Dark tears.

Once, during a time I was very sick, when a Catholic woman worked for me, she taught me two things: "the best way to go through each day is with your hand in His hand. We are nothing compared to Him." I then transposed this to "the way to go through each day is with your hand in the hand of the spirit guiding you." We are such small players on the field of God, tiny hockey pucks in hands; we cannot be safe, but we can be armed. We are part of a larger light.

Christianity was transposed into mysticism by a small Italian girl fascinated by the side curls of the Jewish boys and men—asked, if they have straight hair, do their mothers make them wear curlers? *Am* I a magpie? Not a girl off to First Communion?

Any dark day was one to be escorted up the straight flight of thirty stairs to the attic to rummage. Here, we found old trunks, hatboxes, dolls with eyes sprung out who no longer said *Mama*. (A friend has just written to ask if the doctor's children went without attention. Disorder breaks the heart, and no, I never felt neglected, but I did feel cordoned.)

We met with a handshake when Chel and I visited the practitioner up one floor from our father's. While my heart was being listened to, I imagined our father's rooms in the precise layout of his third cousin Eliot's, whom we visited. In this way, too, we remained hidden children. At the end of a checkup, Eliot would pick up the phone and say, "Ed, the girls are here." It was a rare treat to shake father's hand, after which we'd return with Mother Marcelle to our West End apartment.

Was Father clinical? He hospitalized his own mother for senile psychosis when she imagined she was back in Russia fleeing the oppressors who were after her children. They, too, were hidden. This is like those Chinese boxes, or Russian eggs: one opens a larger one to find smaller and smaller folded inside. Or like the Babushka doll that has another within. It's called *nesting*. A nesting fever for hiding swept Europe in wartime. It's that perpetual wartime which I'll habit and inhabit and re-habit until the end, no doubt.

Occasionally, and with dread, we were scheduled in the hospital for a conference. This meant a head doctor, Dr. Deevers at Haverstraw, led a team of young doctors to clinically review our cases. Totally "exposed" to them, I remained hidden, realizing they saw the event without understanding what happened. I did nothing, quietly quilting over my heart despite my nudity, endured with silent tears, once in a while tasting salt on my tongue.

Saint Paul said to never let the sun go down on your anger, but I didn't know him then. I knew only that a white light waited for me at day's end. I'd seen Bibles and Catholic missals thumb-indexed with gilt-edged pages. For me, they were sullied by guilt.

My book, *Rembrandt's Smock*, arrived in my adoptive country with its import scan at 8:03 this morning. It had its departure scan in Seattle and in Louisville, after starting out somewhere in Tennessee. Adverse weather conditions caused a few delays, kept it hidden.

What did we uncover with greatest delight in the attic on rainy days? A shawl under a shawl on the mannequin / tailor's dummy. The first shawl was purple, the one beneath took us back to Mother Russia and Romania, blood-red.

Blood-red—the vials by my bedside during the acute phase of my illness, when the angel of death pressed on my lean body like a lover. Images of refugee camps in Europe flashed through my mind from Warner Pathe newsreels seen only six years earlier. These were no brief moments for soul-searchers; I had time to dream of being a weaver in a fly-by-night place in Holland. *If you are willing* (I told my angel), *I will fit you in alongside me.* We lived in the same heart, although that heart skipped beats, frequently.

There are greater traumas than I had: parents are shot in front of children.

Mother sublimated her sexual passion, doubtless, to the attention of her children. And rummaging among her hatboxes, endlessly trying on capes and jackets transposed that longing, to some extent. She also lit the magic lantern for "us chidden." For me, after the hospital, where we were like children in Victor Hugo's *Les Miserables*, it shone like a welcome-home beam.

Again, who sought to find me? How to translate myself out of this darkness? I wake with such sadness I cannot swallow, choke on dawn, then make it into day. "What should we do with our brilliant child?" my father said he and mother thought then. He told me, when he paid his last visit in his eighties, failing to cancer (a fact he knew but did not share). *They must hide me, like children in asylums.*

Afraid of being a freak, Mother called others freaks. "People will talk about the Weirdo in #3," she told me, while visiting Sweetheart and me in our small, Canadian, railroad apartment during our thirties and forties. We lived at Jacob's Age on Cook street, with its proper-sounding British name, frayed area carpets, its British ex-pats as lodgers. I was still the hidden child in #9.

But now I'm gathering bits of tinfoil to make them gold—in appearance, at least. *Hidden child, the covers have been pulled off. Step forth!* Today my life is both festive and Lenten. *Child, take infinity and make a robe out of it to clothe your shoulders and straight backbone. Shine!*

More Than Just a Stolid Pump
by Ash Hibbert
from *Journal of Truth and Consequence*

Sitting at a table in the yard under the stars with a dozen dropped matches laying between his feet, my brother's old friend finally makes fire. Brian has invited himself to my place on the pretense of collecting a lighter for his smokes, but the truth is that he is dealing with a fix and needs somewhere safe to mellow out.

I still call this my parents' house, even though my father is dead and his widowed wife the sole inhabitant. I still rebel against him, but on such a subconscious level that it no longer registers. Now I am able to dedicate my conscious energies to rebelling against my mother. So, when Brian asked on his last visit whether he could inject himself in the kitchen, I instantly said yes. The bench became a shooting gallery, water from the kettle disinfected a purpose-made spoon, and a lighter from the local supermarket dissolved the goods.

Alone in the kitchen, I make a coffee for myself and white tea with two sugars for my visitor, who sings outside to the beat of the lounge room stereo and punches the air like Rocky Balboa. After joining him in the courtyard and placating him with the tea, Brian crushes the cigarette butt into the muddy ground. He stands.With pants rolled up and shirt hanging out, he scratches his heroine-induced itch. He will continue to irritate his skin long after his entire body is red, yet with the cold evening air biting, at least his top will not be coming off this time. The dog drops sticks at Brian's feet; neither of them are impressed. Both start to shout at one another, but with the help of the coffee, my own heart is beginning to race and soon Brian and I are comparing martial art techniques and correcting each other's stance. I am hot beneath my coat as we feint and recall similar matches of skill and strength. Then he asks me where he can be sick. I point to the far back yard and he jogs eagerly up the steps.

Back at the table, he sculls down the last of his tea with a grin and sighs. He fingers the box of matches and makes another pile between his feet. I reach out and take his shoulder as he begins to lean forward. While I have never been up close and personal with someone coming down from heroin, I am well versed in the language of melancholia. I do not need a degree to tell me that it was the death of his two sisters in a car accident ten years ago—including Lindy, who I was friends with—that lead him to take up mainlining, and I do not need to be psychic to see that his habit is failing him. He tells me he is down. I tell him that it is time to start rethinking his choice of medication. He questions my choice of the term "medicine." I mention my mother's Bach flower remedies in the cupboard above the fridge. He tells me about the fight that my brother started shortly after our father's death, which left him with a purple face and a limp.

It seems that everyone has his or her own rescue remedy.

I think of asking him for a spare cigarette as a reward for not asking earlier for a taste of his other drug of choice. Even if what I am looking for in such substances is not relief from sorrow but relief from my bourgeois background, I remember that each rescue remedy itself becomes something from which we need rescuing.

I finish my coffee instead.

Brian collects his words like spilled matchsticks from the ground. He wants to talk about his sisters, yet when the dam of his thoughts busts, all he can produce is an indecipherable flow. His feelings, though, are obvious. His pain finds shape in a tongue that belongs to a time earlier than the tower of Babel. I lean back and let him slur. I hope that in the morning he will feel he has offloaded some of the burden weighing down his heavy heart.

After helping him light his second cigarette, I tell him about my friendship with Lindy. He asks me if I *liked* her. I reply that she was a beautiful girl and that everyone liked her.

We think about that for a while and laugh.

While eating toast in my grandfather's kitchen, I realize that all of us are trained by our predecessors to depart into the night. For I now see in my widowed mother the same conversations, the same routines, the same obsessions, and even the same aroma as her father. In three years of living alone, my mother has begun to echo my grandfather's amnesia, deafness, and fascination with the banal that took him decades as a widower to manage.

She is no longer growing old.

My grandfather and I have never had much to say to each other. I am here only on the urging of my auntie and because it is on my route to the city to return library books and make sure that no one has ransacked my apartment. However, today he is glad to see me and we talk of his son-in-law, of the confidences that they shared, such as my father's dark foreboding in the month before his freak death. I try to think what it would be like to anticipate your own extinction. The only comparison that comes to mind is when I am standing near a tram driver's compartment and the doors are closing. I try to anticipate the moment that the tram will surge forward and I sway towards the front of the tram to try to counteract the inertia. Inevitably, though, I misjudge by a second and end up faint.

Anticipation does not always help.

I wash up in the bathroom before leaving. Looking in the mirror, I realize that in the three years since my father died, my head has shed its roundness and my hair, its blondness. I am the so-called baby of the family, and once upon a time, I revelled in the adolescence expected of me.

My reflection tells me that aging is no longer a ride I am yet to take.

That evening I drink my red wine in a lounge overlooking the corner of Brunswick and Johnson, remembering one of the last times my father and I had a night out together. I met him at his hotel in the city and we headed out for dinner on Brunswick Street.

I buy him his tram ticket, as he has never caught the city's public transport. Later, he pays for dinner, as I have never held a job before. We eat Thai and drink whiskey distilled in the waters of the Mekong. As he is a connoisseur of spirits, I ask him what he thinks of it. He tells me it tastes like whiskey.

Afterward, staring out of his hotel room at nocturnal Melbourne, he updates me on his plan to maximize his retirement package. When he is due to retire in ten years, he will do so in name only. I drift into recollections of gazing across a similar height after accompanying my family through a canyon in the Grampians National Park.

Upon reaching the opening to the plateau, I looked out that little entrance like an ant staring out of a nest opening. I watched and waited while my father and brother walked the last hundred meters to the edge of the plateau overlooking the valley below. It was the roof of the world and my father had traveled to the perimeter, leaving me at the portal. One day he would not return and would leave me instead to shine a torch into the darkness of his skull, to ask myself whether that dinner on Brunswick Street was my father's attempt to get to know me on my own turf. In the end, though, all I have is my speculations, and my own terminal ignorance.

I want to know what went through my father's head in the last moments of his life. Perhaps I should find satisfaction in the funeral, where we talked about his life and demonstrated our belief in an afterlife—yet what about the unspoken: that bridge from air to dirt, sky to earth: death?

Lying on the grass at a friend's Brunswick West backyard picnic one Sunday, conversation turns to athletes who suddenly die. Steve himself moves with the grace of one practicing Tai Chi his entire waking life, and speaks with a quiet wisdom of a young Yoda. From the glimmer in his eyes, however, I can tell this epitome of human excellence dropping dead has held a long fascination for him.

I too have often felt exercise to be bad for one's health. Throughout primary school, I saw the fittest and most active of my peers relegated to crutches or plaster from bike or skateboard accidents. Acquaintances return from overseas skiing trips having torn every ligament from their knees, while a high school teacher meets an abrupt end in a solo skydive when his chute fails to open.

Steve holds a smoke in one hand and a bottle of Champagne rests against his chair. Sian, his partner, is in her late twenties, yet he is in his late thirties. Steve has an ambiguous relationship with vitality. While on the one hand he laments his declining empathy with young people, on the other he gains a perverse pleasure from the phenomenon of healthy people dying for no apparent reason.

Doctors call this phenomenon "sudden death."

What caused my father's sudden death? What caused his heart and mind to forget its vital foxtrot? There had been no warning signs. Was it a slow kind of suicide? Had he worked himself too hard? Maybe it was because of coronary artery disease—the buildup of cholesterol in the blood routes—yet people have much higher rates without problems. Maybe it was lack of fitness, but then, cardiac arrest can happen to triathlon winners.

On the other hand, maybe it was something as incidental as touching water. The immersion of his limbs in the ocean off Eden for a routine scuba-diving session could have caused a coronary arterial spasm, triggering an arrhythmia. Coronary thrombosis—the blocking of an artery—may have exacerbated this, which is caused by a build up of plaque formed by cholesterol lining arterial walls that eventually rips off and causes clotting that, within minutes, prevents the flow of blood. This fatty gruel would have been collecting since his birth, yet only upon giving up regular exercise would it have begun to harden to a consistency strong enough to notch a surgical knife. Absorbing passing calcium and coalescing with nearby growths, the plaque would resemble stalactites and stalagmites filling an underwater cavern.

How his heart failed is a reflection of how he failed. Once a strong organ capable of pumping more than the contents of an Olympic pool, likewise, my father had run marathons, constructed houses, and cycled to work. Yet, like the arteries clogging with plaque around his heart, he had filled his days with obligations until he no longer had time for himself. He had thrown himself thoughtlessly into work and tried completing his goals with brute force.

Blood supply to either his heart muscles or its chambers would have slowed. Tight, squeezing, gripping, hard and heavy pain would have spread from his upper chest behind his breast bone, upward into his neck and jaw and possibly into the inside of one or both of his upper arms and down as far as his belly and fingers. While, like very bad heartburn, he would have known something was wrong. He would have begun to perspire heavily under the wet suit. Blood vessels along his skin would begin constricting.

His face appears deathly white, and his hands and feet begin tingling. He reaches out to his diving partner still on dry land. His expression is one of fear, panic, perhaps resignation.

Days later, sitting at the dining table at my parents' place, it is the image of our father or husband sensing in fear that something dark within him is ready to burst that causes my brothers and mother—having arrived from abroad and interstate—to disintegrate.

My own heart remains stoical, and my cheeks dry.

With his heart failing to pump out all the blood that it took in, it would have began to swell and accelerate. In doing so, however, it would have merely quickened its own demise like a driver turning the ignition of a car until the engine is flooded. Without the brain dictating the metronome-like beat, his heart, like a gyro, begins to spin further out of control, to fibrillate. If someone were to dip their hands into his chest and clasp his heart, it would feel like holding a bagful of agitated worms. His lips and tongue may have turned blue, his breath shortened. His lungs may have filled with fluids. He might have felt as if he were drowning, even though his head was above the surface of the water. Blood accumulating in his feet and ankles would have caused them to begin swelling.

His heart stops and the supply of oxygenated blood to the nervous system and the vital organs quickly begins to fail. Pulled onto dry land, his diving partner begins cardiopulmonary resuscitation—filling his lungs every four seconds with second-hand air to supply his brain, and pushing his chest sixty times a minute to deliver it. Those trying to save him, though, are like puppeteers pulling the strings of inanimate flesh.

Four minutes after CPR stops, his oxygen-starved brain ceases to function.

I look for the "me" in the man staring back from the mirror, who offers only what I give him. I try to guess the trend of the protrusions of jaw, shoulder and ankle. I see my brothers in that trend. But only after seeing my father, it becomes clear that our mother's apparent femininity is all that tempers his spirit in them. The wary certainty that one day I will find the image of a dead man staring back at me beyond a few anomalous features through that looking glass drives my desire to solidify my self-image.

One of my brothers suggested that I refused to go back to our childhood home because I was afraid of finding our father. Really, though, I was afraid that I would not find him. As long, perhaps, as I did not open that front door, he would continue to reside there, both alive and dead for eternity.

When I finally return, like a pilgrim entering a temple, I turn the handle to the front door and find the tabernacle empty. My deity is absent, and the offerings within his shrine remain untouched. My father must indeed be in heaven, for these four walls have failed to contain either him or his memory. I walk down the side of the house and find Dad's fernery guttered. I ask the spirit of the place if this is what he would have wanted, but it is silent, for its loyalty is to its new owner and renovator.

While I am but a passing pilgrim, too weak even to plant incense in the sand.

I know now where I will meet my maker. He will not come to me like a thief in the night, but as a sleeper, an assassin or saboteur, slumbering in my cells. He will be a genetic time bomb waiting for my thirty-eighth birthday— the age of my father when I can first recall him. The sleeper will awake and I will stare in the mirror and find my father's eyes looking back, questioning me, offering me hope, admonishing and absolving me.

The American
by Molly Gaudry
from *UpRightDown*

They lunch at L'Olivier, and during her first glass A— says, There was a tourist. Of course there was, D— chides, her disgust for tourists as palpable as the crème brûlée she abuses with her spoon. Was he good in bed, at least? C— asks. Except for the swearing, A— says, yes. Romantic B—, who has obviously never had her heart broken, sighs, So he was an American. Of course he was American, but I courted him, not the other way around. And now he's returned to the United States and you miss him. B— removes a cigarette from her silver case. Please don't light that, A— says, I haven't finished my meal. All right, go on then, tell us about him. When was the affair? C— asks. He went home two weeks ago. You didn't tell us, D— says. I didn't think you would understand. I understand that you're my friend and should have said something. So I was right, you don't understand. I understand perfectly, you haven't finished your wine. I'm not thirsty. Thirst has nothing to do with what I'm talking about. A— drains her glass and cuts her veal into grape-sized pieces. Lifetimes pass between swallows. D— loses patience. Give me a cigarette, she says. But A—'s still eating, B— says. It has never mattered before. It matters now, A— says, it matters now to have friends who will respect me and allow me to make my own decisions. You're letting him off too easily, D— says, they're all the same, especially Americans. Maybe I am, but he promised to write and I'm worried because he hasn't, something terrible must have happened. Why don't you call him, B— suggests. Because I would rather he called me. You could e-mail, C— offers. I have. Just once I hope. Yes, just once. What did you write? Only that I hoped he arrived safely. Is that all? And that I was thinking of him. You're a fool, D says. She's not a fool. Yes, she is. Why do you say such things? Why can't you just listen to her? I've already said it, because she is a fool, and so are they. All four gaze in the direction of D—'s upraised chin and see the same two people but differently. A— sees a happy American couple, happy, she thinks, because they wear their joy meaty on their bones the way the rich wear jewels and the poor their humble rags. D— sees two fat American pigs and wishes she were sitting in B—'s chair, so she wouldn't have to see them. C— sees money, she always sees money where tourists are involved. She has a souvenir stand outside the Louvre, it was her father's before he died, a suicide. She runs the family business in his honor, his name, her memories of him that much lovelier when tourists purchase his postcards. And B—, romantic B—, she sees nothing but the love that passes between two vacationers, U— and I—, who have come to Paris on business, competitors for the same promotion, and what's true is that there is no love lost between them. Then U— begins to choke. Halp, halp, halp, U— gasps between fast breaths. Din't, I— shouts. Halp, halp. Din't tauch hem, watt jest a menit. There's no time, A—, the beautiful one, the one I— has been admiring since entering L'Olivier, says breathlessly, rushing over, heaving her fists beneath U—'s ribs. A mushroom cap launches from U—'s throat onto the floor. A— sits beside U— and smiles. That's better, isn't it? Are you all right? Tank you, U— says, tank you, tank you. It was nothing, A— says. Tank you all the same. When A— returns to her table, two of her friends applaud. You just saved that man's life, B— says. It was nothing. It wasn't nothing. He was going to choke and you saved him. You would have done the same, it was just that I reacted first. You're my new hero, C— says, lips pinched white. And you, do you have nothing to say? A— asks. Forget him, D— whispers, staring at U—'s greasy chin and bulging cheeks, forget him the way that man has forgotten he nearly died but for your pity.

The Right Passengers
by Waqar Ahmed
from *Anderbo*

On his prowl through Manhattan's bar-filled Meatpacking District, taxi driver Nadeem Riaz is looking for the right passengers that will make up for the three hours he spent in traffic on the way back from JFK airport, and another half hour he was tailed, needlessly, by a police car. It's Saturday night, well past midnight, so, actually, it's Sunday morning, and Nadeem is roaming this neighborhood of New York City because, brimming with drunk people exiting lounges and bars, it holds the promise of short, lucrative trips to local neighborhoods. He must avoid another cross-borough trip into Long Island or Brooklyn—or New Jersey, God forbid—otherwise, he runs the risk of returning to Manhattan passengerless: another hour potentially wasted.

The city's sweating on this humid July night. Clusters of young people, the women barely clothed, gather in front of bar doors, huddled in packs, spilling over the edges of the sidewalk. On this Ninth Avenue block, the road becomes tighter, cobblestoned. The bright lights from the clubs and restaurants shout but, higher, the buildings in this section of the city are dilapidated, the dull carbon-colored facades are peeling, though one would have to look upward, and then it's dark anyway, as if someone forgot to turn the lights on upstairs.

Nadeem Riaz cruises on Ninth Avenue between 13th and 14th Streets surveying his customer base. He can't be too picky here. So much time already wasted today. The traffic from JFK he can live with, but those cops that followed him for no reason, probably just trying to make their monthly quota of tickets—following him through three neighborhoods, waiting for him to trip up, maybe take a right on a red light, or double-park to pick up a passenger. Nadeem Riaz was so nervous he stopped picking up fares, switched his taxi light to "off-duty." Still the cops persisted, for half an hour, until they found someone else, speeding. What could Nadeem do? He's an immigrant—with a green card, yes—but still a lowly worker, so he went out of his way to follow the rules.

No, he doesn't have to worry about competition for passengers in the Meatpacking District; the harvest is plentiful here—the body heat of the city doesn't seem to bother this crowd.

The corners are where people, wobbly, wave at taxis, leaning on one another to stay upright. Nadeem Riaz's cabdriver friends, those who drink behind their wives' backs, or *really* drink when their families leave for Pakistan on vacation, have told him that many of his drunk passengers will not even remember the taxi ride—they're in some intoxicated purgatory before they finally, what do they call it, *black out*. Nadeem doesn't worry about that too much. He will try, if he can, to pick the most sober customers, because one time a young woman vomited all over his seats, cutting his night short—he can't afford for that to happen. So, he lets another taxi overtake him to pick up two staggering females in very short mini-skirts.

Now, Nadeem Riaz's taxi is fair game and there are several groups of people in front of him. When he drives up to the corner, a couple enters his taxi. From the rearview mirror he catches a flitting image of brown skin—a fellow South Asian, maybe, and he hears a throaty female laugh, a Caucasian girl—her, he sees. Nadeem Riaz hears legs slide across vinyl, then some more balancing in the back seat. He starts the meter, waits for directions.

"Two stops, uhh," the boy begins, Nadeem Riaz feeling his voice closer. The young man reads Nadeem's name on the permit behind the driver's seat. "Riaz Uncle, let's see.... First, Upper West Side, 105th and West End, and then Upper East Side, 75th and Third." The boy's probably had too much to drink and now he's showing token respect to him, but Nadeem Riaz doesn't like the brash tone of his voice.

At least the trip will be lucrative enough: two stops, on opposite sides of Central Park. The door still open, the overhead light on, he sees the young woman in his rearview mirror again. Curly blond ringlets and skin so pale that it makes her lipstick that much more red. The boy, he can't see. Nadeem starts the meter with a tap. He takes the taxi up Eighth Avenue.

"Faisal," the girl asks the boy. "Why did you call the cabby 'uncle?'"

Now *this*, Nadeem Riaz *really* doesn't like. Yes, he drives a taxi, but, back home, in Pakistan, he owned a spare-parts shop; he was *respected*. He's been in this country long enough to know that, by calling him "cabby," she's somehow associating him with the seedy muck of New York City.

"Oh, he's *also* from Pakistan," the boy says to her. "Just being friendly. I'm in a good mood."

Then Nadeem Riaz hears kissing, the uncomfortable skirmish of cloth. The girl giggles a little and then lets out a slight squeal, perhaps signalling the boy that what they're doing is inappropriate.

"I had a *great* time tonight," the boy says.

"Me too," she says to him in a heavy voice. "Tonight was *wonderful.*"

Then the sound of lips smacking. This time Nadeem hears a natural rhythm to the swish of their bodies, and a more agreeable friction of clothes.

Such sounds, commotion, in the back seat are familiar to Nadeem Riaz. If it's not drunk couples on weekends, it's amorous sweethearts he's taking to or bringing from the airport. Two males sometimes; once, even, just females—they made the same yelping sounds in the rear seat. Strangely, not once in his eight years of driving people has he had such a couple—Pakistani and Caucasian—do such things in his taxi. He has transported several mixed couples like this boy and girl, heard their conversations; some he could tell had been together for a long time, the boy always the Pakistani, usually making conversation with him, the girl sometimes asking polite questions about his background—but never a *hello* "Riaz Uncle" followed by *this* display.

Nadeem begins to take the taxi up the West Side Highway, the quickest route to the Upper West Side, but the action in the back grates on him. He decides to lengthen the journey—pad the meter by taking unnecessary cross streets, even going in circles near busy Times Square—as he often does when there's activity in the rear. He would never cheat sober, well-behaved customers; never take advantage of wide-eyed tourists who wouldn't know Midtown from Harlem. But he feels these two passengers are the right ones for such treatment.

The high buildings of the city are asleep, the upscale stores have their night lights on, but there's an array of yellow scavengers around him on the streets. He jockeys for position with his taxi-driving compatriots—accelerates and brakes suddenly at traffic lights, drives over potholes—if just to disrupt the rhythm in the back.

The boy and girl wrestle behind him; he hears yipping, panting, desperate gasps. He half-swings his head, but doesn't see anything, nor distract them.

He can't tell the age of the boy—the girl looked like she was in her twenties, and, from the sound of the boy's voice, he was probably also in that range. Why haven't his parents married him off yet? Nadeem Riaz wonders if they're in Pakistan, maybe receiving handouts from their son earning dollars! The boy's carefree tone did suggest he's made it in this country. The meter reads $19.50, not bad. No, someone as impudent as this young man, calling him "Riaz Uncle," then brazenly disregarding tribal civility by such shameful behavior, is probably from a rich family; his parents, fat, sated, yet unsuspecting—but Nadeem admits to himself that he doesn't really know, can't be sure.

On his third wide circle of Midtown, he takes a very sharp turn back onto Ninth Avenue, making the girl and boy tumble behind him. He thinks maybe he heard the girl retch a little. On top of everything else he's had to endure this day, he can't afford vomit in his taxi! "Why aren't you taking the West Side Highway," the boy suddenly murmurs, coming up for air.

"Accident on Henry Hudson, gentleman," Nadeem Riaz lies, in a very dutiful tone. The boy goes back under.

The taxi's windows are perspiring, Nadeem doesn't know whether from the humidity or the antics behind him. He opens both rear windows to try to faze these passengers; it doesn't work. He could cut the air conditioner, but then he'd have to suffer as well. He can't even talk to anyone on his phone, because he's too distracted with what's happening in his taxi. Sometimes, to discourage conversation, driving chirpy tourists mostly, he'll switch on the recitation of the Holy Quran on his radio—that usually shuts them up. It wouldn't be appropriate here, though maybe this Pakistani in the back seat might be embarrassed enough to stop defiling his taxi. But Nadeem Riaz can't bear to have God's word recited under these conditions—just like God Himself, who's probably cringing up there right now.

"Are you married, gentleman?" Nadeem Riaz finally asks the boy.

No answer.

"Are you *married*, gentleman?" Nadeem screams.

"What's *wrong* with him," the girl whines.

"I don't know," the boy tells her.

Nadeem Riaz hears the boy adjust himself in the back seat.

"We're still not there, Uncle?" the boy asks, a little loudly.

"I told you, gentleman, traffic on Henry Hudson." Nadeem Riaz can't help but pursue his question. "You didn't answer, gentleman?"

"What's his *problem?*" the girl asks the boy, in a small voice.

"We just met tonight, Riaz Uncle," the boy says happily, even blissfully.

"He isn't going to go *crazy*, is he?" the girl asks.

"Relax, he's just having a bad day, I'm sure," the boy says to her.

Stupid, stupid—Nadeem Riaz, if he were a better man, would kick them out of his taxi, onto the sidewalk. Too drunk, they wouldn't have the good sense to note his driver number and complain. He has already cheated them a little. But no, he still has a job to do—to transport his customers, as requested, from point A to point B. He turns onto 105th Street. He doesn't know who he hopes will get off first. The girl tells him to stop curbside next to a green-awninged building.

"So, next Thursday?" the boy says to her.

"*Definitely,*" she says.

One final smack of the lips and she gets out of his taxi. Nadeem Riaz waits, watches her walk towards the building, adjusting her blouse, tugging her miniskirt down.

"75th and Third," the boy says.

Nadeem shrugs and races the engine. He looks at the meter. $23.50 already, and the trip's still not over.

"Having a bad day, Riaz Uncle?" the boy asks him, with that carefree attitude again.

"Not every person can have good days like you, gentleman," Nadeem Riaz replies.

The boy is musically rapping the vinyl seats, still happy. From the West Side to the East Side Nadeem Riaz now drives, starting to think he really shouldn't bother further with this kid. But $26.50 on the meter—he's doing fine.

"This isn't *Pakistan*, you know," the boy says, his voice not near; Nadeem still can't see him through the rearview, he's probably resting back on the seat right behind him.

"For how much time will you use her, gentleman?"

The boy laughs. "Not as long as you use this country!"

"*What?*" he asks, turning over the boy's answer in his mind again to make sure he heard him right. Nadeem Riaz expected him to say something like, his parents were going to get him married off soon enough, so he was just having a little fun. Or, at least, Nadeem had expected to embarrass the boy into silence.

"You drive the taxi for the time being, I'll go out with the girls for the time being, but we both have our thoughts on where home is, right?" the boy says.

He's just drunk, talking nonsensically, Nadeem thinks, but he will put him in his place yet. "This is hard work, gentleman—I support my family by driving this taxi all night."

"Not the point. You hate being here, yes? You complain to your friends and family about being stuck in this Godforsaken country, yes? You worry what will become of your kids when they grow up in this culture, and that you better save enough to move back? Yes?"

"Gentleman. I am scared one of my children will turn into *you* when he grows up," Nadeem Riaz answers. "The other points you make are correct. I am stuck here and will only be staying for a short time, God willing."

"So you agree, you are using this place?"

"It is a small thing, gentleman, for what I have to tolerate, like activities in the back seat of my taxi," Nadeem answers as they cruise through Central Park.

"What if I am not using this place, like you?" the boy asks, the jaunty tone gone, but his voice getting a little heavy with sleep.

"You were sinful in the back seat," Nadeem Riaz says.

"But I may have honest intentions with her," the boy says, his voice closer. "Maybe this is a start with her with no end? Then what? Who's making out with who now? And even if I'm trifling with her, she's only one American—you're messing with the whole country!"

"You are alcoholic and talking nonsense, gentleman!"

"You know what, forget it, you're right," the boy says and drops back on the seat.

"You will remain with the girl?" Nadeem Riaz asks, softening his voice.

"Sorry, Riaz Uncle. Look, I just want to get home," the boy replies sleepily. "Please don't think too hard about what I said."

"Son?" Nadeem Riaz calls to him. The boy is still seated right behind him, and Nadeem still hasn't seen his face. He turns off the air conditioner, to reduce the hum in the air, to give their conversation another chance. But when he hears the boy snoring, he turns the air conditioner on again.

Funny, Nadeem thinks, being in this country—he's expected to act a certain way, how, exactly, he doesn't know. He gets scraps, hints, here and there, and, just as he's about to put the puzzle together, the instructions, the conversation, ends abruptly. So, then, he'll just continue to do his job.

He stops his taxi on the corner of 75th and Third. The boy is still snoring. With his knuckle, Nadeem Riaz knocks on the plastic partition behind him. "Son, 75th Street," he says. "What is the exact location?"

"Huh?" the boy, in a stupor, replies. He stumbles out of the taxi and shambles away, disappearing into the dark street, while owing $42.80. The taxi meter hiccups a receipt which Nadeem Riaz crushes with both hands. He tosses it to the floor of the cab and starts to look for other passengers.

Krazy
by Roy Kesey
from *Hot Metal Bridge*

A night halfway through a family trip to Xian: my wife picks up a comb and looks at herself in the mirror. The kids are asleep and watched over in their room across the hall. The day's walking and looking, the day's climbing and looking, the day's banal and pointless arguments have left us stupid with exhaustion, and also thirsty.

As my wife combs her hair, she tells me to choose where we will go tonight, and for a moment I think she is baiting me, because whenever I choose where to go, it never works out. Then I see that she is simply tired, simply wants me to choose and there is nothing more to it.

This whole business of me choosing has become a joke between us though it is not at all funny: how can it never work out? And by "never" I mean never: one night a month ago back in Beijing I chose and wrote down directions to five separate bars, and we went to all of them that very night, and the first was closed and the second was closed and the third was awful and the fourth no longer existed and the fifth was closed.

Tonight the odds are still worse, as the Guide only lists two that look worth trying, and of course: the taxi rides are very long and one of the bars is unfindable and the other is inside some sort of hostel that is apparently closed, tonight and/or forever, the gates locked, the doorman's hut empty. Somehow my wife avoids sneering, and I am grateful.

Another taxi into the city center, and we choose a main avenue at random, Dongdajie, and walk. It is fairly lively in spots, and at one point I see a club called 1+1 on the far side of the street. I remember the listing in the Guide: it sounded like a place my wife might like if she were in a dancing mood, which she usually is, but just now I am not, and I am a horrible fucking person and don't point it out. I don't want a club. I want a bar. I am four years old and want a bar, a bar, a bar.

Everything else is closed and we check our watches: eleven o'clock on a Sunday night. On and on to the east, still hoping. Finally we find a bar that is open. We climb up a steep narrow fake-wood-wallpapered staircase, the laminate starting to peel, into a space that is odd and large and dark and empty except for the owner, his wife, and their ten-year-old daughter.

The wife disappears. The daughter watches us, then leaves as well. There is pop music from Hong Kong playing not too loudly. Dirty Christmas decorations are everywhere: tinsel along the banisters, cardboard Santas and reindeer and elves pasted crookedly to walls and pillars. There is also a karaoke machine, and no one singing, and a video playing that is not to the song we are hearing.

My wife asks me to sing to her and because she didn't sneer I agree but first we order drinks: I ask for a beer and she orders a Pink Lady, just to try one. They take their time in coming, and the owner spills both as he sets them down. The beer is fine. The Pink Lady is Children's Panadol on ice in a sherry glass.

I ask the owner for a list of possible karaoke songs, thinking that with luck there will be at least one I know. He shakes his head and shrugs. I try again, my Chinese as shoddy as ever, and mimic singing into a microphone. He nods, smiles, assures me that now he has understood. Then he brings my wife a Krazy Straw.

And this Krazy Straw, brilliant red, somehow it works where everything else has failed: we observe it and smile and shake our heads, start to talk, then to laugh, then to tell old stories, ones the other hasn't heard before. This is fairly rare for us, eight years together now, three-and-a-half years married. It is also a good thing, this reminder that we are not yet wholly known to one another.

Several drinks later it is another taxi home and a sweaty muffled romp; then my wife sleeps, and I sneak out onto the balcony. When the cigarette has burned all the way down, I squeeze the filter until the coal falls out—an obsession of mine—and now the coal trails away, falls bright through two hundred feet of dark air, a tiny skydiver in a day-glow jumpsuit, the smoke like a failed chute and thank god for backups.

Forearm and Elbow
by Amy L. Clark
from *Juked*

She is proofreading a medical textbook all about fractures. Last week it was gastrointestinal disorders. The week before that, *Sexual Function and Dysfunction* had asked her how often she became aroused in the shower, and another one, for first responders, had informed her that taking iodine pills when visiting a nuclear ground zero could help protect against future thyroid cancer. "Yeah," her boyfriend had said, "you won't get cancer. But your face will be melted off."

"We're not talking about me," she had responded.

Tonight he says, "It is your night to do the dishes." Yesterday, when it was his night to do the dishes, he had told her that it wasn't fair. What wasn't fair was supposed to be that he had to do all the dishes, not just the ones from dinner but the dishes that she stacked up in the sink while he was at work and she was at home, freelance proofreading. She told him she didn't think two glasses, a mug, a cutting board and a small plate were really a matter of justice.

She gets up from the table and moves to the sink to do the dishes. The doctors had told her that it is important that she try to do as much for herself as she can. She thinks: her boyfriend will not come up behind her while she is doing the dishes and slip his arm around her from behind. His forearm will not rest against her stomach, the crook of his elbow will not cradle her hip. His cheek will not rest against her hair. It had been his idea for her to get this proofreading job, after the bus accident. But the medical textbooks, he thinks now, are making her morbid. He told her the titles sound apocalyptic. He told her it's no fun when they don't go out.

The next day, when she reads that forearm fractures are more common in boys than girls in children over the age of two, but in older people they are much more common in women, she goes into the kitchen. She holds the mug she drank her morning coffee from over her head and drops it to the floor. The kitchen floor is old linoleum, soft with age. Only the handle breaks off. She sweeps it up into the trash anyway. It has been a month since the cast came off. Her ankle is only stiff in the mornings. After lunch she does the same with her plate. She cannot think what to do with the plastic cutting board so she puts it, whole, into the trash can along with the bread knife. The water glass and wine glass from her afternoon snack are easy. And just before he gets home from work, she takes the trash out and puts a fresh bag in the bin.

"Thank you," he says when he comes into the kitchen. He is looking at the empty sink.

Hive
by Elise Paschen
from *Valparaiso Poetry Review*

— *for Stephen*

Tucked in a cleft of arm you hunt
for milk. Roseate. Areola.

I circumnavigate the signs
pictured on your pajamas. Arrows

point east and west; a violet hive;
bear: tail end up in honey-pot.

Cars drone outside. I comb back tufts
of hair. We burrow in these chintz

pillows, sink deeply down in sofa.
For now, we are a pair spied on

by animals. (A rabbit pokes
its ear, antennae-like, from under

cushions.) I've read "during the summer
honey flow, worker bees will travel

55,000 miles to gather
nectar to make one pound of honey."

A foot kicks off its sock. You sip,
roaming many miles, honey-seeker.

Days tumble. I would like to buzz
into the orchid of your ear.

2 Stories
by Blake Butler
from *Action Yes*

Year of Weird Light

I began to try again—and yet in want of nothing, as there was nothing I could taste. The hall outside my bedroom had grown engorged with dirt frittered full with raspy holes threaded by tapeworms and aphids, eating. I'd crack the door to let the looser dustings shake in so there'd be something I could chew on also. It didn't do much good. My tongue took to the texture of grass but my belly would not stop screaming, and the bug matter hung like gristle, my stomach so weak it couldn't grind. I could feel them moving elsewhere. I could feel the crawling behind my eyes. The old ceiling sat around me. The new ceiling: a smudged sky. In the idea of those unbent stars still drooling—the false hope of short-lived rain—I began to convince myself there would again be something. What something, when, regardless. I waited through the long phantasmic buzzing of the others so long gone, the other flooded rooms (my mother's, the tiny crib space, the basement where my brother went under first). When the sound of scissors filled my forehead I would swallow air until they wore away. I would rock and lick the salt of my kneecaps and laugh aloud and remember math. I'd been good at that garbage sometime. I'd been working on a wall. From my window I could see nothing of the yard—just the pinky pastel upchuck that had spread over everything. No sun. In the floor in the far corner where I'd once stood for being dumb there was a mouth. A man's mouth—I could feel his gender in the bristle of his bridge, the texture of his breath. He was not my father, though I'd buried him beneath the house. When I came near enough he'd whisper, his voice ruined and raspy like beehive flutter. He mostly said only one thing over and over. He'd repeat until the words became just words, until even what short sleep came for me was slurred. To shut him up I'd spit between them and the lips would shrivel, bring a hum. You could hear him suck for hours, my taste some nourishment, a fodder. But soon enough again the wishing—like a hymn.

Finally I took the dirt that would have been my dinner and meshed the lips over to make the floor full flush and proper. Then the world again was hushed and far off. I began to teach myself the words I'd need when things returned: the yes and please and bless you. The *ouch* and *why* and *I remember*. I tried to find my mother's voice in my head, but the sounds from outside and in (me, myself) brought a blur: the electric storms, the shaking, the ice-melt, the itch, the rip. I continued to continue to try. I waited longer and the trying became a thing worn like a hairpin in my heart. Or more aptly like my fingernails—nearly an inch each by now, growing out of me some crudded yellow. In time I'd become sly and slouched enough to eat those goddamned slivers of myself. But before that I'd wish the mouth back. I'd lap the dirt and find a hole. One tiny nozzle down to nowhere, black no matter how loud into it I'd beg or bark or sing.

Gristle

The meat had steeped in vinegar for fourteen hours. Its thick scrim glinted in the light. I stood in vigilance near the icebox with a flyswat, sweating. Somehow the aphids kept getting in. They'd laid eggs in the grass cakes. Burrowed my breast milk. Ruined the lard. We were so hungry. It was the seventeenth of September. I would celebrate my goddamn birthday.

The boys were outside in the deep end, splashing to keep warm. It was frigid for the end of summer. Our skins were still raw from months of sun. In their beds I'd find my babies' flakes like large translucent leaves. Jon was losing hair. His head had huge bumps bulging full of pus. The whites of Timmy's eyes were yellow. I could count my tumors like my freckles from young yard-stuck days in Kentucky.

We had the rot inside us now. Even the dachshund, Roger, hung with fungus. He spent his hours heavy breathing. He'd been a good boy for many years. He'd been a gift.

We were so hungry. Two weeks before I'd watched our field of cattle as they fainted in one long wave. As if God's translucent hand had come and swiped them down. Our whole herd, just gone, demolished. Their flesh had rotted in an hour. In another the field was swarmed with heathen—wasps and gnats and rats and roaches. The whole farm's fortune shriveled black and writhing. My husband Jack and I just stood there staring. We had to hold the dog to keep him from running to the swarm. I thanked God only that the boys were asleep.

It'd gotten worse since then.

Insects clustered at the windows. The wind had ripped our roof off. I could hear the kids in the pool now—giddy, whooping. Malnutrition had made them dumber. They needed protein, sustenance. We'd been eating paper, eating mud. What stores hadn't collapsed by now had been fully pillaged. We had no TV, song or excess light.

When the sun went down enough so birds couldn't see to swoop, I carried the meat out into the backyard. Rain had turned the lawn to slosh. I'd made Jack's Cadillac's hood into a makeshift sort of skillet. The pink hammy flanks of Roger sizzled on hot metal.

I'd explained Roger's recent disappearance by saying he'd gone on to find their Papa; that soon he'd return with our man's hand clenched in his teeth and then again they'd neither leave. Jack, the motherfucker, had found an anvil and jumped in the pool they swam in now. I'd fibbed for that occasion also, said he'd gone to build us a new home: a mansion somewhere sacred, where we'd never wake to shaking, to weird bumps on our backs. When they frittered for more info—*where? how much longer?*—I snapped and smacked their chins. I couldn't help it. He'd given up. He'd left me here alone to raise two boys in a world where at night flies caked the moon.

Jack—the man who'd sworn he'd stay beside me for forever.

Jack—who by the time I found him had been picked clean. I'd identified him by his front teeth: each crowned from boyhood fighting. The gold had gotten us along another week.

But now the plume of cook-smoke from Roger swam around me. The gristle jumped and spat. I started drooling—couldn't help it. I sliced a hunk out of the thigh meat, sucked it down soggy with juice. My stomach screamed in glee. I ate another—*Happy birthday.*

I was thirty-three years old. Same age my mother'd been when she was ripped to bits by incensed cats. I didn't feel so bad eating Roger, as good a puppy as he'd been. I nibbled his bitter liver and his kidneys. Something long gone whooped in my cerebrum.

The wind was picking up. Rain spanked my face like little hands. I chewed so hard I bit my lip a bit. I tasted blood. My body surged.

I ate the whole dog raw.

Afterward I felt giddy, awkward, my stomach bulging as if with child. My heartbeat throttled through my body—*rollercoasters*. I felt embarrassed, somewhat sick.

Before our roof I'd watched the Johnsons' RV ascend. I'd seen whole sheets of land uprooted. Each night the CB blubbed with gossip: how the sky had stole a school bus full of children, our city bridge, an apple orchard. Even the stream that crossed the backyard had one night begun running upward. God was taking things back. Just a matter of time before my boys or me. If not tomorrow, then tomorrow. Things would continue in their way until they didn't.

Sometimes I still see Jack in the cracky black above the bed where I haven't slept right in forever.

My knees now shook beneath me. Saliva dribbled down my cheeks. I turned around to see the boys' bodies flapping, their heads bulging ripe on sallow mass. They looked so happy, even still. It took a minute to recall their names. The wind whipped so strong my hair now stood up over my head. The grill sputtered with the rain. I could feel its sizzle in my stomach—its metal issued through my tissue. I wanted more. It was my birthday. My teeth sweated for my tongue.

The boys. These boys, my babies. These sons who wouldn't ever grow much older. Who before they'd had a chance of love or worship would be combusted, spored. If the rain didn't take us, then the wind would, or the mud, the mire, the cats. They shouldn't suffer such long torture. I couldn't wait for the sky to dive.

With both hands shaking the greasy flipper, drool now curling down my thigh, I called my boys to come in from the rain and sing my name.

An Interview with Blake Butler

Author of *Year of Weird Light* and *Gristle*

1. Some might describe your fiction as intense, immediate, unsettling. What do you think of these modifiers?

I think those are modifiers I can live with. Most often, as a reader, the text I feel most moved by is that which inflicts my brain or body as if physically manipulating me through the paper. Condoning physical responses via the simulative act of language is, for me, in the same mind of the way the body is altered via states entered in sleeping, i.e. you are experiencing and, yes, I think, actually entering interstices that do actually exist, though on a separate, perhaps parallel, sphere of what most people experience on a daily basis. I guess it's in and of my blood that my tendency in this area is for the more visceral or disturbing camps, as for as long as I can remember my dreaming has been haunted with images and motions as brutal or often more so than those that appear among my waking words.

2. So I'm curious: what propelled you to write "Gristle"? "Year of Weird Light"?

As with most impetuses for my makings, I believe it was the sentences that occurred first—they come in through the nostrils mostly. Once I get them in me the only way to get them back out is to force them into my computer. I guess in that way for me often writing is like sneezing, only more intense and more prolonged. For "Gristle," I know that once I got through those first paragraphs the idea of the mother eating the dog occurred to me like something I had done inside me thousands of times, somewhere else and so writing it was as casual as talking about eating Cheerios, though some readers have mentioned that the action, again, was unsettling. "Year of Weird Light" was purely a language exercise, one word dictating the other: I didn't think about what I was doing semantically at all as it was written, which is my most favorite way to write.

3. Just an observation—the narration itself seems to often take center stage in your fiction, whereas dialogue is less present. Care to comment on this (as W would have it) strategery?

Writing, for me, is all about how a thing is said, more so than what it said or what goes on inside it. I like ideas and diction and sound mouths and gibberish much more than more precalculated modes such as character, setting, plot, etc. The old saying "Everything has already been said" I believe applies mostly to the nature of what is said, not how you say it. To get out of the lamp of repeating one story after another, a writer should be speaking his own tongues—if culled at the same time from years of reading masters. Not to say that I don't love a good story, but in the case of all of my favorite writers the story comes from the invocation and not the brand.

4. What are you reading these days?

God, a lot. I think there is more new good being created out there every day now than there has been at any other point, and I think online literature's recent swelling (thanks in part to enterprises like BOTW) has a lot to do with it. Recent authors or works I have loved, new and old: Ken Sparling's *Dad Says He Saw You at the Mall*, Michael Kimball's *Dear Everybody*, both novels by Eugene Marten, Johannes Goransson, Jesse Ball, Gert Jonke's *Regional Geographic Novel*, Vanessa Place's *La Medusa*, Sean Kilpatrick, Sam Pink. I always reread a large chunk of Brian Evenson every year, he's like blood. I also love and read religiously the online journals *Diagram, Elimae, Wigleaf, Bear Parade, Action Yes*, and countless others as well as print.

4. Tell me about *Scorch Atlas*.

Scorch Atlas is a novel in 15 interlinked stories, interspersed with flashes of strange forms of rain in rendered a destructed America, very much in the vein and mind of "Year of Weird Light" and "Gristle." Many of the stories have the same "bleak" texture as the pieces found here, but I think also interspersed with a sense of family and want for preservation, a kind of double-edged evocation of grit and gash and exit. It's got a bit of everything in it, from a story about a baby swelling to fill his parents' attic, to fake insurance claim questionnaires, to neighborhoods sucked under mud. It will come out this September from Featherproof Books. I couldn't be more excited.

The Dance of Curb Chickens
by Joseph Olschner
from *Arsenic Lobster*

For a time,
they scattered
like cotton
popped from a shotgun,
running like leaves
flung from a tunnel
as the rubber and steel rims
of a green Packard
busted
through what had been
a quiet pecking space
but for the road shoulder roar
that would push
beating wings and feathers
back to the packed dirt yard
under ribbons of wet clothes
hanging in the sun.

For a time,
my curbed visit is a quiet one,
rolling into the sidewalk silence
at my once lived in house,
the yellow one where she still lives
and from where she sends the kids out, garnished
in weekend backpacks
and happy smiles for our weekend journey.

For a time,
The wings that flutter here are not feathered
but hang beating like flapping clothes,
drying and waiting to be taken in,
only now
there are less baskets
for them to covet,
less hands to gently crease the seams
and fold them for their own
far flung scattering.

Bounty
by Tricia Louvar
from *SmokeLong Quarterly*

Daddy is a man of tight seams and tanned skin. He can do just about anything. He used to trap coyotes and then cut their heads off. For each head, the county gave him twenty-five cents. In the front seat of the Charger was his jar of money. In the trunk was the bucket of heads. By summer's end, he remembers making about twenty bucks.

A few years later he was sent to Vietnam but he doesn't tell me any of those stories, only the one about the tiger. Waiting in a manhole, a tiger dragged him out one-legged. He shot and shot and shot her between the eyes. When it was over he remembers feeling her soft chuffing sound on his leg and her eyes had a widened sheen of sympathy.

When he returned home, he wouldn't play hide-and-seek with me any more. He said he was tired of surprises, which made birthdays sucky.

He pretty much just works now at the taxidermist manufacturer in the artificial eyes department. He likes the mammal eyes. Testicles & noses and jaws & tongues don't interest him too much.

Sometimes he brings home a grocery store plastic bag filled with defective eyes. The Dalls' pupils are too narrow; the albino eyes are too white; the fallow deers' eyes are too tigerish; the elks' eyes are too toady. Sometimes I organize them by color into little glass jars. Other times I swap out my dolls' eyes for animal eyes. They become beautiful little monsters.

Most days though, before he comes home from work, I brew him some black coffee, pour him a mug, and walk it out the back door and down the hill to his metal shed. I do this special thing where I pour a little honey into his coffee and stir it up real good. I leave it on his workbench scattered with eye tools, like the shapers and the eye socket elongaters. He's trying to become a taxidermist for real. He says believability is in the eyes.

Later in the evening when I get ready for bed, he comes into my bedroom to tell me, "Peaches, another great cup of coffee." He doesn't know my secret. He asks but I don't tell. I love it that a secret can hold on so tight in the rear corner of my mouth.

Little Witches
by Bill Cook
from *The Summerset Review*

Mamma brings home another black man in another pressed blue suit. My sister and I are sitting on our brown sofa, eating dry cereal and pretending to read our schoolbooks. Our bright-colored daypacks are on the floor by our feet. School papers, tests with Ds and Cs spill out of their open mouths like crumpled Tarot cards. We say let's go upstairs, winking at each other. But first, we go into the kitchen, where my sister takes an old metal stepstool and reaches into Mamma's liquor cupboard.

She quickly retrieves two tall plastic cups and two shot glasses while I pilfer the pink lemonade and the big jug of milk.

Hand in hand, we scuttle up the old, creaky stairs, giggling.

Sitting cross-legged on Mamma's bedroom floor, we pour white drinks and pink shots as she entertains downstairs. Soon we hear roaring laughter, Mamma's stamping church-white sandals, then her high, angelic voice, thrumming, "Halleluiah! Halleluiah! Halleluiah!"

We stare at our long blond hairs flung across the wooden floor like perfect silken threads, silent as angels.

My sister gets up, says nothing, and goes to Mamma's closet.

Soon, she's back with Dad's old sport coat and tweed fedora. I wear the dusty hat and my sister dons the big blue coat. It's so large she disappears, and my face as well; my eyes covered, my nose pressed against the fuzzy, warm rim that smells old. There are little frizzes of his hair inside, dark and curled like I remember.

Now we laugh at ourselves, sit back down and soon become groggy and pour everything out onto the space between us. We watch our perfect flung hairs dissolve in flows of pink and white. Then twirling our fingertips like magical wands, we incant, "kaleidoscope... kaleidoscope... kaleidoscope" and fall over.

We laugh some more, but now we're too tired for all that. We roll against each other, sandbagging under Dad's old coat and dusty hat, smelling and giggling. We take turns, telling him our little secrets again and again. We tell him this is where we belong.

Belly
by Glen Pourciau
from *Hobart*

We'd just eaten a steak dinner. I'd handled the salad and the baked potatoes, my husband had grilled the steaks. Bottle of wine on the table, a few drinks for him before dinner. My husband, veteran of many cocktails. As usual, he finished his plate first and shoved it away from him while I was still eating. He lit up a cigar, rolled it around in his mouth as he moved his ashtray in front of him, and then unbuttoned his shirt and rubbed his hairy belly and groaned. He knows I don't like to see his belly at the table, but when he's in the mood he unveils it anyway. I picked up the wine and refilled my glass, and he pointed a finger at his glass and I topped him off.

Puffing his cigar, he began to hold forth. He likes to hold forth after a good meal. My role is to sit quietly, not to ask questions, interrupt, or answer the phone if it rings. If my knife or fork makes a sound on my plate, his eyes go to it. We're a perfect match: he doesn't notice if I don't listen to him and I don't care what he's saying. I'd picked up that he was again complaining about his assistant, a subject I was sick of, but I didn't bother to follow the thread of his latest story. Instead I asked myself what he would do if I pulled off my top and unhooked my bra. I could prop my breasts on the table, dip them in some of the butter that had oozed out of my potato. How would that grab him?

I knew why his assistant was on his mind, knew that he wanted to get her into a hotel room. She was married and had a son, but he wasn't going to concern himself with her family, they weren't on his radar. I knew about some of his affairs, probably not all of them, and I'd seen his assistant and knew what he was looking at. If he put up with being annoyed by her there was only one explanation for it. He'd just fire her if he didn't like the way she did her job, unless he had a reason to want her around. Without listening to details I could tell she couldn't stand him and that she challenged him. I studied his stuffed belly and the pits in his face as he slurped down a mouthful of wine, smoke swirling over us. I pushed my plate away, unable to properly taste my food, but he didn't seem to notice my movements.

146

Based on what I'd heard of his assistant, I liked her attitude. It occurred to me that I might call her up, ask her to lunch and hear what she had to say about him, and what he might have said to her, but I hesitated to put her in that position. She probably needed her job and wouldn't want to say too much and then have to worry I'd rat her out to him. But I remembered that when I met her she'd made eye contact, and there'd been a question in her eyes. I didn't know what the question was at first. I wondered if her eyes could be asking if I suspected her of having an affair with him, but that didn't seem to be it. Her gaze stayed with mine, and I took that to be her effort to estimate the connection between us. She wondered if I was on to my husband and whether I'd show compassion in the way I returned her gaze. I did try to show compassion and I think she looked at me with compassion.

The orator before me continued with his rendition, addressing the air in front of him on the topic of his bothersome assistant. She didn't look like a blank page, and I supposed that she had too much to say of her own to keep quiet around him. I wouldn't know exactly how much I might admire her until I talked with her, and I decided then that I'd ask her to lunch and see what happened. I could get personal if she wanted to or I could be diplomatic if she preferred that, but there would be an undercurrent there, a link, I could feel it already. I thought of places we could go and what I could wear to set the right tone, and I made up my mind that I wouldn't tell him what I was going to do. I didn't want him to get in the middle of us.

I felt a smile coming on, and the smile seemed to muffle his voice. I pulled off my top and took off my bra and threw them aside. I shook my hair back into shape, the smoky air on my breasts. He kept right on talking.

I'm Not Supposed to Wear This Gorilla Costume
by Arlene Ang
from *Juked*

I'm supposed to be on a plane for Gibraltar.
On the back of my hand, I've written keywords

like *natural disaster* and *conscience.*
In the turbulence, I'd be taking the in-flight meal

apart with a plastic knife. It is always up
to the omelet to appear greening in the light.

So what if I've begun to resemble a hair ball
by the hour? I've never gotten paid on time,

never had my nose hair plucked by
a professional. There's supposed to be

a celebration of some sort—pagan
or otherwise—taking place in three days

at the studio of a future spouse.
The expectations of others have little

to do with reality. The way everyone
prepares their clothes to jitterbug the dancefloor

is supposed to make me think everything else
is the alpha dog. I shouldn't even be

following this trail of dead ants, but someone
burned them and left the magnifying lens
in my hand. I have a birthday greeting, too
hidden somewhere in my body. I should stop

fondling all this synthetic hair now. If this is Kansas,
what have I been fighting for all my life?

An Interview with Arlene Ang
Author of *I'm Not Supposed to Wear This Gorilla Costume*

1. Tell me a bit about your writing process.

Writing doesn't come naturally to me so I do most of my first drafts in ITWS, an online writers' community. They have a challenge there to write 30 poems for 30 days. I find that the 24-hour deadline works really well for me.

2. What stirred you to write these two poems chosen for *Best of the Web 2009*?

A documentary on zoo animals and missing my flight (again).

Like the speaker in "I'm Not Supposed to Wear This Gorilla Costume," I also like writing words on my hands sometimes. What have you written on your hands recently?

Actually, that was just wishful thinking. My hands are rather Shar-Pei-ish and sweaty, hence poor writing material.

3. You've become quite a presence in online (and print) magazines. Can you share some of the secrets of your success?

There's no secret really. I submit a lot and get rejected a lot. It's sometimes hard to cope with the latter, especially after getting three or four in one day. But if there are no rejections, then acceptances wouldn't be half as great. Plus, I'm a born pest. And editors know it.

4. Can we look forward to a new collection from you at any point soon?

Cinnamon Press has my poetry book, *Seeing Birds in Church Is a Kind of Adieu* scheduled for publication in 2010. God willing.

Anything Was Anything
by Ryan Dilbert
from *FRiGG*

When she was four, my sister Lily accidentally made clothes out of whiskey.

Uncle Dan was drinking Bushmills and water and going on about how he hated having to press 1 for English.

"Isn't this America?" he said, a gold, strapless cocktail dress hanging out of his glass.

Years later, I drove to her cabin. Cicadas sang their flittering song as I waited at the door. I had to knock three times. Lily answered in a bikini. I asked her if she was going swimming and she just grinned vacantly. I tried to lock the door behind me but she had turned the deadbolt into seaweed.

The letters I had sent my sister over the last few months were stacked neatly at the center of the kitchen table, unfolded and held down by a Greek cookbook. Lily had always been reluctant to use whatever it was she had, and was a shut-in after she dropped out of high school, but this was different. I was dying and she didn't even respond. I knew then that she wasn't Lily anymore.

I offered to make my famous milkshakes but the ice cream was a pygmy kangaroo and it hopped out of the blender. We used to drink them in the attic when my parents fought. Lily was the biggest baby when she got a brain freeze. She wailed and writhed and held her head in agony. I think she did it just to see me crack up.

The pygmy kangaroo jumped out of an open window and disappeared into the slouching oaks that surrounded Lily's cabin. The cicadas droned like old piping.

When Lily first knew she could change things, it pained her. She felt like she was angering God. But if we were going hungry, she'd make food or if Mom was short on rent, she'd take some cigarette butts and squeeze them in her hand until they were hundred dollar bills. It made her cry.

I sat down in one of her chairs and found myself sinking in sawdust. She couldn't control it anymore. Anything was anything and nothing was anything for long.

She had two dachshunds.

"This one used to be my ex-boyfriend, Alvin," she said pointing to the yapper chewing on my shoelaces.

When Lily was little she never used to smile. She smiled all the time now. The pressure had flattened and lobotomized her. I'll bet my family regrets all those comparisons to Jesus now.

I asked her if she could turn my cancer into something less deadly. She smiled like the sun was coming out.

"Lily, I need your help."

She looked down and twiddled two sticks together, two tuning forks, two Barbies, two dead crickets. I had lung cancer and I had never smoked. I imagined that Lily could wave her hand and turn the growth into a tiny fairy that would fly out of me in a puff of gold dust. Lily told me how she fixed a leaking pipe all by herself.

I put her hand on my chest, right on the pain. This is where you change it, I told her.

Her dachshunds were Komodo dragons. They waddled toward me, hissing. I thought they were going to snap at my shins, but they turned into football helmets, into two stacks of Esquire.

"No, here!" I yelled, pounding her hand on my chest.

Lily always just wanted to be a normal kid. She wanted to step back from the spotlight and take care of dogs and find love and eat well and buy sweaters that fit perfectly. She didn't want to evade scientists or constantly be asked questions.

"What are you going to do with it?"

Everybody asked her that.

She turned her poofy, red hair into cornstalks. Copper pipes. Feathered wings. I told her I was sorry for yelling at her and telling her she was wasting her life. I had pushed her as hard as anyone. I was always jealous of what she had even if I saw it drain her like she was getting blood-letted. She wanted nothing more than to shy away from greatness and none of us let her.

I pointed to my right lung and begged her to help me. She glanced up at me with a sliver of recognition. I spoke softly and told her what she had to do. She squeezed down on my skin and I could feel her power surging through me.

She turned my cancer into an anchor. It didn't hurt at first. My arms went numb. I fell over, sinking down into blackness, onto the floor. The anchor burst out of my chest like a battering ram through plywood.

I was afraid to ask her to change it again. So I stayed disfigured, and in great, stubborn pain. I told Lily bye. I limped back to my car. The cicadas weren't making noise anymore. They were nickels now.

Catching Hell: The Joe Holt Integration Story
by Heather Killelea McEntarfer
from *Terrain.org*

Joe Holt's troubles didn't begin the summer of 1957. But when he thinks back, that's where he lingers. Late summer, 1957, his cousin tearing down a country road, crying and shouting: *Lord have mercy!* Late summer of 57: the summer hell slipped the grasp of the devil himself, and settled contentedly in the Holt family home.

It was a Saturday. Joe, fourteen, had been shipped to his father's family in the backwoods of eastern Carolina—a little vacation, he'd been told. That day, his relatives had visited an aunt who owned a television. Joe had decided to stay home. He was a city kid, after all, and television old news. Hardly worth a quarter of a mile.

But then his cousin rushed through the front gate, hysterical. *Lord have mercy!*

"What's the matter with you?" Joe asked.

"It's all over the television! Oh, Lord have mercy, they gonna destroy ya'll's house!"

Raleigh does not remember Joe Holt. The family that made television in eastern Carolina, 1957, slipped from the narrative of a city willingly—or something close to willingly. In a city just as eager to forget, that story fell to fragments. A misgiving here; tight tug of anger there. Typed lines in old records, bound and shelved. A story that, for nearly half a century, no one chose.

You could say that story begins in August, 1956. Raleigh. Two years after *Brown v. Board of Education*, and Joe Holt still rode the city bus across town everyday to Ligon, the black school, rather than the nearby Daniels' Junior High. His parents wanted Joe to attend Daniels'; after all, the law said he could. Local black lawyers hoping to enforce that law were seeking just such a family. Joe was thirteen, entering the ninth grade.

That November, the family made *The Raleigh Times*. They posed together: Elwyna hovered above husband and son and pursed her lips a bit, as if hiding some ironic amusement. Little Joe, as he was known, leaned in on the other side of his father, long face solemn. And in the middle, Joe, Sr. Perfectly straight, shoulders back, eyes narrowed and the hint of a smile on closed lips. "I intend to see this thing through," he said. "We are not going to stop now."

It was a Joe, Sr. kind of a thing to say.

"Perhaps this strikes every boy about his dad," Holt says now, "but my dad stood tall, as a man. It was a matter of pride to him as a man that he stood his ground. To me, he was the epitome of strength, both physically and in character. He was strong, and he stood tall."

Joe, Sr. grew up in eastern North Carolina, where Joe visited that summer of 57. Out there, a city boy like Joe, on childhood visits, could collect attitudes and anecdotes, stockpile them the way children do with random treasures: rubber bands and buttons and shards of colored rock. Hide them in bulging pockets or the folds of a tree; spread them out later for examination. There was the way, in that community, white folk lived among the blacks, if not *too* close. The way you could address a white man by his first name, no Mr. This or Mr. That cluttering up the conversation. You couldn't get away with that in Raleigh. Still, Holt says he never saw his father *subordinate* himself to anyone.

Joe Sr. found a match in Elwyna. She was, Holt says, intellectual, cultured, refined. She knew her rights. A local schoolteacher, Elwyna wrote the application to Daniels', arguing that Daniels' was closer than Ligon. It was—with better facilities and books that weren't hand-me-downs. But for the Holts, admission to the white school was not about convenience, nor even entirely about facilities. It was about their son not being made to feel unworthy. As long as you went to Ligon High School, Holt says, "You still carried with you: this school is for you; *that* school is for our white kids."

Joe Holt's application to Daniels' Junior High was denied. According to the city school superintendent, it was not the time for that.

The next year, 1957, the family tried again. Too old now for junior high, Joe applied to Broughton High School.

This time was harder.

Rules sprang up, thick as kudzu. School transfer policies before 1956 were not particularly complex; school transfer had never posed a problem.

A year earlier, Elwyna sat down in August and wrote the superintendent a letter. School board minutes show that other parents requested transfers in the same way.

But by 1957, things had changed. The Holts had happened. The Board's new Pupil Assignment Policy required forms, signatures, notaries. The Holts made the deadline with time to spare.

But Joe Holt remembers another rule: in order for any school board decision to be made, a certain number of members needed to be present. Joe's application reached the board in June 1957, and it was a funny thing, those summer months: each time the Holt matter came up, seemed there weren't enough board members present to make a decision one way or the other.

June 11, 1957: Upon motion by Mr. Martin, seconded by Mr. Powell, action on this application was deferred until the next meeting of the full board.

So the Holts waited. Meanwhile, the harassment that had begun late fall of 56 reached a screaming pitch. Hate mail, bomb threats, phone calls all through the night, *every* night. What's more, the Holts felt even the black community had averted its eyes. Before his application, Holt says, his parents had been accepted members of Raleigh's black community, their names cropping up on guest lists for events and socials.

And then, this strange silence. We live today in a world that's known the Sixties, a world in which African-American resistance to racism has become an integral shade in the collective hue of American history, American politics: a shade without which we wouldn't know ourselves. That's not to say resistance is new, nor even that it's entirely safe. Just that it's easy to forget how dangerous it was. There were hands in the night that could ring your house with gasoline, pour poison down your well, string you from a tree and set you aflame. *Emmett Till* was whispered as a warning to young boys. And danger was catching: a disease transferred not through a cough, but an unwise smile on the bus. Joe, fourteen, didn't notice it so much. But his parents began to sense that friends were distancing themselves.

Joe Holt understands that distance now—understands the fear. Still, it hurt. Dr. Prezell Robinson served as academic dean of Raleigh's historically black St. Augustine's College in 1957. In Robinson's memory, most of Raleigh's black community supported the Holts. But Robinson also remembers the fear. The "White Citizen's Council," he says, did everything it could to intimidate black people who supported Joe Holt.

The threats regarding jobs weren't idle; by that summer of 57, Joe, Sr. had lost his own job and begun a series of odd jobs that tended to dry up as bosses realized just whom they had on their hands. His periodic joblessness left Elwyna the family's sole breadwinner, her teaching job precarious at best. And as the fight wore on, Elwyna bore the brunt of the verbal abuse directed toward the family. She answered the phone, fielded the name-calling and threats. Joe watched his mother, saw how the very way she moved about the house changed. Jittery, on edge. He swears now that his mother was on the verge of a nervous breakdown.

And Joe? Joe Holt was a boy. In *The Raleigh Times* photo, his eyes catch you. His parents look off a bit to the right, but Joe stares straight at you, eyes solemn and deep. He was a serious, quiet kid. He understood his family's fight, and he wanted it. He says he never wished his parents would just let the whole thing drop. He says he was still able to hang out with the boys, get into mischief.

He also calls those four years the most stressful in his life.

"When you are in a subordinate position like blacks are," Holt says, "you have been conditioned, unfairly, to feel that you have to be perfect in order to be accepted, where a white person doesn't have to think twice about it. I knew that I was like in a fishbowl. I was a black kid that everybody—every black person in Raleigh that I knew—was looking at as somebody special. I felt I needed to be a genius, okay? So that I wouldn't let anybody down. I wasn't a genius. Okay? I was a good student—but I wasn't a genius."

Joe worried about his parents and his grades. But as far as actually *going* to the white school, it wasn't Broughton that scared him the most. Maybe that was too far off in the distance—unimaginable, really, in North Carolina, 1957. Maybe Joe's fear latched on to something he could imagine. At any rate, what scared Joe Holt during the summer of 57, as the school board stalled and his parents worried and the phone raged in the night— what scared him was the prospect of going before the school board for his transfer request. To go to a hearing, surrounded by whites, not knowing what they might ask? Maybe they'd make him work out an equation, differential calculus or something. He didn't know. He knew from intuition and experience that anything he said that didn't satisfy that board would be exaggerated. Maybe headlined in the paper, whispered and frowned over by the black community he believed was counting on him.

The worry followed him out of Raleigh to his aunt and uncle's house, a fear he couldn't say, lest anybody see it as unwillingness. Joe Holt was willing to go to Broughton. But now he had to go to some sort of damn *inquisition*?

And then the trip down east, and his cousin flying down that dirt road, carrying on about dynamite and fire and Joe's parents on TV.

Joe didn't believe her at first. He thought he was on vacation. He didn't know about the woman back home who'd overheard something somewhere and issued Elwyna a warning: *Get Little Joe outta here.*

He shook his head. "You didn't see them on television. C'mon."

The cousin insisted. "They were on *TV*, Joe! They had a picture of them right there at your house!"

It took Joe a while to believe her. When he did, he said, *God.* He'd been trying not to think about anything related to Raleigh or school boards, but the terror in his cousin's eyes was real. Within 48 hours, Joe's parents had joined him down east. They were quiet, and Joe was too. He worried, but his parents were usually open with him. Joe figured whatever they wanted to tell him, they'd tell him.

And if they didn't tell him anything, that meant Dad had it under control.

One night, though, he stood out on the front porch with his father and his Uncle David. Little Joe was silent, but his uncle and father began to speak.

His uncle asked, "Do you think you really need to go through with this thing?"

Joe remembers his father saying, "David, I'm going through with it." And, "Everything'll be alright."

And then his uncle said something that surprised Little Joe. Here was this big strong farmer, formed on the same parcel of earth that had formed Joe, Sr., and both with cores like pillars of oak: big on strength and fortitude, but not necessarily on sensitivity. Little Joe didn't picture his Uncle David as big on reading people either, and he'd been working so hard to hide his fear.

But there was his uncle on that porch, saying, "I'm not sure you ought to put Little Joe in that situation."

Joe was silent. There were words on his tongue, but they could have been misconstrued: a worrisome prospect in a world where a child did not correct his elders. If his father and uncle got the idea that Joe wanted to back off the fight, there would have been no respectable way to set them straight. But in the silence that followed, Joe's father went quiet. Finally, Little Joe *did* speak, something along the lines of, "Well, I wonder what they're gonna ask me?"

His father stayed quiet a while longer. Joe felt him searching, running the words of his brother and son against that oak, as if he'd find an answer carved into some unexpected nook. Maybe he did. When he spoke, it was the Big Joe his family knew.

"Hell, no," he said, "you're not going down there in front of that damn board."

Back in Raleigh, the Holts' lawyers agreed. Listen, they said, we're your lawyers. We have power of attorney. There's no reason for you to go down there. In fact, the Holts' lawyer, Herman L. Taylor, thought Joe's intuition sound.

"In those days," Taylor would say later, "they used every ruse they could find to delay, and one reason we didn't want your father and his parents to go to that school board meeting was that we knew that they wanted to get them there and try to intimidate them, brow-beat 'em, see, and put them through all kinds of torture. And as their lawyers, it was our business to shield them from that."

The decision would prove critical.

The school board finally addressed Joe Holt's application in August of 1957, when it ruled, "*In the interest of the public, and in the best interest of the Raleigh City Schools, and for the welfare of Joseph Hiram Holt, Jr.,...*" Joe would not be allowed into Broughton.

The Holts filed suit in federal court, but in September of Joe's junior year at Ligon, the court denied the application. The official, legal ruling? Joe couldn't go because of the Holt family's "failure to exhaust all administrative remedies before the law."

In other words: Joe hadn't gone before the board.

Failure to exhaust all administrative remedies? The phrase ran through their minds, a taunt laced with guilt and what-ifs: what if Joe had just gone? Would the fight be over? Because, coming when it did, the court's ruling was like high water rising. Not an end; not an answer. A continuation. It meant Joe couldn't go to Broughton, at least not yet. More immediately, it meant that all of the abuse, the phone calls, the threats, the fear, would all continue. High water rising, and nothing to do but tip back your head, grab what air you could, and keep paddling. If the family thought of stopping, they did not say it. But they were tired.

Once again, they fought back. Their lawyers appealed the ruling, and finally in fall, 1959—Joe's senior year—the Eastern District Court upheld the *Administrative Remedies* ruling. The Supreme Court would not hear the case; the Eastern District Court was the final recourse. A few months later Joe graduated from Ligon, and the matter was over.

Or the court's decision made it seem that way, for a while.

Raleigh does not remember Joe Holt. Raleigh tells another story—one that brings the city pride, and, in some ways, deservedly so. Joe learned about that story in September 1960, three months after he graduated from Ligon. At the kitchen table one day, he picked up the *Raleigh News and Observer*—and there, on the front page, a young black child smiled back. Seven-year-old Bill Campbell, the first black child to be admitted to a white Raleigh school.

There'd been no fanfare. The article was small, set beneath the fold. A few days later another article, tucked into the inside pages, recorded the milestone: "Raleigh's public school system was peaceably integrated Friday...."

And it had been. On September 9, 1960, second-grader Bill Campbell arrived with his mother at Raleigh's Murphey School. In a photograph accompanying the article, a few parents and children stood along the sidewalk, watching Bill Campbell and his mother leave. They watched as though mother and son were curiosities: lonely members, perhaps, of an already-passed-by parade, this child with the pressed plaid shirt and white socks drawn up high, and the mother who clutched his hand and bent over him, protectively. They watched, and in the photograph a little boy behind Bill Campbell cocked his head.

They watched. But they were only a handful.

That week, a few letters to the editor derided Bill Campbell's admission. At the Murphey School, a few parents withdrew their children.

Within a few days, most were back.

In Little Rock, angry crowds chased nine black teenagers from the lawn of Central High. In New Orleans, six-year-old Ruby Bridges was "integrated" into an empty classroom. And in Prince Edward County, Virginia, school leaders closed down every public school in the county for five years, rather than integrate any one of those schools.

In September 1960, Raleigh's local papers focused on Hurrricane Donna pummeling the Florida Keys. Letters to the editor focused on the relative propriety of a Catholic running for president.

Three years earlier the Holts fled this city for their lives; in 1960, the public record portrays Raleigh's introduction to integrated schools as a sidenote. According to Casper Holroyd, a white Raleigh parent in 1960, that's just about right. Bill Campbell's acceptance, Holroyd says, "didn't seem to be any outlandish thing."

The claim invokes a public front. Within the Murphey school, five years passed without one black face for Bill Campbell's eyes to rest on. Within the family home, the phone erupted with threats from which the family fled, unable to trust the police. And every morning on Raleigh's streets, a small group of citizens escorted mother and son to school, protecting them from taunts, shouts, spit. Every morning a white woman called down from her porch, "*Nigger, why do you want to go to school with those children?*"

There is, to be sure, the public front—one that does justice to neither Bill Campbell nor his family. But the public front has become the story that's survived, one that takes on its own importance: the story Raleigh claims. The story of a city that had its controversies over race, no one denies that—but a city that can also point to relative calm in a time when the state and the South and the country all seemed to have gone just a little bit mad.

Bill Campbell's admission should have been a right, a good thing— and it was. But coming on the heels of the Holt family ordeal, that admission also became a twisted sort of mirror—one in which the Holts' reflection came out poorly. If the school board was willing to accept a black child in the fall of 1960, why should it not have been in the fall of 1959? Bill Campbell's acceptance lent *failure to exhaust all administrative remedies* a new legitimacy, in the black community and the Holt family. That *failure* became the story told in hushed tones: black children in Raleigh couldn't go to white schools because the Holts screwed up.

In the years that followed, the entire experience—most of all, that decision not to go before the board—haunted the Holts, silently. The late fifties became a time not talked about. A time worked over on the inside. *If we had just....If I had only....*

Meanwhile, Raleigh's black community beheld Bill Campbell with a kind of awe: this child who carried so much into that school. Centuries of pain, and the promise of all they could imagine. Everybody needs heroes, Joe Holt says. And if the young Bill Campbell embodied an up-and-coming city and an up-and-coming people, he seemed—for a while—to have made good as an adult: in 1993, Atlanta elected him mayor. Campbell's name even cropped up on lists of potential running mates for Al Gore in 2000. When Campbell spoke at the 2002 commencement of Raleigh's historically black Shaw University, President Talbert O. Shaw told him, "You are a favorite son of Raleigh. As a boy, you were so brave."

And behind all of that: Joe Holt. Seventeen years old in September 1960. Soon he'd earn honors at St. Augustine's College. Airlift materiel into and out of Vietnam with the Air Force; forge a career; retire as lieutenant colonel. Raise, with his wife, three children who would give him three grandchildren.

But in September, 1960, he sits down at the kitchen table, unfolds the paper, and *What in the world is this?* Who *are* these people? What did they do that *we* didn't do?

The questions tormented Joe. Bill Campbell was seven years old; the timing was not the child's fault. And Joe Holt, then and now, is not by nature a vengeful man. But now, when he speaks of his family's story, and particularly of the Campbells, his voice rises in pitch. *The fiery Ralph Campbell:* that's how black people in Raleigh would come to describe Bill Campbell's father. And any thought directed by Raleigh toward the Holts? Not much, and always filtered through the Campbells: See, the people would say, they did it right.

If it weren't for Deborah, the story would end there. A family disgraced and then replaced in the collective memory of a city. But Deborah Holt, Joe's daughter, knew about her father's experience. And when she needed to produce a documentary to complete her masters, she began making phone calls, and rummaging through boxes in basements. What she found offered insight in all sorts of ways. Her father's head shot, for example, in Ligon's National Honor Society book, and the same photo labeled *salutatorian* in his yearbook. The same Joe Holt who speaks, in abstract terms, of segregation's degrading influence seems utterly sincere when he presents himself as merely a "good" student. Dr. Prezell Robinson, from St. Augustine's, held meetings on campus for the brightest black students in the city, including Joe, and remembers Joe's academic credentials as impressive.

And Deborah found something else: the man who answered the questions that had haunted her father's adult life. Of the three school board members who took part in that vote to reject Joe's application to Broughton, only J.W. York was alive when Deborah began her research. Deborah told York over the phone that she wanted to speak about racial integration in Raleigh. He agreed. When she arrived, York, large and jowly, greeted her pleasantly. Unbeknownst to York, Holt sat nearby in the waiting room: moral support for Deborah's most tense interview. He could hear them speak.

York began to speak proudly of Bill Campbell and Murphey Elementary. Deborah told him that was all very interesting, but she'd like to ask about Joe Holt.

J.W. York's eyes got wide.

York haggled, insisting suddenly on legal forms. But he talked. And he offered a rationale for Joe's denial that no one—Joe nor his parents nor their attorney—had ever heard. Joe Holt, York said, had been denied entrance to Broughton High School because of his *age*. "Our feeling was that when we got ready to integrate the schools, we should start at the primary level," York says on the documentary, "so that the children would grow up being used to the integrated schools."

Not necessarily such a bad idea; Holt now believes that had he actually been allowed into Broughton, he'd likely have been hurt. But blame had been placed for forty years on his family. York was rewriting the story before his very eyes. "They never advanced that reason to us at any time during the Holt case," the family's lawyer Herman Taylor tells Deborah on the documentary. "See, they never even mentioned that."

York was backpedaling; Holt could smell it.

Deborah's research inspired Joe. He's read other cases from the time, Raleigh's school board minutes, and the Student Assignment Policy the district passed in response to his own application to Daniels' Junior High.

That policy holds another clue. In July, the school board minutes include "*A motion by Mr. York... that Joseph Hiram Holt Jr., and his parents be requested to be present at the August 6 [school board] meeting.*" But the rules in the Pupil Assignment Policy include no such requirement. They offer parents the right "to be heard and to present witnesses" —but nowhere do they state that to do so is a responsibility. In regards to transfer requests by white families, the minutes include no details about who was present. The Holts were "requested" to be present, yes. But that request stood up in federal court as if it were a rule.

Holt now believes that his denial into Broughton had nothing to do with *administrative remedies*, and everything to do with the fear that gripped white school boards in the years following *Brown*. He thinks district leaders hadn't decided *what* they were going to do, other than make damn sure nobody was going. He believes the acceptance of that story, in the black community and his own family, comes down in part to the timing of Bill Campbell's acceptance—and in part to history.

"The black community," Holt says, "was, at that time, not as... conscious, politically, let's say, as we later became, many of us. Many people did not want to really know the particulars, and I'll tell you why. The black man in the South lived under a system whereby he was subject to the whims of the white man; he was subject to the white man's capriciousness. During slavery, black people learned to know as little about anything that the white man found disfavorable in respect to race situations—to know as little about it as I can. 'I don't know anything about that.' You learned to distance yourself—because if you don't know anything about it, you can't give away, even unintentionally, any information. Nobody can sense by watching you, or baiting you.

And everybody was so interested, certainly, in a breakthrough, and the breakthrough was supposed to begin in the schools. And blacks just like me felt like, if the white man says that there's something that you should have done and you didn't do it, then damn it, you should have done that. It makes us all look bad if one of us doesn't comply with the man's rules."

Slavery's legacy in Raleigh was like a ghost with two hands: one clenched with white fear and prejudice, the other with black fear and self-preservation. In the late fifties, both hands latched onto the Holts and held tight.

What changed by September 1960? History again, Holt says. This was four years after his initial application, six years after *Brown*. Changes had begun elsewhere in the state; Raleigh had begun to lag behind. By 1960, Holt believes, those changes had reached a school board that was comparatively forward-thinking. A board so very forward-thinking, perhaps, that no one thought or had the courage or the compassion to look back: to examine what had been done, what had been said, and who'd been hurt.

What Joe Holt wants now is for people to know what happened. To remember. He wants to rewrite the story. He and Deborah have begun that work through the documentary, which aired on Raleigh's UNC-TV, and through local speaking engagements. And as a recent Christmas present, his children made him a web site: www.joeholtstory.com.

And so it is largely through the work of his children that Holt finds himself able to honor his parents—which is what he really wants to do. Joe, Sr. and Elwyna are gone now. Joe Holt, Jr. finds himself caught in that old role reversal: protector of the parents who fought so hard for him. He cannot change the past. He can't undo the worry, the isolation, the disappointment. But he can make sure no one else undoes them either. He wants what the Campbells have always had: a place in the history of a people. *Integration in Raleigh did not happen without some people catching hell*, he says. *And my family caught hell.* He wants an acknowledgment that his family played a role, that it *means* something to catch hell—even if hell, and not the glory, is all you ever get. (In the complicated stories of Joe Holt and Bill Campbell, hell and glory may always be tangled: in 2004, shortly after the Holt family received its first hints of recognition, Campbell was imprisoned on charges of racketeering and fraud.)

Joe Holt does not hate Bill Campbell. But he is bitter. How could he not be? In his senior yearbook, the boy in the valedictorian picture smiles, a little shyly. Joe stares. Four years of public scrutiny, public torment, rocks hurtling toward the house and here he still is. Salutatorian. He tilts his head upward, as if he wants to take the photographer on. Only when you freeze the frame do you realize that his eyes are the same eyes that haunted *The Raleigh Times*. Joe Holt is hurt.

Nearly forty years later, in the waiting room outside the office of one of the many men who said no, Holt hears the conversation take a nasty turn. A turn that won't make the documentary's final cut, but will call up ghosts forty years old—an old story, and all its pain. A turn that will nearly send a reasonable man flying through an office door.

"After all," York says, "Bill Campbell went on to become mayor of Atlanta. What'd your *daddy* do?"

Joe Holt recounts the story. He's a teacher now, retired colonel. Former high school salutatorian. Civil rights pioneer. Husband, father, grandfather. He repeats the words, grimaces; they're poison in his mouth.

What'd your daddy do?

No Knocks
by Stephen Dixon
from *failbetter*

I go out into the street. Finally, it's a nice day. Rains came, went; sun now. I say hello to my landlord. Next-door neighbors. Wave to Mrs. Evans behind her window. Mr. Sisler sitting on his stoop across the street. Rob's boy walking their dog just before he goes to school. Mary Jane Koplowitz dumping her family's garbage on her way to work. Children, workers, cyclists, pedestrians, mailman. "Howdy-do. How are you? I feel great. Lovely day. What a relief after so much rain. Hiya. Morning. Hope the good weather holds. See ya. Take care. Hope you have a nice day." I walk down the block and say more of the same. "Hello. Morning. How's it going? So long. Have a great day." Friendly street. Living on it for years. People know who you are, what you do. What do I do? They know I do relatively nothing. Just about nothing. Nothing. They know. In other words, they also know what you don't do. I don't work. They know. No home projects or work for other people that keeps me home. They know that too. I walk, talk, read. I get up first. I have breakfast, wash, shave. Shower every day. No shower in the morning, then an evening shower. Then I go downstairs. Not after my evening shower, though I might do that too, but after I do all those morning things. I never bother checking the mailbox anymore, on the way out or when I come back. There's never any mail. I'm waiting for the day the mailman says "Mr. Rusk, your mailbox is jammed full. I can't stuff any more mail inside. Please take the mail out so I can have room to put new mail in. At least take some of the mail out so I can have some room to put new mail in." That'll be the day. Day I might even look forward to. Do I? No, though I once did. But it'll be a day, all right. What'll those letters be like? Say it happened. And who'd write? Nobody. I know no one other than from the street and around the immediate neighborhood. No relatives, friends, old acquaintances. And I tell people who move off the block or out of the neighborhood "Just come back and visit if you want, but don't bother to write. I never bother opening my mailbox, so I'd never get your mail. Only day I'll open my mailbox is the day

166

the mailman tells me it's too full to get another piece of mail in, but that'll be the day. But say that happened. I might only take out a few pieces of mail, or just one big one, to make room in the box, so I still might not get your mail." And I pay all my bills by cash and personally and on time. So no need for mail. I've none. No need for it and no mail. And the mailman's instructed not to put any junk mail in my mailbox. The instructions are on the building's vestibule letterbox for the mailman not to put any junk mail into my mailbox. Or they're on the vestibule mailbox for the mailman not to put any junk mail into my letterbox. One or the other. I'll go to the library one of these days to look up the difference in the dictionary between those two. If there isn't one, I'll find that out too. A difference. Mailbox and letterbox. Both I get my mail in, but which is which? And if the vestibule box that houses all the tenants' smaller boxes for mail is called a letterbox and those tenant boxes are called mailboxes, or vice versa, then what's the box on the street called that people put their mail in? Not only people. Yes, only people. I was going to say "Not only people but children too." But children are people too. Children are people, period. I don't know what could have been on my mind when I started to say "Not only people but children too." Caught myself this time. Other times also, but my mind's particularly sharp today. Not particularly. Not even sharp. Mind's just functioning a bit better than yesterday. Not even that. I can't really tell if it's functioning any better today than yesterday. Mind's functioning better now than when I woke up today. That's for sure, so that I can at least say. But now I'm at the corner.

I look around. No one I know here. People, yes, but no one I know to talk to when I feel like talking to someone. I look all four ways. Up the block I just came down. Down the next block of this street that I don't think I'm going to continue on. Both ways along this avenue I'm now on. Though who's to say where the avenue begins and sidestreet ends when one's standing on the corner where the avenue and sidestreet meet? I'm sure plenty of people can say. I can't. Not right now at least. But all four principal directions, in other words. East, west, etcetera. No one I know. No one who knows me. There's a difference there. Lots of people— Not lots. Several. A few, I'll say, claim to know me when I don't know them. Not claim. But they say they know me. They'll come over to me or just stop me and say "Hello" or "Good morning (etcetera), Mr. Rusk." In other words, that etcetera: all depending on the time of day in the time zone we're in. If, for example, they say "Good morning, Mr. Rusk," when it's obviously evening, then I figure they're joking or confused or even crazy or they made a simple word-reverse mistake, and I react according to how I feel at that moment about why they greeted me this way by my last name. If they use Mrs. or Miss before my last name, then no matter how accurate they are with the time of day, I ignore them or question them about the use of that conventional title of respect. But say they do say "Good morning, Mr. Rusk," when it's morning or close enough to it where I don't think the greeting is strange. If I look at them as if I don't know them—and usually when I look at them this way, I don't know them—they'll say "I know you but you don't know me." Sometimes they'll greet me and immediately say that about my not knowing them, even though I do know them and they know I do. And sometimes when I know them and they know I do, though they'll say I don't, I'll look at them as if I don't. Why will I give them that look when I do know them and why will they say I don't know them when they know I do? Couple of reasons, at least, that I can think of. But today none of that happens. So no one to talk to now unless I stop someone I don't know and who I know doesn't know me and start to talk to him, something I don't like to do.

If I walk uptown on this avenue, which is north, the chances of stopping someone I know in proportion to the number of people on the street will be much less than if I walk downtown, which seems to get more crowded the further south you walk. The chances of stopping someone I know in proportion to the number of people on the street would be greatest if I walked back to my block and kept walking up and down it and especially on my side of it, but I don't like going over the same route so soon after I came off it. I could cross the avenue and continue west along this same numbered street. But partly out of personal reasons, which I won't go into, and because the chances of stopping someone I know in proportion to the number of people on the street would be no better walking west than walking uptown, west seems the least likely direction to go except if I didn't want to stop or be stopped by someone. I could, of course, create many other routes other than just walking straight in one of the four principal directions. I could go north four blocks, then west till I hit the river; or south three blocks and east one and then south again till I get to the heart of the city; or south two blocks and east three and across the park and continue east till I hit the river that runs along the other side of the city, and so on. But I think the best chance, without going back to my side of my block and walking up and down it, of stopping someone I know or being stopped by someone I know or don't know but who says he knows me, is to walk downtown on the avenue I'm on.

So I walk south. I see no one I know on this avenue and am not stopped by anyone. I keep walking. Chances get less with each step that I'll meet someone I know or don't know but who says he knows me. I walk five blocks, six. Chances get even less, and after four more blocks, almost nonexistent. Then I'm so far away from my neighborhood—sixteen blocks— that I feel if I want to talk to someone now, and I think I do, the only way would be if I stopped someone I don't know, and chances are almost nonexistent here that he'd know me, and start up a conversation with him despite my dislike or reluctance or apprehension, or whatever it is, in doing so.

First person I see on the street, and now I'm twenty blocks from where I live, who I think I'd like to stop and talk to is a man. Not because he is a man. Though maybe because I'm a man I prefer to stop a man stranger to a woman, since I think a man would be less alarmed at being stopped by someone he doesn't know and feel more willing to talk to a stranger than a woman would, though I could be wrong. Are women less likely to be bothered or frightened by women strangers who stop to talk to them than by men? I'd think so. And what about men in regard to women strangers who stop them because they want to start up a conversation, or even for other reasons, like asking change for a dollar, let's say, or asking for a handout, or a donation of some kind? I'm not sure. But this man. I might now know why I prefer stopping a man I don't know, to a woman, but I'm less sure why I think I'd like to stop and talk to this man out of hundreds I've passed. It could be his clothes. One reason. He's dressed in a sports jacket and slacks, boots, big wide-brimmed western hat, and is carrying a closed umbrella and flat package, and has an overcoat over his arm. But closer I get to him from behind, more I think the flat package is a thin book and the jacket and pants are a suit made of a heavy fabric and the overcoat is a parka and the umbrella a black cane. When I get right up behind him and then am walking alongside him on his left, keeping in pace with him now, I see that the flat package is a book, on cytohistology, its cover says, another word, if I remember it and remember to look up, I should look up at the library one of these days. The other was what? I forget, though it came to me today and could come back. The cane's the closed umbrella I originally thought it was, but beige rather than black. Boots are western and well polished and recently heeled and have intricate stitching on them that looks like a lot of lassos. Parka is several djellabas that I suppose he's taking to a store to have cleaned, though that's a wild guess. His hat is still a Stetson-type, though leather instead of felt. Shirt's almost the same color as the suit and seems to be made of chamois cloth, while the suit's suede. Brown suede. Light brown. Darker brown leather buttons in a hatched pattern. Flap pockets. Same kind of buttons on the pockets. Or at least the left flap pocket has that button; the right one could be different or have come off, for all I know. A tie. Red. Stickpin. Gold. Cuff links. Just initials or one word: DAD. Or at least the left cuff link has those initials or that word; the right one could say MOM, for all I know, and also gold. "Hello," I say.

He stops. "Do I know you?"

"No. Do I know you?"

"Not as far as I know."

"That's what I should have said. Not 'No.' But 'Not as far as I know.'"

"Then we definitely, or almost definitely, which could be undefinitely but not nondefinitely, don't know each other as far as we know, could that be right?"

"As far as I know it can't be 'We definitely don't know each other,' but on the other one you're right. Now as far as knowing each other, my memory does fail me sometimes. So we could still know each other. If we do, I've forgotten, and I'll have to leave it up to you to remember."

"My memory does fall short of me also," he says. "No, that's not the word. The words. My memory does fail me also, as far as I'm concerned. And that's not the expression. My memory occasionally fails me also, as it does everyone, but I'm almost sure I don't know you. Years ago I might have. But there comes a time when I have to say about someone I knew long ago but since then haven't spoken or written to or heard from in any way, or seen, and if I did see him, didn't recognize him, that I don't know him now."

"So we could have known each other once, you're saying."

"Possibly," he says. "But our faces could have changed so much since then that we don't recognize each other now. And our eyesight, in addition to our faces or apart from them, and to a lesser degree as a recognizing factor, our voices, mannerisms, appearances and clothes. Anyway, to boil it down to the minimum: if I once knew you, I don't recognize you in any way now. How about you?"

"Same here all around. So how are you?"

"Do you mean, since I last saw you, if I ever did see you, or last heard from you, if I ever have?"

"Yes."

"I'm fine, since we last spoke, wrote or saw each other, if we ever did. And if we didn't, I can still say I don't think I've had a bad day that I can remember since I was born. That's not to say I haven't. My memory again. What it does say is that as far back and as much as I can remember, I haven't. Had a bad day, I'm saying."

"I can't say that."

"Well, it's over now, whatever it was, isn't that right?"

"I can't say that either."

"Broken love affair? Family tragedy? Professional or affinal crisis? Illness? Malaise? Something you read in the newspaper? Got in the mailbox? Witnessed from your window? Saw in the street? Personal experience or experiences? Is one of those it, or are some to all of those them, and which can't be broached, right?"

"Personal experience, yes."

"A woman?"

"Can't be broached, yes."

"Yes, a woman."

"Can't be broached."

"The woman? The subject?"

"Can't be broached, can't be broached."

"Too bad, then. That it happened. And that she or it can't be broached." Sticks out his hand. "Lionel Stelps."

"Victor Rusk."

Shaking of hands. Nicing of days. Changing of weathers. Preferences of sun to rain, city to suburbs, streets to parks, busier the better. What do you dos? Where you off tos? Going my ways? Okays. Walk, Talk. Seems he likes almost nothing better in life than to walk the streets too. To talk to people he knows or doesn't know but who know him, or to people he doesn't know and who don't know him but who like almost nothing better in life than to walk the streets and be stopped by people they know or don't know, and for many of the reasons that he and I do. Because we like people. Talking and listening to people. Because we like to be outdoors and preferably on the busy and hectic streets of the city with many kinds of people of both sexes and all sorts of age groups and occupations and pursuits. He's very much like me, in other words. Maybe that's why I wanted to stop him, when I ordinarily don't want to stop anyone I don't know and who shows no signs of knowing me. Not just his clothes. Not that I could have known much what he was like or what he almost liked doing best in life just by his clothes. Not that I really could see what his clothes were like, and especially the front part, from so far away in back when I first spotted him and thought I might want to stop him. Not that I even like to stop people who are like me in any way and who like almost nothing better in life than walking the streets to stop and talk to people or be stopped by people they know or don't know but who know them or show some sign they do. And as far as I know he isn't like me except for what he almost likes to do best in life and that he likes what helps contribute to it: mild weather, good health, sufficient sleep, crowded city streets, etcetera. His voice, face, hair, build, height, weight, age and just about everything else about him, and especially his clothes, aren't like me or mine at all. He's well-kempt, -shoed, -spoken, -bred, more mildly mannered than I, it seems, and he wears a hat. I don't own a single headpiece. Not even a winter cap, or hat with a brim of any kind to keep the sun off my face. Must be lots of people who do what we do, we say. Streets, walk, talk, people, stop, like to be stopped, and so on. Now the sun goes. I probably got a bit of a burn on my face today, which he didn't because of his hat. Continue to talk. He's lived a few more years in his apartment than I have in mine. Streets get less crowded, and not because we've passed through the heart of the city or it's that time of day. Bad sign, we say. Clouds come. We continue to walk. Three more blocks, four. Sky darkens. Talk about what we don't like to do most. Stay inside on nice days like this one was, for one thing. Not talking to anyone for hours, another thing. Day after day of unrelenting rain is probably the worst thing. Wind. Store awnings quaking. People hurrying. Signboards swinging. People running. They sense something. Finally, we do too. Or I just sense it, because it's possible he already did and wasn't saying. Maybe because he wanted to continue talking. "Pity," he says. Pats my shoulder.

"Pity is right," and I pat his shoulder.

"Though nice chat we had."

"Yes, while it lasted. No, that's not what I wanted to say or how I wanted to say it. One of those, not both. But I think you know what I mean without my going into it or repeating what I wanted to say the right way."

He doesn't say yes or no or nod or shake his head. He smiles, a weaker smile than the ones before, and sticks out his hand. I stick out mine and we shake. It starts to sprinkle.

"See you sometime," he says. "But I better run. Don't want to ruin my clothes."

"I guess I don't mind getting—" I begin to say, but he walks away. Put up his umbrella and is heading further downtown. That where he lives? Maybe he was shopping in midtown. But he had no package. The djellabas. But they weren't bagged or wrapped. Maybe he came to midtown to get them from a friend, or even the umbrella or book or hat or he bought something that can't be seen in a pocket or around his neck or wrist. Or even his ankle. Men sometimes wear ankle bracelets, though that's the least likely prospect I mentioned. Or maybe he strolled all the way to around where I live and possibly beyond, and just to stroll—for exercise, let's say—and I caught him walking back to his home downtown. But that doesn't explain the djellabas. The book he could be carrying for any number of reasons. For instance, just to read in a stopping-off place like a café. What was the subject matter of the book again that I was going to look up? Forget. Such a long, complicated and unfamiliar word, and I doubt I'll ever be able to remember it. Maybe he hurried off with that rain excuse because he knows something more about this area than I. I rarely get this far from my block. The last time was when? Can't remember. Well, lots of questions, and nothing like a little mystery in one's life. What's the mystery in mine? That personal experience I brought up and didn't explain? Bet he's wondering about it now. Woman, hmm, I can see him thinking. Actually, I can still see him walking downtown, the umbrella still protecting him. He's a block away but not many people between us. Then he disappears. Maybe he ducked in someplace to get out of the rain. Doesn't even want a few drops on his clothes, if that excuse was the truth. What I was going to tell him before he left was "I guess I don't mind getting caught in the rain as much as you." He would have asked why. I would have said "My clothes are quite old and used. First old, then used. I mean by that: made old by someone else, or who knows how many people, because who knows how many thrift shops they were in, then further used by me. In plainer language: I bought all the clothes I have on in a thrift shop. Several thrift shops, but they all came from one. Meaning: several different thrift shops, but they're all thrift-shop clothes. In even plainer language: they're worn, shabby, very cheap clothes that were the only ones I could afford in several very cheap thrift shops. What could be called work clothes if I worked. Worked at a laborer's job where one didn't need good clothes. In the plainest language possible: I don't mind ruining them; they're already ruined."

I look in all four directions. I seem to be one of the few pedestrians on the streets, and those that are on them are protected by rainwear or umbrellas or both. But why get wet? It's pouring now, so I mean why get wetter? I duck under a store awning. But why duck? Ducks take to rain, don't they? That might have elicited a laugh from that man. A good joke, I think, and I laugh out loud. Oops. Someone's under the awning with me. A woman, also with no umbrella or rainwear.

"Howdy-do," I say to her. "Nice day, eh?" She gives me the fisheye, looks away. One of those. Meaning: she is.

"Just a joke," I say. "Minor. Harmless. Didn't mean anything by it. Just the good mood I'm in. But some rain. Cats and dogs, yes? Bats and hogs, no." Fisheye, looks away. Still one of those. No letup. She nor the rain. Me too, I guess. Strangers. But maybe I'll get to her yet. In a good way, I'm saying. "Okay, I understand, madame. Takes all kinds, and I love that it does. But must say good-day. I must, not you. For ducks take to rain as they do to water, don't they? In fact, rain is water. Rainwater, of course." Fisheye, mutters, clutches her handbag closer to her, moves two steps away from me but still under the awning. I laugh to myself, but inside this time. Sort of to balance the last time I laughed out loud, which was to an inside remark.

I salute her goodbye and step into the rain. Really pouring now. Buckets. I start running north. Every so often I duck under a store awning or building overhang and try to make talk with someone there, and the awnings and overhangs I choose I choose because someone's there, but have no luck. Could be the clothes and that I'm so wet. And more I run, wetter I get. And there's nobody I know under these overhangs or who seems to know me. If they do, they're not saying, something I can also understand. A man so drenched and who keeps running in the rain without any protection can seem crazed. I run a few more blocks, keep ducking under overhangs, more because I'm tired than to talk to anyone, so some of the overhangs I duck under don't even have anyone there. Run a lot more blocks, but I'm really just jogging now, and walk fast and then at a normal pace the last five blocks till I reach my sidestreet. I run down the block—there's nobody out or at the window to wave to—and go two steps at a time up my building's stoop into the vestibule, where the landlady's mopping the floor under my mailbox or letterbox I don't open but do peek through and see nothing inside.

"Some day out," I say, but she's in no mood to talk. And when she's mopping while it rains she usually gets less in the mood with each succeeding dripping tenant. "Have a good day, though," I say, and run up the three flights of stairs to my apartment to do some undressing, showering, maybe soaking in a tub, drying, dressing, wet-clothes hanging, eating, resting and sleep. All that and more till later today or early tonight or tomorrow or tomorrow night or sometime this week, depending if the rain stops and if it's not too late in the day, I can go out again.

To All Those Who Say Write What You Know
by Kate Petersen

from *Brevity*

I will just say this. I know a river or two, the easy ones—the Thames, the Danube and Seine—quick to give their beauty to everyone who nears their banks. I know others who keep more to themselves—the Hudson and Snake, the Elwha—content to take and carry your secrets with their own, they leave you for the sea, though you keep watching the eddies for some answer that is not quite love, staying past hope, the way you stay every Sunday for the singer's last song in the bar on Fourth and Lafayette because that voice, you think, will finally give her away.

I know the silver ready of takeoff and the unearned divinity of cruising altitude. I know, too, the melancholy rush of final approach, of returning, as we knew we must, to earth. I know the allure of always going somewhere else.

I know the winter hush of a cathedral, the effect of prayer on stone, light through stained glass some sort of proof, and the dare of my own footfalls in the nave, how they become a sudden hallelujah. I look up, the echoed nowhere, *Sanctus.*

I know girls who still love their bodies, who let their hips draw commas in the air before them, paving the way. I know women who used to, whose hands and teeth and shoes are asking always: *how do I get back there.*

I know noise: car alarms, steamed milk, sex, baseball crowds, last call, the drone of mortar fire on an unwatched TV, a train abiding its rails.

I know sounds, too: the crystal wink of a champagne toast, a bedsheet lifting at lights out, a dead piano key, a breath held, the surprise of insects on summer screens, the quick applause of embers from flame, snow underfoot, a flicker of birds in the cemetery trees.

I know the smell of juniper, the bright gin and tree of it, and of unbathed bodies, street-heavy and ripe with someone else's shame. I know in these streets our sadness.

I know something of desire. I know the blue spell of afternoon on his skin, the way a minute's kiss can absolve one hundred wasted days. The plain chance of bodies I've been willing to mistake for fate, like playing cards found facedown on the sidewalk. I know the words—the yes and the sorry and gone—that stand in for other things we can't say. The constellation of freckles on my left arm I am waiting for someone to read me like tarot. I know the aftermath of want.

And past the cemetery fence on the hill above Southstoke, I know a gray horse, his nose in grass, mud to his fetlocks, dappled with the threat of rain. I was there four years ago now, every afternoon in that cemetery deep with strangers, because I did not know any more to write. And now I find myself there more nights than not, dreamwalking over the bone soil, the gray horse standing between me and another profane morning in the world.

Sensing me he lifts his neck, a movement slow and improbable as marble, and nickers a welcome, the kind that says he knows I will not stay, for I am just passing by. And yet in his voice there is the recognition that we've met somewhere before, and we have—I swear I know him, though from where I couldn't say. I stop for a moment, though I do not reach out. Touch is too easy an answer.

In the town below, certain windows have been left open, letting in the sky. Rain nears. The streetlamps stand at ease, waiting for night to come again and bring them purpose. I can feel the light inside the churches shifting its weight. Breath between us, little else. Across the vale in Landsdowne, all the greens confuse themselves, bleed willingly into storm.

With no warning, a lark lifts itself out of the boughs, rising against the rain, which is coming now, still weightless. The headstones grow dark with water. Aloft, the bird waits, buoyed by an updraft off the hillside or by some other unlikelihood, maybe the one that has kept me here, too, past sundown all those evenings ago and now, years later, still tethered by some sweet reluctance to this field of stones, to the memory of this lone bird in the green transept of my unmade cathedral, waiting for the *Ave*, for the first winging chords of a song I want so badly to know.

How Catholic
by Terese Svoboda
from *Brevity*

You've seen the movie: white convertible, uncle with slicked black hair, woman with Cleopatra eye shadow and a neckline, poodle instead of child in back. Okay, two poodles, big ones. Peach-colored, smelling of money. Not sprayed peach but given some pill the way pet doctors, even real doctors, dispensed them so freely then, some pill that wasn't trouble.

Did I say the dogs were four hands high? I was a neck taller and had just learned how horses were measured, fell off one and looked up at all those hands. These poodles leapt out the second the convertible pulled into our sickle of a driveway, trotted around us like horses. They didn't lick.

We stood, all assembled, probably an accident of summer chores, and gawked. Six of us, with three more on the way—well, really one on the way. I wished for triplets, though my mother would have them singly. Triplets! That would be fun. Instant Kennedys.

Mom came from seven siblings herself—four brothers—but no uncle ever visited. This one—the first—had hair like Mom's: thick strewn and strong, willed flat but wind wild from the open car. Its glaring white metal sheen set off the woman about to be released. Skin cream-powdered-white, she did not move until he leaned over her and wrung the door handle open. Honeypot, he said but not the way you would to a wife.

She turned her kohl-rimmed coal-black eyes to him. *Get out and open it*, she said so we could all hear.

What a surprise, Mom said. Dad already had his hand stuck in over the car door. *Not since our wedding*, he was saying, *long time, where're you on your way to?* The rest of us were struck dumb, the better to hear.

He had three kids of his own, lore I was privy to, having helped Dad write Christmas cards making fun of the ones other wives send out in boasting. No one mentioned that card-like state during their overnight stay, how long Mom whispered she could stand it while Dad mixed drinks loudly, but not too loud. Or was it their decision, the two of them arrayed at our barbecue, meat flesh sizzling in Western welcome, the best piece offered and refused by the woman feeding the juicy bits to the dogs, eating only the French bread, as if she were French. *Dolce vita* she did say once and laughed like Mom had been there too. Everyone drank but us.

He looked like her father said Dad to no one.

I cleaned the bathroom after they left, picked up her towel from the floor. Two half moons of green eye shadow over smudged caterpillars of black dirtied it, a shroud of Turin. I doctored the stains with straight All and stuffed it into the washer. I knew better than to present it to Mom as a problem.

It wasn't much later when Mom hatched out those last three singly, year after year after year, one retarded, two otherwise, then went on to age well in a gold Cadillac Dad bought her, thick leather, seats heated, windows sensing the dark and light of life passing by so quickly. Eventually she said to all of us assembled: I have wasted my life.

My uncle never returned.

A Floater on the Course
by Marge Barrett
from *Hot Metal Bridge*

A rope hangs from a butternut tree—I swing out, cut through the water. I smell wildflowers: sweet clover, wild rose and geranium, goldenrod. Cardinal lobelia, my favorite, brightens shady riverbanks. Named after the robe worn by a Catholic cardinal, it blazes red in August, arresting red, like the deep cochineal dye of a Navajo Indian blanket.

Thousands of years ago, in the last ice age, it rose: a small spring, narrow and shallow, in a channel created by glacial melt-waters. Joining other streams, it carved, through volcanic rock, a wide valley. It grew deep. The Ojibwe and the Dakota in wigwams and lodges along its banks held the sounds of bird songs, reeds in the wind, animal runs and calls. The Native Americans canoed the water, rich with game, fish, and rice.

My cabin sits above the main channel of the river near Marine on St. Croix, Minnesota. Looking out from any window or deck—imposing sky, water, shores. The house also overlooks an island; that view is more contained, intimate. I come to the river to both wonder and touch. In the spring, I watch light rise and fall on terraced bluffs. Swamp maples cede to oaks, waive to soft white pines. The woods brim with jack-in-the-pulpit, skunk cabbage, bloodroot, cowslip, trillium. Birds and animals, fragile and fierce, showy and secluded, sing out, call. I rejoice in deer, wee shrews and skinks, fat toads in horsetail reeds, skinny tree frogs, osprey, hawks, hummingbirds.

Hundreds of years ago, the river served as an important trade route, first for the Native Americans, and then the French, English, and American fur traders. Voyagers paddled the canoe highway from Lake Superior, down the Bois Brule, across the St. Croix to the Mississippi, singing lively rowing songs, ballads and laments. They built fires for meals and heat. Smelling of smoke, sweat and beaver pelts, they met in teepees and trading posts, lodged in forts or in the open air, surrounded by sounds of white or still waters.

I pontoon in the summer to waterfalls and gorges, dalles and cliffs. I canoe to marshes and meadows, to swamps. On beaches, I plant my feet, feel the swell of sand, sink in my heels. I pick pebbles from the shore, spin some into the St. Croix River, plunge rudimentary rock into sedimentary sand. Ripples swirl in concentric circles. Sparkling grains of quartz whirl, twirl, submerge with the swiftly flowing current. I wade into the channel from sedged sandbars and feel the shore shear off. Peering into clear water, bronzed by tannins, I follow underwater trails to observe rare mussels with lustrous linings. I explore islands, discover stones and bones.

Fir trade followed fur trade. With stovepipe hats and long poles, loggers drove huge log rafts down the river, cursing, carousing. They lit dynamite to break up jams, built dams and iron flumes to float the logs over falls, through narrows, to mills where turbine wheels turned the logs to lumber, lath and shingles. In 1890, a peak achieved: 450 million board feet of lumber and logs. A forest sea.

Autumn arrives in yellows, rusts and oranges. I happen upon a flock of wild turkeys following a path into the village. The gobblers eye me, strangely uncurious; they saunter over dead bent grasses, chew khaki plants. I look up to see an eagle circle in widening arcs around a dead birch. Down below, the blue heron bends a gangly-poled leg, holds steady, old as the river.

Pioneers—French, Yankees, Scandinavian, German—with names like DuBois, Pepin, Allen, Lee, Hanson, Bjornson, Krueger and Mueller—settled states, Wisconsin and Minnesota, founded towns on either side. Women with bonnets strolled plank board sidewalks, their children casting hoops alongside. They progressed down to the general stores, up to the wooden churches. Everyone bustled to the booming landing when flags flew and folks shouted, "Boat's a-comin!" Steamboats churned. Paddlewheels slapped. From those floating wedding cakes, deep-throated horns hooted and calliopes whistled. Dark smoke trailed.

I cross-country ski on the river in January and February. Grateful for a flat trail, I glide along in a great, white, silent space. I trek onto land, examine paw prints and scat, muskrat holes, beaver dams. Frozen waterfalls cast magical colors; minerals leached from rock walls streak the ice emerald, turquoise, copper and golden.

At the turn of the century, new machines started up with a roar and sputter. Motorboats. Later, speedboats, pontoon boats, jet skis and snowmobiles ran alongside canoes, kayaks, sailboats, and skates. The different explorers sought the same pools and rapids, swamps and lakes, the same tumbling waterfalls and gorges.

For fifteen years, in all seasons, I revel in the river. Like a child who fills and empties a pail of sand, I sieve out the city's work and worry. Aware that the sand is ground from ancient basaltic rock, I'm attentive to breaks, days—my tiny time—spent in this vast valley. At my spot on the river, I try to filter in the grand, to join those before me singing whole body notes, buoyant on the waterway.

Alopecia and the grizzly bear
by Arlene Ang
from *Arsenic Lobster*

It began with the geometry of cages. Stainless steel bars.

He recounts these things as he takes his hands from his pockets.

To ascertain there is no mistake. And he likens it to rattlesnake.

Multi-skinned: a blues musician's eye electrifies the neon lights.

He is in captivity again. He is the dream in the wired guitar.

This contact lens on the floor, cracked and unseeing.

The honey has crystallized, the dead lake frozen.

It's too late for sleep under the pulp of blood oranges.

Away from the sun, newlyweds honeymoon in a snailshell.

A short slip dress, a nebula of smoke.

They are irretrievable: instant cake mix down the chimney.

The body is weightless, its protective membrane rips easily.

Shimmering like salmon in his hands.

There is no coming to terms with loss.

The Stare
by Davide Trame
from *Convergence*

The shallows along this narrow sandbar
tell you about plain stillness,
the spellbound time of salt and marshland.
There's a half-sunk chair covered in marsh green
and an old engine's rusty gears
and the usual scattered tins and plastic bottles,
the hard to avoid here-and-now, our dumped selves
we can't get rid of.
But almost unimaginable behind Torcello's
bell tower, in that cleansing aloneness.
The rubbish, you tell me, has always been there,
one with that stretch of mud.
For a reason, I think, for some unageing
particular carelessness.
Part of the picture by now, part of the quiet.
Part of these mute outlines on the slippery path.
Where long ago I saw a boatman walking towards me,
wearing a grey muddied coat and clogs,
retirement, isolation—I remember I thought,
rowing in his early days along weeds
that didn't hide the nakedness of the channels.
The lapping. The still mud. The stare.

Our Father in the Belly of the Fish
by Peter Markus
from *failbetter*

Us brothers, we go down to the river to look for our walking-out father. Our father, us brothers, we believe this, he is down by the river, he is down here, a part of us believes, at the bottom of the muddy river. When we call out to our father his name, when that word father comes floating up and out from out of our open boy mouths, we are fearing that the sound that our mouths make, those burbly sounds bumping up against all of this muddy river water, we are afraid, us brothers are, that these sounds that we are making, our hunting hollerings out of, father, where are you, father? father, come out, come out, wherever you are: we are afraid, us brothers are, that these words that are ours are going, that they have gone, by our father, by our father's ears, unheard. And so, what we do is, instead of us keeping on with this calling out to our father our father's name and having that word make nothing but some muddy sound that not even the fish can make out what it is that us brothers are trying to say, we get it into our boy heads to start to look and to call out to our father the way we have heard it said that deaf people, those of our world who can't with their mouths make the sounds that are words, who can't with their ears hear the sounds that words make—yes, we have heard it said, yes, us brothers, we have seen it said too, that these people who are not like us, who don't talk like us, who don't hear like us, but they can, yes, they can and they do talk with their fingers: they make words come to life with their fingering hands. You have got to see it, if you haven't seen it, how beautiful it is to see these people speak without making a sound. How beautiful it is, it must be so beautiful, to be able to make words out of fingers that are made, by a twist of the wrist, by the bend of knuckles—these fingers that are made to look like to us brothers, they turn into letters, sentences made up of silent words, an alphabet made out of bone. And so, us brothers, we take up our bonied boy fingers, we make with our mud-dusty hands, shapes that we hope can do, here at the river, here at the bottom of this river that is ours, what our mouths seem unable to say when they try to mouth out that word, father. Look here. See how Brother, with his hand, he is closing it right now to make it into a fist. Hit is what this fist of his is saying. Or else: back off. Or, maybe yes: Brother I am ready to take it. My hand, this hand of mine that I say hello with this hand, with a wave of this hand that is mine, this hand that I pick up stones with and send them skipping across the muddy skin of this river that runs its way through this dirty river town: this hand that I hold the hammer with is what I am really wanting you to see: see this, it is the hand that I open it up so that the fingers on this hand are all five of them finning and fanning out. See my hand, see with my hand: it is a starfish that has risen up from the bottom of some long ago rivery sea. This hand, it is a star calling out to our father his name. Us brothers, we each of us take turns fingering that word father so that our father might see it, so that he might rise up towards, a river-bottom fish swimming up towards the light of the moon: a fish leaping up, breaking through the sky of the river, opening up its fish mouth to take a bite of the moon. Father. We say this word with our hands held up for our father to see, to eat. We say this word father ten thousand times with our bony boy hands, our fingers gnawed down to the muddy nubs. We walk up and down the river's bottom but our father does not hear or see us. Only other fish swim up near to us brothers and come up to us brothers' calling out. The littler fish swim up to us brothers and nibble us on our fingers and toes. It is possible that they believe us to be their mothers. But the bigger fish, they swim up to us brothers and take our whole hands up inside their fish mouths. There is this one big fish that is the biggest big fish out of all of these coming up to us brothers fish. This fish, it is the biggest fish that the eyes of us brothers have ever before seen. This fish, it is as big as us brothers are big. If this big fish stood up on its big fish tail, this big fish, it might even be bigger than the both of us. I can see that Brother can see this too, so I look at Brother with this look. Us brothers, there is this look that we sometimes look at each other with. It is the kind of a look that actually hurts the eyes of the brother who is doing the looking. Imagine that look. Look now at us brothers. We are still looking at each other with this look that we sometimes look between us when we hear some rivery voice say, Boys, look inside. Look inside where? is what I am thinking, and because Brother is my brother, Brother says, out loud, these words that I am thinking. This big fish that is bigger than the both of us, it is then that this fish, it opens up its fish mouth. This fish's mouth, it is big enough for us to stick inside of it both of our boy heads. This is what we we do. We stick our heads into this fish's mouth. When we do do this, when we take a look up inside of this fish, what we see is, we see our father. It's our father on the inside of this fish. Our father, he is down inside the belly of this bigger than us fish. And us brothers, us seeing our father like this, we both know what it is that we have to do next. I hold up with just one finger to say to our father for him to hold on. What our father does to this is, he holds up his hand too, his thumb and be-quiet finger touching to make themselves into a circle, and in this light that is right now shining down from the above the river moon, our father's hand held up in just this make, it makes a shadow of a dog on the inside walls of this here fish. Good, Brothers, is what our father is wanting to say to us, his sons. He winks at us with one of his eyes. With our eyes, us brothers, we look at each other. Brother sticks up and out a thumb. I take this to mean that what Brother is saying is that this big fish, it is a keeper. If you say so, Brother, I say to myself. And then I reach my right hand down inside my right trouser pocket. What I fish out from the inside of this pocket is the knife that us brothers use when we take the fish that we catch out of this dirty river home in buckets rusted with mud. What we do with these fish after we catch these fish, after we walk with these fish back home is: we gut and we cut off the heads off of these fish. We give each of these fish a name. Not one is named Jimmy or John. Jimmy and John is mine and my brother's name. We call each other Brother. So I take this shining blade of this knife, and then I stick, I run it, the blade of this knife, up from the tail end of this fish all the way up to where this fish's gill are good and red and are about to get even redder now with its own blood. Fish, we say, give us back our father. This, I whisper this. This, to this fish, I hiss this into where I believe is this fish's ear. This big fish, it stiffens, it winces with its fish body, but it's too late now for this fish to put up a fight. The guts of this fish are floating up and away, they are heading down the river, because down and away is how most rivers like to flow. Our river is like most rivers in the way that it flows down and away and out to the lake. But it is up, not down the river, where us brothers want your eyes to take a look: to see, no, not the guts of this big fish floating down and away, down the river, but to look, to see, instead, our father, he is up from this fish's big fish belly rising, like a last breath bubbling up and out: this is our father coming back upriver back up to be with us. Our father, he is up from the bottom of this muddy river rising up: our father, he is up towards the light of the moon rising up: he is, our father, a fish looking for a hook, and a pole, and a mud-rusty bucket filled up to its brim with fish. He is looking for us brothers for us to take him back home with us. Because he is hungry, our father says to us. He says this to us with his hands. It's time, our father, he knows this—our father, he is telling us brothers this—to come back home to us brothers, to sit back down, a father to us sons: it is time for us to eat.

Rock Paste
by Corey Mesler
from *Cezanne's Carrot*

When I was a child, a small child, a boy, I wanted to make rock paste. This was really just part of my overall experimentalism, my personal belief system that considered the world a place ripe for change, for alchemy. In my backyard I was a prince, a scientist-prince. This made up for the more public front yard where I was not quite so welcome, where I was called sissy and little girl and worse. But, on the 25-foot cement patio in my back yard on Kenneth Street, I was Curie, Pasteur, Einstein.

Like most boys my age, at this particular time in the 1960s, I had a chemistry set. With it I could make no experiment work. This was probably because I mixed those colorful powders willy-nilly, with no guide. Reading the instructions was for more prosaic minds. And I really believed that I would stumble upon some combination that would engender something miraculous. Wasn't this the way x-rays were invented, by accident? Yes, I saw it on *John Nesbitt's Passing Parade*. I really didn't see my complete ignorance of science as a drawback. I wanted to roll God's dice anyway.

Anyway, I had a theory. My theory said that if I could pound the rocks and stones that I found in the yard, where they were abundant, pound them hard enough with a ball-peen hammer, steadily enough, I could pulverize them (the operative word here is pulverize) and produce a powder so fine that, when mixed with tap water, I would have rock paste. A paste made from rock dust. This seemed to me one of the finest ideas I had had up to that point in my young life.

I took my handful of stones and my hammer and sat on the patio near the faucet. It seemed to be important to be near my water source, as if, perhaps, I might have to add the water quickly before the rock dust changed back to rock. I began to pound on the stones, using the pavement as my mortar, one of my dad's hammers as pestle.

The initial smashing was satisfying. The colorful rocks, as they crumbled, seemed to me to be the very building blocks of the Earth. And I was Lord of it.

But soon, friends, my girlish wrist grew tired. Very soon it grew tired. I looked at what I had crushed. It was far from fine. It was really just rock crumbles. I put a cupped handful of water into a plastic pail and added what I had crushed so far. It just looked silly. It was wet gravel. Wet gravel did not seem a particularly satisfying result to my experiment. And, here I confess: I have never really conducted a successful experiment. Through laziness, lack of focus, and just plain lack of knowledge, I could make nothing from nothing. I was no alchemist. I am no alchemist.

In college, after five years of mostly English and philosophy classes, I was called into my advisor's office. It was there suggested that if a degree I sought, I had better take something other than English classes, namely the required phys. ed., a language, biology, and zoology. I thanked my advisor for his wisdom and insight and shook his hand. I then went home and told my parents that I was through with college. They were disappointed of course. I wanted to tell them that I had made wet gravel instead of rock paste, but, what I really said was, I am going to be a bookseller and writer.

And this is what I became. My experiment with my own life is not finished yet, but it's a safe bet I will no longer pursue the breaking apart of raw materials to try and effect some sort of magical, elemental change. I will only do this metaphorically, on the dreamy page, in my dreamy head. And, in experiments done metaphorically, friends, there are few who know what fails and what doesn't.

Silver and Blue
by Todd Hasak-Lowy
from *Five Chapters*

November 6, 2005

Dear Customer Care:

I'm writing this letter in order to request that the Sunday Ticket component of my DirecTV satellite service be terminated. I realize this may well be a matter one could address by calling 1-800-DIRECTV. I have, as your records will undoubtedly show, called (as well as e-mailed) Customer Care on numerous occasions with questions and concerns, and my queries were always answered satisfactorily. In fact, because of the high quality of both your company's product and support service, I feel you deserve a full explanation of the reasons behind my request. I will try my best to explain.

I was born in 1969, and since that time the Detroit Lions have a winning percentage of .435. Only the Cincinnati Bengals, the St. Louis/Arizona Cardinals, the New Orleans Saints and the Atlanta Falcons rival the Lions' futility over the course of the last three and a half decades. But in truth, since Monte Clark took over as Lions' head coach in 1978, around the time I myself began following the team, their winning percentage has dropped to an even more anemic .405. They have won but a single playoff game in my lifetime. Outside of the 41-14 humiliation at the hands of the Washington Redskins in the 1991 NFC championship game, the closest the Lions have come to the Super Bowl was 1982, the year the title game was played at the Pontiac Silverdome, the Lions' home field at that time. The 2006 Super Bowl is scheduled to be played at the Lions' new stadium, Ford Field in downtown Detroit. Once again the Lions' players, and not just their fans, will have to find whatever solace they can in rooting for another team.

Sports matter because I'm the youngest of four boys. Less than five years separate myself and Brent, the oldest, while Mike and Dave, the twins, are just eighteen months older than me. Childhood was sports, playing them and watching them. Occasionally we ate or did homework. Adolescence included predictable diversions—girls, drinking, and drugs—but for us they were just that, diversions. We were addicted to sports. We loved sports. That was the point.

Before I forget, I wanted to be sure to mention that both Carla (ext. 3440) and Patrick (ext. 3302?) from technical support have been nothing short of stellar: professional, knowledgeable, and friendly. As you must know, your impressive menus and subscription services, while wonderful, can be a bit intimidating. And don't even get me started with the finer points of on-screen programming! Carla and Patrick could always be relied on to walk me through things clearly and patiently. I hope that when reviewing my account, you won't assume that my present decision in any way reflects dissatisfaction with their care. Nothing could be further from the truth. I think each would make a fine manager. My wife used to joke that I was having some sort of affair with Carla. I never found this funny. Thankfully she spared Patrick her cruel jokes. Not that it mattered in the end.

Me and my brothers played all three big sports: football, basketball, baseball. But mostly football. Our house happened to border on an undeveloped lot. A big empty rectangle that subdivision bylaws required be maintained. In other words, mowed. I grew up next to a football field. We considered it ours. Land title aside, it was ours. The Kramer girls, Carrie and Laura, lived on the other side of the field, but would ask us before going out there to practice baton.

Look, here's one way to think of what it means to be a Lions' fan. Since Brett Favre—whom I admire greatly, though I root like hell against the Packers—has been in Green Bay, the Lions have started thirteen different men at quarterback. Sucky thirteen. And the best of them (Erik Kramer? Scott Mitchell? Rodney Peete?) has been average, and that's being generous. Sure we've had some great running backs: Barry Sanders and Billy Sims before him. But does anyone remember Roger Craig? Or Dorsey Levens? Everyone knows that the Broncos got along fine without Terrell Davis. Montana, Young, Favre, Elway. Those are the guys who win Super Bowls. I'll admit it, I was a quarterback myself. But I think I'm being objective here.

Despite your excellent coverage of last year's draft, Jen, my wife, wouldn't let me watch. And that was just as well. I knew the Lions' brass were going to burn it on another high-priced wide-out. But either you got it or you don't, and as much as Joey Harrington is a class act, and probably a decent talent when removed from the violent chaos of a collapsing pocket, he just doesn't have what it takes to be a big-time NFL quarterback. I told Jen to go to hell for telling me what I could and couldn't watch, but maybe she was right. She claimed she was just asking or begging or warning me, not as a threat, just cautioning me that it would only make things worse. But I figure every draft day some team brings a player on board who leads the whole damn team to the Promised Land: Montana, LT, Elway (he was drafted by the Colts, but immediately traded to the Broncos, so he counts). Why can't I dream? Why can't it happen to us? Is our franchise that sick?

Before I forget, if by any chance my November 1st conversation with Carla was in fact recorded and/or monitored for quality assurance purposes, I was wondering if I might be able to ask of you to remove that conversation from your records. Actually, if it was only monitored, never mind. It was following the overtime loss to the Bears (interception returned for a touchdown, of course), and I was in a bad way. Maybe you could forward my apologies to Carla, too, since she's been away from her desk an awful lot since then. If company policy requires it, I'd be happy to submit this request in writing separately. Though I'd prefer not having to specify my reasons any further at this time.

Growing up, I spent a lot of time getting the snot beat out of me by my brothers. At school they would swarm and flatten any bully who messed with me. Ask Kenny Sturtz. But football is football. We didn't play touch. And I wanted to play. Sometimes they had to talk me out of it. When Brent brought home an even bigger kid, like Tom Smolinski or Brian Pavel (walked on at MSU, 1985), they made me watch, for my protection. Smolinski could bench 325, so I couldn't much argue. But if it was just us, what did they care? Brent would get hell from Mom whenever she saw my blood all over my t-shirts (they'd use the hose outside to clean up my face), but if they couldn't find anyone else to come over, what were they supposed to do, play one-on-two?

By the way, the enclosed check is for the rest of this billing cycle. I'm pretty sure it's for the right amount. Honestly, the billing aspect of DirecTV continues to baffle me. Don't get me wrong, this has nothing to do with my decision to terminate part of my service, but I won't exactly miss trying to decode yet one more subsection of your invoices either. Truth be told, I gave up on that a few months back. Another thing Jen gave me grief for. Pay Per View is a mixed blessing, let's just leave it at that.

By the age of twelve, playing backyard ball with a bunch of high schoolers day in and day out, there wasn't a whole lot any middle school linebacker could do to get me frazzled in the pocket. What are you going to do? Sack me? Go ahead, blindside me. My brother weighs 75 pounds more than you, and at Keller Field (that's what we called it) no one wears pads. And so yes, as you might have guessed, I became a quarterback.

Jen has argued that everything bad about me can be traced to my quarterback mentality: I like to give orders, I want to be the center of attention, I don't do anything myself (apparently she's never heard of Steve Young or Randall Cunningham!), I need to be surrounded by selfless people who sacrifice themselves for my protection, I always make sure I can blame someone else for dropping the ball. What quarterback worth his number blames the receiver? I'm not arguing with her about my ability to take responsibility; maybe she's got a point there. It's just why does she have to drag all quarterbacks through the mud along with me? That woman sure knows how to stuff a point down your throat. It's like being married to the '85 Bears. Jen thirty-seven, Rob nothing.

I don't know if you (or your parent company) have a corporate relationship with any chain of hotel or motels, but if you're considering something along those lines, I've been very impressed with Motel 6. My experience with Red Roof Inn left a lot to be desired. But the people at Motel 6 — at least the one here in Wheat Ridge — definitely know how to make their guests feel at home, especially those of us Extended Stay Guests. Granted you have to watch the Broncos every Sunday, but at $218/week what do you expect, the NFL Sunday Ticket Superfan Package?! Anyhow, Dewey's Bar and Grill across the street has a decent satellite set-up. They usually got four or five games to choose from. Not that it matters at this point.

I never had a great arm, and at six feet in heels I wasn't exactly Coach Harrison's dream come true, but I had my upside just the same. Brent, Mike, and Dave all played for him and I went to all of their games and more than a few of their practices and by the time I was on JV I knew the whole playbook chapter and verse. I'd been throwing to Kyle Martin and Jay Jurvis since seventh grade. I knew how they ran their patterns and that Kyle couldn't catch anything across the middle so why bother, but that he timed his curls perfectly and that Jay needed to get at least one pass a quarter or he'd stop trying. Starting JV quarterback. In a year or two I'd be doing the same for Varsity.

Now all this time I'm becoming more and more of a Lions fan. Becoming one and not knowing it, or at least not thinking much about it. It was just happening. Look, I was seventeen, that's when Mike and Dave went off to Western, before I could make my own decisions, before I realized such a thing was even possible. It was another two years at least before I had become my own man. As they say. I know you're thinking: but you're a quarterback, Rob, quarterbacks are leaders. Maybe, but I guess I wasn't that type of quarterback. At least not off the field.

Regardless, our school's a bit of a powerhouse at the high school level, and less than an hour and a half away you've got U of M and MSU, both pretty storied programs, but somehow I fix my sights on the Silver and Honolulu Blue. My brothers' fault. They were crazy about the Lions. Mike knew everything there was to know about Billy Sims: the name of his home town, his favorite movie, what he ate for breakfast on gamedays. Dave slept in an Al "Bubba" Baker jersey the night before each game. Did it for years after Baker left the team. Brent was too old for such rituals or even for simple hero worship. He chose instead to take it all very, very seriously. He believed in them, made it clear to us that we were to believe in them, delivered complex arguments each and every fall as to how and why this was finally going to be the Lions' year: the healthy return of a once-injured Pro-Bowl offensive tackle, the long-awaited maturation of the secondary, the hits our rivals in the NFC Central took in the off-season, and worst of all, the arrival of some new quarterback who had what it takes. I looked up to Brent. While he took his shots on occasion, he also protected me from Dave and especially Mike, neither of whom seemed too concerned with my well-being. Brent didn't tell me to care about the Lions. He made me want to love the Lions by way of personal example, because he loved the Lions and because I loved him. I wanted him to be happy and satisfied, to see all that patient loyalty start paying some long-awaited dividends. When the Lions would score, when they'd win, and the four of us would holler and give each other high fives and act out the whole damn thing afterwards down in the basement, finishing up the pop and pretzels mom set out for us, the couch and armchair worn out from tension and excitement, I made sure to sit near Brent, to listen to his recap of the game, to hear him ask after a certain climax, "Man, how sweet was that?!" To feel the spent warmth that came off his body, to get a good look at the way his eyes would open wide with optimism and relief.

Do you get letters like this from fans living in New England? What must it have been like to live in Dallas or San Francisco in the early nineties? Did a single person cry in Pittsburgh from 1975-1980? What is it like to win, to win it all, to end your season with a victory, with everyone else, people all the way in Spain and South Africa, watching you celebrate, raising that oversized trophy in the air, to remain in your filthy, champagne-soaked uniform hours later, because it's the filth of a champion, and not having to ask yet again what went wrong and what can we do better and how can next year be the year it finally happens? Is that when the pain stops?

It's not that the JV team got much attention, but we were a couple wins better than the Varsity. And they knew it. We were deferential to the Varsity guys, we weren't stupid, but they knew we knew. Mike and Dave knew that their team was turning into a down year for the program. They were 4-3 as Halloween approached, and with the Garden City game coming up the post-season wasn't looking too likely. Meanwhile we had won six straight since the opener, and I was emerging as a leader. And I knew it. You see, when you're the youngest of four and you're thrown into it with them from before you can remember, you've got no choice but to learn and mature quickly, if you have any intentions of surviving. I wasn't an exceptional athlete. But I had Varsity knowledge of the game. I had thrown hundreds, maybe thousands, more passes than your run of the mill Junior Varsity QB. I had listened and even taken notes as Brent talked me through a million situations. And, in our backyard at least, I had learned how to get the ball past defenders way more formidable than anything the tenth graders over at Westville could offer.

A quarterback in control. There's nothing else like it. No other sport involves so much simultaneous human movement. Twenty-two people set in motion at the snap of the ball. What sport created the need for slow-motion replays? Football. For eighteen different camera angles? Football. For the telestrater? You guessed it, football. A combination of contraction and expansion. The lines crush into each other. The wideouts trying to elude the cornerbacks, the cornerbacks shadowing their every step. Only the quarterback stands alone, watching it all, like a fan, waiting for the proper spaces to appear. But as the man with the ball, and the one equipped to make the most costly, the most demoralizing, momentum switching, season-ending mistake in football, the interception, you don't have much time. Because the defense isn't just trying to keep you from completing your passes, they're trying to prevent you from passing in the first place, by doing whatever it takes to bring the team leader, painfully if possible, down to the turf. But knowing this you still stand in the pocket, this improvised, fleeting space you know won't last more than three or four seconds, and you survey your options, taking it all in, until you find that moment when it's time to pull the trigger. And so if you can't really watch you can't really throw, not when you're supposed to and not to the right spot. Which is why when things aren't going right for a QB all that failure just builds on itself. The collapse of the pocket seems not just inevitable, but immediate. The windows that open between your target and the opposition seem impossibly small and then slam shut in an instant. You're no longer seeing, you're not letting yourself see, so you make one bad decision after another until coach sits you down. Which is an act of mercy, since pretty soon your brain was going to melt and run right out through the holes in the side of your helmet. I've pretty much seen it happen. You all beamed it to me from Chicago back in September. How in the world does a professional throw five (five!) interceptions in a single game?

But for me, time passed slowly in the pocket those first seven games. I knew just how much time I had and I used it wisely. It's chaos, but after a while it's predictable chaos. I checked off one, two, three receivers. I could find my tight end or a half-back to dump it off to when protection broke down. Worst comes to worst, I'd scramble for a few yards. You see, most JV units throw the ball half a dozen times a game. Because your passing game is a complicated thing. The routes, the timing, the decision-making, throwing a ball well in shoulder pads, getting the goddamn offensive linemen not to hold. But the JV Hawks had a bona fide air attack. Against Salem I had twenty-one *completions*.

Against Franklin I threw for three TDs, in the first half. Most of the time, if you're coaching a JV defense, you're not really concerned with much beyond your nose guard, tackles, and middle linebackers. It's nice to have a decent safety, but outside of making sure nothing that squirts past the linebackers goes all the way, ninety percent of the time your secondary could sit on their helmets. Because most JV offenses can't manage anything more elaborate than trying to run it between the tackles. Us? We ran eleven straight pass plays against Central. They were so desperate that when we finally ran the ball, a draw play, Brian Kelly waltzed in untouched from eighteen yards out. We were toying with them.

My father converted a couple Betamax tapes of that season to VHS a few years back and gave them to me for my birthday. Jen agreed to watch. She'd heard more than a bit about those days, as you might have guessed (as has Carla for that matter!), but outside of a couple photo albums she'd never seen what it was all about. I'd actually been bugging my dad for some time to transfer the tapes, but you don't want to be too hard on him. The games were pretty much as I remembered them. Maybe my spirals weren't quite as tight as I recalled, but the poise and the leadership, you could still see it. Watching the games with Jen made a mess out of me. Morale was already pretty low at our place. Part of me just wanted to watch the games, but part of me wanted her not just to watch them but to want to watch them, and to watch them close enough to get it, and to love me for ever having been as graceful and as able and as seamless as I was then. I wanted her to turn from the TV to the living me and find the remnants of my tenth grade self in the man and husband sitting next to her. Because there was no way she could fail to love a man tied in any way to that other time and place and person. Against Cherry Hill I saw the fifteen-year-old me throw the ball forty yards in the air to Jurvis, who didn't need to speed up nor slow down. Didn't even need to extend his arms. All the lucky bastard had to do was open them up, just to make a little bit of room for the ball. I didn't pass it so much as place it there for him. At certain moments the line between sport and art gets pretty fuzzy. Hell, you all know that, those amazing promotional montages you put together. That damn Barry Sanders was a dancer, plain and simple. But by this point Jen just didn't have one tenth the patience I had back there on the field. She couldn't separate good football watching from bad football watching. Bad football watching.

Since I've been in Denver, I've met more than my share of serious fans, and we get talking and pretty soon they see that I'm what you might call a football purist. Carla knows about this. And at some point one of these Denver fans will ask me, "But how can you be a fan of a team doesn't just play on turf, but plays on turf *indoors*?" Knowing it's coming I usually just smile, take another sip of beer. And there's no point in explaining, not to someone who was a perfect stranger just an hour earlier. Of course I love football outside on actual grass. Back on Keller Field, in the middle of summer, we'd play some marathon games. Counting up by sevens, touchdown after touchdown, final score 105-84. Eventually, when our own house would already be casting a long shadow halfway across the field, Brent would call some wild play. A Statue of Liberty flea-flicker that led to a screen and then an improvised second pass, this time forward, all the way to the end zone and a pile of grass-stained bodies laughing like idiots, not just the four of us, but some of the regulars, Jamie Miller and Danny Gurchik and Pete Baachi, too. The game would be over, no one had to announce it, and the rest of us would migrate lazy down to the end zone that was marked off by two baseball hats, one t-shirt, and an old shoe, collapsing to the grass, absently plucking out weeds, putting wildflower stems in our mouths, trying to find the energy to get up and head toward the hose, but instead sinking deeper and deeper into the field that was and wasn't ours. I knew that Astroturf was a recent invention, and not a good one. In '82, the Varsity played the State semifinal in Flint on Astroturf, and Brent came home with pink and red burns up and down his arms. He just shook his head, saying it was like playing on cement. I respect the dirt of football, the way football decided long ago that outside of lightning all weather is welcomed, that the season was in fact designed to begin in the grueling heat of late summer and end in the brutal cold of early winter. I knew that the Silverdome was fooling with something that shouldn't be fooled with. Football's version of genetic engineering. I understood all that, but I understood something else, too.

Practices were tense the week leading up to Garden City. Varsity needed to win if they were to have any chance of making the playoffs. The JV were confident enough, but we knew it wouldn't be right if we won and they lost, if we rose to 7-1 with them falling to 4-4. It would be disrespectful and against the proper order of things. But we were going to play Thursday night, a day before Varsity, so there was no way for us to know if we were supposed to win or lose. Mostly we just kept quiet in the locker room. To encourage them would be patronizing and to show them how confident we were, and we were, would be insulting, because they weren't (and shouldn't have been). But there wasn't anything you could do. They were average and we were great and that's just how it was. What the coaches should have done was scrap the Wednesday Ritual, or Wednesday Torture as the players called it. Make up some excuse. How hard would that have been?

While Jen and I were still living in Royal Oak it never occurred to us to subscribe to satellite service. All the road games were carried by the networks, and if a home game wasn't sold out and the network blacked out local coverage, something that happened more and more in the nineties, it wasn't hard to find a bar or a friend with satellite. No big deal. But when I got transferred to Denver we needed a plan. Was I happy to get transferred? I pretended to be proud, and I guess I was, since it was a promotion. New Head of Regional Sales for a major pharmaceutical outfit. Nineteen percent raise and stock options. Half a floor of people working under me. A personal secretary plus an assistant. But the farthest I had ever lived away from Detroit were my four years in East Lansing. I've been to Canada five times, three of which were just across the river to Windsor. Jen put together our honeymoon to Cancun, but that's it. I didn't even know the rest of the world called soccer "football" until last year. Maybe I'm a bit provincial, it never bothered me. Anyhow, we celebrated, and then Jen rewarded me with the whole package. A Zenith 50" Plasma widescreen with HDTV and a home theater system to boot. She had everything delivered the morning we met our movers at the new place. I was high all day. And surprised. Not just because of how much money she decided to spend on me, but because by then we'd already had a few fights about my sports viewing habits, as she called them. But Denver was a big change, and she knew I was nervous, about leaving home and about the new responsibilities, and she did still love me then, and the electronics were a surefire way for her to tell me so. She gave me something that I could rely on when times got tough. Which isn't to say it was a good idea. Because even though times got tough, sometimes they got tough because of this thing I could turn to when times got tough. That day we arrived in Denver was in fact the time I contacted all of you.

It was my good fortune that the next available Service Representative happened to be Patrick, who was kind enough to answer some of my home theater questions, though this obviously falls a well outside his official purview. Thank God for Patrick. The people at Sony make great products, but their customer service has clearly been outsourced and not to the right people.

I don't know what Pontiac looks like these days, but when I was a kid it was out in the middle of nowhere. We'd be driving and suddenly, there it is, the Silverdome's eight-sided, puffed-out white roof looming in the distance. Half enchanted palace, half oversized dessert. Majestic and secretive. It looked so out of place the outlying forest landscape seemed transformed, as if our destination were actually some mutated medieval castle. All that unlikely architecture just for football. Air pressure kept the roof from collapsing. At the end of a blowout, and there were a few, the four of us would go play by the exits. We'd open a regular door, instead of the revolving ones you were supposed to use, and soon find ourselves fifteen feet down a walkway leading to the parking lot. The science of all that air pressure. But the magic was being let in, not getting shot out. Settling into your very own seat, Section 134, Row 25, Seat 19, looking up and out and seeing how you're an integral part of the 80,000-plus who have come to see the Lions. And the crowd and the game were only the beginning. After all, over 100,000 assembled a half-dozen Saturdays a year not an hour away in Ann Arbor. What made the Dome special was right there in the name: a fully enclosed sporting facility. Watching the Lions in a single room occupied by more people than you'll meet in your entire life. Just you and 80,462 other people closed off from the rest of the world, no planes or even clouds passing overhead to bother you, not a single thing reminding you that another world exists. The awesome impossibility of climbing into Spaceship Roar turned all the supposedly negative features of the Dome into its transcendental virtues. The absence of real grass, of dirt, it wasn't fake or sterile anymore, it was pure. The predictable air, 69 degrees year round, the studio-quality lighting, the game deserved this concentration of technology. The regal parabola of the tumbling pigskin on a kick-off, or better yet the sight of a Hail-Mary climbing higher and higher into the air, the crowd screaming with insane anticipation, this kind of magic deserved the invention of a brand new place. The Colosseum is 2,000 years old. Piling thousands of people into a single structure to watch men hurt each other according to the rules was nothing new. Football is a recent invention, one perfectly suited to our age. The sophisticated equipment, the improbable complexity, the intricate language of war that suits it maybe a bit too well. Professional football needed a place like the Silverdome. When a player finally got behind the defense and the whole damn field opened up before him, a single man running a perfectly straight line down an absolutely flat stretch of green chemical carpeting marked off into yard-long segments, the crowd rose with a joy that in its immediacy had to be private. Something the so-called purists can't understand.

Today's a Sunday, and according to my company's laptop it's 11:19 p.m. The Lions traveled to Green Bay this week. ESPN's Sunday Night Game. The Packers are having a down year, but I imagine they're still nearly a touchdown favorite. No matter. I disconnected the cable wire from my room's TV. It's in my trunk. This computer's modem would happily climb aboard the wireless signal the good people at Motel 6 offer free of charge, giving me instant internet access to Real-Time Updates, including all the stats. I might even be able to find a highlight or two of the game still in progress. But the cable is in my trunk for a reason. I'm writing this letter for a reason. I'm living in a Motel 6 for a reason. Now's not the time for updates.

The Wednesday Ritual began when the JV starters walked up the small hill leading from our run-down field to where Varsity practiced. And then onto a short scrimmage between their second string and our first. Traditionally the Ritual just meant the JV starters getting their asses whipped up and down the field for twenty minutes. Looking back on it, I can't say I understand the rationale behind the Ritual. Make the second-string feel better, since they spent the rest of the week getting their own asses whipped up and down the field by the Varsity starters? Maybe the coaches thought that for the JV squad it was the equivalent of strapping five-pound weights around a sprinter's ankles the day before a big race. Since the next time we suited up it would be to play regular old tenth-graders and not a bunch of put upon eleventh-graders who wanted nothing more than to remind us of the natural pecking order, to for once not be on the business side of all that brutality. Maybe it was just one more sign of how a football team is like an army. Sadistic hazing in the name of sadistic hazing. But you see, what I knew was this: a lot of playing football is just coming to terms with doing whatever it is you're supposed to do while in a lot of pain, and while your opponent is trying to make you feel even more pain. Once you make your peace with that, that you hurt and will soon hurt more, it gets easier to concentrate and fulfill your duty to the team. Which is why fear, though perfectly rational, must be overcome. So I looked at the Wednesday Ritual as an opportunity to get past being afraid and hurt. Having basically lived the Wednesday Ritual with my brothers day after day for years on end in the unofficiated field next to our house, for me this wasn't all that much of a challenge. Here at least I had pads and my very own helmet. Plus, I knew that dumb luck had made the eleventh-grade players sub-par as a unit, whereas we were playing at a very high level. My fellow JV starters took a while to realize all this: to stop tightening up the moment they climbed the hill, to figure out they could do more than just try to survive the next twenty minutes, to take a little pleasure in seeing if it wasn't possible to score against the Varsity right there on their own field.

Watching a football game on a 50-inch Plasma High-Definition TV complete with a six-channel high-end home theater system isn't all that different, as far as poor substitutes go, from seeing a game live and in-person at the Silverdome. The experience, in terms of seeing and hearing, is pretty complete, and what you lose by watching it alone in your remote and isolated living room, you make up for with the close-ups, the instant replays, the in-game highlights, the back-to-back-to-back games, and, most of all, the viewing options provided by your unparalleled NFL Sunday Ticket Superfan Package. Sure, your wife cooks quiet frustration in the adjacent kitchen, she suffering through her Denver exile every bit as much as you. Sure your own home office sits impatient at the end of the hallway, where emails wait unanswered, where the specs for the November trade show sit neglected on your desk, even though the National Director of Marketing was expecting them the previous Thursday. But when you have a $1,700 reclining leather arm chair positioned just so in the sweet spot at the center of your six speakers plus sub-woofer and a meticulously programmed universal remote that can control seven different big-ticket items, then the moment you close the door that once opened up onto your wife and your office and the rest of the world, not because you want to keep them out, but because you want to seal this in, then you've built your own private, hermetically sealed Silverdome, capacity: 1. The Rob Keller Dome hosted home games every Sunday and played another on Monday nights for good measure. By our second fall in Denver the RK Dome drastically expanded its operations, having opened its doors for the college game, HBO's "Inside the NFL," two to three daily doses of ESPN's "SportsCenter" along with an endless stream of copycat programs, Major League Baseball's pennant stretch, the NHL preseason, Davis Cup tennis, the Buick Open Golf Tournament, the X Games, high stakes poker, women's college volleyball, the World's Strongest Man Competition, rodeo, and log rolling, all of which you, DirecTV, thought I might enjoy. And I might have.

Meanwhile, in 2001 the Lions had hired Marty Mornhinweg, the one-time offensive coordinator for the San Francisco 49ers, as their new head coach. As far as credentials go, a man could do worse. Half of losing is not scoring enough points, so you can't blame owner William Clay Ford for thinking that bringing the West Coast Offense to the Midwest would finally turn the ship around. Mornhinweg would coach the Lions for two seasons, leading the Silver and Blue on to the field for thirty-two regular season games. Of which the Lions won exactly five. A .156 winning percentage. The worst two-season stretch in franchise history. A lifelong Lions fan learns quickly not to expect too much. He tries to be satisfied when his team remains in playoff contention through mid-November. He takes the moral victories along with the real ones, he tries to agree with the head coach, who, during a post-game press conference, complete coverage of which you, my ever reliable friends at DirecTV, provide as part of the NFL Sunday Ticket Superfan Package, says with a straight face following a 37-9 loss to the Indianapolis Colts, "I thought we played competitive football for the better part of three quarters." A lifelong Lions fan tries not to stay awake each night for weeks on end in order to construct an elaborate set of theories explaining Barry Sanders' inexplicable decision to abruptly announce his retirement at the height of his game a paltry two weeks before the opening of training camp. But to be a fan is to care. And to be a lifelong fan is to care without ever having decided to care, to care before you knew you were caring, to care despite yourself, to care at your own expense, to care in a way exhausting and demoralizing and soul emptying, to care involuntarily even when your wife is sliding curt notes under the door informing you that dinner is on the counter and that she is going out with someone named Gail or Dale and that she's not sure when she'll be back. And to be a lifelong fan of a chronically rotten team is to decide against your better judgment to watch them play 1,800 miles away from the hi-tech solitude of your living room, twenty years after you at least had the blood close company of your similarly cursed brothers to pass around and swallow together the still thick and bitter taste of disappointment, brothers who have since scattered themselves to preposterous places around the world, to Nanimo, British Columbia, to Nowhere, Bolivia, to a fishing boat in the South Pacific, brothers who once had the sweet, innocent luxury of taking for granted the ever-present love and self-sacrifice of a high-endurance mother, who went from never having so much as a cold in thirty years to dead from breast cancer in fifty-three days, brothers whose father, just like them, fell straight apart afterwards, having never learned how to love each other or anyone else for that matter without the flimsy crutch of rooting for a deformed team that played a violent game their own bodies could no longer tolerate.

By the week before the Garden City game the Ritual had been turned upside down. Week after week I stood indifferent in the pocket, taking my licks, but also managing to climb through the tiny windows that still popped open, windows leading to quick outs by the sideline and, just the week before, a streaking Jay Jurvis who caught Doug Machino stumbling at the line of scrimmage. That sixty-four-yard score undid the whole point of the Ritual. The Juniors had been humiliated, and we had so completely overcome our fear we forgot to act surprised. If the Ritual was foolish before, it was now foolish and pointless. Breaking from the first huddle, I looked across at the Varsity squad to see what you get when a cocksure sense of entitlement transforms into an anxious resentment that comes from having to once more endure whatever it was that stole your cockiness in the first place. They knew we were about to rub their faces in it, in other words. Pity and compassion being the only alternatives, neither of which appeared anywhere in the Hawks' playbook. But I threw the first ball at Kyle's feet on first down anyway, and was glad to hand-off on the next play. On third down, Coach called the same play we scored with the week before, only this time Jurvis was supposed to run a Flag pattern instead of a Post. The idea being, I suppose, that poor Doug Machino would be a bit too determined not to repeat his previous mistake, leaving him ripe to bite on Jay's initial sale of the Post. Sure enough, Jay was soon running all alone with the strong safety nowhere in sight. Did I wait to pass to see just how far I could throw a ball on the Varsity field? Was I hoping for the coaches' sudden intervention, having made our point once again?

If I am to make one thing clear here, it is not that DirecTV is a bad thing, but it is no small thing either. Trust me, I know exactly what it's like to sell that most rare of products, the kind people actually want more after they obtain it than they did before. But so much has to go right for your team to win. Sacrifice and teamwork and effort are too small as words. The moment you truly understand just how wrong it can all go, the very possibility of victory, of seeing everything come together, well, after a while the best you can do is try and remember that for every loser someone else is a winner, so maybe this is the week. Maybe the Lions have learned this week how to bring their A-game, how to take it to the opponent, how to come up with the big plays, how to avoid the big mistakes, how to suck it up, how to play their hearts out, how to overcome adversary, how to grind it out, how to show some character, how to win one for the fans, how to earn the right to repeat the happy clichés and not the sad ones. But I'm doubtful, and more than that I just don't want to know anymore. I've been a winner and loser, often in that order, and it's time for me to hang it up.

I had learned to see from the pocket, but I still wore a helmet and all the poise in the world wasn't going to provide me with much in the way of peripheral vision. What I could see was Jurvis receeding alone, a giant smile burning through the back of his bonnet. By the time the blitzing cornerback and the entire right side of their defensive line got to me I had run out of time to remember how to be sacked correctly. Which is a skill, as all Lions fans know too well. As horizontal became vertical, the very real dirty grass of the Varsity practice field replaced Jurvis. My collarbone was asked to do some things it could not and it cracked to tell me so. Between the sound and the pain I waited, deep inside the safety of my helmet, preparing myself for another loss, something I had already learned a thing or two about on Sundays with my three brothers, two of whom had to be removed from the pile before they could replace that pile of players with one composed of silent coaches and worried teammates and remorseful brothers and, eventually, a pair of medics. The clearest thing I'll ever remember was that moment between the sound and the pain, because somehow I saw forward and backward, all of it, in that instant. Of what I had done and what I wouldn't do again.

Somehow I knew this was it for me. The collarbone healed by Christmas, but my throwing motion was never quite the same. I got a bit caught up with being mad at myself and others, at the program and maybe even at Mike and

Dave. I still played my Junior year, but my head was no longer in it, and I only got a handful of game snaps. Senior year, which should have been my year to take us to State, I didn't even suit up. Delivered pizza. Tried to get down Katie Bowers' pants. Watched a ton of TV. The thing I still can't figure out is if that moment, the one between sound and pain, was a good one. Because nothing hurt then. I knew it was going to, but it didn't yet. And though I knew things were about to get very bad for me, seeing my whole damn life right there was more than a bit of consolation. Truth be told, it's the most alive I ever felt, right there all alone before the pain. You see, I don't know that the Lions lost today.

Please do not suspend my satellite service completely. Though Jen claimed she got it for my benefit, I caught her more than once lit up opposite the screen on those nights I came back late from work. She can't get enough of those reality shows. If I'm due any sort of rebate or refund, make the check payable to Jenifer Keller, or Jenifer Gelfand, I'm not sure of her allegiances these days. Regardless, that's one 'N' and one 'F.'

Thank you for your attention to this matter.

Sincerely,

Robert L. Keller

Amputation
by D.A. Feinfeld
from *Entelechy*

After that surgery, my name seemed to me to be no more than a
loose rubric under which at intervals, aspects of myself
occasionally reassembled and functioned. — Larry McMurtry

After drugging and cutting,
split sinews, veins lopped to tree-stumps,
he finds one unplanned side effect:
amputation of his given name.

He dreams in the colors of pain: red bands
over his eyes battle black sunspots.
Half-awake, nerve-cords loosed
from their mooring, he collects
arms or legs for shocked instants,

and, blinking in blood-mist, gropes
along a strange street each house
like the others, iodine brown,
same spread of corners and lines.
No numbers or door-signs, box
follows box; no bell chimes;
none answers his timid knock.

In this town names are snipped away
by slow scissors that twitch across
the fabric of sleep; frayed clouds
blur the edge of the wound.

Who are you? echoes in a blind space
not yet packed with gauze, not filled in
with the seeping ooze of identity.
There's no one –
But you know this already.

The body I touch is no longer mine.

I spend my time changing words –
translation in a cloud of smoke.
The piano is Bach, Goldberg Variations.

This hotel, with its hint of plush,
massive, severe, is mostly empty.
In the corridor, a passing troupe of dwarfs,
the last one in death mask,
is my pretense for loneliness.

Under my window, a scrawny horse
whose ribs could spell my name
pulls at a wagon, loaded with junk
to sell, over the narrow, dirty street,
from one lost intent to the next.

Cannibal Love
by Lindsay Merbaum
from *Our Stories*

The things a fat woman will do for her lovers: the nipple twisting, the safety pins, the cucumber-made-dildo snug into its comdom. But Harvey sends me a cassette tape and says he is coming in a week. He wants to see progress.

When we were on our fourth date or so he told me liked big women. But he said it in an inverse way. We were having dinner in some cheap Italian place that dims the lights in an attempt to create a romantic atmosphere but the chairs were uncomfortable, the waiters sullen, stains on their shirts. The table was too small, a forced intimacy, and our knees touched when we didn't want them to. You had to wonder then if the lights were dim because the owner wanted to save a buck on electricity. But Harvey didn't seem to notice any of this. He ate his dinner slowly, first cutting his chicken into little pieces, then raising each bite towards his mouth, his eyes watching the food en route, considering it. His jaw moved cautiously. In between bites he looked at me, snatching glances at my bust which, for someone my size, is surprisingly inadequate.

"I don't like skinny women," he said sheepishly. The top of his head reddened where his hair is starting to thin.

"Oh yeah?" I said and picked up my wine glass. I'd heard this before, usually from people who didn't really mean it.

"Yes," he said, leaning forward. Suddenly his eyes seemed to open wider; their color in the dim light was shrewd. I saw a flash of what this man, successful in his business, must be like at work. His nose protruded brazenly, aiming at me. This was a man, I realized, who was used to getting what he wanted. I pulled at my napkin in my lap.

"In fact," he said, "though you're beautiful—lovely—you're a bit small for me." Then he leaned back in his chair and smiled. One incisor had an edge, tapering, as if it had been filed to a point. He placed his hands on his stomach, a slight swell.

I held my wine glass, filled my mouth, then continued to hold onto it. He saw this and reached for his own glass. "Cheers," he said. He angled his glass towards mine without touching it and took a drink. He looked at me through the goblet, then squeezed his eyes shut for a second as he swallowed. When he opened them again I realized that they were two different colors: one blue, the other gray, silvery. I stared, forgetting that he could see me.

The waiter appeared, frowning at us. "Would you like some dessert?" he asked flatly, looking at me.

"Yes she would," Harvey said, and grinned.

He took me home and fucked me hungrily, grabbing fistfuls of my flesh, seeming to want to touch all of me at once, pushing at me, his mouth open, sucking at mine as if he wanted to enter it, to hold my jaw open and clamber inside.

It went on like that for a few weeks, maybe a month. He would call me at work and say, "Meet me for lunch," in a whisper, as if he was saying something illicit. I would blush, cross my legs beneath my desk. I work for a small-circulation magazine called *Big Sista*. It is a magazine made by and for fat women who are big and beautiful and lead big, beautiful lives. The women I work with have made careers out of fatness. They have sour mouths. Their clothes are often too tight. They cannot afford to shop at the stores we feature. The single ones, like me, carry hefty plastic bags full of celery and carrot sticks.

"You gotta boyfriend?" they asked me, watching me hurry out to my lunches.

I smiled, shrugged in response and jogged to the elevator.

But soon something changed. The mid-day calls ceased. During our dinners out he seemed sullen, his knees withdrawn. One evening, sitting on his couch watching a movie, the hand I held was flaccid, indifferent.

"What's wrong?" I asked.

He sighed at me, rubbing my arms. "It's not your fault."

Instinctively, I thought, I've gained weight. Panic rippled like hunger in my belly.

But with all the sex and the skipped lunches, I'd actually lost a few pounds. The difference was imperceptible to me, but not to Harvey.

He gave me a hurt look, his hair wispy on top of his head, his hands folded in his lap, like a child who thought he was getting a new toy but has actually been tricked into going to the dentist.

I rubbed his shoulder. My heart was galloping in my breast. Really, I have to admit that I started the whole thing. The blame is mine. I am the one who said, my voice trembling slightly, "Let's order a pizza," and he beamed. "Good idea." He pinched my breast. "There's a nipple in the air," he said and leaned forward to kiss me, his hand sliding over my neck.

Now, a month later, he is in Michigan. A temporary displacement. A business trip that was unexpectedly extended. Without him, I go to work as usual. I eat apples at my desk, editing articles on 250-pound women weight lifters and plus-size maternity wear, my glasses resting low on my nose, my feet clad in comfortable shoes.

"Where's your boyfriend these days?" Shar, the woman in the next cubicle, asks. Her hair is in a permanent bun, a knob at the back of her head. On her desk are framed pictures of skinny, aggressive-looking boys. There are little bows glued onto the frames.

"What boyfriend?" I say flatly, removing my glasses so I can see her.

Her frown folds outward from the middle of her face. "Mm hmm," she says.

At night I listen to the tapes he's sent me. He doesn't like the phone, nor will he write letters. He says he can release his thoughts best when talking to himself. That's what the tapes sound like, a record of someone's inner dialogue. He talks in a muttering hush that I sometimes can't decipher. Occasionally he says my name, but he sounds like he is talking about me, not to me. At times his voice is distorted, crunchy, and I think he might be eating something.

In the last tape he sighed and said, "I am almost out of here."

I sat up. I was lying on my bed in my fuchsia bathrobe, a cup of decaf coffee on the floor beside me. "In a week," he continued, "I'll be home. And, oh, how I can't wait to see my honey bear." I had begun to think he had lost interest in me, that he was choosing not to come home, that the tapes would come less frequently until I got one that said, "I'm staying here forever."

"I bet my honey bear is gonna look so good for me." He made a smacking sound.

I jumped off the bed and furiously pressed the "stop" button on the tape recorder.

I am not an over-eater by nature. A chubby child my portly, good-natured parents wistfully named "Willow," my body blossomed into fatness in adolescence. Now, in my thirties and a size eighteen, my metabolism has begun to slow. I do

212

not get enough exercise, it's true. But in my despair I have allowed myself to go without meals, to leave unopened bags of low-fat cookies in the cupboard. I am not a woman who stuffs her face when her boyfriend goes on a seemingly never-ending business trip. Rather, depression fills me with emptiness and the hunger—a meek pang—feels satisfying, a kind of dull companion. Really, I would have made a fantastic anorexic.

Consequently, I have not gained an ounce since he has been gone. When he was here, he stuffed me in bed, a veritable buffet on the nightstand. He poured honey on his own body until it dried in his chest hair and became painful to remove. Boxes of expensive chocolates appeared in my mailbox. Together, we shopped for new clothes for my body. "Something that shows a little leg," he said to the saleswoman, hitching up his pant leg slightly and laughing. He bought me big, pointed, lacy bras with cups I can't fill.

And now he's coming back a week from the day he sent the tape, which means, since I have already received it, that he will be home in a few days.

I go to the grocery store and push the cart like a bull, my head down, feet stomping heavily, my face turned towards the shelves. I collide with other women, thin women in heels that look too heavy for their ankles.

"Watch it!" they shriek.

I turn my face to look at them. Quickly, their eyes run over me, appraising instantly the way only women can. If their boyfriends are in the store somewhere, they are not worried. But when their faces meet mine, their expressions drop. I am scowling but is there something else there, beneath my hair, that is actually naturally blond or in the points of my green-brown eyes? Some over-confidence that could mean I am crazy, that I am capable of anything? Perhaps. Quickly these wafer women turn, their heels clicking as they move away from me, pushing along their near-empty carts.

My cart is full to the brim. The check-out woman, her belt long enough to strap her to the roof of a car, belly voluminous, shaking slightly with each motion she makes, mechanically rings up the ice cream, the boxed cakes, crinkly bag after bag of chips, then looks me in the eye, her mouth thrust forward by the robust push of her soft cheeks. I chose her over the skinny adolescent in the next row. Now she's looking at me, fatty-to-fatty. She nods at me and her nostrils flair. Then she asks me if I want all this delivered.

"No," I say. "I can manage myself."

At home the going is tough. Fifteen pounds, I thought at first. By the time he gets back he'll have been gone for almost a month and a half. Fifteen pounds is the very most you could expect someone to reasonably gain in that amount of time. Now, sitting on the couch before the TV that is laughing at its own jokes, I am beginning to think ten is more reasonable. He can't expect more than that. I am a busy woman, after all. I don't have time to just sit around all day and eat. Ice cream and chips roll over in my stomach. I am full, very full. Still the spoon moves to my mouth.

"No pain, no gain," I say to myself then swallow hard against a gag. There is still a boxed cake waiting for me in the kitchen. "Oh God," I whisper, and let the mostly-melted carton of ice cream fall between my knees to the floor. It tips over, spreading its milk over the carpet.

I see Harvey's face in the television, watching me, the colors of his eyes reversed like a reflection in the mirror; now the left one is gray, the right, blue. "Come on, baby doll," he says, furrowing his brow, his mouth puckered into a pout, "Just a little more. Just for me. Wouldn't you do this for me?"

"Yes, yes," I say, and flub backwards against the couch cushion. My throat feels thick. "Of course I would."

I dream of biology tests involving live, convulsing frogs.

"They're having seizures," the teacher says. He's tall with round spectacles and paces the aisles of the lab. "You must fix them. The procedure was covered in chapter seven of your text book."

But I have forgotten about the test. I haven't studied or even read chapter seven and now my frogs are hurling themselves against the glass sides of their fish tank, their tongues rolling out of their mouths.

I glance at the other students but they are quietly at work with their tools that look like pens and tweezers. Their frogs have stilled.

When I wake up, it takes several minutes for the numbers on the VCR clock to come into focus. When the message does finally get through, I mumble, "Shit." Even if I leave right now, I will still be late for work. In my mind's eye, my body has already jumped off the couch and is hurriedly rushing around the apartment, panty hose attached to one leg, a hairbrush in hand. But in actuality I have not yet risen. I feel anchored to my flesh, which overnight has somehow merged with the couch so that now, if I want to get up, I must take the couch with me as well. But I can't carry the weight, so instead I sink into it. The cushions fold over me like my own soft flesh, additional buttocks and foamy breasts I have nurtured and grown with processed flour and preservatives.

When I finally arrive at the office, it is past noon. In my panic, I have confused the food suitable for the office with the stuff I am eating at home, and stuffed my bag full of cookies and greasy chips and dry packets of hot chocolate.

Shar watches me hustle to my desk. "Well," she says with one eyebrow raised, "good morning to *you.*"

"Yup," I say and turn on my computer. It makes slow, laborious start-up noises.

"Late night with your boyfriend?"

I see again the image of Harvey's face on the television screen, the deliberate slump of his eyebrows. Oh God, I realize, I have been hallucinating. I have ODed on sugar and carbohydrates.

"I'm not feeling so well," I whisper to Shar as I slide my glasses over my face.

She looks away from me, mouth pursed with disapproval. "Mmm hmm," she says. Then adds casually, "Jenny came by looking for you. She wants that article about the weight lifters on her desk a-sap."

"Shit," I say. Though her face is turned away, I can feel Shar smiling.

It is the same thing tonight. I am eating a cherry pie, fork in hand, but I can't finish it. I can't even get half way. My mother raised me to always leave something on my plate. "That's what ladies do," she said. She had a fat, buttery face.

I don't dare weigh myself.

He will come back and find me the same, perhaps even slightly smaller. Then he will dump me.

I slump forward in my chair at the kitchen table, pushing the pie away. My tongue is coated with crust. I lean my face sideways on the cool table and cry into it, the gaping, doughy mess of my mouth.

I have not had a lover in a long time, it is true. I have never had a lover like Harvey.

I could call in sick tomorrow and spend the day filling myself up. Then I would not have to rush. I could drink milkshakes. Yes, I think, Milkshakes!

Instead I leave work in the early afternoon.

"Doctor's appointment," I whisper to Shar and shrug.

She stops typing and rolls towards me in her swivel chair. "What, going on the pill or something?" she hisses.

215

"What?"

She shakes her head. "You better watch yourself, Willow. You don't look right these days."

I stiffen, my back arching. "I'm fine," I say. "I'm great. Butt out."

Shar raises one penciled eyebrow then swivels away, self-consciously patting the bun at the back of her head.

My entire life my body has rebelled against me. Things are no different now. I kneel over the toilet and vomit steadily a lumpy, sick-sweet mixture into the bowl. This is how the milkshake experiment ends. Since I got home from work I have been lying on the couch, eating. Eating stale croutons and a can of olives after I finished off the provisions I bought expressly for this purpose, drinking powdered milkshakes all the while like water, one after another. Now I think of the Greeks and their Vomitorium. What a lot of fun that must have been.

At the grocery store I sway through the aisles. The bodies beside me are quick-moving blurs, their voices distant, distorted as if coming from on high. But I don't understand what they say. I push my cart and fill it up, pulling boxes haphazardly off the shelves. My body is heavy, slow. An invisible barrier encases me, like a cocoon made of sheets of plastic, an alternate universe.

When I get home I find that the door to my apartment is unlocked. Did I forget to lock it? "It's the landlord," I think, my heart a rabbit. "Please God, let it be the landlord."

I step gingerly into the kitchen as though trespassing. I grip the bags in my hands, though I have ceased to be conscious of their weight, swinging slightly beside my calves. Everything looks the same.

"Hey, baby," a man's voice says. It is a familiar voice. Is it coming from somewhere within the apartment? A voice with a body attached, certainly. I put the bags down on the floor. I often hear the people next door talking and moving; it sounds as if someone is in my apartment, clomping around in my bedroom closet. But then I hear another step and the floorboards creak. I suck in my breath.

When he sees me, the smile will fall from his face, breaking into an open mouth, the one sharp incisor protruding slightly, his eyes like zinc. "What have you done to yourself?" he'll want to know. "What did you do?"

And maybe I will answer with something sharp like, "Eat me," only more clever and dignified, that will not speak to the things I have done but will say without saying, "I am my own. I'm fine, Harvey, I'm fine."

Absent Without Leave
by Michael Baker
from *Convergence*

I took little from San Francisco:
a bitter smell of almond, signatures
of Chinese suicides, women pierced,
a woman named Anne, one leg missing,
pounding our cement with steel crutches.
We would openly stare on the stoops
of our Mission wrecks, knowing she knew
we were amateur peeping toms
at the sight of a free-swinging stump.

Fearful of genetic mishap we returned
to escape plans centered on cigars
and Lower Haight fog. We too had crashed
fathers' cars into elms and we too missed
vital items: Ohio's terrain, the relentless
Atlantic, reasons to get up in the morning.
Even as children we loved that which was gone.
No matter how much we sweated
in the Baja heat on our Yamahas
we came back, whole and hipper.

Our mothers, teachers near Youngstown,
are too tired to call: the three-hour gap
mystifies them. The entire world
limps now we write to them. Their students
stay blind to the bliss found
in permanent repairings. We merely inhabit
our street—deep in garages, tools
for casual tinkering in hands, our boots
sink into the spilled motor oil.

On Saturdays, in cafes, we study
The Autobiography of Malcom X.
We will share directions south soon.
We see Anne steal pastry from her new lover,
another rich white guy from San Jose,
a manchild soon to wander Divasadero
on Mondays, lust
where once his blue eyes shone,
now scarred with certitude from lessons
learned firsthand: Oakland fires
will die out before they harm us and death-
trap desires will return soon
because of everyone's lofty slippings.

When He Died
by Anne Germanacos
from *elimae*

Dyed Hair

"Why are they still bringing food?" For months Madeline hadn't cooked. Grocery bags of noodle soup in cartons, whole chickens, chocolate chip cookies—there was always something on the top step. Sometimes the notes blew off and she had no idea who to thank.

"They're taking care of me. You know how it is on the airplane? First put on your own oxygen mask, then help your children?"

"So are you going to let me, Mom?"

He was used to getting his way, but the sudden possibility of magenta hair silenced him.

"You still want it, don't you?"

"Yes!" Then, he went silent in yearning. No thought of his dead father.

The next afternoon, Dustin took the stairs from the garage two at a time, pushed his brother, August, out of the way and hit the bathroom light switch. For a month he'd wanted magenta hair so badly he'd dreamed about it. When he'd told her, she'd said, "Well then, maybe the dream is enough." But it hadn't been.

His pudgy face, brown eyes, skin that always looked tan. Red lips that were sometimes an embarrassment. His mother's face and big bones. No one could beat him up; no one bothered trying.

"Mom, I think it's perfect. Don't you think it brings out my personality?"

"You're right: perfect." Perfection they had learned to cultivate, relegating fear to transient moments. The ten-year-old was inordinately brave. She put her hand in his thick, neat, once-brown hair. Pulled a little.

"Hey!"

"Just checking."

Show and Tell

After the second morning recess, the other children started standing up, one by one, to show what they'd brought. August controlled himself, kept his hand down: he wanted to keep the best for last. But he could barely sit still. Danny was trying to tie a balloon into a long weiner dog, but the balloon kept bouncing back into a balloon. He looked like he might cry.

When the others were finished, August jumped up and ran to his cubby. He picked up the thin wire hangers where they were held together with a rubber band and carried them to the place beside the teacher's desk.

"This is what I brought today. My Dad's shirts. My Mom says I can keep them so I can wear them when I'm older."

August was the only child in the class who could hold up the weight of his body with just his hands. The children looked to their teacher to see what she made of his presentation.

He looked at his classmates. "Do you think they're nice shirts?"

One girl answered. "Yeah, they're okay. My Dad has shirts like that, too."

"But these are special because my Dad wore them. He died before I turned six. I didn't even know him for six whole years."

The teacher was the only one who spoke. "They're beautiful shirts, August. Do you keep them in a special place?"

"Of course."

"Where?"

He didn't answer but let the shirts drag on the floor as he walked back to his chair. The bell rang and the other boys ran out noisily. He put his head on the shirts against the cool desk. Little by little, the blood inside his cheek warmed everything. The shirts came alive against his skin.

Love Song

After dropping the boys off at school, she turns around and drives back in the opposite direction, away from her office, toward home. The streets are almost empty of cars, and the ones on the road seem to be driven lazily, as if their drivers are listening to dreamy songs on the radio. She pulls into the garage, scraping the side, taking off one more gray chip of plaster and paint, and runs inside.

The song playing inside her head: *How did you slip out of our lives so quickly?*

Past Dustin's painting of a basketball player that goes on for three lined, taped-together pages, past the humming dryer, she opens the door to her heart, a leather suitcase. Her heart and breath catch on each other. *If you're not there, I'll be desolate forever.*

The night she folded the clothes, alone and planning, she hadn't known it would be so soon that she'd need to come back and unfold them. She kneels now on cold cement, presses open both brass latches, and, closing her eyes, plants her face in the clean wool of his sweaters. *Where are you hiding?*

She pulls out the red wool sweater they'd given him on his last birthday, the gray and blue striped one, the beige hat he wore until the end. *Can't I touch you one more time?*

She wants the leather of the suitcase to give way, open onto another life: he would be there.

Fuchsia

While he was alive, fuchsia was the last color on her mind. Looking back, she might have said that fucshia was always there, at the edge.

Her first fuchsia dress, ever. It was sleeveless, silk and linen, low cut, tight. Fit her like a modified glove, room for a finger to press between fabric and skin. Whose finger?

Six-year-old August seemed to read her mind: "Mom, you're too old for such a sexy dress." Pushing miniature soldiers into the ruts of the dark green carpet. "Isn't this perfect for grass, Mom?"

A field to roll in. "Yes, Augie." She looked in the mirror. "Not right for Grandma's?" "Definitely not, Mom," Dustin intervened.

Dustin, just ten, had been the man of the house for almost eleven months. The boys' father had died in the hospital, weighing less than Dustin, more than August. By the time he died, the only things complete and untouched, nearly perfect, were his striped shirts, his swimming medals.

She was in love with a color: fuchsia. "Boys: gray slacks, blue button-downs and navy blazers. Ties only if you want them. This is how I'm going—they'll have to take it or leave it."

August threw a handful of soldiers at her. Ballistic in five seconds, hysterical in less than thirty.

"Don't talk about leaving!"

She gathered each tiny soldier, fifty-two of them, like a deck of cards, like their father's age before he died.

Purple Pen

It was because of his brother that it happened, his brother's clawlike grip on the Action Man with all the dogtags around his neck, that came down on Dustin's back, making a long bloody scratch through his t-shirt and pants. The new babysitter made him take off his shirt and he took off his jeans as well, and in the hole of the boxers he insisted on wearing, there was a hair coming out, staring at him like it had a face and eyes. He was not yet eleven; he wasn't supposed to have that kind of hair.

Now he takes showers with the door locked and brings clean clothes into the bathroom with him. He remembers the luxury of wanting magenta hair and getting it as if it were the depth of his childhood.

One evening in the bathroom he searches for the curly hair but it's not there. He panics without it, pulls up his pants, finds his green flashlight, turns it on and twists it to the sharpest point of light, searches, as if the lone hair were a ship on a foggy morning. Finds it at last. Still there. Startling. He has no idea why it avoided his eyes a minute before. He finds a purple pen on the floor. Paints a circle round his lone dark hair.

Telling Time

After the hiatus of a long winter, she went quickly through spring to summer. She had several men, not at the same moment but at the same time, like a smorgasbord after a time of fast. She'd fasted for long enough.

This one was taking her through a vast supermarket, vegetables and fruit arrayed like paradise, a whole wall of candy. She picked up her clear bag and made ready to gather more chocolate and jelly beans (some, perhaps, for the children,) when her cell phone rang and she had to answer it, out of breath, not quite yet out of her head. She'd promised her son August that he could reach her any time of day or night.

"Yes, darling? . . . Having dinner. . . . Well, it's still early. We ordered a little bit ago, and I think I see the waiter with our salads. Yes, I do. . . . I'm fine, honey. How about you? . . .Yes, you can ask me anything you like. . . . Do you think we could discuss that in person? A watch is an expensive item. . . . Sleep well."

When she hung up, they were in the mashed potatoes department. Together, they worked their way back into more interesting aisles. They passed the candy again and headed past the vegetables, which were nicely steamed and delicious most of the time, but she required something more than a vegetarian diet. She found herself at the meat counter, out of breath, his mouth on her neck and biting hard enough to make her groan, when the phone rang again. She thought, even before saying hello, that everything was over, that nothing like this was ever going to work. Their bodies were slick with sweat, hardly distinguishable.

She attempted schoolteacher cheerfulness coupled with a sense of boundaries.

"Yes. I know you bought the watch with your own money, and yes, I do allow you to give away your toys, sometimes, when they're not particularly expensive. But do you remember how much you paid for the watch? . . . Yes, it was almost fifty dollars. Don't you think that's a lot? . . . I know Dan is your best friend, but is a fifty-dollar watch worth a drawing?"

He was confusing her, or her state of mind wasn't allowing her to think properly, and she had to get off the phone. "All right, it's your thing, do what you want. And August? Do you think you could let me eat my salad now? It's just arrived, and it looks delicious. . . . Some kind of vinaigrette. Thank you. I love you, too."

By then the sweat was dry and she was at a loss, but he was unusually talented, and before several moments had passed they were at the meat counter once more, as if they'd never left, ordering steak, thick-cut, and not daring to touch one another for fear of what might happen, right there in the supermarket, where they seemed to be alone but couldn't be sure. They stood like that, near one another but not touching, for what seemed several very long moments.

And when the phone rang again, she wasn't sure if it was the bell that customers press in order to bring the butcher from the back of the counter. But it was August. "Haven't we already discussed this, August? Just a few minutes ago? . . . No, we're still on the salad. Well, to tell you the truth, the waiter just came and took away our plates but because I keep talking to you on the phone, I wasn't able to finish it. . . . Yes, it's too bad, I agree. So what is it now? . . . Yes, you do have a large collection of watches, and giving one away so you have one less isn't such a big deal. But does it have to be the expensive one? Didn't you save for it — for months, if I remember — because it was the watch you wanted more than any other? . . . No I'm not trying to make you feel guilty. It's your decision. Just go ahead and decide and then do it."

Hanging up the phone, she thought it would be over, the man's pleasant blue eyes would tell her it had been a nice idea but wasn't working out. But he was upon her, almost smothering her, and they were back in the wanton supermarket as if they'd never been away, and before she had another thought, her body mingled with the oranges and reds, the yellows, the smoothnesses, the honeys and jams, until it all burst forth. Then she found herself entwined with him, two bodies on a bed in an apartment above a city street.

I Would Tell You
by Hari Bhajan Khalsa
from Avatar Review

how I woke in a jagged ball, the image spliced so you don't see my face, any part of my body, just the oars dipping into the sea in a steady back and up, out of the frame; how there's an island with palms in the distance, sun, and the raft moves to the right quickly and in its wake the churning, pale eddies of blood. It's the million tiles, cut and placed just so, that are hard to talk about, how they are mortared together until I'm sitting in the room with the medium on Wednesday and the next day the acupuncture needle searing my heart meridian and the book I was reading that proclaims everyone has something vital to say. When the camera zooms in, all you will see is a woman on her bed, her dog at the foot, light from the street slicing through.

The Unrealistic Philosopher
by Jimmy Chen
from *Prick of the Spindle*

Because of Heidegger, he didn't have time to floss. He didn't have time to buy toilet paper or Palmolive dish detergent, so he let his wife do those things. He didn't have time to take out the garbage, pay the electric bill, and all other "ephemeral" things. He would read and read about being and time; being and sense; sense and semblance; what *what* was; what *is* is; etc. Such ontological questions and their incongruity with touchable matter plagued him. Still, he would read and read, until the air around him hurt, until it felt like he was scraping the inside of his scalp with a spoon, the way one might eat half a cantaloupe.

His gums bled in the morning, the result of grinding his teeth at night. Consequently, he had a receding gum line. His dentist gave him a mouth guard to wear at night. The mouth guard smelled like ass, according to him— during a very brief phone call he had with the one friend he had—so he refused to wear it. His wife upon their marriage, initially attracted to his intensity and earnest existential inquiries, quickly got used to attending dinner parties alone because he just couldn't deal, he told her, with the asinine conversations so commonly overheard at social gatherings. Slowly, she resigned to having regular dinners at home alone as well. He needed time to read, time to think. When asked what she felt about Heidegger, she replied "asshole," not exactly sure who she was referring to.

His one friend would worry about him because he, who read Heidegger, also had a flare for exaggeration. His friend would be at work, and he who read Heidegger would call him on the phone and say "Meet me at the bridge in forty-five minutes." His one friend understood this meant that he who read Heidegger was proposing that the two of them jump off the bridge, in order to commit suicide. The reason he who read Heidegger felt comfortable saying such things to his one friend was because their friendship, since college, was built upon a sort of amateurish philosophical discourse, in which both parties would ponder—for entire evenings in the dorm lounge while others were getting laid or enjoying a drug's effect on one's perception—difficult abstractions, especially concerning the "absolute." Their inability to define and settle once and for all exactly what the "absolute" was, led to the smashing of lamps, and tearing down of curtains.

He who read Heidegger, in his quest to resolve the "absolute," joined a religion. He was adamant that this religion was not like any other religion. The other religions failed where this particular religion succeeded, because this religion asserted that it was the consolidation of all religions, and thus the only true vehicle in which the "absolute" could be rendered and manifested. His one friend told him he respected that, but didn't want to join this religion, which he who read Heidegger encouraged him to join. The latter continuously broached upon this matter until his one friend's patience was so strained that he could not help but cite possible incongruencies between Heidegger's existential implications and said faith; he may have even used the word "hypocrisy." An argument broke out, a very bad and drawn-out argument which only ended because both parties' throats were so hoarse from arguing that they had to stop. In the silence, they looked at each other with confusion.

His receding gum line had receded so much that his teeth wobbled in his mouth. He claimed to his one friend that any pressure from his tongue, even by the pronunciation of a hard consonant, would displace his teeth. By this time his one friend had curtailed emotional investment into the friendship because, frankly, he was a little hurt and put-off by he who read Heidegger's continuous judgments about his character—veiled as concern for his spiritual fate—and could only afford cliché placations over the phone such as "that sucks man," or "damn bro." He who read Heidegger was emotionally intuitive and could sense the nonchalance. This resulted in another running argument: that his only friend didn't have the spiritual capacity to be interested in he who read Heidegger's life because he, the non-spiritual friend, wasn't a member of said religion. The arguments became blurry, interchangeable, and so exhausting for his only friend, that he began screening his calls in order not to converse with he who read Heidegger.

He who read Heidegger, suspicious that his one friend might be screening his calls, grew so indignant that he would violently beat his pillow, imagining it was his one friend's face. This was often accompanied by the listening of loud and abrasive industrial music. He asked his wife to call his one friend as a means to test whether or not he would pick up. His wife, by this time resentful about things in general, told him to leave her out of his ingrown neurosis, to which he replied that any woman who owns the amount of shoes and handbags that she does must be too shallow to empathize with a man whose one noble task in life is to resolve the "absolute." He then threw a tangerine at the wall. The splatter marks looked like fractals, though she would not understand. His one friend and his wife often supported each other by conveying the details of any particular incident in which one of them was either hurt, annoyed, or offended by the latest thing he who read Heidegger said or did.

He, who was not able to finish Heidegger because of a nervous breakdown, prayed a lot—especially near the end. There are no transcripts for such prayers, but one may assume that they would contain many exclamation points and passages typed out in caps lock. Feeling a little guilty, his one friend bought him a new book, which non-incidentally, was beckoned by Heidegger. He, who just started Sartre, is now being taken care of in a hospital. A special request was put for a single room, because the ranted prayers, while mitigated with tranquilizers, are still incessant, mumbled through a mouthful of loose teeth and yogurt. If one were to visit he who started Sartre, one would not need to bring flowers, due to their lack of phenomenological description and one's inability to deconstruct them on a hermeneutical level.

Ball Lightning
by Karen Heuler
from *Oxford Magazine*

My uncle Al was hit by ball lightning while watching his TV, which was near a window. The relatives said it wasn't the window that brought the lightning, but the fact that Uncle Al had put foil on the rabbit ears on his TV set to improve the reception. He was watching the Ed Sullivan show, and while Señor Wences was doing his act, the TV gave a little pop and a bright flash, and a ball of light swept out of the screen and ran straight across the room. Uncle Al said it came to the mirror, smashed it, and made a turn to the right before slamming into a wall and turning it black. He heard thunder as it whacked him on the side of the head—but he didn't know if it was the thunder from outside or whether it was a noise from his own interior turmoil.

My aunts visited him in the hospital, and they were suspicious. "Were you drinking?" Aunt Etta asked. "You're always drinking. Could it be it was an alcoholic stroke or something?"

"Go look at my TV," Uncle Al said. His head was completely bald and he kept touching it.

"It will grow back," Aunt Louise said. "Why did they shave it?"

"They didn't shave it. It got burned or something; it all fell out. They hooked me up to electrodes to see if there was any brain damage."

The aunts waited.

"I have the brain of a 19-year-old," he said.

The aunts went to Uncle Al's apartment, and indeed, the place was burned black in a line from the TV to the back wall and then in a V to the side wall. They looked at the chair Uncle Al sat in, and it had burned to a crisp. How come Uncle Al was still alive?

"I had just gotten up for a beer," he said. "I don't like Señor Wences that much. Besides, it was raining so hard just then that I wanted to check the windows were shut. I just got up. I was right by the mirror; I saw it coming straight at me. It just hit my ear. They say it's a miracle."

"I understand ball lightning isn't as strong as regular lightning," Aunt Etta said, pursing her lips. "Now if real lightning had hit your apartment, I don't think there'd be anything left. If real lightning had hit you on your ear, I think your head would explode."

Uncle Al glared at her. "My hair exploded," he said angrily. "Every hair on my head exploded. Isn't that enough?"

"You were losing it anyway. How much was really left?"

Uncle Al and Aunt Etta had always had a testy relationship. Uncle Al got the big bedroom because he was a boy. Aunt Etta and Aunt Louise had to share a room because they were girls. My mother had her own little room behind the kitchen because she was the youngest by ten years. She was babied and petted and never part of the sibling rivalry.

"I can't believe you're jealous that I got hit by lightning and you didn't," he finally said.

"You didn't get hit by lightning," she huffed. "Just your ear. The ear is hardly even a part of your body. Not even skin and bones, just cartilage."

"Lean over," he said, "let me cut your ear off and see if it's a part of your body."

Aunt Etta didn't lean over, but she wasn't about to let her brother stay in the center of attention. In the next year, she traveled to Florida, Ohio, California and Maine. She went to the Museum of String, the Crystal Caves, the World's Biggest Quarry, and the Last of the Sequoias. She had a list of all the people she'd met, and where they'd come from originally. She had it laminated.

On the first Sunday after Christmas, the whole family got together and showed slides of important points in the past year. Aunt Etta had boxes of pictures; she showed herself sitting on a big rock, standing under a big tree, staring over a quarry ledge, and standing at the start of a string labyrinth.

Uncle Al showed the slide of his room after the lightning struck, and the headlines of a local paper: "Rare ball lightning attacks local man." Then there was a TV documentary on strange but true cases, and they interviewed Uncle Al and his doctors. He got a reel from the producers and showed it as a home movie on the projection screen. Soon after that, Aunt Etta said she was thinking of moving to Washington state. She said no one ever talked about lightning over there; it was a matter of small interest and even less use.

My uncle Al was tone deaf until he was struck by ball lightning. When it happened, he was knocked off his chair and lay on the floor. His ears rang. He saw lots of blue around him—boxes of blue hung in the air. He shut his eyes and the boxes became purple.

Uncle Al was single, but he had good neighbors. Of course, most people were home watching Ed Sullivan, and in fact, the ball lightning had shorted out all the wiring in the building. The people below him heard a crash, the lights went out, and they took their flashlights and ran upstairs to bang on the outside of his door.

Uncle Al crawled to the door and let them in. They thought he'd been robbed, at first. Uncle Al kept shaking his head slowly—he suddenly couldn't hear anything—but then they noticed the TV, which had burst outwards and was still smoking.

They sent a kid to run down the street and call an ambulance.

Uncle Al was deaf for three weeks. Then, when his hearing cleared, he heard noises all the time. At first they bothered him, but then he realized something.

"They're notes," he told Aunt Louise, who liked to listen to show tunes. "I think I'm hearing scales of notes. Didn't you used to play scales when you took piano lessons?"

"Sure," Aunt Louise said. "Everyone has to play scales. Like this." And she hummed some Chopsticks for Uncle Al.

He shook his head. "No. Not that." He listened for a while and then he hummed what he was hearing.

"That's a scale," Aunt Louise said. "I think it's a minor scale, but really, I only took four lessons. At any rate, it sounds good to me."

Uncle Al went to music teachers then so he could learn to play what he heard in his head. Mostly, no one wanted to see him more than once because he couldn't play anything except what he heard—the notes in his head confused him if he tried to practice anything else. So the teachers became formal and disinterested. Except for Miss Gutcheon. She asked him to hum things, and then she wrote them down. And then she held his hands over the keys and made him repeat it. She taught him all the scales, and then she would call out a key to him and he would hum it. And then she wrote little duets based on what he heard. "You have perfect pitch," she said. "It's a rare thing. Of course, you have to learn what the notes are called first, before you can sing them. But you're perfect once you do."

Uncle Al was amazed. "I never had it before," he said. "Couldn't hold a tune at all. People told me to shut up—at least my family did."

Miss Gutcheon smiled. "But you sound beautiful now. I love to hear you." She blushed.

Uncle Al told his sisters what Miss Gutcheon said, and Aunt Etta looked at him thoughtfully. "Perfect pitch? I've heard of it." She thought for a moment. "But what good is it?"

Uncle Al was a machinist for the subways. He usually had oil on his hands (maybe that was why the ball lightning went for him?). He had never been interested in music, didn't much listen to the radio, liked funny songs rather than good ones, and had no idea what the point of perfect pitch was. But he had it, and he was proud of it. He went to Miss Gutcheon's recitals for children and adults, and he could tell when they played a wrong note. He knew what her range was: her laughter was in C, her disappointments in A, she soothed children in B-flat. His sister began to suspect he was in love.

And then one day he lost it. First his hearing had gone, and then it had come back in a wonderful way. And then the wonderful way cleared up as well. No more scales, no familiar pitches. When he heard music, it just sounded nice or annoying, not recognizable.

It was devastating. Miss Gutcheon was sympathetic, but without that one thing about him, Uncle Al didn't seem all that exciting anymore. She was delicate about saying it, came up with pretty excuses not to see him, and little disappearances out of town, but Uncle Al knew enough to stop going to her recitals, and she took back the recording of medieval chants (pure human notes! she had once cried out) she had lent him.

So life went back to what it was. His sisters chipped in and got him a really good television, one that didn't need tinfoil to pick up the signals. He never saw Miss Gutcheon again, as far as I knew, and that didn't satisfy me. I would race down the block when I knew a storm was coming, and stand across the street, watching his window. When the thunder cracked and the sky got dark, I would see him open the window and lean out. Sometimes he'd hold out his hand. I found this unbearable, and beautiful, and I'd imagine that someday I too would be broken by a strike of love. I couldn't leave it that way, however, so I took the wires I found from discarded lamps on the street, or useless toasters—any electrical appliance—and I made long, thin, uninsulated strands that I brought with me when I went to visit him.

When he went to the bathroom or to the kitchen, I'd sneak my newest wires out and attach them to the wires I'd already laid around his apartment. One line ran from the phone jack, another from his doorbell. One came from his floor lamp, another from the new TV's grounding wire. All the lines ran toward the window, where they met in a single wrapped strand that I snaked out the window sill and then separated outside. There I extended them, pressing them into the ribs of the brick exterior, splaying out. I was careful to observe from across the street whether anything showed, but nothing did.

By winter I had constructed a kind of spider web around his window, wires wrapped around wires, thin filaments designed to give back to Uncle Al what he had once had: Magic. Love. Life.

Nothing ever happened. One or two of the wires were removed—I imagine one of the aunts found them and discarded them silently, quick to assume it was a clue to her brother's mania.

I thought, for many years, that I had done him an immense favor, by trying to trick him back into the life he loved. It wasn't until I myself was old, and knew that love wasn't always magic, that I realized he must have known about some of it at least. He wasn't unobservant. And I know, too, that until he died he went to the window whenever there was a storm, and looked at the sky, and placed one hand firmly on the wires I had run through the window frame. He would have known that a second strike could kill him, even if I didn't know it. But he let the wire reach his skin, let the chances arrange themselves in the thickening air because even though he wasn't strong enough to act, he was strong enough to believe. And he believed for the rest of his life, alone.

Geographies
by Carmelinda Blagg
from *Avatar Review*

He believes if they were to cut his body open, they would find all kinds of maps inside. He sits in his blue wingback chair surrounded by boxes. His daughter, Eva has been busy packing his things all morning. He knows what she thinks. That he cannot live on his own any longer.

Perhaps she is right.

An old topographical map of frayed and yellowing silk is spread out in his lap. It shows the Pyrenees with their jutting, undulating ridges and cartoonish halos of clouds shrouding the tallest peaks. Stains the color of tea freckle across its sheen. When he lifts it up to the light, he can see the threads separating, the blotched faded images of mountains and sky wavering against the bright air. With a palsied finger he traces its lines, remembering the gray winter landscape of France, his stomach flat against the earth, his cheek resting against his rifle. He had floated down to earth; the dome of his parachute spread open like a vast apron in the sky.

He remembers the open grave they had ordered him to dig, the clumps of dark, muddy earth on his shovel, his face sweating in the freezing air. He remembers the smell of the earth.

Eva is playing a CD of Mozart arias, her voice softly echoing the soprano's. She sounds like her mother. He closes his eyes, drops his head back. He dreams of the open grave, thinking of his escape. Harrowing. The stuff of novels, which he had turned it into. Six years of work. Now it is just a thick dusty manuscript, thanks to that sorry New York agent who couldn't sell ice cream to a six-year old.

"Poppi?" Eva touches his shoulder.

He opens his eyes, looks around. Bare windows. The room feels strangely unfamiliar. He looks up at her face, her quiet eyes, her slight smile. She has her mother's voice, her pale beauty.

"How about some lunch?" she asks.

He nods. "Did you know when your mother left me, she not only took you and Niels, she took the good silver, too?"

Eva drops her face, purses her lips, shaking her head. "Oh, Poppi, that's so long ago! You know how she was. She just couldn't stand being away from Vienna."

"She couldn't stand not inflicting her own kind of punishment."

Eva laughs. "For God's sake, Poppi" she sighs. "Why do you always drag yourself back through all that ancient discord?"

"Ancient what?" he mutters, feeling irritated with Eva as she turns, heads back to the kitchen, singing along softly again, *Exsultate jubilate*. Beautiful B flat above a C.

"I'll make you a sandwich," she says, partly jubilate.

"You know I only tell you these things now to make you laugh," he says. Her voice rises again. She chides him as she spreads mayonnaise on bread, laying slices of turkey and tomato on top.

He looks at the silk map. The sky is a flat blue, but he remembers it as something at once deeply iridescent; something you could travel through without ever hoping to get to the other side.

Sonya still remains a bruising mystery. He had met her in Vienna after the war, when her star as an opera singer was rising. She was from Linz. He would watch her at the Statsopera backstage. His vigils had been many, the bouquets he had delivered to her dressing room elaborate. His patience, his adoration had ultimately proved persuasive. They were married in a ceremony at the Votivkirche, the church founded by a grateful Franz Josef. By the time they crossed the Atlantic together, she was pregnant with Eva.

It was a world no longer at war. They were happy. They flew to America. He promised to build a house for them by the sea.

❀

There are things for which a transcript does not exist. Things which belong only to him. It is hot in the small hospital room. The window is open, only partly, because there is no screen. There is, occasionally, a breeze, but it is so hot, so utterly stifling it makes breathing painful. His right thigh burns. The pain emanates through a dense, morphine-induced slumber. It is the kind of pain that stuns him into a deep silence. The hospital is in Naples, and from some of the windows, other soldiers can see Mount Vesuvius, calmly rising from a mist in the distance.

He cannot see the volcano from where he lies. Beyond his window is a gray building. Lines of laundry hang in startling profusion; row after sagging row of white bed sheets and lace underwear, T-shirts, a man's khaki pants, a woman's cotton scarf that carries a pattern of roses, children's socks that look like the tongues of animals. The building next door was bombed, but this one has remained, and the women here still insist on hanging the laundry in the sun.

He sleeps. It is not yet the future for him. The wound on his thigh has been cleaned and stitched. The torn ends of his skin have not yet fused. The bandage is large and wraps around his thigh like a woman's girdle hugs her waist. His knee is a swollen yellow knot, twice its size.

He hears Eva, it must be Eva, moving boxes, muttering and sighing, but it feels as if she is miles away, like a vector on a distant horizon; and it is only possible to discern the aura of her fretfulness, her disagreeable love.

He dreams. He is swallowed by that dream. The dream of the boy who is running, always running. He runs across a field, wearing dark shorts and a white shirt, arms waving in the air. There are large gray clouds above, blocking the sun. The landscape is flat and brown and open, and there are trees, fruit trees, pear and apple, that look small against the sky and in the sky the gray has swallowed the blue. There is a low fence, the fence he built to enclose the orchard, and the boy runs alongside it, his fingers grazing the white wood as he races towards the house. The arrangement of tree and fence and field and sky have become distorted; stretched and expanded so that everything is smaller and too far away. The boy is too far away and it would not be possible to run after him. Now he cannot see the boy, cannot see how small he is as he loses his footing where the ground slopes downward. But he remembers where that shallow dip and rise of earth occurs, how easily it breaks one's stride, there just near the orchard. He knows that before the lightning strikes the boy, he will cut his knee on a sharp piece of rock as he falls, before the force of the lightning throws him, leaving him lying there stunned and motionless out beyond the last pear tree. The telegram rests, like a folded handkerchief, on his bandaged thigh. He remembers seeing the words about the boy and about the tree—which he imagined to be the pear tree he planted when they first bought the farm—and about the lightning. There is nothing about the boy's bleeding knee, nothing about the swallows that he knows would have been there, flying mournfully above, fleeing the storm clouds; nothing about the boy's face, startled and mute.

It is not yet the future for him. He remembers the telegram, but was it in the dream? Or did it make the dream? A breeze lifts the telegram and it falls away from his bandaged thigh, floating to the floor. The sound of Eva's voice; something that brings him back, something that locks him in time. One summer many years later, he sits on the balcony of his small apartment on Amelia Island watching the sea. Eva is there, sitting across from him, quietly peeling an orange. She asks him about this boy who, had he lived, would have been her half-brother. He is quiet at first, but then, in a low voice, he tells her the facts of what happened. He talks about how the boy just tripped, a freakish accident, and then the lightning struck. Eva listens, nodding, her mouth drawn down as slowly, carefully, she lays pieces of orange peel in a neat pile on a small glass table between them, his tumbler of bourbon nearby, ice melting in the sun. He remembers the simple declarative words of that telegram; how his incomprehension betrayed their clarity. And the dreams that followed. Always, those birds are there circling the skies, always that unbidden premonition of how quickly the sky darkened, how the drops of rain gathered, pouring through the trees in the orchard as the boy's breathing ceased.

The sea moves in, retreats, making a sound like breathing, over and over again.

Little Mother
by Amber Cook
from *Toasted Cheese*

My mother's wedding ring taps the steering wheel in time to the dull melodic strains filtering through the speakers. One tap, two tap, three taps and I want to throw myself from the window.

"I always loved this song. It's so...springy."

Springy. I ignore her and focus my attention on the sidewalk flying by outside. Girls with pink book bags and light-up sneakers walk in pairs, skipping over cracks and laughing so loudly I can hear the noise over my mother's incessant tapping. One stands aside from the rest, a science book pressed against her developing chest. It flattens the barely visible lumps I know are behind it and my heart strains. She is me, a younger me, and I want to scoop her up and tell her everything will be all right. I'm one of them, or I was, once. I don't know anymore. Maybe I'm just a shell of what they are and what I used to be.

Tap, tap, tap.

My mother, she sings. God help me. As if the tapping weren't enough to bear. In time to the music her foot presses the accelerator and the bags and blinking shoes turn into a melded blur of white and pink and light. My stomach turns and I have to look away.

"You're carsick. I told you to stop looking out that window."

She knows. A creep of panic flutters through my stomach. No, she can't know. She repeats the same statement every time we get into the car. I cover my legs with my coat and pull down the visor mirror to check out my reflection. No sign of green or water retention. We're safe.

She's watching me and it feels like she's been doing it since the day I was born. The checklist is being covered in her mind, I know, as her eyes dart from one inch of my body to the next.

Shirt—no profanity or visible cleavage.

Check.

Skirt—knee length and of a reasonable tightness.

Check.

Teeth and hair—brushed and combed.

Check.

If she could lift up my skirt and measure my underwear for full coverage, she would. She is the imperial involved mother. No foul language or g-strings shall pass by the maternal walking radar in Bill Blass flats. Her ultimate pride comes in knowing every aspect of her children's lives and balking at the lack of parental skills in the mothers around her. At least once per newscast, she will raise her voice loudly and proclaim if the carjackers and drug dealers had been under her raising they would have been at home in bed instead of warming a jail cell on block C.

Tap, tap, tap. It's a case of tragic irony, I guess.

I feel suddenly naked beneath her stare and pull my coat a little higher. Coats shield everything. They hide what needs hiding and cover up those little stains that can ruin a day. Today, it will cover my stain, and maybe tomorrow too. After that, words will have to be said that I don't want to say and she doesn't want to hear. But, until then, I will live in my silence and she in her happy bliss and together we'll both be content for at least a day or two.

She sings again. Her voice fills the SUV like water and I close my eyes for a moment to listen. She sounds like fuzzy wool sweaters and denim straight leg jeans. I tug my coat a little higher.

I'm the good girl, or the bad girl, or maybe a little somewhere in between. I have good intentions that sometimes don't pan out and good morals that ultimately get compromised here and there. It doesn't make me a bad person, but that doesn't stop the guilt from seeping in. My resistance is just a little too thin, or lax, maybe. She would call it a case of "severely impaired judgment," but it doesn't sound right to me. Judgment had nothing to do with it, though it will now. It just won't be my judgment she'll have to worry about.

The song changes and the rhythm of the wedding bands slow down a beat or two. I resist the urge to turn my head to the passenger window and stare out the front one instead. White paint lines rush toward us then shoot beneath our feet and disappear in the rearview. We rush ahead and she's pressing the accelerator a little harder. Life comes too fast, too soon, and with too much reality and I just can't handle it. Again, my stomach turns and I close my eyes and rest my head against the seat.

"Life goes on..." My mother chirps like a bird.

I can't breathe. The seatbelt is tight against my chest and it's leaving a red imprint in my skin. It's binding, cutting off my air. I pull it away and breathe deeply in, out. That's better. Beside me, a car passes by with a child's face pressed into disfigurement against the backseat window. He sticks his tongue against it, making moist swirls and ripples on the glass. Such innocence. There could be any number of deadly germs breeding on that window and there's no telling how many fingers have touched it, but he doesn't care. He is a man living in the moment and after his tongue leaves the glass it will probably find some dirty fingers to wrap itself around. It's all in a day's work for him, and I feel a surge of envy twist my insides. I want that kind of innocence. I want it back. It left so quickly, and I never even noticed it gone. No one told me it happened like that, without any sign or warning.

It was supposed to be the epitomizing moment of my life, my awakening, like some sort of Jackie Collins-narrated sexual enlightenment. I would journey from childhood to high heels and big breasts in one defining moment and my whole world would be changed for the better.

What a disappointment.

Things have changed, but not for the better, and I certainly don't feel any different. Except, perhaps, a little more regretful than I was last week. I'm not a woman, and if I am I don't know it. Maybe I'm a woman in a child's body or the other way around. I don't know anything anymore.

"Sing with me, Stephanie. You have such a beautiful voice."

I ignore her. The light ahead changes from green to red with no in-between and my mother slams on the brakes with every ounce of force in her lead foot. My stomach turns again and this time there's no stopping the party. In a flurry of fingers my seatbelt is flying against the door, which I fling open wide. Next breath I'm leaning over the wet pavement spilling a Cheerio and English muffin cocktail into a drain gutter. The sight makes my stomach turn again and I have to close my eyes. I spit twice, cough, and crawl back into the SUV before the light turns green. I don't want to open my eyes because I know what I'll see. But I do, anyway, and I was right. My mother stares at me with shocked curiosity and blinks three times slow.

"Are you feeling all right?"

I wipe my mouth with the sleeve of my jacket. "I'm fine. Much better now."

She stares a moment longer. "All right."

There will be more questions later, and probably a doctor's appointment. God, help me.

The light turns green and we're on our way again. I glance at her and pull the coat over my torso again. She'll know soon enough. For now, there's a parent-teacher meeting and I failed my last history exam. She puts on the turn signal and turns carefully into the school parking lot. I sigh. Here we are. Two little mothers.

She'll know soon enough.

January in December
by Matthew Derby
from *Guernica*

Church was bunk. Scarves were bunk. The cold was bunk. Robert Fancer's grandfather, the man he was wheeling back from afternoon service in a crappy chair, was massively bunk. There wasn't a word for the level of bunk Fancer's grandfather was. Especially when the wheels of the chair were coated in brown, gritty slush, like they were just then, on the way back from the church, and the grandfather was trying to tell him shortcuts that didn't even exist anymore, places that had been bricked up years before, or fenced in, or protected by loud dogs, and his grandfather smelled, and he was losing his mind, and he apologized even though he didn't mean to apologize, even when he was trying to do the opposite of apologizing underneath the apology.

"If you had turned down that alley, we'd be home by now," he said, pounding his fists against his thighs.

"That wasn't an alley—that was a newsstand."

"I'm sorry about that, Robert. But if there was an alley there, and there should be, we would be home."

Before, Fancer's mother had taken care of everything—the catheter, the vinyl sheets, the runny bowels—all of the horrible things that happened to Fancer's grandfather in the course of a day. She executed these tasks with such precision that they attained a transparency. Until she died, Fancer had no idea how profound her influence was over the apartment, how much discord had been held back by her fierce, silent vigilance. She was dead, though, and he could no longer pay for the Pakistani nurse to come, the one whose voice was thin and sweet, always on the verge of song. She would come once in the morning and again in the afternoon, and when she came the second time her voice was always lower, as if weighted down. Fancer missed the nurse, missed the wind she carried through the house, the brief flurry of activity, sheets snapping,

242

halving under the direction of her slender, sure hands as she stood next to his grandfather's bed. Fancer wanted to ask her where she had learned to do these things with such dispassion, under what circumstances she had happened into his life, into the small, brown apartment from a place too far away for him to imagine. He wanted, most of all, to hear the voice, to drape it over himself like a shawl, but he could barely muster speech in her presence, and so he never asked, just left the money in an envelope on the small table by the front door.

Then he got fired from the supermarket for crashing a delivery truck packed with snack cakes, and he had no more money. He called the agency that sent the nurse, asking for a temporary extension of credit, but they did not do credit, they were a cash-only establishment.

They made it back to the apartment building. Fancer bent down and helped his grandfather, who weighed less than a stick, onto his back. This was the only way they could get up the stairs, because the chair would wobble when he tried to lug it up backwards, and Fancer worried something would break or that he'd lose his grip on the rubber handles and the old man would tumble down the long, narrow flights, crumpling into a sinewy mound in the lobby.

"You're good for doing this, for making sure I get to mass," his grandfather said, clinging to him with feathery arms. "I'm very thankful. Do I seem thankful to you?"

"Yes."

"I want to make sure you know I am thankful. I was never thankful, not to your mother or to your grandmother before her. They both died resenting me, I know it."

"They did not. It's fine."

"That's nice of you, Robert. But I can tell. I can feel it. I can feel them looking down from heaven. I can feel the pressure of their eyes above me, bearing down."

Fancer carried his grandfather into the apartment, laid him out on the special bed, covered him in a crocheted afghan, and turned on the news. The first story involved a group of nuns who had been raped and murdered by soldiers in El Salvador. Father Gregory had mentioned the women in his homily. He told the congregation to turn their anger into prayer, because the sentiment would multiply like the loaves and fishes and spread out into the world in the form of peace. After the story about the nuns, the news anchors talked about the hostages in Iran, a warehouse full of abused cats that had been discovered in White Plains, a new advance in heart medicine, and the Dallas Cowboys. The male anchor made a joke about the Dallas Cowboy cheerleaders at the expense of the female anchor. The female anchor laughed, concealing a grimace, and the news ended.

"Why didn't they mention the election? When does the election happen?" Fancer's grandfather asked, clicking laboriously through the channels. The wand worked only intermittently, and only when you rolled the batteries back and forth while clicking. Mostly, they kept it on the same station and hoped.

"Grand-dad, come on. Already happened."

The grandfather stopped clicking. "You're serious."

"Yes. You saw it."

"Who won?"

"Come on, Grand-dad. Reagan won. You know this."

"Oh, god. I hate this head. It won't work." The grandfather blinked, wiped a veinous hand across his scalp, smacking with his elbow a Tupperware bowl full of unpopped and half-popped corn kernels left over from the day before.

Fancer knelt on the floor and began picking the oily kernels out of the carpet pile. He could feel his crack showing.

"I'm sorry, Robert. About the mess I've made. Not just there, the mess on the floor. I mean the mess inside me. I hate when that happens, when I forget."

"It's fine."

"But I really am sorry. You can't understand what it's like. I have these huge holes in my head where all of the memory goes. Like down a drain. Do you understand?"

Fancer paused, crouched on his elbows and knees. "Stop apologizing, please."

"But I want you to know. My life is going away, slowly, down these holes."

"Please stop. That's what happens. There's nothing to apologize for."

"Don't let your life fall away from you like this. It's pathetic."

"Stop it."

"When you're done with that, could you bend the TV over this way more? That yellow spot—the reflection from the hall light—is making it hard to see."

Fancer moved the television for his grandfather. On the program, there was a detective investigating an assassination. He wore a thick moustache and rubbed his chin vigorously, pointing with his free hand at a crumbling apartment building across the street. It looked like Fancer's neighborhood, but no building he recognized specifically.

"How much longer do I have to stay awake today?"

"You don't have to stay awake."

"Be good and bring me some of the drink."

"When it gets to commercials," Fancer said, but went to the kitchen anyway, because he knew he wouldn't be able to bear sitting through the detective program while his grandfather stewed in the special bed. He went to the refrigerator and mixed some vodka into a tall glass of orange juice. He handed the drink to his grandfather, who began immediately slurping away the pulp from the surface like a young boy. Soon his attention drifted back to the television.

Fancer retreated gingerly to his bedroom and lay down on his stomach on the bed. He reached under the bed for the long red box and carefully dragged it into view. He opened the box and looked at the rocket launcher. It looked like nothing, like a big black tube with a trigger and a stock. He picked up one of the rockets and hefted it in his palm. It was freezing cold in his hand. He breathed on it, which only made it wet. He put it back into its foam, rocket-shaped hole. He sometimes bought weapons for Craig, who couldn't buy them himself since he was arrested that time in Queens. But he'd never bought anything as enormous or complex as the rocket launcher. Craig would be coming for it soon. Fancer wondered what it would take to convince Craig to let him keep it. He thought about the rocket launcher constantly. Its presence in his room forced a clarity to erupt through the measured torpor of his life; it revealed, for the first time in years, a sense of purpose. He wanted to use it for something big, something that only big people did, the ones who took up huge chunks of the world, crowding out everybody else. He was ready for it—he'd compressed and sharpened his years of isolation into a jagged courage. He just needed a target.

⁂

The bell rang. Fancer's son, Thuan, was at the door, holding a paper bag with his things. Fancer had made the boy with a captured Vietnamese resistance fighter named Binh, whom he'd guarded at the prison camp in Bienhoa. Binh was addicted to some sort of diet pills that were actually really high quality speed, and she was across the street in her car, rolling up the driver's side window as she pulled away. Thuan was named after Hai Thuan, who was someone important to the Vietcong. Thuan, the boy, had happened to Fancer and Binh after a lengthy, botched interrogation session. The investigator could not get any useful information out of her. He threw a thin, stiff towel at Fancer's neck and left the room, disgusted. Binh huddled in a corner, panting, her wrists and fingertips browned with dried, crusted blood. When Fancer went to pick her up she fell into his arms, a motion he interpreted as a sort of resigned, fatigued passion. A few days later, she was removed in a prisoner exchange, so that Fancer didn't find out about his son until 1977, when she tracked him down in Harlem. He remembered little about the morning Thuan was conceived, just that Binh mumbled in slushy, fractured sentences, and that one of her arms was just barely shorter than the other. There was a mustiness to her, a robust and impermeable scent, like a soiled wool coat. It was the scent of prison, of communism. She glowed in the shady periphery of the windowless interrogation chamber, and when he embraced her it was partially to shut out the light that seemed to emanate from her naked torso.

"Hey," Fancer said.

The boy looked up, and said something that sounded like "google."

Both of them watched the car turn the corner and disappear.

Binh was the boy's mother, but Fancer was only Fancer, despite a series of early attempts to bore his way into the boy's world. Binh brought the boy out to him whenever she needed to be in the city. The bell would ring, and Fancer would hurry down the steps to the front, where the boy always stood, holding a paper bag with his things. Across the street, Binh, in a battered Le Baron, would roll up the window and drive off slowly.

"Can I have a cigarette?" the boy asked.

"How old are you now?"

"Ten."

"That seems too young to smoke."

"It's not."

"Let me think about it."

The boy opened his bag and carefully removed a crumpled pack of cigarettes. "I will hold these while you think about it."

"What do you want to do today?" Fancer asked.

"Just play video games."

"Okay."

They walked three blocks to a narrow, poorly heated arcade. On the way, the boy slid a flattened cigarette from the pack and lit it.

"I didn't say you could have that," Fancer said.

"I get tired of waiting."

"Could you put it away? It looks wrong."

"What does?" The boy held the cigarette expertly between his forefinger and middle finger, and when he exhaled he blew the smoke discretely away from Fancer. The boy had a point—he looked oddly mature. Fancer had stopped smoking when his mother died, mostly out of respect, since it was the peach-sized tumor in her throat that killed her. But he hated to quit, and thought often about the sweet burning in his mouth, the light, drowning sensation.

"You just look too small to be doing that. People are staring at us."

The boy did not respond, just took a long drag and exhaled through his nose.

At the arcade, Fancer changed a five-dollar bill for a handful of quarters. The boy made it through seven levels of Galaxian on a single quarter. Fancer didn't really know how the game was played, but the boy commanded the furious pixels with such exactitude and determination, immobile except for the pair of synchronous, spastic hands, that he felt his heart rise up against the walls of his chest.

Afterward they bought wet, translucent fries from a Middle Eastern man on the street and ate them in a vacant lot where four girls were trying to jump rope with a partially unthreaded telephone wire.

"How did you learn how to play those games?" Fancer asked the boy, who was sitting on his hands.

"I don't know. I just tried them."

"I try those games sometimes," Fancer said. "I always die right away."

The boy nodded, staring into his lap. "You're older."

"Maybe, you know, you could teach me how."

Thuan didn't answer, just fished for something in his jacket pocket. He looked uncomfortable.

"How is school?"

"It's just school."

"Any bullies?"

"What's that?"

"Kids who mess with you. Push you down. Call you names. Like that."

Thuan shook his head slowly, as if unsure.

"Anybody there that you just wish you could take out?" Fancer said, rolling a charred pebble around on the blacktop with his heel.

The boy, smoking again, inhaled and just held the smoke inside, like he was trying to store it for later. "You mean who I would kill? That kind of thing?"

"Yeah."

"Why you asking me this again?"

"I've asked you this?"

"You ask every time I come."

"Oh. Shit, sorry." Fancer slid his hands between his thighs. He could feel his cheeks going sour and red.

"You don't remember things."

"I said I was sorry."

"Can we go somewhere else now?"

There were many things in Fancer's life that he did not like. Being told by someone he had taken part in creating that they knew more about him than he himself knew was maybe the thing he hated most. It made him want to get up and leave the boy there, on the park bench. He wanted to walk away forever, to escape the city, to lose himself in a thick forest somewhere. It would be a glowing place, and he would walk barefoot, and feed deer from his cupped palm, and he would no longer have to change the fetid bedsheets of his grandfather, or listen to a small boy he loved tear him down on the small, rippled half-circle of cracked pavement behind the arcade, crisp sunlight flashing brilliantly in the mounds of dry snow.

They walked down to Central Park in silence, the boy taking the lead, tapping things with a twig he'd torn from a tree. It was too cold to walk, and way too far, but Fancer didn't want to spend money on bus fare, and anyway, they had a whole day to get through.

Thuan started walking with his eyes closed. "Hey," he called back to Fancer, "yell if I'm about to hit something."

Fancer closed his eyes as well. He could only get four or five steps before chickening out. Then he started to walk with his head pointed straight up. He craned his neck back so far that he could see the tops of the buildings. He wondered how far the rocket launcher could fire. He wondered if it could go higher than all the buildings in the city. A feverish urge to smile cascaded through his insides, but he did not smile, just cued the laugh track inside his chest while a smaller version of himself mugged and took a bow in front of a studio audience.

Up ahead, he saw a very well-known singer signing an autograph for a young woman on the sidewalk outside a fancy hotel. The singer was someone Fancer had admired for many years, as far back as he could remember. Fancer considered the singer a top-notch performer, maybe the best in the world. He looked hard at the singer for a long time to make sure he was right. There was no question—it was the same narrow, hook-nosed face he'd pored over on album covers and promotional posters for years.

"Hey," he said, rushing up behind Thuan, poking him gently. "Look there —it's..."

Thuan squinted. "I don't know who that is."

"Come on, sure you do."

"No."

Fancer had followed the singer's career for many years, had even seen the singer perform once at Madison Square Garden. Fancer was twenty-four at the time. He hadn't been back in the United States for very long—he still felt, at night, the dizzying claustrophobia of the jungle canopy as he lay absolutely still on the grandfather's sagging old bed. The singer had changed greatly from the well-dressed young man Fancer remembered from his adolescence. He had grown his hair long, and mockingly wore an olive drab uniform shirt onstage. But his performance made Fancer feel something he couldn't explain—a giddy trembling at the back of his head, right at the base of his neck, something he had never felt anywhere else, at any other time.

The singer's hair was short again, and he wore a white T-shirt beneath a faded denim jacket, an outfit that seemed outrageously unseasonable. The young woman, whose dark, pageboy hair accentuated a punchbowl face, was wearing some sort of gingham peasant skirt. Her brow was furrowed in concentration, as though she were working very hard to record every detail of the transaction—each word a separate parcel to be numbered and shelved, each brief, hysterical reflective streak in the record's shimmering plastic wrap to be drawn and redrawn later in some sacred headspace.

He was close enough to touch.

It felt as if the moment had been hovering there in the future all along, waiting for Fancer to find it. It was like a note someone had written to him—a note or a set of instructions, a document that would be revealed to him only when he was ready to receive it. Maybe someone had written it there on the night that Fancer had seen the singer walk out onto the stage, dwarfed by the cacophonous rioting of the young people in the aisles, or maybe even since the day Fancer was born. Maybe the moment formed as he exited his mother's womb, crystallizing in whatever city the future is stored, just waiting for him to stumble upon it and find the anchor point for his life's trajectory, to recognize the truth—that when he did the big thing—when he carried out the detailed plan that was slowly unfurling inside his head—the rocket launcher would come apart into a million pieces in his hand, and inside would be a small, pure song, like a bead of light.

When they got home, Fancer's grandfather was on the floor, asleep. He was holding a plastic jug of Magic Shell ice cream topping. He'd been drinking it straight from the bottle.

"What the—hey, get up off the floor," Fancer shouted, swiping the container from the old man's hand. The grandfather opened his eyes briefly and then shut them again.

Thuan went into Fancer's bedroom and closed the door.

"Hey," Fancer said, giving his grandfather a sharp, restrained kick in the thigh. "I mean it. I'm done picking you up after you've done something you're not supposed to. You got to learn to stop that."

The grandfather opened his eyes again, but did not look at Fancer.

"My kid saw this. My son saw this. How am I supposed to explain this to him?" Fancer bent down and lifted his grandfather back on the bed.

The grandfather rested his forehead against the metal bars on the side of the bed, the ones that were there to keep him inside. "I'm sorry," he said, and closed his eyes again.

Fancer went into the kitchen and riffled aggressively through the cabinets looking for a meal that the boy would eat. There was nothing he could combine to make a full meal so he broke off a hunk of frozen peas and ate it over the sink. On the radio on top of the refrigerator, someone was talking about the raped, dead nuns. There was an interview clip of one of the family members, a father who sobbed incomprehensibly. Then a song came on, a song by the singer, and Fancer stopped crunching the brick of peas to listen. He remembered how close he had just been to the singer; that the singer was, right then, moping around in the same air mass, moving objects around in the same city. The coincidence of the sighting and the song rose up sharply inside Fancer. It was possible, suddenly, to see the two separate incidents as the interlocked hemispheres of a vast, shadowy world in which he found himself increasingly entangled.

"Hey," his grandfather called from the next room. "Turn off the radio and come in here. I haven't seen you all day. Where did you go? I was calling for you. And why did you try to kill me? You almost killed me with that jug of syrup."

"You drank the syrup."

"Come here and tell me what happened today. Bring the boy."

Fancer let the shard of frozen peas fall into the sink, where it shattered and slid in wet chunks down the disposal.

"What was that?" his grandfather called out.

"Nothing. Peas."

"Peas?"

Fancer opened the door to his bedroom. Thuan was already lying on the floor, setting up a tiny group of articulated plastic figures on the burgundy shag rug.

"Do you want to watch TV?" he asked, leaning over the threshold, one hand on the knob.

The boy shook his head and reached in the bag for a vehicle.

"Your grandfather wants to see you."

Thuan continued to move the figures around on the floor.

Fancer went into the T.V. room and turned on the set.

"Leave that," said the grandfather.

"No."

"You're going to tell your grandfather what you did today, so turn that thing off."

"No way. The Muppets are going to be on."

The grandfather fell back against the pillow and let his head roll back and forth a little. His mouth was still ringed with half-dried Magic Shell syrup. "To think that a boy would sooner watch a puppet than tell his own grandfather about the world. It's horrible. I've been here all day, in here, stuck in this damn," and then he stopped, aware that Fancer was no longer listening to him.

※

The woman behind the counter at the narrow, breathy newsstand slipped the magazine into a plain brown bag and slid it toward Fancer, purposefully avoiding eye contact. Fancer had been out for most of the afternoon, looking for "help wanted" signs in shop windows, sipping dry, rancid coffee, paging through monthly magazines in store after store, picking up bits of stray newspapers left on half-smashed benches, anything to destroy the empty hours of the day. He'd seen the magazine behind the counter, the magazine with an exclusive interview with the singer, and, even though it was a dirty magazine, even though he was blowing lunch money for the next couple days, he'd weathered the embarrassment of the purchase for a chance to read what the singer had to say for himself.

He walked for a long time before finding a busted-up plastic toy kitchenette behind a dumpster where he could read the article without being discovered. He drew the magazine slowly from the bag, noticing immediately the date: January 1981, even though it was only December. This was a startling, liberating impossibility. The future—a month Fancer hadn't even lived through yet—had already been documented. No matter what Fancer did, he would survive.

He hunched forward on the flimsy plastic furniture, which collapsed slowly under his weight. The magazine's cover featured a half-famous actress dressed in a tattered nylon dress, but Fancer was not interested in the woman or her body. He skipped straight through to the feature on the singer. The interview went on for many pages. Fancer read each line carefully, fingering each line of text, even though his hands ached from the cold. He didn't want to miss anything. He knew it was ridiculous, but he kept sensing that the singer might suddenly mention his name; that, somehow, he had been on the singer's mind as much as the singer had been on his. As he read, the probability of this increased, until, at the end, it seemed inevitable, so that, when he was not mentioned, he felt belittled and cheated.

He chucked the magazine under the lid of the dumpster and started erratically down the street, no longer sure where he was, in search of a pay phone.

"Hey, is this Craig?" Fancer said softly into the receiver.

"That you, Bobby?"

Craig was someone Fancer met on the way back from the war. He was just a person who talked too much on the plane, who kept writing letters to Fancer after they landed. He worked for a company that was trying to get computers small enough to fit in a house, and sometimes, when he was in the city for a convention, they went to bars together. He also liked rare weapons. He'd send Fancer a package with directions to a grayed tenement rubber banded to a cigar box stuffed with bills. Craig needed the weapons, he told Fancer, because they were like a bridge between the two parts of his life he no longer cared about, the before and the after.

"I was wondering—That thing you had me get you, right?"

"Yeah, the RPG-7. I said I would be by tonight to pick it up, didn't I?"

"Yeah. I was wondering, actually, if I could keep it for a while longer."

"No way."

"Can I, like, rent it from you?"

"No man. That is a Soviet piece. Totally impossible to get. Do you know how hard that was to get? Way hard."

"Just—how long will you be in town?"

"Three days."

"Okay. Can I just—can I keep it until then?"

"Man, I kind of have to think about that. I don't feel right about it."

"Please."

There was a sound like glass breaking on the other end of the line. Then a girl laughing, talking in another language. "Hey," Craig said, finally, "I sort of have to go. Can you meet me at the car rental place the day after tomorrow?"

"Yes."

"Okay. You can keep it 'til then."

✳

Fancer opened his eyes without moving the rest of his body. Just opened his eyes and, without blinking, looked at the ceiling, trying to figure out what the scratching sound was. He listened to it until it turned into something else, a faint, ancient voice, telling him he had no more time to waste. He had only hours left before he had to meet Craig—so few he could taste them each, individual gumdrops in his mouth, slowly dissolving. Anxiety welled inside him as a staticky dirge, seeping painfully from every pore.

He sat up in his bed. Thuan was asleep on the floor next to him, half off the foam mat. The noise became more pronounced. It was erratic, desperate—it came from another room.

"Hello?"

He opened his door. He could see, down the short hallway, into the TV room, the grandfather's feet, crossed one over the other, like a dead bird.

"No," he said. "Please not today."

The grandfather was stretched out on the floor, trembling, one arm extended underneath the emerald recliner next to his bed. His eyes were mashed shut. Fancer knelt and rolled him over onto his back. His face was all wrong, like the flesh had come loose from the sinews or ligaments or whatever kept skin tight against the skull. His lips were wet and rubbery, and a little bluish. The scraping sound was the grandfather's fingernails against the cardboard underside of the recliner.

Fancer went back to his bedroom. Thuan was sitting cross-legged on the floor, his eyes thick with sleep.

"Hey, Pop-Pop's really sick. We have to go to the hospital right now."

"Okay."

"I have to call an ambulance or something. I need to think about what I'm supposed to do."

"Okay."

"But don't get alarmed or anything. Just hang out in here. Just stay here until I come back in and say it's okay. Okay?"

Thuan sat down on the bed, resting his bag next to him.

✳

Fancer walked Thuan over to the area the emergency room attendant had motioned to, a set of fused orange plastic chairs next to a vending machine that sold hot drinks. They sat at opposite ends, Thuan leaning against the machine with his eyes closed, steam from the photograph of hot coffee seeming to rise directly out of his small head.

They waited for a long time. It was impossible for Fancer to tell how long because, from where they were sitting, they could not see the single wall clock mounted behind the help desk, and there were no other indicators of the passage of time anywhere. Just a loose constellation of people waiting, splayed out on identical chairs, some bloodied, others just shaking or slowly, silently wailing in slow motion. Without any real sense of time's passage, it was almost like there was no time happening at all. It was as if he and the boy were fixed in a fluorescently lit diorama, just sitting there, outside time.

An attendant, a young man with feathered hair, emerged with a clipboard. He told them they needed to run another battery of tests.

"Can you give me a ballpark figure of how long it will take?" Fancer asked, chewing at a hard, pebble-sized lump on the inside of his cheek.

"Sorry, not at this time."

"Do I—that is, would I have time to run some errands while you do this—these tests?"

The attendant looked hard at Fancer. "Please stay close, in case things get worse—not that they will get worse, but—just, it would help all of us if you could stick around."

Fancer sat down next to Thuan.

"What did they say?" the boy asked.

"Nothing. They don't know anything. They're doing more tests."

"Oh."

Fancer crossed his arms and bent over, resting his forehead on his knees. He pursed his eyes shut until he saw colors. Then he whipped back, making himself dizzy.

"I have to go out for a few minutes."

Thuan stood up, zipping his coat.

"No, I need to go by myself."

"I'm going to stay here?"

"They might have news about Pop-Pop." Fancer took a brief survey of the room to see if anyone was listening.

"I don't want to stay here."

"You'll be fine. It's safe here. That's why it's called a hospital."

He held the boy's head in his hands and kissed his forehead.

"Be good," he said, and handed over a one-dollar bill and some change.

He took a cab back to the grandfather's apartment, using the money he'd saved in his breast pocket specifically for the plan. It was startlingly dark outside, or maybe it just felt dark because Fancer had been in the bright hospital waiting room for so long. Looking out the smudged window of the cab, he saw only the occasional flare of a neon sign between the black buildings and trees.

"When we get to my apartment, can you wait outside and then take me someplace else?" he asked, hunching over in the seat. Fancer had never asked this of a cab driver before, but he'd seen it done in the pictures. The driver made an indecisive motion with his head and shoulders, one that told Fancer nothing, but that also discouraged him from asking any further questions.

The driver pulled up in front of the grandfather's apartment. Fancer sprinted up the concrete steps, winding himself by the time he made it to the door. As he steadied his hand to fit the key into the lock, something hot and sharp rose up in the back of his throat, something like relief, or shame, or both, vying for a spotlight in his head. He was close enough to the plan, now, to feel its heat. It was a real thing, surging through him.

The floor in the hallway was scuffed and splintered from when Fancer and Thuan had hurriedly dragged the grandfather out to the stairwell. This was what they would see afterwards, he thought. These rooms would be photographed, samples would be taken, evidence collected.

He entered his darkened bedroom the way a stranger would—cautiously, one foot touching down delicately in front of the other, sliding his hand along the wall to search for the light switch. Lit from above by a single bulb, it looked like a room someone went to do something illegal, which was a new way to look at the hot, dense space in which he'd languished for the past six years. He squatted before the bed and yanked out the red box. Taped on top was a sheet of ruled paper. On it, the boy had written, in smudged, boxy script, "IS THIS FOR REAL? Please check one: Yes; No." He folded the paper and put it in his pocket.

Outside, the driver was standing beside the running cab, legs crossed, flipping a pack of cigarettes repeatedly on his thigh. Fancer rushed down the steps, hugging the red box with both arms. The driver, who had been staring upwards absently, slowly dropped his head as Fancer approached the cab. Fancer finally saw the man's moon-shaped face in full. Each of his features mirrored the spherical contours of his head—round, heavy-lidded eyes, round mouth and lips, rounded nostrils.

Without speaking, they both entered the cab. Fancer sat up straight in his seat, the red box in his lap, his hands resting evenly on its surface.

They had to stop often for red lights. Fancer watched the pedestrians swarm around the cab, toting holiday gifts in thick paper bags. Soon they would know him, would understand the terrible, terrible thing he had done, and never forget his face.

At 72nd Street, the driver slowed down. Fancer's heart, which had been pounding furiously against his chest cage, slowed suddenly, cooled to a low, even drone, as he recognized the spot where he'd seen the singer that day with Thuan.

He had the driver pull up across the street from the hotel, near a stand of well-trimmed bushes. The red box was cumbersome, but he managed to drag it to a patch of dry, packed dirt, worried to a porcelain sheen by sleeping bums. He opened the box and assembled the rocket launcher in the amber half-light cast by the streetlamps. He was cool and efficient, his hands steady in their work, just the way he'd practiced.

Cars passed on the street. An older couple, well dressed, walked quickly by, pretending not to notice Fancer's head peeking over the brush. He didn't care if he was seen. Better, he thought, if he was seen. He imagined the couple the next morning, the woman briskly unfolding the paper, reading the account, asking her husband whether he remembered the funny looking man in the bushes, the one with the lopsided head and small, pointed eyes, working on something made of metal.

The cold began to wear at him. His toes stung inside useless, flattened combat boots. He longed for a meal. He thought about the dollar he had given his son. He hoped the boy was eating, or blowing on a waxed paper cup of piping hot chocolate. He hoped a nurse would come and take pity on the boy, maybe play a game with him while they waited for someone to come along and claim him. Maybe, when no one came, the boy would end up with people who could actually take care of him. He imagined the couple who'd just passed by—they would read about the abandoned boy in the newspaper and feel vaguely responsible for his welfare. They'd adopt the boy, move him out to a well-appointed neighborhood far from the city, a green and iridescent place, steeped with helpful, friendly people, the aisles of the supermarkets stacked with heartbreaking precision. Someone, Fancer decided, would love the boy fiercely, teach him actual, like, things. Maybe, then, Fancer, crouching in the bushes, waiting to blow up a person he'd never even met, was putting the final touches on his only fatherly gesture.

A long, black car pulled up in front of the hotel. Fancer knelt, just the way he had seen in the manual, and shouldered the weapon. He saw the singer's wife emerge from the car, and then the singer himself, wearing the same outfit as before. He traced their movement through the reticule of the rocket launcher. Everything inside him tightened.

When he heard the first shot, Fancer thought he'd pulled the trigger himself, though there was no heat or exhaust, and the warhead remained loaded. Across the street, there was a man in a dark overcoat, braced in combat position, holding a pistol. Fancer had seen the man earlier, loitering outside the hotel, reading a paperback book. As he brought the man into focus, Fancer saw the barrel of the gun burst through the night four more times. Ahead of him on the sidewalk, the singer was sprinting erratically, waving his arms, followed by his wife, whose mouth was open. Fancer could hear him making gurgling sounds, like a loud balloon losing air underwater. The singer somehow made it inside the hotel before collapsing, his back dark with blood. The singer's wife threw herself on top of him, covering him with her body. Sound started to come out of her mouth, a tight, high-pitched tone, rich with distortion. Fancer looked back at the man on the sidewalk, who stood under a street lamp, lifting one hand and then dropping it again, as if unsure what to do next. Then he removed his hat and overcoat and threw them into the bushes. The hotel's doorman appeared. He approached the man without a coat. "Do you know what you've done?" he shouted, again and again, as if calling out into the wilderness, while the man tittered like a goofy adolescent and shuffled backwards, leaning against the brick hotel wall.

Fancer set the rocket launcher down on a mound of hard snow and rose slowly, the street lamps illuminating his lower half in dishwater light. He had failed to put into motion even this, his last attempt to push something back out into the world instead of taking it, once again, in. If he had been a better man, a more reasonable man, hardened by life instead of merely weakened by it—if he had been a man who planned out a day instead of mincing his way through, bitching out the hours one by one until they disappeared up the steel column of night, he might have made something of the moment, put his signature on it. He might have set a special, public fire. But this other man beat him to it. He felt a clean tremor of recognition then—clean because it was like the wispy white center of an ice cube—at what the man across the street had done, what he had failed to do himself. The man had cut a hole in the history of the world, and fallen in, and Fancer was standing at the freshly cut edge, peering down.

The police came and surrounded the man, and he did not resist. They led him away to a squad car that was hastily parked halfway on the curb. The man lay down in the back seat, hiding from the officers and bystanders that surrounded the car, but Fancer could swear he saw the man's terrified smile still hanging in the place he'd just been standing, burned into the night air, the way you could see, on the evening news, ghostly white trails from the flashlights of the search crew in El Salvador, examining the site where the nuns had been killed—a bright reminder of the video camera's shortcomings, an impression of the world as created by a faulty, primitive system. Fancer stared hard at the smile, blinking against the chill, trying to wipe it from his vision. The mouth opened, then, and seemed to say, "There is nothing left to do with a life but wait." It was nonsense—there was no mouth. There were no words. It was just a failure of the senses, an illusion, a string of garbage that became something else, something real and heavy as it took shape before him, staining his eyes for good.

Two Among Many
by Philip Holden
from *Cha*

Then Raffles said, "O Sultan, hear what is enacted by English law. The murderer according to it shall be hung; and if not alive, the corpse is hung, notwithstanding. Such is the custom of the white people." Then at the same time he ordered the corpse to be brought and put in a buffalo cart, which was thereupon sent round the town of Singapore to the beat of the gong, informing all the European and native gentlemen to look at this man who had drawn blood from his Raja or Governor; and that the law was that he should not live, but in death even he should be hung. When they had sufficiently published thus, then they carried the corpse to Tanjong Maling, at the point of Telok Ayer, where they erected a mast on which they hung it, in an iron basket, and there it remained for ten or fifteen days, till the bones only remained. After this the Sultan asked the body from Mr. Raffles, which was granted: Not till then was it washed and buried.
—Abdullah bin Abdul Kadir, Hikayat Abdullah

She will not meet him for two years. But when she steps forward, when the alarm sounds under the lintel of the metal detector, when the brisk woman in her crisp blue uniform comes forward with hands extended to pat her down, it's decided. The date remains to be fixed, but it is certain that they will meet.

She has waited in Singapore Changi airport for hours, after the crowded flight from Phnom Penh, bumping through turbulence over the Gulf of Thailand. Her connecting flight delayed, she's walked the pastel corridors with their low lighting, taking in the purple orchids, the koi pond bridged by a narrow, parsimonious arch. It's cool here. Quiet. The heat outside must be just like the heat of the cities she's visited before—Hanoi, Ho Chi Minh, Bangkok— but she's insulated behind glass, like the quick fish in the tank in the waiting lounge. Outside the planes bake on the concrete, gleaming white, wings sharp as knives.

She's passed through the airport once before to change planes, just as she is doing now. Today's different, though: she's much less certain of herself. More time to think things over. As much as she would like to forget, she cannot quite avoid her purpose here. She's calm, but it's a willed calm, carefully maintained, like the pruned beauty of the palms in the light well. This submerged nervousness leads her to seek familiarity, and she searches for comfort food. She finds a stall selling Starbucks, marooned like an island in a vast expanse of purple carpet. She orders a latte; they take American dollars, but return change in an unfamiliar currency. When she sits down, she sorts the coins idly with her spare hand. Different colours, different sizes, but all mirroring each other: on one side a crest, on the other, flowers.

His housing estate has corridors too, lined by planter boxes of purple bougainvillea and trim palms, maintained by an invisible army of workers who vanish each morning. It's in the north of the island, connected to its fellows, to the city centre, and to the airport by the arteries of the MRT and highways. He likes the fresh paint, the well-scrubbed tiles of the estate, the bus that always comes on schedule, the solid pillars of the Light Rapid Transit system. Everything is cared for. When the LRT passes blocks of flats its windows mist over automatically, shielding balconies lined with washing and potted plants from the prying eyes of passengers. Yet when he goes to the kopitiam each morning he's looking for a sanctuary from this overwhelming newness. Not that the coffee shop's so old, but in the twenty years or so since it was built it has already acquired reassuring layers of grime. In one of the angles where a pillar meets ceiling, a pair of swiftlets have made a nest, a small pocket of feathers and twigs glued to the walls. Today he pauses momentarily to watch one of the birds return with food, noticing the high-pitched chirping of the young birds in the nest, the way the yellow rims of their unformed beaks open and close. He's glad that no one's thought to clear the nest away. Then he sits down gratefully at a formica table worn white by the scraping of plates, finds that his hands tremble when he unfolds the newspaper. He's gestured for coffee; they know him here, and the kopi o arrives promptly.

He has counted out the change for the coffee vendor carefully in preparation, but he still fumbles when he picks it up. His palms are sweaty, and the silver and gold coins cling together, eluding his fingers. More haste, less speed. Then he pulls them free. Next the roti prata arrives, a pillow of folded, crisped dough, and he repeats the performance with greater success.

He arranges everything on the table precisely, like a surgeon preparing for an operation. To his left the newspaper, unfolded to the letters page, weighed down in one corner with a bottle of chilli sauce so that the overhead fans will not turn the pages prematurely. Nearer to him the kopi in a heavy china cup printed with English flowers, a fading colonial memory caught beneath the glaze, mismatched with an orange plastic saucer. He stirs it so that the sugar will dissolve, takes an experimental sip. The handle is tiny and difficult to grip; he pinches it tightly between two swollen fingers. Finally, he reaches to his right. He eats the prata with spoon and fork, pulling the layers apart along hidden seams, dipping a small piece into the curry sauce, feeling its soapy texture on the tongue followed, after a moment, by an explosion of taste.

At Starbucks, she drinks her coffee, reassured how it tastes the same as in any other airport. It will also taste the same in Sydney, when she arrives late in the evening or now—in all probability—early the next day. The accompanying croissant is dry in her mouth; she chews with deliberate slowness. Later, in the interview room, she will tell them everything about her that they want to know. Who she met in Australia before she left. Who paid for her trip to Cambodia. Where she went. Who she met there. Eventually her whole life, from the beginning. She was born in a refugee camp on the Thai border; her mother had fled from Laos, but she's not Laotian: she's ethnic Chinese. Teochew. She never knew her father. They—her mother, herself, a younger brother—migrated to Australia when she was four. She cannot remember much about her childhood. But later life was hard: she couldn't afford to go to university. She did sales and marketing, but her brother got into debt. Into trouble. He needed money. And so ...

Now she returns the tall glass with its plastic stirrer, the empty plate speckled with crumbs, to the barista. Not the woman who first served her, but a young man with a mullet and a tattoo that curves down from the neck until it's hidden by the collar of his shirt. He nods to her, but doesn't speak. He can't place me, she thinks; he doesn't know what language to use. And I won't help him. Here I am one among many. In Australia, every now and then, a stranger can burst open my sense of belonging: the man in the shop who tells me I speak English very well; the immaculately dressed old lady who asks me if I am an "Oriental," and, when I nod, speechless, continues "Oh well, dear, never mind." In the few days I spent in Vietnam , the taxi drivers knew from the way I dress that I was from somewhere else; once or twice they thought I might be vietkieu, overseas Vietnamese, and gave an experimental greeting, only for me to answer them conclusively in my mangled phrasebook pronunciation, my broken tones. It is just here, at this airport, that I fit in, in transit between lives.

When she shoulders her pack she feels the tug of the packages taped to her lower and upper back.

He is also one among many. She's flotsam, moved across continents by the currents of the world. He's like a limpet. He has stayed here, stubbornly, while the world has changed around him. First the British, under whom he started working. Mr. Grouse, the Superintendent, taught him well. In his teens, in his twenties, everything that was solid began to melt: colonial retreat, insurgencies, elections, merger with Malaysia, and then, in 1965, unlooked-for independence. He remembers the press conference on a flickering television screen, the prime minister who paused to wipe away tears at the failure of a life's work. And then, when he was still married to his first wife, a reverse process: the sudden solidity of the nation-state, the deep freeze of post-independence politics. Through all this he's kept his job, kept up his standards. Some things never change. He still uses, in his work, the 1913 tables that the British devised but long since abandoned. He's tried unsuccessfully to pass on his skills, trained two successors who each left the service when the time came to shoulder responsibility. Even if he's supposed to be retired now, the government still calls on him when he's needed.

He sips his coffee.

They are both Catholics. She went to church faithfully, every Sunday, for as far back as she could remember. At ten she took her first communion. Even when she returned home from uni, after her brother had said he wouldn't go any more, she would accompany her mother to Church, performing the masquerade of a double life. But she, like her brother, has long since ceased to believe. Forget other worlds: the business of living in this one is more than enough. She remembers. Money to help her brother? She could go to Cambodia, pick up a package through to Sydney. Through Singapore? She laughed in incredulity. You don't understand, the man had told her: they don't mind if you take stuff through, in transit. They just don't want it coming into their country. Here's the name, the phone number, when you're in Phnom Penh.

In Cambodia, even on Tonle Sap they have churches, boats with a high pitched roof and a wooden cross that float across the lake. In two years' time, before the meeting in the prison, they will ask if she would like to see a priest;

she'll acquiesce, and they'll talk, separated by glass. Even in prison she'll play this masquerade again: on the surface she'll be numbly calm; on the inside something will move restlessly within her, like a bird beating itself against glass. She will allow the priest to think he has comforted her.

He goes to mass faithfully, every Sunday. He likes the grandeur, the ceremony, the statue of the Virgin Mary garlanded with flowers as he climbs the steps in the morning heat up to the church that has no walls, the nave supported by pillars only. His first wife said to him, haven't you read the Ten Commandments? How can you carry on doing the job you do? But for him it has never been like that. Your life is a series of compartments, like the segments of the oranges his Chinese neighbours give him at New Year. When government service calls him, he will leave his flat in the cool of the night, go to the prison, spend hours checking that everything is in working order. After it's all over, he'll return in the midday heat, sink into the soft leather of the couch beneath the ceiling fan, pour himself a single glass of brandy.

When she walks towards her waiting flight the corridor narrows. She tries not to think too deeply, to drink in sensations of the present: the purple carpet, the potted palms, the advertisements for credit cards and frequent flier miles. On either side, the gates in orderly rows, dimly lit, like empty glass tanks. Or cells, she thinks. As she reaches the brushed silver walkway it sighs suddenly into life. And as she's propelled forward, she becomes conscious of the soft music. Lennon's "Imagine," without the vocals. She smiles: a protest song become Muzak, oiling the smooth flow of money through the airport. For a moment she remembers again: the packages on her body, the white crystals reduced to powder in the cheap hotel room, the door locked, the fan switched off in the gathering heat. Keep walking. Don't think. By the gate ahead the early crowd is gathering. When she steps off the walkway she feels calmer again, as if she's entered a ritual, like one of the masses of her adolescence. Her body moves forward—it does not disrupt the ceremony—yet she is propelled towards her destination by habit only. She notices herself join the line at the gate.

When he stands up he's wearied by the sudden weight of his body. It's hotter now, and he can taste acid in his mouth; his right knee creaks in protest on the first few flexes. Strange, he muses, how he can control all bodies other than his own, weigh each one, subtract the weight of the head, calculate the exact length of rope for the clean, momentary fall into darkness. What he does is not the most difficult thing to do. Think of the doctor who is always waiting. If the organs need to be harvested, Doctor Yeh will wait two minutes, then go up a free-standing ladder next to the corpse that is still not yet quite a corpse. He'll lean forwards, hold body still, put stethoscope against the heart, and listen: only then will the doctor give signal to lower the body down. Compared to this, what he does is nothing. There's a mirror on one of the pillars in the coffee shop, and as he passes he catches sight of his reflection. Still a full head of hair; a fuller belly. He doesn't look his age. When he comes out from the shade of the awning the space between the buildings seems less like a corridor than a conduit, a storm drain filled up to the brim with a surge of light.

Before they meet, there'll be a process. First the court case, then the failed appeal, then letters to the press, fruitless representations from politicians and celebrities for clemency. A war of images: her old passport photo; her mother in tears; lawyers at the prison gates; the Prime Minister with his awkward smile. A war of terminology, also: barbarism, colonialism, sovereignty, rights. Her face slowly becoming invisible, written over with layer upon layer of words.

He keeps his mind active. His grandson taught him how to use the Internet. He likes those sites where you can find an address on a map, and then zoom out, from a block of flats to the town, and then to the whole island of Singapore caught in an indentation in the tip of Asia, snagged like a corpuscle on the wall of a vein. Reclamation has long ago softened the island's shape. It's rounder, fatter: Tanjong Maling has been swallowed up by the wharves and gantries of a container port. But he's still struck by an uncanny symmetry here: how the impossibly large resembles the impossibly small. The lines of silt that trail out into the Straits of Malacca are viscous, like venous fluids under a microscope.

In public life, too, he's haunted by unacknowledged symmetry. This is something that he senses but can't articulate, why he celebrates the new but seeks out the old. He does not want to think further, and yet in this gleaming, brilliant city he always feels unclean, something that persists beyond the daily rhythms of showers, clean tissues, or the careful soaping of hands. The memory of something else swells beneath the skin of the present, something before, when he was younger, when a nation was coming into being. There were words he and his friends heard often and were not ashamed to speak: equality, rights, socialism, democracy, justice. If he searches hard, he can still detect traces of them in the present, but they are almost erased, written over by the crisp new language of social order, economic imperatives, retribution, discipline, punishment. He's not sure how to picture this change. You think the city is perfect; visitors love its shining schools, hospitals, factories and shopping malls. Then you look more closely, and you see scar tissue, like the keloids that grow on your arm after an immunization jab. Imagine a scarified body, its skin like armour, memories and desires sealed up within it, their retrieval an impossible effort. Yet these perfect scars are also not without their beauty: they are hard, and can resist the storms of the world.

In this particular storm, they will both be in places of calm. She behind reinforced glass, thick concrete walls. Even her mother will not be allowed to touch her hand. He, and so many others, behind other walls: routine, the soft intimacies of family or of friends, the forgetful business of living.

At the end of the island, next to the airport, there is a prison. It is clean, modern, well planned; its corridors meet at perfect angles. Like the airport. Like the estate.

They will meet there, in two years. Two among many.

Mandible
by Donna D. Vitucci
from *Front Porch Journal*

His license named him Manfred, but my little sister and me, we called him "Mandible" from the time he started hanging around. He'd sleep over with Mama, this scary, big-headed, sharp-jawed cartoon guy, who we imagined was made of metal. The guy's face was all jaw. He was too long of arm, with a slick, black pompadour. Who, in the 21st century, still worshipped Elvis? Manfred did, and other guys in Hebron, Kentucky. So me and Jennie nicknamed him "Mandible," and we cracked up whenever we said to his ugly mug: Hey Man, yeah, we're good. How 'bout you? He had a shameless smile, and he flashed that grin at us—probably thought he was buddying up with his woman's wisecracking son and daughter.

"I'm a man can stand his liquor," Mandible bragged against all evidence otherwise. I moved his bottle and cup from where he set them down, playing a switcheroo game, stumping the bastard when he reached for a gulp. He wobbled over the chair he pulled out to sit in, ended up kissing the floor.

Just keep your hands off my sister, I thought. I knew better than to say it—get knocked across my teeth by someone or another, Mama doing her part because she had her own prospects to harbor, so maybe a double sock-it-to me, right side then left side, lip busted equally, twin black eyes. Not the first time the mirror would have shown me my beat-up self, courtesy of Mandible Jones.

※

Mandible brought with him two big dogs, one beautiful German shepherd and one black Lab. When he released the tailgate and the dogs leapt out, he pointed and said, "That one there's got some Rottweiler in him, so don't get him riled up," but he was no fearful thing. The black and the tan, they played like puppies, they were puppies, less than a year old. They romped, kicking up tufts of grass with the toenails of the fat paws they'd grow into. They bit each other's necks but never to hurt, they rolled around in the fenced yard, and they tracked mud through the house when we let them in at night.

Mama ranted about that, but then Mandible murmured at her low and soft, "Could we just lie down?" A tobacco man pitching woo, he led her by clutched, praying hands into the back bedroom, where he evoked from her another, more piteous sound, Mama's love tumbling down to meet Mandible's.

Jennie and me sensed what they were doing—we'd watched enough Cinemax and HBO—but we looked off in different directions, la-di-dah humming as we went out to play with the dogs. The dogs were the best things Mandible brought us. At eleven and twelve, we might have been too old for pretending, but it helped when nothing else did, and so we pretended we were canines—me and Jennie galloping around, wrestling with each other, wrestling two against two with Blackie and Tanner. We loved them like brothers.

We tracked as much dirt inside as the dogs, but the adults didn't rise to chide us or play their in-charge roles. They let us live this disaster. They lived it, too. We were mostly, as the school counselor noted over the phone to Mama, "unsupervised." Mandible called us each, at different times, "wild child," but he spoke the words softer and scarier in Jennie's direction. The alcohol glitter in his eyes could have been poured straight from the bottle.

In kinder, pre-Mandible times, Mama had called me her Guardian Angel. She would scratch my head while we watched TV on the couch together. We'd sit, me in Mama's lap and leaning back into her soft breasts and gone-soft stomach, and Jennie leaning into me, her big brother, the three of us stacked like cups in a cabinet. Mama had done steady, ill-informed choosing since the day she was born. Her worst choice brought Mandible through our door.

"We aren't needing a daddy," I told Jennie because Mama wouldn't listen, and my sister and me made a pact affirming our battle against Mandible in the gloom of the basement bathroom.

Jennie looked up at me with her brown eyes, the eyes of a small forest animal, and I guess that's what she was, a hunched, hood-eyed rabbit-girl, wary of anything bigger than herself, submissive, flinching, playing dead if she had to. And me protecting her.

"We will never take Mandible any more seriously than a cartoon," I said. "Now you say it," I told Jennie, and she did, most solemnly, most reverently, before we busted a gut laughing. We crossed hands in the convoluted method I invented from movies I'd seen. I twisted her this way and that by her arms and she let me do it, no meanness in either of us.

When Mandible moved in, Mama demoted Jennie and me to second class citizens. On the couch, with the TV light flickering in Mandible's glassy eyes, Mama leaned across his chest, covered only by an undershirt. To me and Jennie, wedged on the other side of the cartoon man, she said, "Ain't this cozy? Like a real live family?" Her hopeful voice, married up with her gin-tilted smile, turned me suspicious. We didn't need Mandible to make us more than we already, satisfactorily, were.

On weekday mornings, before Mama left for the day shift at Care Crest Retirement, she wrote our list of chores in the margin of the home-delivered coupon magazine and left it on the counter by the cereal box. Get yourselves off to school; pick up the house; feed the dogs and yourselves; clean your clothes. Jennie was good at the household stuff, and I'm not being prejudiced or whatever they call it when guys admire girls for doing girly things. She was simply better at keeping the whites white and the colors from bleeding, expert at cracking eggs without having to fish out pieces of shells. She remembered to switch off the oven when the fries were crisp.

I once left the oven lit all night and Mandible threw me down the basement steps, railing about "burning the goddamn house to the ground with all we know and love in it."

Mama said, "You know that ain't happening."

Mandible yelled, "And stay down there," which I was glad to do.

Mama's voice, muffled through my ceiling, told him, "Go find some other food."

No one brought a meal to me, while I touched bruises.

I heard Jennie refuse to eat if I wasn't. "All's I want is water," her voice bleated.

"Well, get from this table then," Mandible said.

Her chair erupted, her feet pounded above my head, she slammed the door to the room we shared. I could hear dishes fall into the drying rack of the sink.

"That boy's on my bad side," Mandible said.

"Not your bad side," Mama said, "just your opposite side."

"What's opposite good other than bad?"

"No-account?"

I knew they'd been drinking, probably since noon. That night and the whole next day I huddled on the concrete floor of the basement shower because it was the farthest I could slink away and still be housed. I was mapping an escape for me and Jennie, assembling evidence and the intelligent kind of pleading that might free us but also wouldn't have Social Services tossing us from the frying pan into the fire. They missed me at school until the third day Mama wrote an excuse note claiming I'd had a headache, and sent me back.

※

After the stair-pitch, I carried my Swiss army knife with me always, got kind of hooked on knives in general, checked them out at flea market stalls—the pointed and the pearl-handled, the dull, the ebony, and the rusted. The long and the short of it, I imagined Mandible saying, his sharp jaw-jutting jeer. Well, he could wait and see, how long or how short.

With my eyes I bored devil ray-thoughts into Mandible when we'd come upon him after school, leveled flat out on our couch watching or dozing through ESPN, smoke-bombing the house with a lit cigar or spilling potato chip crumbs into creases between the cushions because he was too hung over or too drunk to find the gaping stink-hole he called a mouth. I hoped my evil intentions would open up flames in his gut. Thirteen-going-on-fourteen, I was deep into horror films—chainsaw massacres, possessed souls, dead back to life, death or the devil incarnate, blood curdling fear paired with maximum blood letting.

The few knives I had I worked at nailing into our storage shed from across the backyard. What a clean, clear thwack when they wedged into the wood with the force I'd manufactured. Mrs. Lowen, our next door neighbor, watched me from our mutual fence. I felt her gaze from over my shoulder. Finished with one round, I turned and demanded, "What?!"

She said, "Is that your daddy I've been seeing?"

I snorted, guessing she was referring to Mandible. "Hell, no." I was a proud, tough delinquent cussing in the face of this beautiful woman, who'd been mostly abandoned, I'd noticed, by her traveling husband in the three months they'd occupied the house.

Mrs. Lowen dragging cans to the curb on garbage night or pinching dead tops off flower stems were snapshots my mind had lingered over. Without my being aware, Mandible had helped sharpen my focus. I'd heard "Let's Give Them Something to Talk About" drifting from Mrs. Lowen's upstairs window onto the roof of our prefab ranch house. Her crying, too, was part of what rained down.

I said to her, "Jennie's and my dad, he's either dead or run off." I wondered at the flat October sky. "Or maybe we're the runners-away." If Mrs. Lowen could only see the burning in me, the smolder, she would know me in a way more pure than Jennnie or Mama, who were diverted from me by Mandible's stumpy fingers at their jaws, insisting, "Look. You're two peas in a pod," him pointing out their pretty, look-alike faces in the mirror next to each other.

Within a few days of our fence conversation, Mrs. Lowen actually stepped inside our chain link, fending off the dogs with hands held out in front of her.

"Mrs. Lowen, you're awesome with knives," I said, after she helped herself to my collection and threw them. Only two of her five stuck anywhere on the shed door, but I'd learned from observing Mandible how to build a girl with praise.

She blew on her fingertips like they were the hot end of a just-fired gun, and smiled. "Call me Allison. And you are?"

"Whit."

"What?"

"Whit. Whitley. Named after my grandma's side, all dead now."

"Jeez, Whit," she said, full of the right kind of sympathy.

I wanted to hug her for taking time out of her life just to say my name. Instead, I shrugged, threw my slew of knives at the big "X" on the shed door. Standing beside Allison caused a humming in my ears, a humming that commenced in other parts of me as well. For the first time in my life, worry did not occupy the center of my day. And neither did Jennie. Allison had displaced them both.

Mama watched us, nose-twitchy from behind the kitchen curtains, Jennie said.

"Your sharp knives are cutting up my backyard." She was supposedly mimicking Mama, but Jennie herself had elbow-thrusting in her voice.

How I wished Mama would take the time to step outside and wrench me back from Allison, ground me, even beat me like before, as she did under

Mandible's influence. I could imagine the man's powerful jaw biting off the words: Make that boy behave, wrangle him back from the lure of the neighbor woman twice his age.

Though for Mandible, age was no matter.

"I'm mostly hitting the mark," I said to Jennie. She'd report back to Mama whatever I said.

Before Allison, I could have walked off into the sunset without notice. Suddenly everybody seemed to hone in on Whitley Holcombe, including Allison's husband, whose latest business trip ended at my front door.

"I'm not threatening to break your arm here," Mr. Lowen said—my arm that had steadied his wife's pale one and tried to show her how to throw a knife. As he made his wishes flat-out known, Allison stood at the fence line, on her side, squinting at us. Mr. Lowen was no Mandible-bully, but a husband had rights, he said. And I was just a punk, he said, who better steer clear. Embarrassment crawled across my skin, not because of Mr. Lowen's murky accusations but because with Mama at work, Mandible sagged in the recess to the living room, playing the half-hearted role of stand-in parent. While Mr. Lowen rattled on, Mandible eyed the TV, his mind focused, I'll bet, on returning to the couch where Jennie sat sipping a Coke. In no way did he defend me, but he didn't snake up and hit me either.

I trawled the fence line where Allison pretended to dig dandelions during Mr. Lowen's next out of town jaunt.

She said, "What're you gonna do?"

It wasn't a question concerning my next move, since there was no next move. She'd said it as an expression, the way people do, her voice jokey and full of resignation. Until then, we'd barely touched, except when handing the knives to each other. I grasped the chain link fence. Allison passed her muddied, weed-green fingers across my knuckles, then went into her house. With dandelion juice drying my skin, I stood there until Blackie and Tanner nudged my knees and inserted their big bodies between me and the fence.

Mandible powered down our storage shed with a bobcat he'd borrowed from a buddy. He turned the shed to a pile of rubble and rotting lumber. Then he poured gasoline and lit a match to it. When the flames shot up to eyebrow level, Mandible rubbed salt in my wound, said, "Addie, rustle up the weenies and the marshmallers," in his best hill country accent.

Adalyn is Mama's name, which he never used full and lovely in the way it should have been spoken, the way I'd spoke "Allison" when the occasion arose. He had the nerve to wink at me. What you going to do about that, boy? his wink seemed to dare.

✳

Because of Mama, because of Allison, because of Mandible—oh, who the hell knows why? maybe just the passage of time and boredom with the pose—the all-black-wearing boy-of-death I'd been for almost a year cleaned up, straightened up, secured a summer job at Video Village at the Silver Grove Market, which was just a strip of stores: Guardian Bank, Donray's TV Repair, the video rental, and the Quick Mart with its gas pumps and beer cave.

I grew beyond knife-throwing, stored the knives in a shoebox under my bed. A phase, Mama termed it, discounting my time spent with Allison. She sometimes sounded like a social worker when she'd try categorizing me or diagnosing me, but sooner or later she'd quit and light a cigarette, increase the volume on the Court TV. This cued up her next line, "Whit, you're beyond hope," which she had declared countless times.

Toward the end of her Mandible Period she didn't even bother with speaking, she let the cigarette flame and the television knob do her talking. By then she was divorcing us—she'd taken up with a guy named Roger and was in the process of moving her most important possessions little by little whenever Mandible was out cashing his disability check. When Jennie and me saw her wedge the hot rollers against the plastic tub of her nail polishes in the back seat of the Fiesta, we knew it was her last trip.

As we watched her mincing steps up and down the concrete slab to the front of the house, halfway slipping in her slip-ons, loading up her valuables, she said, "A mother can be as no-account as a son."

She had several pithy sayings that erased the snappy comeback I'd maybe been planning, robbed it right from my mouth, left me vacant as a cleared-out bank vault.

It was important for me to focus on the consequences of her move and how they affected me and Jennie.

"We're not changing schools again," I said.

She shrugged. "Have it your way."

To me and Jennie, Mama said, "You can stay, but keep up the place or it'll never sell." All her last week she avoided eye contact with Mandible; probably she didn't have the guts to tell him to "get," so she was getttin' instead.

He didn't appear to care if she was present or gone. You could still find Mandible Jones, squat and tough and smelly, rooster-ing around our house, even after Mama moved with Roger to his farm down in Union. One thing you could say about Mama, she ever preferred abandoning a mess to tackling it. With her out of the picture, on paper, Mandible—get this—was the responsible adult.

To Jennie and me he said, "Just because your bitch of a ma's gone don't mean I'm moving on. Place is home to me now."

What could we do? It was where we lived, the three of us, uncomfortably through my freshman winter—Jennie, me, Mandible, and the two dogs, until Blackie jumped out of the moving truck bed and got hit on the Blue Rock Highway.

Mandible again said, partly as homage I think to the dog in his half-froze grave, which, to Mandible's credit, he dug in our backyard: "Place is home to me now." This repeat drifted until it sounded like he bit off the ends of the words. He patted the door jamb more fondly than he'd ever petted the dogs, implying Blackie in our ground sealed the deal. Implying that, same as with Blackie's bones, we could never unearth the scaly roots Mandible had managed to set down here.

For a while I'd strayed from my devotion to Jennie, but under examination, it'd been less love for my neighbor lady than thirst for the whole big world out there to kiss and kiss off, including Allison Lowen, Jennie, Mama and even Mandible Jones, also all the social workers, counselors, jailors, and parole officers I'd yet to meet.

"Wisdom," Mandible often said, "lies in knowing where to stick your dick."

Jennie turned a beautiful thirteen while Mama was gone. I marked counting on the calendar so I wouldn't forget how long we'd been motherless, because ours was a house prone to forgetting. Blond Allison, in the pink and grey track suit she wore when she threw knives with me, had already blurred to a silver spot in my mind.

❈

I turned fourteen and Video Village took me on again for the summer, pay always under the table since I didn't have a work permit. Getting Mama, or God forbid Mandible, to vouch for my age and status wasn't worth the aggravation or the allegiance either would demand. It was hard enough tracking Mama down when official school forms needed signing. We all played a role keeping up the "family" charade for district officials who might drive by the house, investigating, hoping to declare once and for all our residency and our family configuration, narrowing down exactly who was in charge. We qualified for the school's free and reduced meals, though by then Jennie was working on skinny and refused everything but the lunch line applesauce.

The part in her blonde hair, when she stood up straight, reached Mandible's nipple. Yes, the man insisted on walking around without a shirt on, especially in summer. Yes, Jennie took to leaning against him, her back to his front, when he stood at the screen door observing the fireflies and the occasional snake curled on top of Blackie's grave he had to rush out and take a hoe to. Jennie, standing there with him, wore collapse in her body's attitude. My sister could make it so she had no backbone and you didn't fault her for it, as she'd been watching and learning from Mama all her life.

I used to bask in Jennie's sweet weight against me. We'd walked to school countless times when it would be raining and us with one umbrella to share. As the taller one, I held it, more to cover her than me, my arm unbent for maximum stretch and tiring terribly from sheltering her.

"Lean with the umbrella," I'd say. That meant lean in to me, too, and she did. So few joys, but this was one.

Now her and him, and I was to stop it?

Movie channel visions of sex plagued me, but I was scheduled for the late video shift so I spit what rose to my tongue. "I'll leave you two to console each other about Blackie, or Mama, or whatever you're using tonight for an excuse."

"Gonna bust your mouth, boy, you talking to your sister like that."

"Talking to you," I muttered.

Mandible spun me around and punched before I'd even had a next thought. Jennie pulled at his arms until he let her hold me and he drifted to the other room.

"Go to work," she whispered, swiveling her attention from him to me and back, her shoulder a barricade between us. She insisted, "Please, just go." Her loose and untied hair had crossed her lips in the tussle, and some caught there, looked like she was eating straw.

I said, "Gladly." But there was no gladness, and there had been none for me since the glimmer of Allison winked out. I shoved past them and through the doorway. Loyal Tanner tried following, but I yelled, "Stay!" and locked his bewildered face inside the fence.

Stay. Or I could leave for work and not come back. The moaning I did to Mama about not switching schools had been for Jennie's benefit because she had little knack for making friends, and I'd wanted to spare her starting over, but I could see it spooling out: she was going to quit school and set up house with Mandible. Little details were accumulating, beginning with her sipping Coke while Mandible let me twist in the wind of Mr. Lowen's tirade, neither of them coming to my aid.

I projected the scene in my busy head until the details of their flirtation made me sick. I used to imagine flames opening holes across Mandible's middle, but they traveled south to burn up my belly instead.

At Video Village I poured popcorn and hot oil into the old fashioned popper we had for the customers. It was our gimmick—giving away a free tub of movie theater popcorn with the rental of five videos. I was a popcorn popping, movie scanning robot. I smiled a robot's smile.

While the popcorn popped, inside my head the gears were whirring and clicking. This is how the counselor in juvie explained it to me: Kids in strung-out circumstances will adapt to survive. They imagine themselves as other children, tended by other, good, people; they invent characters to save them. They fabricate scenes other than the ones stuck to them—golden scenes, truly. She knew my history, the circumstances, it was all there in the file. She tailored her interpretation to me. "The kids," she said, "romp around like dogs, dumb things provided food and shelter, who aren't kicked too much, who sometimes get a scratch behind the ears that draws their mouths up in satisfied doggy grins, teeth showing. In their imaginations, these kids—kids like you—they manufacture a better life, a life that cancels out the one scraping up their knees and their knuckles."

I know it's where I lived half the time, an imaginary place where Jennie had the knife in her hand and she was going to use it, where she was still on my side. In my dream I would take it from her, but first she'd pretend to fight me, as our hands slipped into that twisting, turning memory of our childish handshakes from the 'hood that we'd invented to affirm our solidarity. She'd grunt as she fought me and I'd hold her in a wrestling lock, shielding her body from the blade with my own hand, my voice calm but my muscles screaming, hate urgent and rising inside me so much I could taste what the knife was made of. Yes, urgent, because the moment required urgency. If I didn't act now I'd lose my nerve.

I'd swallow my metal-tinged spit and shush into Jennie's ear: "You'll wake him. Is that what you want?" We hadn't been this close since Mandible, in the absence of Mama, folded Jennie under his wing.

Every pop of the popcorn popper was a gunshot, but we had no guns I knew of, only my knives resting under my bed. When I got home I checked on their storage. An empty box waited for a pair of shoes. In fact, our whole pitiful place housed emptiness and expected fulfillment. Blackie's bones in the ground out back shifted. Tanner howled for his lost brother. Jennie had a knife in her hand and she was going to use it unless I moved to stop her. It was a long walk down the hall to Mama's bedroom—now Mandible's set-up—and I didn't know if my legs would carry me there. Angels helped, I guess; a Guardian Angel, I heard Mama say. Her hand in my memory closed down on my head; I felt her fingernails tickle my scalp. We'd been okay before Mandible, and we'd be okay once he was gone. His elimination was a given, a must-do, but I wouldn't let Jennie take the blame for sticking the knife in him, because it was my eyes razoring holes in his gut, just as I'd imagined from the day we'd been introduced.

I took my time walking that hallway, put my fingers to the bumps on the wall where hairs from the paintbrush had stuck and dried on with the paint, ahead of me sounds that could have been sex or dying, and Jennie taking care of it either way. I lived in the minutes of not knowing, which I wished would tick on forever, the way a brother-sister bond could last a lifetime, but they quit.

New Joe
by Benjamin Buchholz
from Story*GLOSSIA*

1.

From dizzy-distance high up in fluorescent video background flickering Joe dreams this mudbrick stick and donkeyshit dust of streets no one, not even little sisters stuck in a seventh-grade gullible memory of duct-taping them to chairs and pushing them over to laugh at them and then leaving because he could, would think nice, not these streets, rubble, tatter t-shirts tie-dyed and some hairy white mandress strung from telephone lines patched and spliced and webbed from electric-service thievery of who is this, the goodbad guy, anyway?

Well, Joe won't care.

Joe thinks dreams slip past muddy like Tigris mid-rain with gallow great bridges creaking on pilings in concord such cartwheels as have always thumped thump still just now over new Stryker ruts cutting banks built, berms built, mudbrick by mudbrick, dissolved in the tides of flood like time dissolveth soul, 'til these berms dust away and these shanties dust away and these people leave shadows same as Hiroshima dogs caught sunning on a few stacked stones.

Heightening Joe, heightening him, not a sense of him, but him completely, utterly, as if exploding a cicada in the burlesque of June, this stasis: he is, he is tall, he is looming. Joe all fair sandhaired and a few years near twenty but somewhat hardridden in barfight cosmetic hunched in his turret tough-eyed gray-irised hidden behind darkened sunglasses like TV commercials for Army and youthleading now now in his turret water-moves, syrup-moves, sees the ascensions from PacMan to Doom to today what were they video playing?—warrior-games, dark bloodbaths of yes I can have new life now even though I but half-tried and was maybe blithe moments master of something greater than me, while near in the street a six year-old leans out balconies become no longer balconies but gapes,

278

and falls, and this happens fast, too fast, because Joe sees it, every turning torture of it, slowly, crisscrossing no Matrix-scifaiku shrapnel dodging of it but a darting darning punch-hole cleavering, beating her backward in the blown-wide air, all legs camelopard-tan hem-fluttering in a framing of dress the apostate of a parachute, and from three stories she flattens, holy-chested, marbleized, and Joe maynot/cannot reset.

Joe.

Joe, hey, Joe!

Smoke pops, sizzles, Joe hears sizzle, spewed purple like sprayed unholy-colored carnation in Mr. Vanderhoeven's lapel, a cloud, a wry deep wheezing breath Joe cannot breathe and beneath it Sunday-scratchy collars and starchy pants and sweat and being shoulder-pulled to the narthex and the glittergold bellrope disappearing upward into what before his disquiet comingofage he could imagine a heaven to hold but as if punctuation to it Mrs. Vanderhoeven barfed dentures, let sputter on the ground flossed marbles in a stained glass shine near the tread of Joe's father's foot.

Joe, Joe!

Joe dreams mouth-moving speech as squad leader, who, whom, Latin, screams, parse it, high school, he remembers, who, accusative, come on, mount up, mount up, Joe, come, get in, we're clear, Joe come, kiss me Joe his girl, his first girl, before the playbar nightlies when he worked hot machineshop summers hating it but not backthen working with that clatter racket like .50 calibers always snick-snackering and heated, backing up, earlier, simple, simple time before knowing, just experiment, labrat-boy, kissing her, that girl, a Jenny, he dreams some copper-strange tasting remembrance of her tongue and how could anyone like it, kissing, and who, who, who was he?—who was Joe growing up at all even now, here, there, when this did not happen, even though he knew, maybe exactly because he knew, knew deep and denied dredgingly down in his soul-licorice stash because he had no twitch trigger fast enough to stop a six-year-old turning into a puddle of herself. No. He had not stirred, he had not moved, he had not reset, rewound, relived: who was he?

Joe, come along now, my Joe.

2.

Ur.

Deepening.

Joe cleaned and unarmored and toe home within witchy twilit haze of desert fringeland of oilfield burning and salt-airing here and there where marshes once marsh-people millennia cradle-tombed now bellicose erect amongst it tri-strand and berm built from marsh-dust, gravelly truck paths punched up to motorpool kr-krunching, mortar pits, porto-pots, guylines strung whip tight to commstowers and all flown with little white flags waist high that Joe will not trip them in the hotblue suchness of nightwandering.

As if an amen Joe sits humbleleg asprawl on the near lean underneath of the lee tower close to a stretching shade slanting unto him up berm pebble sands from a black electric hum smelling shack, shine on the wipe sweat drip lines of doffed goggles now knee-strapped and dangling where the dustdark hand hangs and between fingers airy half-forgotten as himpart Joe notes the absence of a cigarette.

Joe doesn't smoke.

Or a cellphone.

Joe doesn't talk. Not much to home.

Home is Vanderhoeven remote like thinkthings like cottoncandy sickle sweet but unfilling dissolving saying same things only over and over of missing and wanting and what will we do what fun will we have where will we go and I can't wait until you are back when, in truth, Joe is back, or had never been, and the now and the here and the twitchy nothing horizon blueness of Hummurabi and time are Joe. The rarer, rarer and stranger, like mistaken chord wheezed on attic organ cloth covered and forgotten when the elbow strikes it looking for fishing rods or memoirs, rarer daily the confession connection something near, true, real, spoken, written, text-messaged, instant-messaged with those Vanderhoevens he remembers from through the far fog sea of his coming ashore.

Joe thought more and more he craved, craved and needed, such think things when they were less and less and so he wrote and wrote and spoke and spoke and fretted with head bulging in the burrowed bedcrease against a cool sweating canvas airconditioned inside of sleep. Now, from Baghdad southing

through shot perimeters in stages day and day until here home in the bubble
bristling he sits and sits and listens and listens and has come zen unwitting
nearer to thee, who, whom, ever are.

Shall we speak of it, or sing, now Joe?

There, climbing toward you, a long-sung simpleness of feartruth's being:

And here face down beneath the sun
And here upon earth's noonward height
To feel the always coming on
The always rising of the night

To feel creep up the curving east
The earthy chill of dusk and slow
Upon these underlands the vast
And ever climbing shadow grow . . .[1]

Like singsong the nothought of staring 'til pink purples and purple
blues and the whole thins and shines 'til it is black and besmirching a gilt aeons
immeasurable smallmaking man who cannot fall even upward into aether, who
cannot console himself with his simpleness, Joe has no comfort in nothought
but only a sense of its utter newness and who is he-ness and Joe begins to cry.

3.

This is not to say Vanderhoevens have no worth in the world Joe but
the shellgame begins this berm sun setting stillness of within him. For some
cicada soulform of what he was is the himlimit of any newness, base before
belltower, Krishna/Vishnu, surely as the belltower dusts back into the risen
base and all begins from the beginning of the end: but here.

Joe, have a shoulder, have this bitterblack I brewed in the TOC with
the harp whirl of the mapboards glimmering in their pushpin acetate unknowing that pushpin peoplesymbols are people and pushpin towns but families

---

1.) Excerpted from "You, Andrew Marvel" by Archibald MacLeish and pushpin strikelines show the figure of death striding new upon a long bled bending land, no, I knew you Joe needed time space and now coffee and the sort of silent togetherness that no one who has not warred and lost can know of manfriendly unspeakable bonding. And so, after a moment, because the abyss stares equally into me from above and below and from out in the saltpan waste darkened and howling allsides unending, I will speak so that wetogether from this pebble bank break our fast and flee peace and solitude to take with us some measure of the new into the world mundane that must be lived, age-old, cicada rhythm, of doing and doing and doing and never except in strikeforce blow to the mind can it disfunction long enough to grow.

Joe.

I say that first, just: Joe.

And I wait.

The cigarette absence in the airy finger space clicks.

It was a damn shame, says Joe.

I don't know what you saw, man. (But I do).

It was a damn shame, he says.

I was thinkin' of our girls, I says. I was thinkin' of them all the way back in the HUMMV as I drove, (this in brogue, thick, a show, to maybe make a little laughter, a lewdness, I'm finger motioning to demonstrate slack jawly the taste of a kiss and feeling of my mouthpart on neck and then down in the suppleness of woman that has been so far from me, us, but near me in my thinkthings 'til it is hallucinatory everywhere and troublesome) I drove thinking, gawd, wouldn't I like a little of my Annie tonight and I thought that that Joe, my friend Joe, up there in the turret a-swiveling and keeping me safe, I thought, man, Joe must be just thinking about the same damn thing about his Kim and how maybe we should go bowling just for the hell of hearing the balls crack and to taste the beer and then we'd take our two cars different ways but secrethandshake glance at each other when leaving that alley cause we'd know what would/will come next.

I hit him on the shoulder, a mooncalf chuckle punch.

Yeah, Joe says, yeah.

And I think, in the darkness, Joe smiles.

Four Alabama Seasons
by Michael Martone
from *failbetter*

Winter

Even when the fans are not running under power, they feather in the breeze.
Turning over, the blades mill wind. Flatbeds stacked with chicken cages piled
two stories high pull in behind the wall of fans parked for a turn at the loading
dock. White chickens stuff the black wire cages. The fans start up, turn, blur.
The air pushes through the cages, and feathers spit out the other side. Everywhere
on the ground are loose white feathers. The feathers blow across the street, cars
stirring up the feathers, catch in the breeze that has not been manufactured.
Breeze that is breeze. The feathers form a drift of down next to the red cedar
slat fence of the city's junkyard. Balls of feathers, hefty as chickens and as
plump, tumble into the ditch. Up north, a fence like that would be strung along
a highway to knock the snow out of a blizzard. Loose feathers swirl around
wrecked police black and whites in the lot, begin to tar the car, coat the surface
of muddy puddles left by the rain.

Spring

Spring and all is new green grass drowned by new white, white sand of the golf course
groundskeeping. The rain puts a crust on the traps that must be raked until they
shimmer, a sawing corduroy seen from a distance, a breeze chopping up the surface of
a scummy pond. Pollen, the gist of the season, tarnishes every surface, takes away its
shine, a mat of grainy finish. But today, see? Spilled sparkle of sand curved through
the blacktopped intersection out front, traced a dump truck's too-tight turn. Already,
house sparrows bathe in the fresh dune, intermittent puffs of dust along the drift, a
moon's crescent in shadow. There, the white sand turns black. A mockingbird on the
strung cable mimics the neighborhood's air conditioners. All emit this compressed

chatter as the sun clears the stand of oak soaked with wisteria. It will rain later and the sand will melt, forget itself. That dawn's gesture's just grist.

Summer

Sundays, a white city pickup truck steams slowly through the side street spraying for mosquitoes. The fog machine's engine, an insect, drowns out the sound of the engine of the truck, a steady gearless whine. The fog itself leaps back from a funnel trailing off the bed, appears to propel the truck alone, a jet of clouds under pressure. The white spray dissipates, gets grayer as it spreads and, heavier than air, it trails the truck, a wake that spreads and skirts the curbs of the street. It spills down the hill, fills the hollow, evaporates like that afternoon's rain turning the concrete to vapor. Later, the truck crisscrosses the grid in the neighborhood, the sound muted and amplified by the spaces between houses, the trees, the yards, and the residue settles into the bunkers of the golf course, a ground blizzard sweeping over the greens, a fluid tarp. Above, the moon breaks up, fogged in the fog as it sets through it. The summer air twice thickened.

Fall

White pine. The new needles replace needles that fall as straw, rake into springy piles in the gutter. The hardwoods stay bare-limbed, leaves exhausted. Clouds of mistletoe are caught in the branches, twig mist. The spindly azalea under-story. Too far north for Spanish moss, the trees trap trashed plastic bags, look like shit. But in the crevices and corners and on the stripped branches, lint from the cotton fields gathers. On the scored red brick and the dull mortar in between, woolly cotton patches of the stuff stuffs the joints, points the grout, a seeping spun sugar. The lint escapes the screened-in trailer trucks of the raw harvest or gets kicked up by the gleaning in the fields and threads itself into the wind, winds up coating anything with a burr enough to stick. It snows, little squalls of it accumulated in the niches, the pockets fall has turned out. It is snow that is not snow, a white reminder, until it dyes itself with all the other detritus, becomes the glue of bark and twigs and leaves, leaving nothing but filth, tilth, a kind of felt.

Second Sunday
by Alex Dumont
from *Fawlt Magazine*

There is a little scalpel that sits on my desk, for making very straight cuts in paper. It is part of the work that I do, making the straightest cuts that I possibly can. People find it surprising that you can make a straighter line with a scalpel than with scissors, with one blade than with two. Usually more of a thing makes that thing do its job better. Or when you can get on both sides of a thing, as with scissors, then you yourself can do your job to it better. But I have found the single blade and the steady hand to be the best and simplest instruments at my disposal.

When my mother comes over to clean the apartment from time to time she always eyes that scalpel suspiciously. She looks at it, then at me, and says, "Don't get fancy!" by which she means: Don't kill myself, either on purpose or by accident. No indication has been given that this might happen, but my mother knows that indication means nothing. For the child to die before the parent is a crime against Nature, my mother likes to say, though when my mother ever started caring so much about Nature, I don't know. When she sees the scalpel, she does not see the potential for care and precision, but a latent carelessness or violence, or a dangerous proximity of the two. That isn't even the truth, really. Here is the truth: The truth is that my mother would not clean my apartment if I paid her.

My mother is a very sensitive woman, and in the position, both difficult and enviable, of being a beautiful woman growing old. You can tell she was beautiful both because she is still at least really good looking, handsome even, and because she conducts herself like a beautiful woman does, acting a little crazy or stupid or mean because her looks have made her lazy and there is no reason to do the work of goodness if it isn't required of you. Sometimes when I see my mother flirting with an innocent member of the service industry, I want to stop her, maybe cover her with a sheet. I never do though, because really: She can get us into movies for free. Still! If I were a certain kind of man that my mother likes I would say admiringly, "What a woman," and by this I would mean that she still has it, it is still there, whatever it was. Just to keep the same shape, after awhile, constitutes accomplishment.

But she is susceptible to everything, and liable to crack under the weight of things that a bigger, better woman would kill through laughter.

My mother's sensitivities have presented certain problems, as sensitivities do. Certainly they present the problem of obscuring each other, that is: sometimes there are so many things that might have upset my mother that we don't know what the problem is. For instance, when she was young my mother had her wisdom teeth removed. Her oral surgeon did not suture the wounds in her jaw, for reasons mysterious to everyone but him. Instead, he told her to bite down on gauze until the bleeding stopped. "When you run out of gauze," he said, "Use tea bags. They feel just the same." My mother did what he said, and after 15 minutes of tea bags, she vomited and then fainted. But here was the thing: My mother had both a horror of her own blood, and a total intolerance for caffeine. So she never did know if it was the sight of blood or the tea bags that did her in.

My mother, though, is not a useless woman, nor a helpless one. She has a power all her own. And she is ruthless, but in a way most people call dedicated. If she had had a child just slightly different from myself she would have taken vicious, tremendous care of it. She would have scrubbed skin raw, enforced strict television watching hours and homework times, demanded torrents of extracurricular activities and thank-you cards for all gifts given on all occasions. That child would have been a force, a power; polished like a gem and burning with ability. My mother could have unleashed something on this world. If she had been able to, she could have really made something.

When I was a kid my family used to go over to my cousins' house for dinner once a week, and in the summertime we would eat in the garage where my aunt thought it was cooler, though it never seemed to be. We ate with the garage door open part way, because if you ate in the garage you had to leave the door open or else you would die from gas fumes, my aunt believed. This was my father's sister, my mother's sister did not believe things like that, and anyway she was dead before the time I am thinking of. My mother was a smoker then (although this is now something we share a hatred for) and my aunt made her sit out in the driveway to smoke, partly because my mother had never managed to win the affection of any of my father's five (five!) sisters, and partly because my aunt believed that my mother's cigarettes would ignite the greasy oil and gasoline spots on the garage floor. My aunt, you see, had many beliefs. When she wanted a cigarette, my mother would sigh, always, and take her folding chair out to the dark of the driveway where she would sit with her good, left side facing the garage. This was largely for the benefit of my father's sister; to show her what she might be with a little effort. My mother did not like my aunts all that much either, for what it's worth. But it isn't worth much, and here's why: it is not even really the point of the story.

The point of the story is: Sitting in the driveway, with her lower half all lit up by garage light, and her upper half in the dark, was a woman, my mother. She presented her profile carefully, even though none of us could see it, denied as it was the light that the rest of us sat under. All we could see was the ember at the end of her cigarette hovering like an insect near her throat and face. And when she was almost finished smoking she would saunter down to the end of the driveway and carefully take the last drag before tossing the butt (unfailingly, unerringly) into my aunt's rose bushes. The light of the ember made a line; a pure, clean cut into the darkness. Impossible, then, to love a better woman; and impossible to love even the worst one more.

The Fridge
by M. Thomas Gammarino
from *The Adirondack Review*

Bill works harder than any other worker I've ever had the misfortune of being married to. Ray worked hard too, but Bill works harder. Bill leaves early and returns late, so late it's usually early again. I don't know where he goes. To be honest I don't much care. I cared when it was Ray. Poor Ray. He got to me too soon. I had all sorts of dreams in my head back then. Twenty-two is too early. I wish someone had told me that. But they didn't tell you that sort of thing back then. They might have told you seventeen was too soon, but twenty-two was considered right on track. A woman should get married in the twilight of her good looks, not the dawn of them. I was in the dawn. Now it's the wee hours and I rather like being Bill's wife. Not that I care what he does. It's unhealthy to go around caring about things all the time. His job description and the hours he puts in don't jibe. I'm no fool. Bill does quality control at the factory. I've asked him what they make, but he just says "widgets." I tell him to bring home a widget for me to look at, but he insists that I wouldn't understand because actually it's not widgets they're producing so much as parts for making widgets. I told him he was probably right, I wouldn't understand.

Ray was a veterinarian. He used to have to jerk off horses. He had a pretty good sense of humor, that's what made me fall for him in the first place, but make a crack about his being gay or a beastophile and he'd get all bent out of shape. He was so sensitive about it I had to wonder if he really wasn't one of those things after all. That's not why I left him. I left him because I met Bill and botched things up and when the smoke cleared all that was left was Bill. Back in those days Bill didn't work the way he does now. Oh, he worked, but he made time for me. I'm fine with it though. I get so much pleasure out of just being by myself these days. I've always been pretty much a homebody anyway. I like baking. I can't hardly eat any of the damn things because of my cholesterol, but I like watching them rise and I know there's probably something of the maternal instinct in that, seeing as how I never did manage to have any kids and I'm well past the threshold now. Not that it bothers me at all. I always thought the idea of a kid was probably better than the reality of one. Which is not to say I opposed it outright. I'd have done it with Ray, and I'd have done it with Bill. It just never worked out for some reason. And that's just fine by me. I don't regret a thing. So long as I can sit on the porch each morning and drink my coffee and listen to the thrushes, I'm about as happy as I can imagine being.

I make dinner for Bill, eat my half and put his in the fridge because I never know when he's going to be home. He doesn't call. I don't require it of him. If he's having an affair, good for him. That's the kind of relationship this has turned into. I'm pretty sure he's not going to leave me at any rate. It wouldn't make any sense at our age. There's more meaning in sticking it out. Anyway, even if he did, I don't think I'd be sad. I got bored with sadness a long time ago. He'd live nearby. We'd probably see each other about as often as we do now. I don't think either one of us has the energy or ambition to strike up an argument anymore. Maybe he has left me, I don't know. But I'd say there's about a ninety-eight percent chance the gratin I put in the fridge this evening won't be there when I go in to take out the butter for my bagel in the morning.

There's a park on the other side of the trees there. In the springtime you can hear the little leaguers pinging. Bill grew up in this house. I asked him once if he ever used to play ball over there and he told me about his first at-bat ever, when on the very first pitch of the day he hit one clear into the creek, and then how everyone acted deferential around him for the rest of the day, and then how he never got a hit again.

"What's your sense of time like?" I asked Bill once.

"Time is money, honey," he said. I knew that was going to be his answer, but that wasn't really what I meant and I didn't know how to explain what I did mean. I didn't really know what I meant. But I knew that Bill's sense and my sense were different senses. For me, time's like a river, a flowing thing. For Bill, I think time's probably more like a big block of something. It's all happening at pretty much the same time. When he tells you about that homerun, you'd swear it had happened yesterday, whereas when I think back on my time with Ray, I'm pretty sure I was a different person then. If I had been the me I am now back then, I never would have mucked things up and Ray and I would still be together probably. Not that I regret it, because I swear I don't really feel this kind of thing too acutely the way lots of people would. I do feel bad for Ray though, sometimes.

His mother phoned me up when it happened. He'd been riding his motorcycle down the turnpike when he pulled over, parked the bike, lay down face up on the shoulder of the road, and died. "Did they say what got him?" I asked her, and she said, "Death, honey."

Was it heartache that got him? It's crossed my mind, but I don't really think so. It was fourteen years after the fact and he'd remarried too. He had a golden-haired little girl. I'd see them out walking together in the State Park sometimes. That was one pastime neither of us could abandon. We didn't actually walk together, but we were always there at the same time Saturday mornings. We'd greet each other and catch up for a couple of minutes and I often wondered why neither of us was willing to alter our schedule. What was it we couldn't bear to let go of? That went on for twelve of those fourteen years, and then one day he just stopped coming, and then two years later he lay down on the side of the highway and died. I don't know what happened to make him stop coming to the park when he did.

Bill never wanted to go to the park with me, even when he wasn't busy, which was sometimes back then. "Fat comes with age, it's unavoidable," Bill says. I don't believe that but I don't argue with him. It's all bound up in his sense of time, which I tell you is a block of something, limestone maybe, or saltpeter. For me it's more like a ribbon, a spool of pink shimmering ribbon that someone's holding out the door of an airplane while it zips about the world.

❧

May's my best friend. That's one thing I can say for certain. She's the best friend I'll ever have in this world. It's a damn shame she never wanted to have a family because she would have been one hell of a mother. I sometimes think that's why I married her. My mama died when I was a teenager, the day after I got my driver's license. I never got along real well with my pa, so I really felt something missing when she was suddenly gone. But the day I met May at the driving range, I felt that space fill up in me for the first time in a dozen years. I gave her some pointers on how to drive and she winked at me and all of a sudden it was like I was living life instead of being lived by it. Ray was there with her, and we were old friends. We went to high school together, and I never would have thought I'd have been capable of doing him the way I did him, but

May was just too important to me to let her go. I was terrible. I'd pick her up at work and take her out to dinner. That was before cell phones, so we'd spend the whole time thinking up newer and brighter excuses for her getting home so late. Then we started going to motels and skipping dinner altogether. We both lost weight. I felt bad for Ray. He never suspected, I'm sure. And he was a good guy, no one ever doubted it. But I blocked him out, I had to. A man's got to live his life, and May was just indispensable to mine. Ray died six or seven years later of a stroke.

When I met Anna, though, that was a different kind of thing. I'd found my mother in May, but what I found in Anna was my Venus. The girl knew how to wear a stocking. We met at work. Both of us were doing quality control on carburetor parts. The rest is history. We never once went to the motel where I used to take May, I made sure of it. I loved May, still do to this day. I made that clear to Anna right up front, that I was all for spending some time with her but there was no way in hell I was ever leaving May. She said she understood, and I was amazed she really did seem to be on the same page as me, and it might have ended nice and clean, or continued nice and clean, if I hadn't gotten careless one drunk Indian summer afternoon and gotten her pregnant. The worst part was I couldn't even tell her to abort the thing. I wanted to keep it more than she did.

Now these days I know May's got to be thinking I'm living a double life, and in a sense I am, but the lion's share of the time when I tell her I'm working, I really am working. I'm trying to juggle lots of balls at the moment, and overtime doesn't kick in until after eight hours of work and that's the only time the money really starts to add up. That and weekends and holidays. I feel pretty bad about it, but May's been wonderful. No doubt she's got a good inkling what's going on, but she doesn't give me hell about it. When it comes down to it, I think she probably just wants me to be happy, which is the same thing I want for her. Oh, she gets a little sulky sometimes, but that started long before any of this did. Right around menopause, I'm inclined to think.

Anna's a different story. She's always giving me hell about how I should just leave May and come live with her and Henry. She says May wouldn't even care, and what's weird is I think she's probably right. She'd have a couple of bad days probably, but then it would go rolling right off her back. I've gotten real close to doing it a couple of times too, but I get as far as the suitcases in the attic when I duck out. May's my girl. She's more my girl than Anna could ever be. It just so happens Anna and I have a son in common. And boy do I love that kid. He's started walking, running actually. Anna called me up on my cell phone and told me how his very first steps were a sprint, a kind of two-yard dash before he dropped on his bottom. He hardly cries. Life's all new for him. He's discovering all sorts of things. I watch him watch the world and I'm always surprised to see what he's seeing that I'd forgotten about, like reflections on the floor of a restaurant, or all the crumbs that are all over everything. I like the way his head smells too.

Anna asked me one time who I was going to be buried next to. That got right at the heart of it. I told her I wanted to be cremated, but I never changed my will, which will have me right next to May in the ground. I probably never will change it. I could live with May for eternity, I think. With Anna, one life is enough. She tires me out. She's a good mom though. But not great. May would have been great.

Yesterday May asked me what my sense of time was. She was in one of her moods and wanted me to say something deep, but I was on my way out the door. "Time is money, honey," I said, and she handed me my lunch. But then something made me pause and I said, "How about another cup of coffee?" and I went over and poured her one too.

"Aren't you gonna be late?" she said.

"Probably," I said.

She smiled a smile like she was back in high school again.

I'd do anything to have known her then.

Spectrograms/Repairs
by Laura Mullen
from *Tarpaulin Sky*

I have no body; the "I" has no body: not in the old way. Zones. Pressures. Here
a structural tension there an underlying ache. Historicities. Phases of disquiet
not clearly demarcated from areas of peace. In the on-going conflict someone
hauling out the slide projector, everyone else preparing—*Here let me freshen
that drink*—to more or less sleep. A test case—not first or last. An intermediary
attempt, closely monitored—they don't say that just to be reassuring. Vital
signs. Mostly to see if what tends to be thought of as two distinct systems
still works, compatible: existing in their uneasy but highly functional state
of irritation. No active rejection on either side. As yet. "As yet" as pulse. The
living space. Into which. Each probability as hypostatized. Dimmed to be lit
by the proof: the question of damage held open too long inadvertently.
Reassurance wired in, probably, to excite a mirroring response? Static. In
another room: preparations, earlier versions, later models, mistakes. A
Sentimental Journey. No sudden movements because the upkeep takes time
and effort. "See, it's a *sand* painting." The dream of being perfectly understood
coagulating briefly into grainy legibility among doses of light. Interstices of
approval, the *two* systems (because they're easier to see that way), sitting down
at the [televised] table, in dialogue at *least* the analysts echo for an audience
tuning in late—"This is us in...where was that darling...Darling?" Next

Who's the "we" in "We were so civilized"? Another holiday. I across
you articulate. A distance. Hydraulics of syntax only part of what's involved.
Sections of greasy steel appearing out of nowhere suddenly. Mash notes as
scribbled calculations in the margins of the blueprints, if you read them
carefully: "I have no body." Structural coincidences. Soldering so delicate you
could miss the seam. Nobody. Two days in what's known as 'the shop' to refrag
the memory; ten hours each day of "surgery." A flare or amplitude of *feeling*
could freeze the whole thing, fixed in position awaiting the arrival of those
paid attendants zoned-out on the drugs that make it possible for them to

handle me. This is us at the airport, the train station, in a—what did they call them there?—...a kind of illness, a taxi. Hysterical mixture of actual flesh and gone memory. I'm an example, a warning. With drugs and only after intensive training: a hand that's steady. In the slippages slick places of cited pain replace "me." Relieved at last to be left to my own devices, as they say. As the saying. Frequencies. Only only

Constant breakdowns built in: still shocking. At an early stage of the research, flesh "sensing" the machine as too cold, machine—reacting badly to its experience of the meat environment or 'locker': read as oppressively "hot," even dangerously.... *Relocate.* Refocus. *Who wants another drink.* To call the system dual is to intensify an error but I or we continue to so describe the opposing unstable interfaces. The snacks, their itinerary, a lay-over. Intervening. Parts of parts of things, halfheartedly inventing themselves, utilizing available evidence in combinations at once tired and totally unforeseen. Source and resource sheer materiality. Openings. Migrations. Stalled near the screen. That one's backward, just look at the writing. Discrepancies. Etched in lightly at the edges exactly the edgy confession they'd been seeking—to sign. Expecting

Surface roughened. "Rubble" as if seen from a satellite away. Resonant influences. Omitting the non-relevant features of the phase. Smooth twist of the prefabricated substitute in the meat sheath. Casual kindness causing a more or less ragged check in the gliding hum of *I don't feel anything* under the mantra-like hiss of the chorus which is Accomplishment. Even the lightest, most casual, rudeness might be too much for the delicate interlockings already under strain, frugal lubrications—doled out by the-system-that-knows-best— sizzling off already. Wisp of *What the....* Cordite tang. A 'thin skin' fries the finger a clumsy mechanic waves in the air, like a lit match: "Fuck!" An uninflected frame walked empty through the air: space for a question that doesn't get asked. Work of processed regret, incomplete collections of details in some inadequate assemblage calling attention to the unfinished: "We always meant to go back, but...." Shifting in the dimness. Deleted to meet you. Hot, isn't it. Complex shapes patched in as requested, wetting down the blistered digit in his mouth so it actually comes out "Whuck!" An interface degrades at timed intervals to keep the fragile assemblage from rejecting its components. A prototype. Not, I repeat, a success. Not "yet." Always room for improvement the technicians say in passing giving one side of the thing a whack with a spanner, for luck. Built to spec. under constant

Description: a sequence of condensations and cloudy orbits, wind-animated expanse, granular beliefs launched in overlapping elliptical drifts. Shadow-crossed this visible drag of hesitant glottal stops veering off into an ether of scrimped and unlikely guess. "Well it looks like...." I'm the manual ('in the flesh') wherein to read is to dissect. Skimming back off the burn point. Translate. To be frank they left the leaving mechanism inside to go after the always retreating detritus: *You knew what I meant* etc.. Another tourist trap. Pale scraps of mangled information and then another invasive procedure on the site of a *well-educated* guess. Stifled laughter. To sit again through the trip. Bodiless. A coded function totals what always gets left out. *Here's looking at you.* Detailed to the point of incoherence. Mumbling the sentence's outline back down into tape hiss. Dissolved to resonance: that ever I was marketed here to. Set. The profit

Pressure checks the loose stuff; blank screen signing a resistance as they pull the acoustics out through the perforations. With tremulous fingers you reach up: "I can't believe it's not...." Reference. A snake pit of extension cords taking over the studio where they blow dry the ethical subject for the sound bite. No way to find out what it's really worth. Try not to collaborate? Some part constantly being replaced so identification requires a complex and increasingly lengthy series of weary procedures. A sort of rosary: "This is us at...." But I trust you. Amplitudes. Increasing fortifications of a fragility that already bores us: those circuits removed or rendered useless. A pissed-off technician pulling a double shift whacks hot metal once, hard, with whatever comes to hand though the machine isn't why he burned himself. Abjure the single. Explanation. *Don't* replicates

A tear in tangled masses of optic fiber: somewhere a gap and for a few days it's down, out of reach. Multiple intensities and then numbness. More photographs. A certain stiffness in the seen comes to stand for how real it seemed, once. Before the crash a wheezed scramble of signals: each term infecting the other in an augmented receiver, unable to hear what separates. Wait. Where meat meets wiring what's nobody's fault flinches once and lies still: "In the pines, in the pines, where the sun never...." Sizzle. Notified presence: a wavering program finding its way through the forest alone, darkling. Shove(d) uncurling cables back in and solder(ed) the left side down: an afterimage of sparks still burning between us. Watched them slamming the lockers, clocking out. Fizz of the fire-punctured air. Holes in the cage *big enough to*. A collection of "residual ideologies" drains away as that window moves past

As if what didn't work more certainly exists and in its non or malfunctioning draws an inflamed attention to itself and (retained in the next stage as irritated memory "tissue") stays frozen in that configuration in the harmonics—despite constant fixing, assurances, and the apparent lack of further problems—to be remembered as broke. Traces of "forgiveness" suspend even those most committed to solutions coming from outside the damaged set. Loosen that nut. "As if" among the elements. Voiceless. That cathedral of light—upside down—hangs precarious for an instant and (one story about where the time went not even half finished) a smiling sun-burnt couple apparently fall headfirst with it into emptiness; laughed off. Strained analogies the actual substance; you are right there *is* something wrong. Certain possibilities viscous in the adherence of what can feel like presence to what was abandoned once

Where the steady tick tick shifts attachments. Currents. Formant. Gradually old meanings rewired or cut off: the registered data. "I," insisted on—(bodiless) (urgency) trying to call back. Longing to meet you. Crashing the memorial service. Waits for reappraisal, reassemblage, reactivation, running some tests on my own initiative. Under the unchanging light they insist on for their work. One goal to "feel better" than this. Each operation involves a series of delicate calculations taking both crisp untenanted future and soggy past into account. Constant expansions and contractions factored in in cracks and panics. Lights. But—complete silence—you'd hardly spend so much time in the shop if. What works sounds likes (laughter) and then I am myself also (trying to laugh). Come(s) to me. A field of inscription, some critical section falling to the oil-stained concrete floor with a defeated clank. *Time for a smoke*. Obscene, the organic aquiver in its saline bath. Recess(ed). They lift the thing out and look at it disgusted for a moment. Miss me? Gleaming lack of access or a pattern water might make on the underside of a bridge, allowed landscape. Damp eyes of the authorized mourners. Sheers past—that shimmer—on the wall as they throw it out. It. Something to think (about)

Broken for inspection, totally replaceable, every interchangeable part infinitely replicated among other variations. Up for sale, marked down, must go, amid the similar, assembled on the cheap. Under a section of foreign sky:

pretty and desolate. The point *likeness*. Wind. Rustling through shreds of stained plans and lists. Available memory stumbles into the sunset filling in the blanks for the guests. Gratitude dissipates in a reflective surface tarnished to allusion—whose vanished breath. Shattered firmament or shattered glass. Philosophers in coveralls, nails broken and black, where ethics is craftsmanship. A *sense* of the past. No death now could move us. Burning off the residue of an interior attempted as time lag, evidenced as an effort to catch my. Escaping in that abruptly stifled bright laugh. Whose vacation was it? No death now could move us like

Knickers
by Tom Sheehan
from *Wheelhouse Magazine*

I was fighting it all the way, wearing knickers, me, twelve going on thirty it felt some days, dreams about Ginnie Wilmot practically every night now, the morning dew being the vague remnants my father spoke about with a smile on his face, new hairs in my crotch, my mother wanting her boy *to look neat*, my father looking at the horizon almost saying *this too will pass*. It was his one-shoulder shrug that carried verb and noun in its arsenal. I had early discovered that he did not need a lot of words.

My mother was looking at her choice of two hats, checking them out in the mirror on her bureau. A dried flower was creased in cellophane in one corner of the mirror; I'd heard some reference about it but had declined interest. My father's picture, him in a Marine uniform, was framed in a second corner, my sisters and me in another, in our Sunday best a year earlier. A palm frond from Palm Sunday twisted itself across the top of the mirror. I think the hats were as old as I was. I knew she would pick the purple one. Her eyes announced the decision prematurely; again, an article of speech. Much of the time we were a family of silence, where looks or shrugs or hand gestures or finger pointing said all that was needed. My cousin Phyllenda had given the hat to her. "You'll look great in this one." I could never tell my mother Phyllenda's boyfriend had swiped it from a booth in Dougherty's Pub in Malden Square where he'd go of an evening or two. I'd seen them talking an evening on the porch, Dermott's hand up under Phyllenda's dress and it not yet dark.

A May Sunday was a bit snappy this early with the sunrise. "There will be hundreds of people at Nahant Beach today." Both the radio in the bedroom and the kitchen were on; her music almost mute in the background. She looked out the window across Cliftondale Square, across the green of the traffic circle and the new green of elms already leaping at full growth against the sky. On the third floor we lived, yet not as high as some of the elms. Gently a nod was spoken, an affirmation. "They are waiting for summer at the beach," she added.

"They go walking on the beach looking for it. It's over the horizon a few weeks yet. We will go right from church. You will wear your new green suit." At length it had become her trip-hammer approach, the hard music. In that voice I felt the agencies of iron and slag at a mix. "You don't know how proud I am of you in your new suit. And two pair of pants, at that." For sure, iron and slag in her words, the new and the dross. At her lighting up about the new suit, I cringed. *Two pair of pants* seemed eternal, would carry me into high school, into football, the mold of the locker-room, pal-talk growing the way my older brother would nod, owning up to all I had heard. Hell, there'd be knickers, for God's sake, for girls, lots of them prettier than Ginnie Wilmot who once sat across a log flashing her white underpants at me so that something happened in my throat, something so dark and dry and dreadful that I can taste it yet.

Simon Goldman it was who sprung the suit on my mother, little shrunken Simon with the poppy eyes and the red face, on Saturday morning collecting his due of pennies she yet owed on a parlor set. "It's green herringbone tweed, my Helen," he said, in that possessive delivery he must have developed early in his game. "It has two pair of pants. For you yet cheaper than anyone. Resplendent he will be in it. Resplendent. No boy in this whole town has a suit like it. And the famous golfers wear knickers, I've seen them in newsreels at the theater. Hogan and O'Brien and Downey, McDevitt and Fitzpatrick, McHenry and that Shaun whoever from Swampscott." He was inventive, you had to admit. I'd have said a liar as well as a schemer. "Two pair of pants. Green. Herringbone. Think of the message."

His eyes almost fell out of his head, dropping Ireland almost at his feet, dropping it at her feet. I almost pushed him down the stairs, he was at it again, selling her, saying it was a bargain, saying you people are climbing the social ladder on my advice and merchandise. Truth is, she cautioned me once, only once, on how I should remember Simon. "I found him," she had said, "he didn't find me."

The worst part of it all, putting on the suit, the knickers with knee length socks, was having to take off my sneakers. I thought they were welded to me. I thought I'd wear them forever. I belonged in sneakers, foul or fair, "But not in your new suit." It was as if her whole foot had come down on the subject. My father lifted his chin, flicked his head aside, gave off a mere suggestion of a nod, shrugged his shoulders. *This too shall pass.* With a knife he could not have carved it deeper.

In my new greenery we headed for Nahant Beach, me in my green knickers, four sisters all dolled up in the back seat of the old Graham, the titters and snickers behind their hands, my unsworn vow becoming animate at the back of my mind, a prowler on the outskirts of a campground.

Up front, in her purple hat, a purple dress with a big collar, a black pocketbook with an over-scored but lustrous patina, my mother looked straight ahead, playing now and then with the knob on the radio, trying to catch La Scala or New York out for a morning stroll.

She stared at nothing she might wish to have. Beside her, between her and my father in a car borrowed from my uncle, was the second pair of green herringbone knickers. Not knowing why they were there, I nevertheless felt my father's hand in it. I wondered if there had been an argument's movement along with the package, or behind it. Arguments I had heard, about dozens of things, then quiet discussions. Once it had been about the radio one could hardly hear. "Music has shaped me," my mother once said, "from the very first touch to the very first clench of fist." That's when I knew she loved the brass of a band or an orchestra, not just the oompa of it, but the cold clear energy of horns clearing their throats with melodies one could only dream of.

"Toot the horn," my mother said. "Now there's Dolly Donovan." Her wave was thorough and friendly. No message hung on its signal. "She'll be at the beach. Maurice will bring her." I did not deflect a message in that pronouncement: it came anyway. Maurice bid and Maurice done. Some laws, it seemed to say, were carved in stone. It could have said *Life is more than being made to wear green knickers*, but I wouldn't let it.

In the rearview mirror I caught my father's eye. "We might as well see what Forty Steps looks like today, and then come back to the beach." The gears downshifted as he swung the corner down Boston Street in Lynn. We had come over the bridge spanning the Saugus River. In my nose the salt was alive, and pictures came with it. The gulls, by the hundreds, whipped a frenzy. Waves dashed on the rocks of Nahant, especially where Forty Steps climbed upward from the froth of water. The lobster boats, working yet, bobbed out on the Atlantic. Under sunlight majestic white sails of sloops and schooners and sailboats from Elysium, Islands of the Blessed and Marblehead darted like skaters before the wind. On that same wind brigantines and caravels and corsairs leaped from my reading, taking me away from green knickers and

Nahant all the way back to Elysium and Ginnie Wilmot, the salt spray clean and sprightly and the dry vulture of taste yet in my throat from one glimpse of white underpants. Would that mystery, that sight, never go away?

The Graham, brush-painted green, lumpy for the tour of Nahant where Cabots and Rockefellers and Lowells and Longfellow himself once sat their thrones, cruised along the Nahant Causeway. In the slight breeze you could feel the sun bleaching stones, sand, the inner harbor's glistening rocks throwing off plates of light like the backs of hippopotami caught in a satin lacquer. People dressed for church and late dinners and nights on the town walked along the beach, their best clothes akin to badges of some sort. "My, look at that white hat with the huge brim," my mother said, pointing out a woman holding a man's arm, three children at their heels. The girls were still giggling behind their hands, restrained while my father was driving, on their best behavior. Once on the beach they would become themselves. And I would set about de-suiting myself.

When we strolled over to the Forty Steps, the waves talking to us, the crowd of people on all approaches, I saw other boys in knickers, but no herringbone green tweed. No iron mother holding her whip and her pride in one hand. A few giggles and *harrumps* I heard, the way my grandfather could talk, making a point or two on his own. No question in my mind they were directed at my pants more than the whole suit. These people could also nod, shrug, gesture, make sense without words. I wondered what made me want to read in the first place, seeking all the adventure of new words, in this wide world of the body's semaphore, so expressive, so legitimate.

I knew it wouldn't take long, not at Nahant, not at the edge of the great ocean itself, not here where the Norsemen and Vikings and Irish sailors were flung across the seas with Europe behind shoving them relentlessly. My parents, arm in arm, walked on pavement, the girls broke free with yells, I fled down to the rocks at the ocean's edge. With an odd gesture, my mother lifted a hand to her face, as if surprise dwelt there to be touched, to be awakened, to be lifted for use. That's when I knew she was the smartest person in the whole world. She had seen it all coming, had practically choreographed the whole thing, and my father thinking he was in control all that time. At last she had measured me against all other boys in knickers. And found something wanting.

Green is as green does, I could almost hear myself say as I slipped on the rocks heavy with seaweed still with salt, still with water, still with an unbecoming dye residing pimple-like, blister-like, pod-like, in its hairy masses. It was more like sitting down in puddled ink, that intentional trip, trying to be a loving son, finding it so difficult in green knickers, obeying more primal urges.

"What a mess you've made of yourself," she said when she saw me, that hand still in surprise at her face. "Go up to the car and change your pants. I brought the other pair along," *so you could get rid of them also*, she seemed to say. My father had found the horizon to his liking, the thin line of boyhood and manhood merging out there on the edge of the world; no shrug of the shoulder, no sleight of hand, but a look outward that was as well a look backward. I saw it all.

I'm so shit lucky, I said to myself, loving them forever, and then some.

Notable Works

Coming to America - A Remix
by Chris Albani
from *Tarpulin Sky*

Mystery Train
by Sherman Alexie
from *failbetter*

Rick Green
by Stephen Aidon
from *Five Chapters*

Armadillo Hunting with an Old Man
by Joby Bass
from *On the Page Magazine*

The Folk Singer Dreams of Time Machines
by Matt Bell
from *SmokeLong Quarterly*

Here, Not Here, Here
by Aaron Burch
from *StoryGLOSSIA*

Lighthouse
by Dan Chaon
from *Hot Metal Bridge*

Notes from an Underground
by Stephan Clark
from *NOÖ Journal*

All That Is Solid
by Susan Daitch
from *Guernica*

Price of Hard Fish
by Hardy Jones
from *Dogzplot*

Mediterranean Prostitute in Sirocco
by Matthew Kaler
from *Fawlt Magazine*

Wax and Gold V
by Kerry Krouse
from *Mississippi Review*

The Difference between Home and Here
by Robert Lopez
from *Sno*Vigate*

Huevos
by Lou Matthews
from *failbetter*

The Deer
by Fred McGavran
from *StoryGLOSSIA*

Our Town
by Corey Mesler
from *Menda City Review*

Speaking Portuguese
by Darlin' Neal
from *Keyhole Magazine*

Waiting
by Gina Ochsner
from *Freight Stories*

How Much
by Matthew Olzmann
from *The Cortland Review*

Hard Canvas
by Ryan Smithson
from *Identity Theory*

Pharmacy
by Jay Snodgrass
from *Juked*

Trinity Site
by Stacey Swann
from *Memorious*

How to Perfect a Cliché
by Katherine Taylor
from *Five Chapters*

Surface Properties of the Moon
by Jessica Trudeau
from *Menda City Review*

Hogs
by J.A. Tyler
from *Prick of the Spindle*

Two Short-Short Stories
by Laura van den Berg
from *Guernica*

The Golden Dragon Express
by Laura van den Berg
from *Storyglossia*

The End of the World, the Wend of the Lord
by Kellie Wells
from *Diagram*

Hammer
by Kevin Wilson
from *Waccamaw*

Intellectual Property
by Angela Woodward
from *Monkeybicycle*

Contributors Notes

Waqar Ahmed lives and writes in Brooklyn. He is currently working on a novel and a collection of short stories.

Arlene Ang is the author of *The Desecration of Doves* (2005), *Secret Love Poems* (Rubicon Press, 2007) and *Bundles of Letters Including A, V and Epsilon* (Texture Press, 2008), co-written with Valerie Fox. She lives in Spinea, Italy where she serves as a poetry editor for *The Pedestal Magazine* and *Press 1*. More of her writing may be viewed at www.leafscape.org.

Michael Baker, once from Ohio, now New Jersey, is an award winning poet, a teacher of university composition classes, a frequent contributor to *Trouser Press* and *Zisk*, and a writer of extended *Perfect Sound Forever* essays on The Kinks, Cleveland in the 1970's, and Alex Chilton. He is working on essays about Rita Dove, the band Family, John Ashbery, and the use of doorways in the films of John Ford. He has a perfect son.

Marcelo Ballvé was born in Buenos Aires and now lives in New York. His essays have appeared in the *San Francisco Bay Guardian*, the *San Francisco Chronicle*, the *Baltimore Sun*, and NPR. In 2007, he co-founded community newspaper *El Sol de San Telmo* in the Buenos Aires historic district.

Marge Barrett received an MFA from the University of Minnesota. She was the former editor of *River Images* for the St. Croix ArtBarn and faculty advisor of *Ivory Tower* for the University of Minnesota. She has published prose and poetry in numerous magazines, most recently in *SN Review*, *The Broome Review*, *Dust and Fire*, and online with hotmetalbridge.org and hotmetalbridge.net. She won the Marcella DeBourg Fellowship at the University of Minnesota, creative work awards from the College of St. Catherine and grants to writing programs in Prague and St. Petersburg. Currently she teaches at the Loft Literary Center in Minneapolis, Minnesota.

Carmelinda Blagg's short story "Geographies" first appeared in the online journal *Avatar Review* and other of her fiction has been published more recently in the online journal *Halfway Down the*

Stairs. She has also written a number of poetry reviews for the literary journal *Poet Lore*. She received her MA in Writing from Johns Hopkins University and lives in Bethesda, Maryland where she is a member of the Writers Center.

Benjamin Buchholz is a US Army officer. He is currently attending the Defense Language Institute course in Arabic Language. His story "The Cabalfish" appeared in last year's *Best of the Web* anthology.

Blake Butler is the author of *EVER* (Calamari Press) and *Scorch Atlas* (forthcoming Featherproof Books). His work has appeared in *Fence*, *Ninth Letter*, *New York Tyrant*, *Willow Springs*, etc. He lives in Atlanta, edits HTML Giant, and blogs at blakebutler.blogspot.com.

Jimmy Chen maintains a blog and archive of his writing at the Embassy of Misguided Zen. He lives in San Francisco. Please visit him at www.jimmychenchen.com.

Amy L Clark is an assistant professor of English composition at Pine Manor College. Her work has appeared or is forthcoming in several literary journals, including *Hobart*, *Quick Fiction*, and *Action Yes Quarterly*, and her collection of short short fiction *Wanting* is part of the book *A Peculiar Feeling of Restlessness* (Rose Metal Press). Amy has always secretly wanted to be an astronaut.

Amber Cook's work has appeared online at *Toasted Cheese*, and is forthcoming elsewhere. She lives in Nashville, TN.

Bill Cook's recent work has been published in *SmokeLong Quarterly*, *elimae*, *Right Hand Pointing*, *Tin Parachute Postcard Review* and other online journals. "Little Witches" was originally published in the 2008 Spring issue of *The Summerset Review*.

Michael Czyzniejewski grew up in Chicago and now lives in Ohio, where he teaches at Bowling Green State University and serves as Editor-in-Chief of *Mid-American Review*. His fiction has appeared in many journals and on my many websites, including *waccamaw.com*. His first collection of stories, *Elephants in Our Bedroom*, debuted in February 2009 from Dzanc Books.

Matthew Derby is the author of *Super Flat Times: Stories*. He lives in Pawtucket, RI.

Ryan Dilbert is a writing teacher, a sometimes stand-up comedian and the editor of *Shelf Life Magazine*. His stories have appeared in *FRiGG*, *Bartleby-Snopes*, *White Whale Review*, and *decomP*.

Stephen Dixon has published twenty-seven books of fiction, fourteen novels, and thirteen collections of short stories. His next, a three-volume story collection called *What Is All This?*, is forthcoming from Fantagraphics Books.

Alex Dumont lives, and was raised, in Brooklyn, NY. She is co-editor of the forthcoming journal *The Wild*, and her work can be found in *The Bard Papers*, *Fawlt*, and *Chapter and Verse*.

Claudia Emerson earned her BA from the University of Virginia and her MFA from the University of North Carolina at Greensboro, where she was poetry editor for *The Greensboro Review*. Her poems have appeared in *Poetry*, *Smartish Pace*, *The Southern Review*, *Shenandoah*, *TriQuarterly*, *Crazyhorse*, *New England Review*, and other journals. *Pharaoh, Pharaoh* (1997), *Pinion, An Elegy* (2002), *Late Wife* (2005), and *Figure Studies* (2008) were published as part of Louisiana State University Press's signature series, Southern Messenger Poets, edited by Dave Smith. *Late Wife* won the 2006 Pulitzer Prize for poetry. An advisory and contributing editor for *Shenandoah*, Emerson has been awarded individual artist's fellowships from the National Endowment for the Arts and the Virginia Commission for the Arts, and was also a Witter Bynner fellow through the Library of Congress. She was awarded the 2008 Donald Justice Award from the Fellowship of Southern Writers. Currently serving as Poet Laureate of Virginia, she is Professor of English and Arrington Distinguished Chair in Poetry at the University Mary Washington in Fredericksburg, Virginia.

D.A. Feinfeld's work has appeared in many journals, including *Ploughshares*, *JAMA*, *Atlanta Poetry Review*, *RE:AL*, *The Hollins Critic*, *Sulphur River Literary Review*, *Heliotrope*, *Slant*, and *Centennial Review*. He's had poems published in four anthologies: *Blood and Bone* (University of Iowa Press 1998), *Verse and Universe* (Milkweed Editions 1998), *The Practice of Peace* (Sherman Asher Press 2001), and *Private Practice* (University of Iowa Press 2006). He has also published three books of poetry: *What Do Numbers Dream Of?* (University Editions 1997), *Bestiary of the Heart* (Fithian Press 2000), and *Rodin's Eyes* (Fithian Press 2004).

310

Contributors

Marcela Fuentes has published stories in the *Indiana Review, Storyglossia, Vestal Review,* and in *New Stories from the Southwest,* (Ohio University/ Swallow Press January 2008). Recent work is forthcoming in the fall issue of *Blackbird.* She is a Teaching-Writing Fellow at the Iowa Writers' Workshop. She lives in Iowa City and is completing her first novel.

M. Thomas Gammarino has an MFA from The New School and is most of the way through a Ph.D. at the University of Hawaii. Some of his recent fiction and essays have appeared in *The New York Tyrant, Word Riot, NOÖ Journal,* and *Elimae.* His first novel, *Big in Japan: A Ghost Story,* is due out November 1, 2009 from Chin Music Press.

Cassandra Garbus's novel, *Solo Variations,* was published in hardcover by Dutton in 1998, and Plume published the paperback in 1999. Her short essay on race relations in New York City private schools appeared in the Op-Ed Section of the *New York Times* in 2000. In addition, she has written for several parenting magazines.

Molly Gaudry edits *Willows Wept Review* and Willows Wept Press, co-edits *Twelve Stories,* and is an associate editor for *Keyhole Magazine.* Find her online at mollygaudry.blogspot.com.

Anne Germanacos' work has appeared in over sixty literary reviews and anthologies. In 2010, a collection of her short stories will be published by BOA Editions. She lives in San Francisco and on the island of Crete.

Matt Getty, the self-proclaimed world's best writer ever, is the award-winning author of *You Will Behave,* the first book-length work of fiction written entirely in the second-person future. Getty's short fiction has also appeared in *Opium Magazine, FRiGG Magazine, Pindeldyboz, Rainbow Curve, Tatlin's Tower,* and *The GW Review.* He lives with his wife and two daughters in Pennsylvania, where he maintains www.mattgetty.com, a Web site filled with what he describes as "free entertainment for people who are smarter than me."

Todd Hasak-Lowy was born in Detroit and raised in its suburbs. He has been a Detroit Lions fan his whole life, sometimes enthusiastically, often reluctantly. In addition to attempting to survive his melancholy Sundays, Todd is an assistant professor of Modern

311

Hebrew Literature at the University of Florida. He is the author of a story collection, *The Task of This Translator* (Harcourt, 2005), a novel, *Captives* (Spiegel & Grau, 2008), and an academic study, *Here and Now: History, Nationalism, and Realism in Modern Hebrew Fiction* (Syracuse University Press, 2008). He lives in Gainesville, Florida with his wife and two daughters.

Karen Heuler's stories have appeared in anthologies and in dozens of literary and speculative publications. She has published two novels and a short story collection, and has won an O. Henry award. Her latest novel, *Journey to Bom Goody*, concerns strange doings in the Amazon. She lives and plots in New York City.

Ash Hibbert is something of a creative writing degree junkie. He has recently finished a novella for a Master of Creative Arts at the University of Melbourne in Victoria, Australia; he has completed a Postgraduate Diploma of Creative Writing, and an undergraduate degree in Professional Writing with honours. The English-Arabic journal *Kalimat* and the University of Melbourne journal *Strange2Shapes* have published his work. He also co-edited the Deakin University literary journal, *Verandah 15*. Hibbert is the resident writer of his own web-log, acoldandlonelystreet.blogspot.com.

Philip Holden has lived in Britain, the United States, China, Taiwan, Canada, and Singapore. He currently teaches at the National University of Singapore, and is the author of books on W. Somerset Maugham, autobiography and decolonization, and Southeast Asian literature in English. With Shirley Lim and Angelia Poon, he is currently editing *Writing Singapore*, the first historical anthology of Singapore literature in English. His fiction has been published in *Prism International* (Canada) and *Cha* (Hong Kong).

Roy Kesey is the author of three books: a story collection called *All Over* (Dzanc Books), a novella called *Nothing in the World* (Dzanc Books), and *Nanjing: A Cultural and Historical Guide for Travelers* (Atomic Press.) He recently won the Jeffrey E. Smith Editors' Prize in Fiction at *The Missouri Review*, and his work has appeared in more than seventy other magazines, as well as several anthologies including *Best American Short Stories*, *The Robert Olen Butler Prize Anthology* and *New Sudden Fiction*. He presently lives in Syracuse with his wife and children.

Hari Bhajan Khalsa's time is split between the fast lane of Los Angeles and the mule deer and red-tailed hawks outside the little town of Sisters, Oregon. She is a Life Coach, workshop facilitator and writer of poems and personal essays, married, with one son. She graduated from Vermont College with a B. A. in Creative Writing in 2005 after a hiatus from school for 30 years. Her poems have been published, or are forthcoming in *Fulcrum*, *HazMat Review*, *New York Quarterly*, *Red Rock Review*, *Snow Monkey*, *Wild Violet*, *Roanoke Review*, *Tiger's Eye*, *Schuylkill Valley Journal* and *Phantasmagoria*. In poetry and in life she's always looking for the word, the inspiration, the connection.

Tricia Louvar, born in Iowa, is a writer, editor, and poet. She lives in a bucolic area of Los Angeles. For more of her work, please visit www.tricialouvar.com.

Peter Markus is the author of a novel, *Bob, or Man on Boat* (Dzanc Books), as well as three short books of short-short fiction, *Good, Brother* (Calamari Press), *The Moon is a Lighthouse* (New Michigan Press), and *The Singing Fish* (Calamari Press). A new collection of stories, *We Make Mud*, is forthcoming in 2011 from Dzanc Books.

Michael Martone's new books are *Racing in Place*, essays, *Double-wide*, collected stories, *Not Normal, Illinois*, an anthology of peculiar fictions from the Flyover, and *Michael Martone*, a memoir made up of contributor's notes just like this one.

Heather McEntarfer teaches developmental and creative writing at Niagara University. A graduate of Hiram College, she earned her MFA in creative nonfiction at the University of Pittsburgh. "Catching Hell" is part of her nonfiction manuscript, *High Water Rising*, which details the experiences of families involved in a current desegregation controversy in Raleigh, set against the re-segregation of US schools. Heather lives in Lewiston, NY with her dog, Bailey.

Lindsay Merbaum received her MFA from Brooklyn College where she was a winner of the Himan Brown Award for Fiction. Her stories have appeared in *Sojourn, the Brooklyn Review* and *Our Stories*. In 2009 she was nominated for a storySouth Award. Lindsay currently lives in Quito, Ecuador and is at work on a novel.

Corey Mesler has published in numerous journals and anthologies. He has published two novels, *Talk: A Novel in Dialogue* (2002) and *We Are Billion-Year-Old Carbon* (2006). His first full length poetry collection, *Some Identity Problems* (2008), is out from Foothills Publishing and his book of short stories, *Listen: 29 Short Conversations*, appeared in March 2009. He also has two novels set to be published in the next year. He has been nominated for the Pushcart Prize numerous times, and one of his poems was chosen for Garrison Keillor's Writer's Almanac. He has two children, Toby, age 20, and Chloe, age 13. With his wife, he runs Burke's Book Store, one of the country's oldest (1875) and best independent bookstores. He also claims to have written "These Boots are Made for Walking." He can be found at www.coreymesler.com.

Laura Mullen is a Professor at Louisiana State University. She is the author of five books: three collections of poetry—*The Surface, After I Was Dead*, and *Subject*—and two hybrid texts, *The Tales of Horror* (Kelsey Street Press 1999) and *Murmur* (futurepoem books 2007). Prizes for her poetry include Ironwood's Stanford Prize, and she has been awarded a Board of Regents ATLAS grant, a National Endowment for the Arts Fellowship and a Rona Jaffe Award, among other honors. She has had several MacDowell Fellowships and is a frequent visitor at the Summer Writing Program at the Jack Kerouac School of Disembodied Poetics at Naropa. Her poems have been widely anthologized and has recently appeared or is forthcoming in *Octopus, 1913, Bomb, Hotel Amerika, the Corpse, Ploughshares*, and elsewhere. Mullen's work is included in *American Hybrid*, just out from Norton. Recent prose has been collected in *Civil Disobediences: Poetics & Politics in Action*, and in other anthologies, and the *Denver Quarterly* published her essay on the poetry of John Yau. Jason Eckardt's setting of "The Distance (This)" (from *Subject*) premiered at the Miller Theater in New York and was performed at the Musica Nova festival in Helsinki.

Darlin' Neal's story collection, *Rattlesnakes and the Moon*, was a 2008 finalist for the New Rivers Press MVP award and a 2007 finalist for the GS Sharat Chandra Prize. In the last three years, her work has been nominated seven times for the Pushcart Prize, and appears in *The Southern Review, Shenandoah, Puerto del Sol* and numerous other magazines. Her work has been selected for the forthcoming anthologies *Online Writing: The Best of The First Ten Years*; *Dogs Wet and Dry: A Collection of Canine Flash Fiction*; *In Our Own Words: A Generation Defining Itself - Volume 8*; and *Southern Poetry Anthology: Volume II, Mississippi*.

She is assistant professor of creative writing in the University of Central Florida's MFA program and this year's final judge for *Wigleaf*'s Top 50 Flash Fiction.

A carpenter by trade and profession, **Joseph Olschner** has worked on his poetry, his music, his graphic arts in the wee hours, raised 4 beautiful girls for 11 years until asked to find another address by a great gal. Because he was lucky enough to have been a surfer on the Outer Banks for the past 58 years, he has learned not one thing worth remembering unless it is how connected we are to the movement of change. And part of that change has come upon this acceptance, his first professional publication of one of his songs. Thanks to *Arsenic* and cheers to all rank strangers.

Jeff Parker is the author of the novel *Ovenman* (Tin House Books) and with William Powhida the collection of art and stories *The Back of the Line* (DECODE). A short story collection, *The Taste of Penny* (Dzanc Books), and a nonfiction book, *Where Bears Roam the Streets* (Harper Collins), are forthcoming in 2010. With Mikhail Iossel he co-edited the anthologies *Rasskazy: New Fiction From a New Russia* (Tin House Books, 2009) and *Amerika: Russian Writers View the United States* (Dalkey Archive, 2004). He is currently the Acting Director of the MA in Creative Writing at the University of Toronto.

Elise Paschen is the author of *Bestiary* (Red Hen Press, 2009), as well as *Infidelities*, winner of the Nicholas Roerich Poetry Prize, and *Houses: Coasts*. Her poems have been published in *The New Republic*, *TriQuarterly* and *The Hudson Review*, among other magazines, and in numerous anthologies. She is editor of *Poetry Speaks to Children* and co-editor of *Poetry Speaks Expanded* and *Poetry in Motion*. Paschen teaches in the Writing Program at the School of the Art Institute of Chicago.

Elizabeth Penrose lives in Pittsburgh and teaches adults for a social service agency. Together with her husband, the novelist Barton Paul Levenson, she is a member of the Pittsburgh Worldwrights writers' group.

Kate Petersen lives in Somerville, Massachusetts and works in Boston, where she writes about pharmaceutical conflicts of interest. Originally from Arizona, Kate's work has previously appeared in *The Iowa Review, Quarterly West, Phoebe, Hayden's Ferry Review, Pearl,* and

Brevity. "To Those Who Say Write What You Know" appears also in *The Fourth Genre: Contemporary Writers of/on Creative Nonfiction,* 5th edition by Pearson.

Glen Pourciau's short-story collection *Invite* won the 2008 Iowa Short Fiction Award and was published by the University of Iowa Press. His stories have been published in *The Paris Review, New England Review, The Barcelona Review, failbetter.com,* Hobart online, *Mississippi Review, New Orleans Review, Ontario Review,* and other magazines.

Sam Rasnake's poetry has appeared in journals such as *MiPOesias, Pebble Lake Review, Literal Latté, Boxcar Poetry Review, Snow Monkey, Siren, The Dead Mule,* and *Poem.* He is the author of one chapbook, *Religions of the BloodNecessary Motions* (Sow's Ear Press). He edits *Blue Fifth Review,* an online poetry journal, (Pudding House), and one collection, (http://www.angelfire.com/zine/bluefifth/index.html) and blogs at sam of the ten thousand things (http://samofthetenthousandthings. blogspot.com).

Jonathan Rice's poems have been published or are forthcoming in *AGNI Online, American Literary Review, Colorado Review, Crab Orchard Review, Notre Dame Review, Sycamore Review,* and *Witness,* among others. His work was selected for Best New Poets 2008, the 2008 Gulf Coast Poetry Prize, the 2008 Milton-Kessler Memorial Prize from Harpur Palate, the 2005-2006 AWP Intro to Journals Awards, and was twice nominated for a Pushcart Prize. He received an MFA from Virginia Commonwealth University, and will begin Ph.D. candidacy at Western Michigan University this coming fall.

Tom Sheehan's books are *Epic Cures,* 2005 and *Brief Cases, Short Spans,* November 2008, from Press 53 of NC; *A Collection of Friends,* memoirs, 2004, and *From the Quickening,* March 2009, from Pocol Press of VA. His last book of poetry was *This Rare Earth and Other Flights,* in 2003. A proposal for a collection of cowboy stories, *Where the Cowboys Ride Forever,* is in the hands of a western publisher. Another collection of short stories, *Out of the Universe Endlessly Rocking,* is also making the rounds. In-process works are *Epic Cures II,* and novels *Murder from the Forum, Death of a Lottery Foe, An Accountable Death, Death by Punishment, The Keating Script,* and *Death of the Final God.* His work is currently in or coming in *Ocean Magazine, Perigee, Rope and Wire Magazine, Qarrtsiluni, Green Silk Journal, Halfway down the Stairs, Ad Hoc Monadnock, Hawk & Whippoorwill, Eden Waters Press, Ensorcelled, Canopic Jar,*

SFWP, Eskimo Pie, Lock Raven Review, Indite Circle, Northville Review, Pine Tree Mysteries, and in selections in books coming from Press 53, *Home of the Brave, Stories in Uniform,* and *Milspeak Memo.*

Claudia Smith's stories have appeared in several journals and anthologies, including *Failbetter, Sou'wester, Elimae,* and Norton's *The New Sudden Fiction: Short Short Stories From America and Beyond.* Her collection, *The Sky Is A Well And Other Shorts,* won Rose Metal Press's first annual short-short chapbook competition. Ron Carlson judged and wrote the introduction. The collection was later included in the anthology *A Peculiar Feeling of Restlessness.* Another collection or book is forthcoming from Future Tense in August 2009. More about Claudia's stories can be found online atwww.claudiaweb.net.

Lynn Strongin b. 1939 in New York City is the daughter of first generation Eastern European Jewish parents. After an education in musical composition at The Manhattan School of Music, she went on to study the poetry of E.E. Cummings, and to work with Denise Levertov in Berkeley during the political ferment of the sixties. For the past thirty years she has made British Columbia her home although she considers her language profoundly American. Sixteen books, most recently *Star Quilt* (a novel), and *Cape Seventy* (A book of poems.) Forthocming books are *Indigo* (A poet's Memoir), *Spectral Freedoms* "Selected Poetry Prose & Criticism." A biography is being written of Strongin's life; it's working title is *Elegant Necessities.* A Griffin AWard nominee, five-time Pushcart Prize nominee, she is at work on a new lyrical novel and a volume of poems.

Terese Svoboda's third novel, *Trailer Girl and Other Stories,* is coming out in paper this fall, and her fifth book of poetry, *Weapons Grade.* She's just passed the 100 published stories mark!

Jon Thompson teaches in the English Department at North Carolina State University, where he edits *Free Verse: A Journal of Contemporary Poetry & Poetics* and Free Verse Editions, a poetry series. His most recent books are *The Book of the Floating World* (2007) and *After Paradise; Essays on the Fate of American Writing* (2009).

Davide Trame is an Italian teacher of English, born and living in Venice-Italy, writing poems exclusively in English since 1993; they have been published in around four hundred literary magazines since 1999, in U.K, U.S. and elsewhere: *Poetry New Zealand, New*

Contrast (South Africa), *Nimrod* (U.S.), *Orbis* (U.K), and *Prague Literary Review* among them. His poetry collection as a downloadable on-line book was published by www.gattopublishing.com in 2006.

Donna D. Vitucci raises funds for nonprofit clients in Cincinnati, Ohio. Her stories have appeared or are forthcoming in dozens of journals, including *Natural Bridge, Hawaii Review, Meridian, Gargoyle, Broad River Review, Hurricane Review, Front Porch Journal, Beloit Fiction Journal, Storyglossia, Smokelong Quarterly, Turnrow, Juked, Night Train,* and *Another Chicago Magazine*. She writes about the assumptions and unexpressed love that tangle families, friends and lovers. "Mandible" is one of her all-time favorite creatures.

Helen Wickes lives in Oakland, California where she worked for many years as a psychotherapist. She has an MFA from Bennington. Her first book of poems, *In Search of Landscape*, was published in 2007 by Sixteen Rivers Press, a co-operatively run press which publishes poetry from the Bay Area watershed area.

Kathrine Leone Wright's work has appeared in *Cincinatti Review, New Orleans Review, La Petite Zine, Small Spiral Notebook, Weber Studies,* and elsewhere. She holds an MFA from Florida Atlantic University, where she received the 2007-2008 Howard Pearce Creative Thesis Award. Kathrine edits the online literary fresco, *Words on Walls,* with Ariana-Sophia Kartsonis and works as a Corporate Communications Manager for a medical software company. She and her family recently moved back to her native Utah.

Once, long, long ago in the Dark Forest, **Jordan Zinovich** heard Baba Yaga singing and glimpsed her walking hut—a vision that utterly arrested his maturation. Through the passing years he has grown younger, and smaller, desperately pursuing her trail of glimmering words. Compulsion is all that remains. He doesn't ask for pity.

　　Jordan Zinovich was born and raised in British Columbia. He left Canada in 1974 to live in Europe, West Africa, India, and New York City, where he now resides. He has published eight books: two historical biographies—*The Prospector: North of Sixty* and *Battling the Bay; Semiotext(e) CANADAs* (as Project General Editor); the novel *Gabriel Dumont in Paris;* the poetry collections *Cobweb Walking, The Company I Keep,* and *Chronicle of an Unverifiable Year;* and the poetic radio play *John Chapman's Harvest*. His work has been translated into

French and Dutch, and has been performed on the radio in New York, Western Canada, and Amsterdam. He has read widely across Canada and the United States, has a modest following in Holland, and is a senior editor with the Autonomedia Collective, one of the more notable and active English-language underground publishing houses.

INDEX OF ONLINE JOURNALS 2008-09

The Battered Suitcase
www.vagabondagepress.com
F. M. Neun, editor
submissions@vagabondagepress.com

Beltway Poetry Quarterly
www.washingtonart.com/beltway/contents.html
Kim Roberts, editor
Does not accept unsolicited submissions

Big Toe Review
www.bigtoereview.com
Joshua Michael Stewart, editor
joshuajoshs@aol.com

Big Ugly Review
www.biguglyreview.com
Elizabeth Bernstein, editor
fiction@biguglyreview.com
poetry@biguglyreview.com

Big Bridge
www.bigbridge.org
Michael Rothenberg, editor
waterblue@bigbridge.org

Blackbird
www.blackbird.vcu.edu
Gregory Donovan, editor
transom@vcu.edu

Blithe House Quarterly Review
www.blithe.com
Aldo Alvarez, editor
blithehouseqtly@aol.com

Blood Lotus
www.bloodlotus.org
Stacia M. Fleegal, editor
bloodlotusfiction@gmail.com
bloodlotusnonfiction@gmail.com
bloodlotuspoetry@gmail.com

Blood Orange Review
www.bloodorangereview.com
Stephanie Lenox and Heather K. Hummel, editors
submissions@bloodorangereview.com

Blue Fifth Review
www.angelfire.com/zine/bluefifth/
Sam Rasnake, editor
bluefifth@lycos.com

Blue Print Review
www.blueprintreview.de
Dorothee Lang, editor
doro21@gmail.com

The Blue Route
www.theblueroute.org
Jamie Gibbs, editor
fictiontheblueroute@gmail.com
poetrytheblueroute@gmail.com

Born Magazine
www.bornmagazine.org
Anmarie Trimble, editor
editors@bornmagazine.org

Bosphorus Art Project Quarterly
www.bapq.net
Aydin Bal, Jennifer Bal and Zeynep Kılıç, editors
bapquarterly@bosphorusartproject.org

BOXCAR Poetry Review
www.boxcarpoetry.com
Neil Aitken, editor
boxcarpoetry@gmail.com

Brevity
www.creativenonfiction.org/brevity/
Dinty W. Moore, editor
brevitymag@gmail.com

Cadillac Cicatrix
www.cadillaccicatrix.com
Benjamin Spencer, editor
submissions.northernpros@gmail.com

Contemporary Rhyme
www.contemporaryrhyme.com
Richard Geyer, editor
Currently not accepting submissions

Contrary Magazine
www.contrarymagazine.com
Jeff McMahon, editor
Submissions through online form

Convergence
www.convergence-journal.com
Lara Gularte and Elaine Bartlett, editors
editor@convergence-journal.com

The Cortland Review
www.cortlandreview.com
Guy Shahar, editor
Submissions through online form

Cosmoetica
www.cosmoetica.com
Dan Schneider, editor
cosmoeticapoems@gmail.com

Creative Nonfiction
www.creativenonfiction.org
Lee Gutkind, editor
Does not accept email submissions

Cricket Online Review
www.cricketonlinereview.com
cor_editors@yahoo.com

Damselfly Press
www.damselflypress.net
Jennifer Taylor, Lesley Dame and Rebecca Cleaver, editors
jennifer@damselflypress.net
lesley@damselflypress.net
rebecca@damselflypress.net

The Danforth Review
www.danforthreview.com
Michael Bryson, editor
danforthreview@rogers.com

Dark Sky Magazine
www.darkskymagazine.com
Adrienne Antonson, editor
editors@darkskymagazine.com

The Dead Mule School of Southern Literature
www.deadmule.com
Valerie MacEwan, editor
submit.mule@deadmule.com
deadmule.poetry@gmail.com

decomP
www.decompmagazine.com
Jason Jordan, editor
decomp.magazine@gmail.com

Defenestration
www.defenestrationmag.net
Andrew Kaye, editor
submissions@defenestrationmag.net

Del Sol Review
www.webdelsol.com/Del_Sol_Review/
Michael Neff, editor
poetry-dsr@webdelsol.com
knight.lori@gmail.com

Delaware Poetry Review
www.depoetry.com
Michael Blaine, editor

Diagram
www.thediagram.com
Ander Monson, editor
Submissions through online form

Diode
www.diodepoetry.com
Patty Paine, editor
submit@diodepoetry.com

Expatlit
www.expatlit.com
Heidi Charlton, editor
joseph@expatlit.com

Expose'd
www.exposweb.net
Mike Green, editor
Submissions through online form

Externalist
www.theexternalist.com
Larina Warnock, editor
fiction@theexternalist.com
poetry@theexternalist.com

failbetter
www.failbetter.com
Thom Didato, editor
submissions@failbetter.com

Fawlt Magazine
www.fawltmag.org
*E.C. Belli, Ryan Joe, Veronica Kavass, and
Alex Palmer, editors*
editor@fawltmag.org

Fickle Muses
www.ficklemuses.com
Sari Krosinsky, editor
fiction@ficklemuses.com
editor@ficklemuses.com (all other)

Fiction Attic
www.michellerichmond.com/fictionattic
Michelle Richmond, editor
fictionattic@gmail.com

Fiction Weekly
www.fictionweekly.com
Jason Reynolds, editor
submissions@fictionweekly.com

Five Chapters
www.fivechapters.com
David Daley, editor
editor@fivechapters.com

Flashquake
www.flashquake.org
Debi Orton, editor
submit@flashquake.org

Flutter
www.freewebs.com/rarepetal
Sandy Sue Benetiz, editor
sandyb1070@msn.com

The Foliate Oak
www.foliateoak.uamont.edu
foliateoak@uamont.edu

For Poetry
www.forpoetry.com
Jacqueline Marcus, editor
submissions@forpoetry.com

Fou
www.foumagazine.net
Cate Peebles, David Sewell, Brad Soucy, editors
fou.submit@gmail.com

Free Verse
english.chass.ncsu.edu/freeverse/
Jon Thompson, editor
freeverse_editor@chass.ncsu.edu

Freight Stories
www.freightstories.com
Andrew Scott and Victoria Barrett, editors
submissions@freightstories.com

FRiGG: A Magazine of Fiction and Poetry
www.friggmagazine.com
Ellen Parker, editor
webmaster@friggmagazine.com

Fringe Magazine
www.fringemagazine.org
Elizabeth Stark, editor
fringefiction@gmail.com

Front Porch Journal
www.frontporchjournal.com
Tom Grimes, editor
Submissions through online form

Identity Theory
www.identitytheory.com
Matt Borondy, editor
poetry@identitytheory.com
fiction@identitytheory.com

Inertia
www.inertimagazine.com
J.M. Spalding, editor
www.inertiamagazine.com/submissions.php

In Posse Review
www.webdelsol.com/InPosse/
Tatyana Mishel, editor
mskomega@aol.com
sdt11@aol.com

Innisfree Poetry Journal
www.innisfreepoetry.org
Greg McBride, editor
editor@innisfreepoetry.org

Insolent Rudder
www.insolentrudder.net
Tim Ljunggren, editor
administration@insolentrudder.net

Istanbul Literature Review
www.ilrmagazine.net/en.php
Gloria Mindock, editor
submissions@ilrmagazine.net

Jacket
www.jacketmagazine.com
John Tranter, editor
Solicitation only

Jerseyworks
www.jerseyworks.com
Ron Gaskill, editor
jerseyworks@comcast.net

JMWW
jmww.150m.com
Jen Michalski, editor
jmwweditor@gmail.com

Journal of Truth and Consequence
www.journaloftruthandconsequence.com
Miranda Merklein, editor
truthandconsequence@netzero.com

Juked
www.juked.com
J. W. Wang, editor
submissions@juked.com

Kaleidowhirl
home.alltel.net/ellablue/
Cynthia Reynolds, editor
kaleidowhirl@gmail.com

Katrina Review
www.katrinareview.com
Christine Lee Zilka, Sunny Woan, Jason Wong, editors
fiction@katrinareview.com
poetry@katrinareview.com
essays@katrinareview.com

Keep Going
www.keepgoing.org
Blythe Hurley, editor
thefarm@keepgoing.org

Kennesaw Review
www.kennesawreview.org
Robert Barrier, editor
Does not accept email submissions

Keyhole Magazine
www.keyholemagazine.com
Peter Cole, editor
Must sign up at www.keyholemagazine.com/submissions

KGB Lit Bar
www.kgbbar.com/lit
Susan Y. Chi, editor
submitlit@kgbbar.com

The King's English
home.comcast.net/~wapshot1/
Benjamin Chambers, editor
thekingsenglish@comcast.net

Konch Room
www.ishmaelreedpub.com
Ishmael Reed, editor
uncleish@aol.com

Konundrum Engine Literary Review
lit.konundrum.com
Pitchaya Sudbanthad, editor
prose@konundrum.com
poetry@koundrum.com

Lamination Colony
lamination.deadwinter.com
Blake Butler, editor
laminationcolony@gmail.com

La Petit Zine
lapetitezine.org
Jeffrey Salane and Danielle Pafunda, editors
lapetitezine@yahoo.com

Laura Hird
www.laurahird.com
Laura Hird, editor
hirdlaura@hotmail.com

Lemon Puppy Quarterly
www.lemonpuppy.com
Michael Tesney, editor
fiction@lemonpuppy.com
poetry@lemonpuppy.com

Literary Fever
www.literaryfever.com
Kristie Langone, editor
Submissions through online form

Literary Mama
www.literarymama.com
Amy Hudock, editor
lmpoetry@literarymama.com
lmfiction@literarymama.com

Locuspoint
www.locuspoint.org
Charles Jensen, editor
Solicitation only city by city

Lone Star Stories
literary.ericmarin.com
Eric T. Marin, editor
submissions@ericmarin.com

LOST Magazine
www.lostmag.com
Peter Joseph, editor
fiction@lostmag.com
nonfiction@lostmag.com

M Review
www.maryhurst.edu/mreview/
Vandoren Wheeler, editor
mreview.editor@gmail.com

Mad Hatter's Review
www.madhattersreview.com
Carol Novack, editor
madhattersreview@gmail.com

Media Cake eMagazine
www.mediacakemagazine.com
Tess Lotta, editor
editor@mediacakemagazine.com

Memorious
www.memorious.org
Rebecca Morgan Frank, editor
submit+poetry@memorious.org
submit+prose@memorious.org

Menda City Review
www.mendacitypress.com
Terry Rogers, editor
editors@mendacitypress.com

Mezzo Cammin
www.mezzocammin.com
Kim Bridgford, editor
kbrigford@yahoo.com

Mi Poesias
www.mipoesias.com
Amy King, editor
jrussellhughes@yahoo.com

Midway Journal
www.midwayjournal.com
Ralph Pennel, editor
The Editors, Midway Journal
PO Box 14499
St. Paul, MN 55114

Milk Magazine
www.milkmag.org
Larry Sawyer, editor
milkmag@rcn.com

Miranda Literary Magazine
www.mirandamagazine.com
submissions@mirandamagazine.com

Mirrors
www.mirrorsmag.com
Julie Yi, Sunny Chao, editors
art.mirrors@mirrorsmag.com
lit.mirrors@mirrorsmag.com

Mississippi Review
www.mississippireview.com
Frederick Barthelme, editor
Submissions sent to each issue editor

Modern English Tanka
www.modernenglishtankapress.com
Denis M. Garrison, editor
submission@modernenglishtanka.com

Monkeybicycle
www.monkeybicycle.net
Steven Seighman, editor
websubmissions@monkeybicycle.net

Moria
www.moriapoetry.com
William Allegrezza, editor
submissions@moriapoetry.com

Mudlark
www.unf.edu/mudlark/
William Slaughter, editor
mudlark@unf.edu

Narrative Magazine
www.narrativemagazine.com
Carol Edgarian, editor
Submissions through online form

Necessary Fiction
www.necessaryfiction.com
Steve Himmer, editor
editor@necessaryfiction.com

New Works Review
www.new-works.org
Jonathan Sanders, editor
timhealy@hal-pc.org

Newport Review
www.newportreview.org
Kathryn Kulpa, editor
submissions@newportreview.org

NOÖ Journal
www.noojournal.com
Kyle Peterson, editor
submissions@noojournal.com

No Posit
www.kenbaumann.com/noposit.html
Ken Baumann, editor
noposit@gmail.com

No Record
www.no-record.com
submit@no-record.com

No Tell Motel
www.notellmotel.org
Reb Livingston, editor
submit@notellmotel.org

Not Just Air
www.sundress.net/notjustair/
Christina Wos' Donnely and Parris Garnier, editors
transom@notjustair.org

November 3rd Club
www.november3rdclub.com
Victor D. Infante, editor
nov3rdsubmissions@yahoo.com

Nthposition
www.nthposition.com
Val Stevenson, editor
val@nthposition.com

On the Page Magazine
www.onthepage.org
Nada von Tress, editor
Currently not accepting submissions

Open Letters Monthly
www.openlettersmonthly.com
John Cotter, editor
submissions@openlettersmonthly.com

Opium Magazine
www.opiummagazine.com
Todd Zuniga, editor
Submissions through online form

Oregon Literary Review
www.oregonlitreview.org
Charles Deemer, editor
ficted@gmail.com (fiction)
charles@oregonliteraryreview.org
(plays and screenplays)

Our Stories
www.ourstories.us
A. E. Santi, editor
Submissions through online form

Oxford Magazine
community.muohio.edu/oxmag/
Karstin Painter, editor
oxmagfictioneditor@muohio.edu
oxmagpoetryeditor@muohio.edu

Panamowa: A New Lit Order
newlitorder.blogspot.com
Michelle Morgan, editor
mmpottlehill@yahoo.com

Paradigm
www.paradigmjournal.com
submissions@rainfarmpress.com

Past Simple
www.pastsimple.org
Jim Goar, editor
submitto5@pastsimple.org

Pemmican
www.pemmicanpress.com
Robert Edwards, editor
pemmicanpress@hotmail.com

The Pedestal Magazine
www.thepedestalmagazine.com
John Amen, editor
pedmagazine@carolina.rr.com

Per Contra
www.percontra.net
Miriam N. Kotzin, editor
percontra05@yahoo.com

Persimmon Tree
www.persimmontree.org
Nan Fink Gefen, editor
editor@persimmontree.org

Pequin
www.pequin.org
pequin1000@gmail.com

Pindeldyboz
www.pindeldyboz.com
Whitney Steen, Grace Bello, Nora Fussner, Rohan Bassett, Nicole Derr, and J.A. Tyler editors
submissions@pindeldyboz.com

Place
www.placethemagazine.com
Submissions through online form

Poemeleon
www.poemeleon.org
Cati Porter, editor
editor@poemeleon.org

Poetic Diversity
www.poeticdiversity.org
Marie Lecrivain, editor
Submissions through online form

Poetserv
www.poetserv.org
James Cervantes, editor
cervantes.james@gmail.com (poetry)
lynda.schor@gmail.com (fiction)

Poor Mojo's Almanac
www.poormojo.org
Dave Nelson, editor
Submissions through online form

Prick of the Spindle
www.prickofthespindle.com
Cynthia Reeser, editor
pseditor@pickofthespindle.com

Prism Review
prismreview.blogspot.com
prismreview@ulv.edu

Pulp.net
www.pulp.net
Submissions through online form

Quarterly Conversation
www.quarterlyconversation.com
Scott Esposito, editor
scott_esposito@yahoo.com

r. k. v. r. y.
www.ninetymeetingsinninetydays.com
Victoria Pynchon, editor
vpynchon@settlenow.com

Ramble Underground
www.rambleunderground.org
fictioneditor@rambleunderground.org

Rare Petal
www.freewebs.com/rarepetal/
sandyb1070@msn.com

Raving Dove
www.ravinggdove.org
Jo-Ann Moss, editor
editor@ravingdove.org

Rhythm
rhythmpoetrymagazine.english.dal.ca
Mary Kathryn Arnold, editor
rhythm@dal.ca

Rise Converge
riseconverge.blogspot.com
Jeff Crook, editor
wordartsinc@yahoo.com

River Babble
www.iceflow.com/riverbabble/welcome.html
Leila Rae, editor

Roadrunner Haiku Journal
www.roadrunnerjournal.net
Jason Sanford Brown, Scott Metz and Richard Gilbert, editors
jason@roadrunnerjournal.net
scott@roadrunnerjournal.net

Robot Melon
www.robotmelon.com
robotmelon@gmail.com

Rose and Thorn
www.theroseandthornzine.com
Barbara Quinn, editor
baquinn@aol.com

Round
www.roundonline.com
Beth Bayley, editor
Submissions through online form

Rumble
www.rumble.sy2.com
Craig Snyder, editor
rumble.microfiction@gmail.com

Salt River Review
www.poetserv.org
James Cervantes and Lynda Schor, editors
cervantes.james@gmail.com
lynda.schor@gmail.com

Santa Fe Writers Project
www.sfwp.org
Cate McGowan, editor
sfwritersproject@gmail.com

Saw Palm
sawpalm.usf.edu
Daniele Pantano, editor
sawpalm@cas.usf.edu

The Scrambler
www.thescrambler.com
Jeremy Spencer, editor
editor@thescrambler.com

Scruffy Dog Review
www.thescruffydogreview.com
Brenda Birch, editor
submissions@thescruffydogreview.com

Segue
www.mid.muohio.edu.segue/
Eric Melbye, editor
segue@muohio.edu

Shit Creek Review
www.shitcreekreview.com
editor@shitcreekreview.com

Shred of Evidence
www.shredofevidence.com
Megan Powell, editor
editor@shredofevidence.com

Silenced Press
www.silencedpress.com
submissions@silencedpress.com

Siren: A Literary and Art Journal
www.sirenlit.com
Sara Kearns, editor
sirenlit@gmail.com

Six Little Things
www.sixbrickpress.com
Bard Cole, editor
editor@sixbrickpress.com

Slope
www.slope.org
Ethan Paquin, editor
Submissions through online form

Slow Trains
www.slowtrains.com
Susannah Indigo, editor
editor@slowtrains.com

Smokebox
www.smokebox.net
fuel@smokebox.net

SmokeLong Quarterly
www.smokelong.com
Dave Clapper, editor
Submissions through online form

Snakeskin
homepages.nildram.co.uk/~simmers/
George Simmers, editor
editor@snakeskin.org.uk

Snow*Vigate
www.snowvigate.com
Doug Martin, editor
snowv@snowvigate.com

SNReview
www.snreview.org
Joseph Conlin, editor
editor@snreview.org

Softblow
www.softblow.com
Christopher Ujine Ong, editor
editor@softblow.com

SoMa Literary Review
www.somalit.com
Kemble Scott, editor
submit@somalit.com

Sous Rature
www.necessetics.com/sousrature.html
Cara Benson, editor

Speechless the Magazine
www.speechlessthemagazine.org
Suzanne Lummis, editor
suzanne@speechlessthemagazine.org

Spindle
www.spindlezine.com
Guy LeCharles Gonzalez, editor
submissions@spindlezine.com

Spooky Boyfriend
spookyboyfriend1.weebly.com

Steel City Review
www.steelcityreview.com
Julia LaSalle, editor
editor@steelciryreview.com

Stickman
www.stickmanreview.com
fiction@stickmanreview.com
poetry@stickmanreview.com

Story*GLOSSIA*
www.storyglossia.com
Steven J. McDermott, editor
editor@storyglossia.com

storySouth
www.storysouth.com
Terry Kennedy, editor
Submissions through online form

Stride Magazine
www.stridemagazine.co.uk
Rupert Loydell, editor
submissions@stridemagazine.co.uk

Sub-Lit
www.sub-lit.com
John Casey Keyser, editor
laurahnraines@yahoo.com

Subtle Tea
www.subtletea.com
David Herrle, editor
doomsinger@subtletea.com

Summerset Review
www.summersetreview.org
Joseph Levens, editor
editor@summersetreview.org

Swink
www.swinkmag.com/online.html
Darcy Cosper, editor
swinkonline@gmail.com

Switchback
www.swback.com
Rosita Nunes, editor
submissions@swback.com

The Sylvan Echo
www.sylvanecho.net
Mel Jones, Andriana BInder, Apinya Pokachaiyapat, Bill Garnett, Desiree Kannel, Kristing Stoner, Laurie Barton, Mariel Howespian, and Patrick O'Neill, editors
editor@sylvanecho.net

Tarpaulin Sky
www.tarpaulinsky.com
Juliana Spallholz, editor
Not currently accepting submissions

Terrain.org
www.terrain.org
Simmons B. Buntin, editor
review@terrain.org

Tertulia Magazine
www.tertuliamagazine.com
Rosa Martha Villarreal, editor
submissions@tertuliamagazine.com

Thick with Conviction
www.angelfire.com/poetry/thick-withconviction/
Sara Blanton, editor
twczine@yahoo.com

Thieves Jargon
www.thievesjargon.com
Matt DiGangi, editor
submissions@thievesjargon.com

Toasted Cheese
www.toasted-cheese.com/ezine.htm
Stephanie Lenz, editor
submit@toasted-cheese.com

torch
www.torchpoetry.org
Amanda Johnston, editor
poetry@torchpoetry.org
prose@torchpoetry.org
shorts@torchpoetry.org

Triple Canopy
www.canopycanopycanopy.com
Sam Frank, Alexander Provab, editors
submissions@canopycanopycanopy.com